Praise for Lee Dunne'

*This story is the most ̲̲̲̲̲̲̲̲
alcoholism ever written in this country. In any other
country, it would be regarded as didactic. Here it is
branded as "indecent and/or obscene" because it reveals
exactly and honestly what it is really like to be an alcoholic*
John Broderick, Hibernia

A bawdy porter and sex-filled classic...
The Evening Herald

*The classic tale follows the fortunes of ambitious
Paddy Maguire and his determination to rise above
his circumstances, make some money whilst
enjoying a heady brew of porter and sex.*
The Mirror

*Dunne's virtue is that he writes in the absolutely
authentic voice of Dublin...*
Sheffield Morning Telegraph

Paddy Maguire is a wonderful creation.
State and Columbia Record

Brilliantly written
Alan Sillitoe

About the Author

Lee Dunne was born in Dublin in 1934. He has written twenty-two books, including the critically acclaimed novels *Goodbye to the Hill* and *Does Your Mother*. Seven of his novels, along with two films, were banned in Ireland.

An extraordinarily prolific writer, he has written an astonishing 2,000 radio and television scripts, for shows such as *Harbour Hotel*, *Fair City*, *Konvenience Corner*, *Callan*, *Troubleshooters* and *Kennedys of Castleross*.

At the age of 69, Lee earned an honours Masters Degree from IADT. He is currently working on a new book to be published by Killynon House Books in Winter 2006.

Paddy Maguire is Dead

LEE DUNNE

This novel is entirely a work of fiction. The names, characters and incidents portrayed in this book are the work of the author's imagination. Any resemblance to actual persons, living or dead, events or localities, is entirely coincidental.

First published by Arrow Books 1972

This edition published 2006 by Killynon House Books Ltd

ISBN: 978-1-905706-02-0
ISBN: 1-905706-02-2

Paddy Maguire Is Dead © Lee Dunne 2006
The moral rights of the author have been asserted.

The Labelling of Lee Dunne © John Broderick 1973
Reprinted with the kind permission of the publisher of Hibernia

Copyright for editing, layout, design © Killynon House Books Ltd

All rights reserved. No part of this publication may be reproduced or transmitted in any form or by any means, electronic or mechanical, including photography, recording or any information storage or retrieval system, without written permission from the publisher. This book is sold subject to the condition that it shall not by way of trade or otherwise, be lent, resold, hired out, or otherwise circulated without the publisher's prior permission in any form of binding or cover other than that in which it is published and without a similar condition including this condition being imposed on the subsequent purchaser.

A CIP catalogue record for this book is available from the British Library

Cover design and text layout by Agnieszka O'Toole

Printed and bound in Denmark by Nørhaven Paperback

Killynon House Books
Killynon House, Turin, Mullingar, Co. Westmeath, Ireland
Website: www.killynonhousebooks.com

*This book is dedicated to
the memory of John Broderick*

Also by the same author

Books

Goodbye to the Hill
A Bed in the Sticks
Does Your Mother
Dancers of Fortune
Seasons of Destiny
No Time For Innocence
Barleycorn Blues
Requiem For Reagan
Ringmaster
Harbour Hotel
Maggie's Story
Big Al

Plays

Goodbye to the Hill
Return to the Hill
The Full Shilling
Bless Them All
Does Your Mother
Tough Love
Busy Bodies
One Man's Meat

Films

Wedding Night
Paddy
The Pale Faced Girl

AUTHOR'S NOTE

This book has been banned for 34 years. I now dedicate this new edition to the memory of John Broderick, a great writer who was a good friend to me - he alone defended it as a very worthwhile novel, a valuable contribution to the understanding of the disease of alcoholism. John also castigated the Censorship Board for its lack of foresight and much, much more.

Also for my old pal, Vincent Smith who stood beside me in 1972 as I made my public protest against censorship on Grafton Street.

I want to thank Jason O'Toole for publishing this story. It has been my privilege that a great number of people, who got the book in England, felt it had helped them change their lives. The hope is that it might reach even one more person who is currently battling with alcoholism.

INTRODUCTION

The Labelling of Lee Dunne
By John Broderick

The number of authors banned by the Irish Censorship Board over the past forty years is so incredible that it is necessary to set them down again from time to time. They include Joyce Cary, Theodore Dreiser, William Faulkner, Scott Fitzgerald, Anatole France, André Gide, Graham Greene, Knut Hamsun, Ernest Hemingway, Aldous Huxley, Thomas Mann, Marcel Proust, Ignazio Silone, John Steinbeck, H.G. Wells, and the Church of England. This list includes at least seven Nobel Prize winners, and must strike some younger readers as a clear case of lunacy, either on my part or on the part of the censors. For, of course, the works of all those writers were later "unbanned", and are largely available, according to the printing situation, for those lucky young men and women of twenty who can afford to buy them in paperback. However, I can assure them that all those writers, together with a publication issued by the Church of England, were at one time labeled "indecent and/or obscene" by the Censorship Board in this country. All of which would seem to suggest that this mysterious committee was frequently wrong in its moral judgment.

Of recent years this iniquitous law has not been much employed; but it still remains on the statute books; and over the past forty years it has been used to brand the work of practically every well-known Irish writer of merit. We remain the only country in the Western world of which this can be said. I repeat this because I do not think it is sufficiently appreciated and known. Either our writers are particularly immoral persons, or there is something gravely wrong with the Censorship Board. The fact that a great many Irish artists, branded by mysterious officials in their own country as purveyors of goods which are "obscene", but acclaimed elsewhere as honourable members of their craft, would seem to suggest that our laws governing the publication of books are iniquitous and unjust. And to prove the point that the censors are ignorant and undemocratic, it has been deemed necessary to revoke their decisions in very many cases over the years, thus holding the law, such as it is, up to ridicule and contempt.

And these mysterious officials are still at it. When, as the popular song has it, will they ever learn? Last November Mr. Lee Dunne's latest novel *Paddy Maguire is Dead* was banned, and quite recently this "judgment" was upheld by the Appeals Board. Mr. Dunne is a professional writer, whose books in paperback have a large circulation in Ireland, thus making it possible for him to live here, in a very modest manner, as everybody connected with writing knows. And now the censors, with a stroke of the pen, have taken this means of livelihood away from him. So much for justice.

This novel was published in paperback first, thus making it possible for a large number of people to buy it. Insofar as one can read the minds of men who ban books in this country, it would appear that this cheap edition had something to do with the banning. What is "safe" for a man with money, is dangerous for those who have to count their pennies. Here again we come upon a situation unique in Western Europe. But the banning of this book poses an even more serious question. Do the censors know what they are doing? And, in particular, do they know what this novel is about? If they do, then they are a truly sinister body; and if they do not, they are an ignorant and arrogant bunch who have once again made the Republic of Ireland ridiculous: the home of obscurantism and imbecility.

It will be argued that *Paddy Maguire is Dead* has many passages which deal with the sexual act between men and women in a manner which might be described as "raw". It has. So have many other paperbacks on sale freely in this country. They are, however, by foreign authors; and their sex passages are just that and no more. Whereas the sexual descriptions in Mr. Dunne's novel are of a special nature.

They reveal together with everything else in the book, the character and temperament of an alcoholic. This story is the most detailed and horrifying exposé of alcoholism ever written in this country. Every incident, every character, every act of the anti-hero, Maguire, is motivated and overshadowed by the effects of this frightful disease. In any other country, it would be regarded as didactic. Here it is branded as "indecent and/or obscene" because it reveals exactly and honestly what it is really like to be an alcoholic. I mentioned above that if the censors know this, then they are truly sinister, because it would appear that they do not want people to know the real truth of this condition. I would, however, prefer to think that they are ignorant. But ignorance of this problem on the part of persons invested with such power is almost criminal. They are confusing sex with disease.

From the beginning of this novel, it is made clear that Maguire is a potential alcoholic. He suffers from black-outs whenever he drinks. His sexual exploits are of a "special nature" because they are not the actions of a responsible man. The desperation, the loneliness, the craving for affection, and the wild pursuit of it, are characteristics of this disease, and are instantly recognisable to anyone who has any experience of it; as is the sense of guilt with which Maguire is riddled. Nothing is glossed over; nothing is made easy for the reader; no aspect of this awful national problem is hidden from us. This novel is the story of the gradual disintegration of a man who cannot control his drinking, and who ends up a mental and physical wreck. Nothing is glorified: his sexual exploits are revealed for what they are, figments of a phantasmagoric world. Some of the scenes are Hogarthian; and all of them take place in a working-class setting.

I doubt if this novel could have been written against any other background. Dickens would have made a great masterpiece of it. Lee Dunne writes in the language of the Dublin slums. Evidently the censors, no doubt well-educated nonentities, disapprove of this. Have they ever really listened to it? Do they know anything of alcoholism? If they do, and then quite deliberately suppress this book, then God forgive them. If they don't, it is about time they learned. Because at the end Lee Dunne indicates how this disease can be arrested; although it cannot be cured. The real worth of the book can, I suppose, only be appreciated by those who have themselves been through this hell; but it would be a very good thing if the many others who have not, but may well be heading for it, could be allowed to read about what may be in store for them.

Nowadays we have many public meetings, many seminars dedicated to the discussion of alcoholism. Bishops have the gall to get up and tell us how terrible it is, one unctuous platitude following another. Yet, when someone writes a book revealing the real truth of alcoholism, it is banned, and labelled "obscene". The real obscenity is to be found among those who say all the right things, and do nothing about it, except to ban a book which might enlighten many who are in need of it. And does so in their own language.

After the rejection by the Appeals Board, I do not know exactly what the legal position is. But there are in the present Government many enlightened and civilised men. Surely it is possible to have this scandalous banning quietly rescinded, and this highly moral novel restored to general circulation. Since the members of the Censorship Board and the Appeals Board are faceless men, they have no face to lose. And if they are really ignorant of the effects of alcoholism as a disease, I know of many people who would be only too happy to explain it to them. After that, unless they are completely ossified, they will see this extraordinary book in a completely new light, the lurid glow of a terrible and widespread disease.

This essay was originally published in Hibernia, 11 May 1973.

BOOK ONE

Chapter One
April 1970

All that guff about the air being for the birds never cost me a thought until the first time I rode in an airplane. And the second time and all the other times.

And as I travelled more and more by what Tommy Manning called "the Electric Sausage" I believed more and more that the Wright brothers and those other lunatics really were lunatics.

All the booze I could drink didn't stop me being the original White Knuckle Flier, sitting there with my hands clamped tight around the armrests, cursing myself for being a bloody fool, and hating those cool, calm bastards that sat beside me.

The safety belt was no help. I mean, there was I, strapping myself in while my eyes sought the emergency exits. I was looking for the quickest way out and not even considering the fact that my mind was in bits to be even thinking of getting out at something like twenty thousands feet.

I remember one of my earlier flights... from Dublin to London late at night, the only plane to get off the ground that day on account of the dyspeptic state of the weather. I'd never have been there at all but for the fact that my presence was badly needed by my bank manager who had been good to me over the years.

I wouldn't have set foot on the plane only I was ossified due to leaning on the airport bar with a glass in each hand, just so that I wouldn't be off balance, for something like eight hours.

The flight was murderous. No smoking... safety belts on all the way.... A head, tail, and side wind battering its way around the plane at a hundred and ten miles an hour... not to mention air pockets that seemed about the right size for an overcoat to fit a rocket to the moon. So I might be forgiven for feeling that I was about to shit green apples at any second.

Just before I started screaming, the woman in the next seat did. And she was so close to my left ear that it went through me like a dose of salts.

Without thinking I grabbed her, mercifully avoiding the no parking zones and she lay on my shoulder like a bad actress in a tenth rate travelling show version of Mrs. Henry Wood's "East Lynn".

She calmed down a bit, and I held her hand, which was no hardship because she was a nice looking lady. I'd slipped into the old Maguire routine....If you're unsure, frightened, or just plain bloody terrified, which I was, go into the comedy act.

In a matter of minutes she was laughing like she was sitting on a door handle. I wasn't sure if it was my impersonation of Groucho Marx (send a dozen red roses up to Lulu and put "I Love You" on the back of the bill) or if the lady had channelled her screaming power into another area of her throat. It didn't matter. It worked, apparently for her, certainly for me. And the more I held her hand the more I felt like giving her one. By the time we got to London she was caressing the inside of my jacket arm as though she'd discovered something special. And I didn't think for one second that she had a hang-up on the old Harris weed.

I won't go into what happened afterwards...it's not important... but I'll say this... A woman frightened out of her knickers who is helped by some equally terrified stiff can express her gratitude in a way that will make the gyrations of Elvis the Pelvis seem like the last twitches of a fella who's downed four quarts of embalming fluid.

Years later I was sitting uncomfortably in my seat when a great, wire haired Irishman sat down beside me. A man with a big ingenuous expression under the steel gray hair. I said,

"Hello," trying hard not to look surprised when he congratulated me on my choice of seat.

"You know your onions," says he, with a wink that one of the Great Train Robbers might have given his buddy as they counted the money before the fuzz came along.

"Oh I know my onions, all right," I said.

"Oh begod aye." He nodded, confirming his original assessment of my intelligence. I learned that I was sitting in the plane's centre of gravity and if the thing started to disintegrate I was in the safest place. I felt like the Marlene Dietrich character in the film "No Highway". That moment when James Stewart, sure that the aircraft is about to fall apart, tells her that the safest thing to do is to "go into the men's room and sit with your back to the wall".

I'll always remember that lovely movie, but I'll never forget, and there's a difference, that way your man assured me I was in the safest place on the plane. He went on then to talk to me about rivets. Rivets for Christ's sake! I mean my lack of concern about their well being hadn't cost me a thought up to that moment.

"Look," your man said... he was some kind of engineer, by the way. "If you were to put your finger out that window at this very second...." We were at twenty thousand feet and moving at four hundred and fifty miles an hour.... "If you did that...." Somehow I resisted the need to say "As If I Would..." "Well," says he... "Sure it'd be torn right off your hand so it would."

I worked hard to look like a fella who wasn't going out of his mind.

"Well now," said the engineer. He paused and I found I was holding my breath. "If there was one loose rivet out there...." He pointed to *my* side of the plane... "Well, sure at this speed the whole side'd be ripped off before you could go by boat." He snapped his thumb across his forefinger while I made a silent prayer to the Patron Saint of rivets, apologizing for the fact that I didn't know the name and swearing that I'd look it up as soon as the plane landed. I was chuffed with my bit of psychology... as soon as the plane landed... implying total belief and implicit trust in the ability, power, or whatever else it took to get the Jesus aircraft down out of birdland and back onto some stretch of friendly, beautiful tarmac.

So I'd had some experience of flying, none of it to be repeated, until April Fools Day a few years ago. I was going to London again and for the first time in my life I wasn't bothered about being off the ground.

I wasn't drunk, and I was being polite to the old girl next to me, nodding my head in the right places, letting her beat my ear about it being her first time ever and how she'd put her trust in the Almighty.

She didn't get much out of me. I didn't tell her...I couldn't... that my wife Phil was lying in the hospital, her life hanging by a thread of her main artery, thanks to an accident down there on the safety of terra firma.

I was fairly numb but I was calm and I was unafraid of flying simply because being afraid didn't change anything. I had no control over the big decisions like who should live and who should die or how and when. So I sat there thinking some about the whole shapeless mess of my life. And I tried not to indulge in stupidity like I wish I cold be down there in the hospital instead of Phil and all that bullshit. She was there, in bits, and all the breast beating, all the hot tears weren't going to put her back the way she'd been at ten o'clock that morning. And that was just thinking about her physical shape. What about how she'd been feeling? I did hope she'd been happy, that she'd been making love somewhere, that her heart was beating for someone the way it used to beat for me.

I loved her. Enough to want her to be happy even if I wasn't starring in the picture with her. Which I wasn't...which I hadn't been for a long time.

I admit to wondering if I'd been home would it have happened? If I'd been home. If If If... If my aunt had balls my grandfather would have taken to the bottle. Which he did anyway. I don't know... Maybe I needed to believe that my presence would have changed something. Or that it might have stopped things changing to point where I was no longer there. Just ego, I guess. Needing to feel a little bit good. Wanting to feel that I made something, anything happen. All bullshit really, because I'd never been any kind of catalyst. I just tripped over, fell into, got bitten in the leg by, situations. So it's no lie to say...everything happened to me.

It helps to put it down, get it out of the system. A sort of confession. Bless me, Blue Eyes, for I have sinned. When I was twenty-one it was a very good year. Even though I felt about sixteen.

Twenty-one...the time when a fella reaches manhood or gains his majority or grows up or whatever.

Maybe some guys do make it by that time. Some mature faster than others as the whiskey taster said to his psychiatrist.

I don't think many Irishmen get there so soon. I know I didn't, but than like most Paddies, I was carrying top weight from the start. Like, it begins with mother and usually middles and ends with mother church.

Chapter Two

When you think about it, what can you do with a woman's breasts? Apart from the mammary gland connection, I mean, when probably for the only time in a fella's life he uses them for the purpose which nature intended them, like to stay alive in those first days after his nine months in solitary confinement.

I guess most breast fed boys take up with girls where they left off, hopefully many years before, with their mother. It's got to be something to do with being warm and comfortable or whatever, because again I ask myself seriously, what can you do with a brace of knockers?

I don't think it matters whether they're of the fried egg variety, crab apple size, bouncer ball in shape and so sure of their firmness that they stare straight at you, or the generous dimensions of the balloon type. Because when you get down to it, and that's not a pun, they aren't really much good to a guy.

Okay, you can touch them, fondle them, pet them, caress them, kiss them, and you can suck them as long as you're not hoping to relieve a healthy thirst. Or if you get lucky and trip over a lady who likes to suffer some, you can bite them. Not that this is intended as a complaint, but that's about it, as far as a fella is concerned.

I'm not unaware that most women get a bang; God, I've done it again; as a direct result of undergoing one or several or all of the variations I've already mentioned. Or that in some ladies it induces the desire to open up. But most fellas, while they realise that time spent making like a windscreen wiper can be of enormous assistance in getting a young and curious nymphet into the scratcher, rarely bother to consider the possibility that she might enjoy it for its own sake.

Those early kisses were something in themselves, when it was all lips with just varying degrees of pressure. In that innocent time when kissing was enough and hadn't yet become a stepping stone, the prelude, to further manoeuvres.

At twenty-one I was, like most fellas, badly hung up on breasts, though I thought of them more as tits or headlamps or knockers, without meaning any disrespect to God's gift to the man who designed the brassiere. That lovely word has become bra, but as we've since added boobs to the language, I don't feel too hard done by.

Anyway, it was this constant application to Jennie's breasts that began to worry me in the year after we lost our baby, and Jimmy Frazer and I had built the new booth for our travelling show.

At first it was just a nagging thing like a periodic toothache. It didn't last long but each time it happened I was more put out by it than I'd been the time before.

I didn't allow it to crowd me, because for once we had something going for us and I wanted to enjoy the feeling as well as pocketing my share of the profits.

The winter had been diabolical, with so much endless bloody snow that I still want to vomit when I hear someone sing "White Christmas". And because of a rednose reindeer called Rudolph, I can't look at piece of venison without wanting to rush out and become a vegetarian.

Any stretch of countryside must look beautiful from the inside of a helicopter, but when you're out in the sticks trying to make a living with a show that isn't going to win any prizes, snow becomes the kind of pain in the arse that makes haemorrhoids seem like a gift from heaven.

In that kind of weather you can't expect people to sit in cold village halls, especially after a day spent fighting to keep livestock from becoming freshly frozen deadstock. But we did expect them and when we could see they weren't going to come, we had to go on hoping.

We attracted some people from the village we were playing but most of those places weren't much bigger than the dining room of a decent sized hotel, so mostly we suffered and shivered and swore. More than once I wished myself back in the insurance office where I'd been so fed up, and that was like praying somebody would give you an injection of polio.

It was just at this time that Jennie lost our baby and though I gagged all the time, trying to take her mind of it, the jokes felt like porridge under my tongue. I felt desolate, but the way I used the situation as an excuse to drink brandy was shameful. Not just because we couldn't afford my expensive thirst. What was so bloody shitty was me insulating myself from reality when she needed me. She never mentioned it. It was her guts, shining in her eyes like beacons on a storm ruptured sea, and the friendship of Jimmy Frazer, that made me snap out of it.

My gratitude to Jimmy (I'd christened him the most rheumatic juvenile in the business) just put a shine on the respect that was already there, and we kept each other going with endless talk about the spring and the way our luck would change once we put our booth, our own hand-built, travelling theatre, back on the road. His eyes would sparkle when he talked about this village or that small town and the crowds that we'd draw, and seeing him smile again was one of the better moments of those years on the road. But I'll never forget his face as we stood in Joe Dominick's shack with our combined dreams in a pile like ashes of our booth in the old open fireplace.

Joe had burned our booth. Burned it piece by piece, to keep from freezing to death while I'd been feeling sorry for myself and drinking brandy.

Jimmy cursed Joe with such vehemence that the poor old bastard, wherever he was, might have been forgiven for feeling that somebody had pissed on his grave, but I know he didn't really blame him. He just felt broken; his face, the colour of the ashes of our booth, a window exposing his spirit which was raw and torn and totally fed up.

I stood there moving closer to the conclusion that everything happened for a reason. Months before I'd given Jennie a hundred pounds to put by for when the baby came. And I'd forgotten about it until she put the ninety two that was left into my hand in her own unselfish way. Because I'd forgotten about it, it seemed like money from home.

Jimmy hadn't moved and went on standing there, his mouth hanging like a torn pocket until I said we'd build a new one.

"What with?" he asked me, "bulrushes?"

I grinned, but that only made him look more frustrated, so I told him about the ninety two. It took a few seconds to register, and then he was making mental calculations, and when we were leaving he was talking about a bigger booth. We hitched up the trailer which, thank Christ, Joe hadn't burned up, and drove out of there laughing together at the idea of just being alive.

When he asked me where the money had come from, I told him it was the remains of the stuff that I'd found in the old trunk that Gary Martin had given to me. We'd been all through this before and he didn't believe me this time either. In a way he appreciated the fact that I was cool enough to make up such an obvious piece of bullshit. To his way of thinking, I was telling people not to ask questions and at the same time, giving them enough to make them even more curious. Anyway he told me I was as dry as a fucking bone, which was a compliment and I let it go at that. But he'd started me thinking about my old friend, my Mister Macabre figure, now dead. Poor Gary, my lovely old man, gentleman, actor, slipping down into the robes of a strolling player, raconteur and feed to Jimmy, who was a lousy comedian, I thought of Gary a long way from the West End, dying in his bed in the sticks....

Chapter Three

Jennie's breasts had me bugged so that by September in fifty seven I had stopped touching them. Which wasn't easy on account of them taking up a fair bit of space in the bed. Nor was it that I didn't want to be having a nibble. Jesus, I wanted to crash dive onto them at all hours, wanted to so badly, that I had to stay away from them.

Of course it was just bloody ridiculous. Like a fella walking around the block to avoid passing a pub. Maybe he doesn't go in and get twisted, but the problem remains right where it was, inside the man.

Naturally, Jennie noticed that I appeared to have weaned myself onto a bottle, and I didn't need to be hyper-sensitive to feel that a lot of the charge had gone out of her sex life. How could she not notice with me having behaved like a team of hungry quads since the first time we'd tumbled into the scratcher together.

I tried hard to put things back the way they'd been, but that only made them worse. I didn't like myself very much and that was a feeling I could have lived without. I was so fed up with the show, so miserable about the way we seemed to remain in a cul-de-sac, that I decided quite calmly to wallow in self pity for a while.

It takes a rare kind of talent to enjoy feeling sorry for yourself, but it was one area in which I was truly blessed. Of course it's unadulterated sensuality, a totally non-sexual experience that is carnal enough to be kinky.

A happy-go-lucky, natural-born iconoclast, a heathen with a positive hedonistic streak might experience it, if say, he went to confession and told the Parish Priest, having just been to bed with the good man's housekeeper, that he'd just had his mind blown by a local lady sexual athlete with an inclination towards cannibalism.

Like anything that even borders on being kinky, it's sad, and though I didn't think about it then, that's just what it was. A natural defensive mechanism trick that was a step towards submerging itself. The tucking away of good old Maguire, getting him out of the way in the hope that if he could avoid things long enough, they would just pick up their knickers and go.

In a way it worked fine. I didn't get into Jimmy about how bad the show was. Nor did I mention, for a time, that I was bothered about not being able to learn anything more. He couldn't be blamed for this, having shown me every chord in his stack, but knowing that didn't help me much either.

With Jennie I went into a perpetual performance, telling her that I was feeling guilty about the way I'd treated my mother, and a lot of other garbage. And being sweet, kind, loving Jennie, she believed me and bled a bit for me. And like a bastard that I was, I got a charge out of letting her do it.

It was a game, and sick or not, it helped me hang on until something happened to save me having to make any big decisions. Making love to Jennie, which I didn't feel like doing any more, was no real hardship because I thought about Maureen while we were actually at it, and for a change, I had a re-run through some of my scenes with my old sparring partner, the butcher boy's friend and benefactor, Mrs. Kearney. Later I smiled over this because Maureen had been very well upholstered, and Mrs. Kearney, Christ! She'd had her own kind of superstructure.

Sometimes I wondered where Maureen might be. With my child. My child, boy or a girl? Where were they? And where was the love I'd felt so deeply? Or the glow that had made me want to marry Pauline more than anything else on earth? And closed still there was Jennie. Lovely Jennie, moving beneath me, fighting to get back what we'd had around the time when she'd conceived our baby. Was it love I'd felt when I told her that no piece of paper was needed to make her my wife? That she was and always would be my wife. Whatever it had been, it was gone like a canary that had flown out through an open window. I felt all alone and I loved the feeling.

During our second week at Woodville in Antrim we got the tail end of a heatwave, and after a couple of days Jennie looked as though she was wearing a dark nylon body stocking. I didn't do any sunbathing. The boozer didn't run to a sun roof, though Paddy Clarke, the publican, did confide that he was considering the purchase of "a wee fridge" to keep a bit of ice handy. His wife had brought up the idea and as she was the kind of crocodile that made him write a formal application for his monthly slice of the legs, anything she said received serious consideration. Otherwise Paddy found the combination lock changed on her chastity belt when next he went to try his hand at opening the safe.

Margaret Clarke was nineteen and if she reminded anybody of her mother, it was only because she looked like her father. From the way she flashed her brown eyes and wiggled her dainty backside, I felt sure that she'd already had a rub of the relic. If she hadn't, it could only have been that she'd frightened the locals off by the way she came on so strong.

Anyway, she had the sap rising in me, and a couple of nights later, I gave her one in a grain barn belonging to her father. Giving her a pull wasn't any kind of achievement, she was the kind the commercial travellers do novenas to meet. But it was something special for me, if only because she was the first girl I'd had since Jennie had started living with me.

It was good for me. She was fresh and clean and could certainly throw some leg. Her enthusiasm for an encore must have flattered my ego because we were tucked up again in no time flat.

The next day she asked me if I'd run off with her. I was so surprised that I ordered only a small brandy, but at least I didn't laugh in her face. Not even when I realised that she wasn't joking. I told her I'd think about it and she poured me a drink on the house.

That evening Jimmy introduced me to an old mate from his early days in roadshows, and right off, I didn't like Barney Whelan. I can't remember why. It was probably something as stupid as his eyebrows meeting. We had some drinks and I listened to him telling Jimmy about the "fabulous gilt" he was getting from slot machines and pin tables.

I'd always hated those one arm bandits, particularly the penny machines, designed specifically to allow the poor to feel that they could grab a little of what was going. And what was going was exactly nothing. Those machines were set with the precision of a time bomb, with all the gravy going to the owner and the hirer, while Joe Soap got just enough to encourage him to have another go.

What disturbed me most that afternoon in Woodville was the way Jimmy reacted to the tales of Barney Whelan and his "gilt" machines. Not only was he impressed, he had a look in his eye that was pure envy. And though we'd been doing well for months, taking decent money, I could see him working it all out, doing figures in his head. I wanted to be sick.

"You don't like it," he said before the show that evening.

He knew how I felt. I'd already told him, and because of that I could see him wanting to drop it. But there was money to be made with those things. During the afternoon, in the early evening before the show, customers could be encouraged to come and try their luck. In remote country places, where shows such as ours caused excitement, the prospect of a little gambling would be very well received.

"Just seems such easy money."

"Thanks for reminding me," I said, "for the tenth time."

I was rubbing make-up into my face, thinking why bother? The punters didn't really care, they couldn't have, not when they could sit through our show night after night. I could see Jimmy grin in the corner of my mirror.

"I never wanted to own a dodgem car, either. Or do you think I use this?" I held up the stick of nine... "because I'm a poof?"

"We'll just forget it."

"Course you won't forget it." I put the stick of nine back in the box. I'd really had enough of this.

"You have the partnership agreement nice and safe," I said.

He nodded into my mirror as I powdered off. He hadn't said anything because he'd been too busy searching for something in my words, in my face.

"Do you fancy buying me out?"

Panic flashed in and out of his eyes, but he was still bothered by what I'd said.

"Fuck sake, Tony." It was always Tony from Jimmy, the name he had picked for me on my very first day. "Just mentioned something that could make a bit extra...."

I thought about him during the show. I liked him but we'd come to the fork in the road. I wanted to act, or I thought I did. I'd nothing against making money as well, but I didn't want to make money running a miniature carnival. More than that, I didn't want to be around people who did. I didn't blame Jimmy. He'd been on the road too long not to be a showman. If things were bad for the stage show buy a few pin machines or slot machines or a projector and show a few movies. He had made up my mind for me - I didn't want to become one of the candy floss people.

And again, if we'd been doing things right, I wouldn't have been able to think all this while I was working in the play. I'd become like the rest of them, simply walking on, saying the lines and making sure I didn't trip over the furniture. It wasn't enough and I was pretty sure that before long I'd be looking down on the audience, sneering the way Gary Martin used to, simply because it was almost impossible to feel any respect for people who could sit night after night through the crap that we dished out.

Chapter Four

Margaret Clarke was in to see the show that night and I nodded "yes" to her as she left the booth. We didn't mean anything to each other. She just wanted to be banged and I needed a little more time away from Jennie and Jimmy, to work a couple of things out. Not that it was going to be any hardship lying into Margaret again. She was tasty enough, about fourteen or fifteen years younger than Jennie. And she didn't make me feel I was cheating because I didn't want to eat her boobies off.

I had the night's take with me when I got to the barn. Jimmy and I took the money every other night in case we ever got turned over. This way we wouldn't lose it all. On Sunday morning we pooled the lot, paid the wages and split the balance.

Margaret was waiting for me and she was like a greyhound out of the trap. I made her hang on while I lit one of her old man's tilly lamps. She believed me when I said I was worn out, and she was only too willing to take her skirt off and walk about in her high heels. She had good legs and the stocking tops were a turn on. But later, even when her toes were pointing to the roof, I was still thinking about Jennie and me. And thanking Jesus we weren't really married.

I hadn't talked to Jennie in a long time. Oh, I'd been making sounds, but it was all part of the performance I'd been putting on for a couple of months.

"Do you love me, Tony?" Margaret Clarke was biting my ear while she pleaded for some sweet king bullshit. I didn't say anything, but I altered my movements and that shut her up because she had to fight for more oxygen.

I knew then that I'd been playing a part for everybody else on the show as well. I'd been giving them whatever it was they wanted to see. Margaret was looking for the magic words again, so I didn't get time to work out whether I'd become all kinds of things to all kinds of people, because they couldn't have take me the way I was, or simply that I couldn't or wouldn't let them see me as I really was. I hoped I'd been doing it for me because it was plain bloody stupid to turn cartwheels and tie yourself up in knots for other people.

"Say it, Tony, tell me you love me, tell me." I kissed her and she thrust herself upwards to meet my weight and for the next few minutes I forgot about everything.

While she was lying back afterwards with her fingers playing with the straw behind her head, I stood up to fix my knickers. She sat up in panic.

"Don't go, please," she said.

"I'm not," I told her, "but just in case your daddy comes looking for you, I wouldn't want to try and dodge him with my knicks down around my ankles."

She laughed, covering her mouth with her hand.

"Daddy wouldn't mind. Anyway, he thinks sex is a great idea...."

I lay down beside her. "What about your mother?" I asked, as if I didn't know. As if the whole town didn't know.

Margaret pulled a face which suggested I had to be joking. And she laughed at some flash of memory.

"Mammy doesn't think about it, that's what mammy thinks about it." Margaret laughed, and I hoped her old man wasn't out looking for her with a shotgun.

"She doesn't think about it before during or after...." She pulled my face around to kiss me on the mouth. Then she said: "But I think about it all the time so that makes up for her, doesn't it?"

I liked her then for her honesty, thinking that in some ways she was like me. And I'm not saying it because we were both hung up on playing parents. Nor do I mean that I was all that honest with most people, but I tried to level with them at all times and Margaret was a bit like that. Whatever side of her she might show to her mother and most of the customers in the pub, she didn't kid herself.

"I'm glad you like it, Margaret," I said.

She pulled me nearer and I moved until I was lying on top of her.

"I don't like it, I love it. And I love it with you more than I ever did with someone else."

I kissed her, stopping to get my trousers out of the way once more. After that I kept my mouth on her lips for a long time. I didn't want her to be giving me any more bullshit. And if it wasn't bull, I didn't want to hear it. What was happening was all right and I was content to take a long time before getting onto the vinegar strokes. While I hoped it was good for her, I didn't need her to tell me that I was any kind of hammer man. Because it didn't really matter whether I was or not. Nobody's good in the scratcher all the time, with the exception, I suppose, of those who spend all their time out of bed, preparing themselves for the next session. But that wasn't, hadn't ever been, and I hoped, never would be, my attitude to getting laid. I liked sex as much as some and more than most.

"Tell me you love me, Tony, tell me...." She was at it again, so I made a little more noise, not wanting her to feel that I was putting her down.

"You don't have to mean it," she promised... "just tell me, tell me...."

I told her and kept on telling her. Why not, when it gave her some kind of charge. But I was surprised, because, up there in the sticks of County Antrim, I hadn't expected to run into a nineteen year old existentialist.

Jennie was asleep when I got in and I moved about very carefully. Not because there'd have been a row if she did wake up, but I was going out again. And not to make any kind of early early show with Margaret Clarke.

I wrote a formal letter to Jimmy asking him to transfer my interest in the show into Jennie's name. I didn't give him any reasons, just saying I had to get up and go.

The note to Jennie didn't come so easily. I felt guilty as a priest in mortal sin, but that wasn't going to help so I shrugged it off and scribbled some lines I can't remember, only sure of one thing. They weren't going to bring any comfort to lovely Jennie.

The dark night was finishing its shift and ahead of me the new day was breaking, pushing it's way up out of time. I walked on, away from them fast, feeling like a thief.

I'd stuffed a few things into a haversack and it felt comfortable behind my right shoulder. A couple of shirts and some socks and underwear, my shaving gear and two books that meant a great deal to me. Everything else, I'd left behind, which might been crazy, but I didn't care. And I chuckled to myself when I remembered leaving Dublin for the first time, with about two pounds in my pocket and not so much as a toothbrush under my arm.

A funny thing happened to me then. I saw myself in London, which I didn't know from a hole in the ground. I was sitting in the waiting area of an office which sold ice cream. As I watched the employees come in, I knew that I had taken a job, that I was going to work in this place. That the manager would be in at any moment to introduce me to my new workmates. I watched them file by and go to their desks and all I could think of was a crocodile of vegetables moving along with a clockwork precision that terrified me. And I was going to work here?!

I knew I didn't have any money and that my cheap suit wasn't going to offer much protection from the winter weather outside. But I couldn't remain in my seat.

I stood up. The door was two yards away. I took a deep breath and rushed at it; if anyone noticed my departure I was unaware of it. On the landing the lift stopped. Through the iron grill the manager saw me, acknowledging my presence with a puppet like movement of his head. I turned and ran down the stairs out onto the street.

Cold wind smacked my face and the need to vomit disappeared. I stood still for about half a minute taking deep breaths and then I was running up the lane. It began to snow. Swiftly and suddenly, great flakes came down, each one touched my face like the caress of Aunt Molly's loving hand. I turned onto the bridge across the Thames and I threw my arms wide like wings. I couldn't fly but I was flying, and when I let go the yell that exploded out of my heart, a man in a bowler hat looked at me from under his brolly and thought I was mad.

Stranger things have happened but not to many fellas on an Antrim road. I walked on, and the further I walked the more my spirit soared. Before long I was singing, and one thing I am sure of, I was singing a hell of a lot better than I'd ever sung during my time touring as a professional through every postage stamp village in the country.

Chapter Five

London knocked me out in the way that my first visit to the movies did. It was exciting, overpowering, and you weren't going to know how it worked. Not in three or four weeks you weren't. But I was sure of two things. I'd fallen in love with the place and I could get along with females in The Smoke even better than I had in Ireland. And that couldn't be a bad start.

To be honest, it wasn't all due to any fantastic ability to pull a bird, though I usually did make a little time when I worked at it. I fell on my feet, and later, on my head, through meeting a bloke going over on the boat from Belfast. His name was Jimmy Finglas and I met him standing at the bar, which is something that seems to happen to Irishmen now and again.

Right away he struck me as a bullshitter, being just half a point too smooth at certain moments. Not that I cared. He was good company, he bought his round, and I was glad to have someone to get drunk with. I needed to tie one on, for however casual I tried to be about walking out on Jennie, I couldn't shake the belief that I was a technicolour shit. And because I believed this, that it was a masochistic urge to suffer, I didn't think it would drift away of its own accord. So the answer lay inside any number of the bottles behind the bar and I was prepared to work my way through however many of them it took to gain the necessary insulation from my stupid conscience.

Jimmy Finglas was easy to be with and the more we drank the more I liked him. He was a fine fella, a six footer, with blonde hair which he wore in a duck's arse style. His all over appearance was what you'd call "with it". His black and white, small check, jacket, cut in Edwardian style and worn very long, was something that I wouldn't have been happy in. But then I wouldn't have expected him to jump for joy at the prospect of spending any time in my bottle green corduroy suit, either.

He smiled at some remark I made about the travelling show and his teeth were even and white, lending a rich quality to the smile that was surely a passport to pussy. He spoke well, too, with an accent that was soft and semi northern Irish, confirming his Monaghan origins.

There were a few girls in the bar who looked all right to me, but Jimmy didn't give them a second look.

"World is full of nothing but birds like that," he said.

I thought he was being a bit hard on them, and bloody cynical for a fella of my own age.

"When you've sampled some of the stuff around Belgravia and Chelsea...." He grinned at me... "I won't say I told you so."

Well, Jimmy Finglas was right, I was only too happy to admit it. He nodded his had, his eyes closing as he granted me benediction for my ignorance, which he didn't regard as culpable. He sipped V.S.O.P. brandy and said in his matter of fact way. "Stick with me, Maguire, at least you'll go out of your mind in luxury."

After a month of that scene I believed he was dead right. It was like being a willing prisoner on a conveyor belt with a bunch of nuts who thought about nothing but having fun.

Having fun consisted of drinking and dancing and fucking all the time. And when I say all the time, that's just what I mean. We moved from pub to club to bed. Or maybe I should say beds, because it wasn't in any way unusual to hit more than one scratcher in the same night.

I wallowed in it with a lust that might be forgiven in a fella who'd just finished a ten stretch in the nick. Jimmy took things a bit easier than I did, but then he'd been living as a professional house guest for two years, and he'd learned how to pace himself.

We were staying in a mews house in Belgravia with an upper crust raver whose daddy was so well heeled that she didn't even read The Financial Times to see how his money was doing. She was a decent bird and once I got used to that accent and a name that read Elizabeth Copse-Chandler, I began to like her.

She was one of the nicest people I've ever met, and probably the most honest. But my chip against anybody who had dropped out of the womb into the lap of luxury didn't allow me to admit this at first. And it was after a weekend of Jimmy and me playing musical beds with herself and two of her girl friends. I've often wondered if it wasn't her natural, disarming honesty that threw me. I mean, if I had an uptight thing about my background and my lack of education, it was more ridiculous than ever because Lizzie, as she liked to be called, didn't give a damn about it. She either liked you or she didn't. If she did, you were her friend whether you wanted to lay her or not, and looking back, I know that on a number of occasions she would have been justified in pulling the ground from under me by calling me a bloody snob. But she didn't because she was incapable of hurting anybody in a deliberate way.

Mind you, she could, like most of her friends, inadvertently walk all over you, but I never knew her to realise that she'd caused pain, or even inconvenience, without being mortified to a measure that was scarcely credible. I think it was this, more than any of her other qualities, that endeared her to me in a very special way. And one night I got drunk enough to tell her so.

She had thrown a party in the house. One of her close friends, Biddy Lennox, had got herself engaged to a nice enough yum yum type in the Guards. Lizzie wanted her to be happy even though "I think you're out of your tiny pointed head, dahling."

It was just another party. I'd been to so many parties in so many different pads in the past few weeks, that it would have taken the arrival of Orson Welles dressed up as a hamburger to make me raise an eyebrow. Or so I thought until I found Biddy Lennox on her knees in front of Jimmy, while her fiancé and a couple of others chortled up and down the kitchen, encouraging her to turn cannibal on "fucking Finglas" or at least to bite hard enough to "nick his pullover dahling".

Well, Jesus! I'm not prudish, but even for me, this was a bit over the top. Jimmy smiled at my expression and I shook my head in disbelief. Not at Jimmy's incredible cool, but at the way the yum yum was encouraging his bird to go around doing blow jobs.

Lizzie turned round to me in bed. Everybody had gone and the house was so quiet that we seemed to be somewhere else.

I could see tears spring into her eyes, hazel eyes, now a deep dark green in the half light from the wall lamps. I started to speak, to assure her that my compliment wasn't designed to hurt her. She stopped my mouth with her slender fingers and I saw her biting her bottom lip. But the tears came just the same and she was clinging to me and begging me to hold her tight.

Later, lying back on her pillow while I smoked a cigarette, she touched my face with her fingertips and smiled up at me.

"You're a poppet, dahling, an absolute poppet, but really, you can't, you mustn't, what I mean is, you shouldn't ever be so kind to anyone...."

I told her that I didn't understand and she sat up.

"Well, it's just too beautiful, dahling, too beautiful to bear.... Makes one think of lovely silly things.... You know... romance and love a la Barbara Cartland, and we all know what a load of old ballocks that is...."

I didn't speak. I had my dreams and I didn't want to listen to anyone, not even lovely Lizzie, making fun of them. I didn't give much room to the thought that maybe my dreams wouldn't stand up to any kind of close examination.

Lizzie moved up until she was sitting with her back to the headboard. "Oh, this is fun," she cooed, "talking instead of screwing...why it's practically kinky." Then without pausing for breath or changing her tone, she said. "Pass me a joint, poppet... there are a couple of sticks left."

When she had it burning I watched her take those long deep drags, looking like she was trying to push it down into her stomach. And for some reason I felt terribly sad.

"Be wonderful, dahling, you know, if there was something to love everlasting... I mean, I simply adore the idea, especially the way those Hollywood shits used to turn it out.... When HE carries HER over the threshold in her virginal white.... But Jesus!" She turned to look at me, her eyes hazel again, and it was so clear that she was serious, that I wished I was somewhere else.

"It doesn't last, does it? I mean, it can't, dahling... a few months, a year... as long as the fucking seems new... but what then? Everybody starts hopping into bed with everybody else...."

"Doesn't have to be this way, Lizzie...."

I refused the joint and she shrugged. "I forgot you didn't like grass; sorry dahling...." She took another long drag and I lit another cigarette. "Be nice, heavenly, I should think, if it was possible...."

"Anything's possible if you want it badly enough," I said this more for me than for Lizzie, who didn't believe it anyway. Maybe I didn't believe it myself but I wanted to.... I had to believe in, hope for, something....

I got up from the bed and started to dress. Lizzie sat bolt upright, her eyes wide in surprise. "Where are you going, love?"

"Just need some air.... I'm going for a walk."

"A walk...." She repeated it twice. Than she wanted to come with me. I needed to be on my own but said she could join me as long as she didn't expect me to chatter. She was up and dressed before me. "Strange one," she said.

Chapter Six

Many things happened to me while I was staying with Lizzie Copse-Chandler as number two permanent house guest behind Jimmy Finglas. And I'm not referring particularly to the endless line of birds that kept me awake nights. Nor the drunken gang bangs and the weirdo scenes, though, the whole lot slung together, would give you the impression that Frank Harris had been recording the minutes of an Episcopalian Church meeting while he wrote "My Life And Loves".

What I mean is that I learned a few things, the most important of which was that I was just plain lucky. And the fact that this revelation came to me in such a roundabout way, gave it all the more impact.

Besides Jimmy Finglas, I'd come to know a lot of other guys, most of them Irish, who were accepted as visiting fringe members of the Belgravia/Chelsea set. And some who were, more or less, permanent fixtures, firmly hooked into that hedonistic conveyor belt which moved around and around, in endless circles.

They didn't wear their hair long and they didn't run about in kaftans, but they were the fathers of today's hippies. They didn't believe in work, they turned on with hash or grass every chance they got. They drank anything that wouldn't stain their lips and they believed in free love, in all senses of the term, except that if the bird had money, they were more willing to take money from her.

I watched a lot of them come and go at Lizzie's place, and after a dinner party one night I caught a character called O'Driscoll stealing a pair of her opera glasses. He threw a punch when I took them away from him, but I bundled him out without too much fuss, and gave him a couple of stiff whacks to take the edge of his aggressiveness. Lizzie came out into the mews and she was upset. Not upset that O'Driscoll had nicked her glasses, but "frightfully distressed" that I had fought over them. And though she wasn't angry with me, I could see she wasn't going to hand out any medals.

She took O'Driscoll back into the house, giving him a drink before she went to find hot water to bathe his face. He raised his glass across the room, and I nodded "no hard feelings". No hard feelings, but confusion, plenty of that, so I just tucked into the booze, and even when I saw Lizzie going upstairs with him, all I did was refill my glass and empty it again.

The next afternoon I mentioned it to Jimmy and I could see he felt it was a load of ballocks. But when he saw that I needed to talk about it, he put the Sporting Life away. He looked at me through the smoke of his cigarette.

"You know these people are mad," he said.

I said: "How do you mean, mad?" I hadn't met anyone who thought he was a corkscrew or a vacuum cleaner or anything.

"Let me put it this way," Jimmy said. "Since we've been here, would you say the people we've met have behaved normally?"

I granted him that I didn't think so and he said "uh huh" and nodded his head. "So, this carry on... all this drinking and fucking and debauchery, which I'm not against, by the way, would horrify the man in the street... he'd be scandalized... by this abnormal behaviour, which surely makes for abnormal people... crazy people... which is what they are."

Maybe he was right. Maybe they were nuts. I thought it a bit strange that he should talk like that when he was so much a part of the scene. And it hit me that if I stuck around it wouldn't be long before I was ready for the same label.

The pussy on the scene no longer interested me. I'd let my appetite run amok and my immediate interest in sex was burned out. I felt good about that because I knew I was going to move on, and I didn't want to get sidetracked by a fresh piece. It was so easy to have a couple of bangs and a few drinks, and come round a week later wondering what the hell had happened.

I felt lucky too, for having that chat with Jimmy. He was right. I was being naïve to expect normal behaviour from people who would regard being normal as social stigma. So that without meaning to, he had shown me that I was a very ordinary human being.

I accepted the thought happily yet realising that only a week before it would have choked me to admit it. And again I was lucky, now that I was going to have enough money left to get a place of my own, and be able to spend a couple of weeks finding some kind of work.

I left the same day with Lizzie yelling "Keep in touch, poppet, I'm flying to have my hair coiffed" and Jimmy telling me that he'd see me around. Jimmy was all right, at least, he'd been okay to me. He was doing his own thing and more than happy for me to do mine. I had the feeling he wasn't sorry to see me go. This didn't hurt me. I was a square and even if he wanted to educate me, just then I had no interest in a crash course on how to be hip.

The more I thought about it the more I realised how fortunate I'd always been. And when I got the first room I wanted in a house at the Notting Hill Gate end of Portobello Road, I felt like having a Mass said.

A lot of kids I'd grown up with on The Hill, hadn't been so lucky, getting themselves nabbed doing the same things I did. We all broke into gas meters and nicked the lead out of empty houses. More from hunger than any need for adventure, we stole food and milk and anything else we could eat. But I had to stop all this when the first of my neighbourhood pals was sent to a reformatory.

It wasn't easy to stop thieving. I mean, it was as big a part of my life as going to the pictures, which I did three times a week. Most of the money I handled came from flogging things I'd stolen. Yet I knew that if I wanted to be certain I didn't get into trouble with the law I had to get honest. It was that simple.

I worked anyway, delivering milk and newspapers, and through a job I did every Saturday in a butcher's shop in Rathmines, I met the one and only Mrs. Kearney, who not only taught me a few things you wouldn't find in the Catechism, but gave me money every time we got into the scratcher.

Again, hating going back to The Hill at night, turned out to be lucky. I'd got to the point where I was angry enough to believe that there had to be something better. That belief turned into a positive desire to get out of there, and though I made a mess of that first beginning, I didn't have to go hungry or sleep on any benches in the park.

I guessed Ma was still in the flat on The Hill and I wondered if she still felt let down. I wanted to believe that time had come to the rescue of her heart, that she didn't hate me too much. But I couldn't tell. Ma was an extraordinary woman and when she said something, she usually meant it. Her last words to me hadn't been the kind you write on Christmas cards.

I lay down on my bed in Portobello Road, bloody glad to be on my own. Maybe Ma was over it by now... once her temper had simmered down.... Sleep moved in on me.... Yeah, I thought, maybe.

Chapter Seven

Right away I fell into a cushy job as singing M.C. in a good pub called "The Horse Trough", off Sussex Gardens in Paddington. I wasn't making a fortune and it was hardly going to be a stepping stone to The Palladium, but it was enough to live on while I found my way around. Apart from having to work only a few hours each evening, I got a skinful seven nights a week, thanks to the endless drinks that the regular crowd set up for me.

The smog bothered me some, getting home after I finished, particularly if I was smashed, which I frequently was, but it did help me steer clear of the professional Irishmen that I'd been running into around Notting Hill Gate. Christ! I got lost so often that by the time the fog moved out, I was ready to invest in a guide dog and a white stick.

Part of my job was to invite the customers to sing a song or tell a few gags, and I never came across a crowd so willing to oblige. Which helped me to realise why, despite buying me drinks, and applauding generously after each of my numbers, they never seemed to be listening when I was actually singing. They came there for one reason only. To get up and entertain each other over a few drinks.

I thought it was marvellous the way they jumped up when I called their names. There was no bullshit about them, no need to coax them. They wanted to do it and they very honestly got up and just belted it out. If I forgot one of them, it wasn't long before I heard about it.

"What's a matter then, Paddy I'm a bleedin' nigger or summing?"

"Andy. Jesus, I left you out." I tried hard to look like a professional pallbearer, grieving for all the injustices in the world, but not forgetting that dignity was an essential quality in the make-up of man.

"Not many, Pad, an' you 'ad that fat bleedin' Cox do free numbers... an' 'e caunt fackin' sing."

"He said it was his birthday," I lied. And I admit I felt it was all a bit ridiculous, but Andy was a really nice man, and it was important to him that he "did his turn".

"Birfday? 'Im? He don't 'ave none, mate. Day 'e was born they saved the afterbirf and frew away the nipper. Coo."

So I had to be careful to keep everybody happy and for a while I enjoyed doing so. It was a happy pub and the tenant, Lenny Caulfield, was a straight, hard working Cockney, who'd been a useful middleweight in his day. He liked a drink so he wasn't a middleweight any longer, but he was still very fast on his feet. I saw him go a bit one night and he surprised me. Some stranger tried to give his wife Elsie a pull and when he drew a blank said something like "Shame, darling, I could have done a lot with those Bristols of yours."

The fella would probably have got away with it if Lenny hadn't been listening to what he said. Elsie wasn't a woman to take umbrage easily, especially when somebody had been drinking, but Lenny chinned your man, anyway, and he was closing the door again, while the man picked himself up out of a shop doorway opposite, all in a matter of seconds.

"There was no need, luv." Elsie always called him that, and though there was a small amount of worry in her face, you could see that she was still potty about him, despite twenty years of marriage.

"Cheeky bleeder," Lenny said. He saw me standing there and he smiled. "Think some of these blokes never saw a decent pair of tits before."

I shrugged and gave him a knowing smile, glad that he'd told me what "Bristols" meant. Years later I checked its derivation and found it was Cockney rhyming slang. Bristol City, titty, hence "Bristols" equalling pair, if you see what I mean.

For the rest of that evening I was like the proverbial Cheshire Cat each time I thought of what had happened. And I was happy to know I wasn't the only one with a hang up on "Bristols". I didn't look for any that night though, because once more I was langers by the time I knocked back all the drinks that were waiting at closing time.

This was the pattern of my night life in those first weeks in London. Most people drank like I did, or so I believed, and I loved it. No matter how much I drank I never got troublesome, and I had a childish pride about getting home under my own steam. Which I did, but a few mornings I woke up fully dressed, lying on the bed in my little room, and this bothered me.

I didn't remember getting home the night before, but I was more concerned about falling asleep in my street clothes. I'd had to sleep in my shirt too many times as a kid, sharing a bed with three of my brothers, wishing through many a cold night that we had a few more old coats to throw over us. At that time my dreams didn't run to blankets and I didn't know the feel of sheets until the first time I went into hospital.

So that, undressing for bed, wearing pyjamas, and being clean at all times, had practically become a fetish with me. And here was I, falling down drunk like some bum. Apart from this, I felt most mornings that I'd been pulled backwards through a keyhole, which was hardly starting the day according to Hoyle. The thought that I should ease up on the gargle, did cross my mind, and I decided that very soon I would. Might even give it up altogether, I told myself. I mean, who needs it, anyway?

I walked the streets of London during the day and I can only say that I felt like Aladdin must have done when the "open oh sesame" trick made him top man in the magic circle. The city was a giant treasure house. So much so, that ten years later, when I had to pull out of it with a finality that cut me down the middle, I was still head over hills about the place.

I never had what you'd call a map reading intelligence, I mean, give me directions and I'd get lost an a coffin, but I was definitely blessed with a great nose for direction. And in the figurative sense again, that same nose was like a Geiger counter when it came to sniffing out which birds *would* and which wouldn't hold onto their ha'penny.

Getting lost, without the smog, was part of the joy of it all. That was how I found the house where Samuel Johnson lived in Gough Square behind The Cheshire Cheese in Fleet Street. That marvellous pub. How can I tell you what it felt like to be standing and having a drink where Chesterton stood and drank and scribbled his copy on cigarette packets and the like. I could almost see him standing there and I could have shed a tear for the wonderful, big, lonely man, but I smiled in my guts at the memory of the story about his mother going to his headmaster at St. Paul's in Hammersmith because she was worried about his school report. Unlike most school teachers at that time, your man could see and feel what was inside the streak of sensitivity that was G.K. Chesterton.

"Treasure him, madam, he's six feet of genius," he said, or words not far removed.

I finished my drink, wishing that I'd been gifted enough for someone to say that about me, even though I was only five feet eleven inches.

My friends in "The Horse Trough" demanded a run down on my days wandering the streets of their own. And being an open book, I poured it out to them, sharing every moment, describing this and that, things a lot of them had never noticed themselves. Elsie would stand behind the bar, frozen in the act of drying glasses, her eyes wide and her lips moving silently, as she caught my enthusiasm.

As you might imagine, some of the things I said were perfect cues for those sharp Cockney characters who have a witty answer to everything. Like me talking about the Tower of London which led to the Duke of Clarence and how he'd been murdered in a barrel of Malmsey.

"Cool," a greengrocer called Terry Hall, said: "Be wastin' their name tryin' that with Old Len 'ere... sup the bleedin' lot 'e would an' come up for a refill."

There was a lot of friendly slagging too, about these flaming Paddies coming over and reminding us Londoners that we know next to nothing about our own manor. Just like myself and Dublin, my own town, about which I knew next to nothing. Because it was there, and part of it was part of you, you took it all for granted, and neglected it with the impunity we only show to those things we love.

When the letter from Ma arrived I rushed back upstairs and stood looking at it for about five minutes before I dared open it. Her handwriting hadn't changed, the same off balance scrawl, hiding her guts and determination, her unselfish charity and her inherent ability to crush and gobble up anybody who didn't do things her way.

I'd send her a couple of pounds and it hadn't come back, which was a beginning. I opened the flimsy paper and found two lined sheets. Ma was well and my father was home again and he had a steady job working for the Electricity Supply Board. She said thanks for the money which had bought enough netting curtain for the two windows in the living room that doubled as Ma's bedroom.

It was good to hear from me, to know I was keeping well. That there was always a bed if I ever thought of going home for visit. I smiled through the tears that pumped out of me, knowing she didn't mean I was welcome only for a visit. I knew her, and could feel all the things she couldn't bring herself to say. But none of that mattered, she'd said enough. The pain had gone the way of all pain in the long miles of memory.

I read those two pages over and over until I knew them by heart and when I finished bawling my eyes out I scribbled a note, enclosing another two lids, and saying that I'd like to come home for Christmas.

A couple of days later I took a day job in an office. I was

employed as book-keeper, would you believe, and me not knowing debit from credit. But my boss was a nice man who seemed to expect having to show me everything from scratch. For me it was the wrong job but it paid twelve lids a week, so I tried hard to get smart enough to take books to "trial balance" or whatever it's called. My boss, an easy going fella from the North Country, as he called it, wasn't looking for any miracles, besides which I wanted badly to hold the number until Christmas. When I did walk through that door at home, I wanted them to know, just by looking at me, that I wasn't short of a few quid.

I told Elsie my news before work that night, and bless her big bristled body, she was up in the air she was so happy about it. She knew all about Ma and me, and she knew a lot of other things I hadn't spoken about to anyone else. But then, Elsie was easy to talk to... a big, sweet, mother woman who'd never had kids of her own. "Not that we didn't do a lot of 'eavy breeving while we were tryin', like." She often said that, her eyes aglow with mischief. It was always good for a laugh, and you can imagine the remarks it encouraged from the regulars. It was the considered opinion of one or two, always expressed loudly enough for Lenny to hear, that all Lenny's power had been in his right cross, while he could only feint with the contents of his shorts. Someone else thought it was his gut getting in the way, that unless he'd been hung like a Nagasaki donkey, he couldn't be expected to get close enough to Elsie.

"You ever finka takin' a bath, Andy, pop rand an' I'll give ye a little punch up the trahsers... see if ye fink it's a bleedin' wart I got 'stead of a choppa... right?"

The cross talk was endless and often vicious, but you could see, and feel, and hear how much those people cared about each other. I'd go as far as saying they loved their mates in the way they cherished the family idea, sticking together, no matter what squabbles there might be, because wife and kids and mates were all that really mattered.

Myself and Elsie had drifted into the habit of talking long after pub had closed, and I was chuffed when she referred to me as "my mate, Paddy". She could let her hair down with me, she said, and because she left the booze alone when she was working, the few drinks we had afterwards meant a lot to her.

I guess I might have been like the son she never had. I know she became sad when she talked of how badly they had wanted kids. She was the eldest of ten and believed desperately in large families, with everybody pulling together. And this great bird had been bypassed when it came to handing out the conception tickets. I thought it was a bloody shame, particularly when so many women at home couldn't even enjoy a ride for fear of having another baby.

It didn't make sense, but then, what did? So many areas in my twenty two years of walkabout had ended up in a shambles, that I'd practically stopped hoping to find what you might call balance.

It was a busy time, and the luxury of sitting round trying to work out answers to world problems was something I couldn't afford. I got on with my work, both jobs, and I tried to ease up on the drinking. I had to, if only so that I could get to the office at nine each morning. And as one December day moved into the next, I found myself trembling with excitement. And I mean that... trembling so that you could see, my heart bursting as I wondered what it was going to be like. Honest to Christ! I was a kid going to the circus for the very first time.

Chapter Eight
Dublin, Christmas '57

One thing that first flight proved - you can be paralytic in London and unhappily shit-scared sober at the Dublin touchdown. And I only wished the head who didn't think I was fit to travel because I was drunk, could have seen me when I stumbled out of the Custom Hall at Dublin Airport. He wouldn't have believed his own eyes.

Mind you, it was rough, Jesus, was it rough? And if I wasn't bad enough, as though I wasn't suffering sufficiently, convinced the pilot was out of the Kamikaze stable, some Biddy behind me jammed her head against the back of my seat and ran through the Rosary non-stop. Except when we hit an air pocket. Then she ejaculated, "Jesus!" which was some kind of swear until she followed it with "Mary and holy St. Joseph, protect me, a sinner." I know I'm being unkind, I should have been feeling sorry for her, but how could I when I had all the stops out feeling sorry for myself.

Dublin didn't mean a thing, if anything, it brought me down. I blamed it on needing a drink and the cabbie didn't mind when I asked him to stop for a minute. He was a nice old man and he had a couple of holy pictures taped to his dashboard. I guess he hadn't heard that bit about "cleanliness being next to godliness" and I didn't bother telling him. I was too busy wishing I could get upwind of him, which is impossible inside a taxicab.

I stayed in the pub longer than I needed, kidding myself that I was enjoying the chat between the couple of oul' ones who were three sheets in the wind and it not yet teatime. I realised this and went back to the taxi. I mean, what in Christ had I to be scared about? Ma had said in her letter that I was welcome, and she knew I was coming.

The Hill. Home, Sweet Home, and the fire black out. The Hill, still there, block after block of grey, stucco fronted rabbit warrens, where the poor remained poor because the system needed a certain amount of fodder, while Mother Church needed more and more Catholics, and never mind whether they were underprivileged, poor, stupid, sick, or just plain helpless. As the cab moved along it hurt to see that things hadn't improved, and I felt like a eunuch in a whorehouse because there wasn't a thing I could do about it.

I took my time paying the cabbie and said something that made him laugh like a drain. That was good for me, helping me to slip into my happy go lucky, always on the ball with the joke, routine. That was it... the way to play it. In the door, a quick hug and a fast remark to break the ice. Ma you look great, your eyes are as beautiful as ever, especially the two on the left. Might even be a good idea to burst into the song. A few bars maybe, just to get me over the threshold. No? Well, anyway, keep it cool and calm. Nice and easy.

Ma opened the door. Her heart was in her eyes and it was beating for me at the moment. She hugged me fiercely and because I knew her so well, remembering how she used to hold me that way when I was a kid, I knew that the pain and the hopelessness of it all was still there inside her, and I held onto her. It must have been five minutes before the pair of us stopped weeping enough for me to bring my Jesus suitcases in off the stairs.

We were all right after that, Ma rushing about getting me something to eat. At the same time she seemed to be trying to tell me all the news without pausing for breath. This was so unlike her that I knew she'd been just as nervous as me, and I felt so warm about her that I'm sure she felt it across the room.

The place had been recently decorated and there was a new glass fronted cupboard where the old dresser used to be. Everything shone like a tribute to Ma's elbow grease, and I had to convince myself that a good clean up was a perfectly natural thing when you had a visitor coming, just so that I didn't start weeping again.

Ma looked well, but then she'd always been healthy and the years of going without food a lot of the time didn't appear to have made any inroads on her constitution. She looked older, and while her hair, the colour of wood smoke, had a lot to do with this, I thought it suited her down to the ground.

I sat listening while she stood over the gas stove in the corner of the room and took in every word Ma said, although memories crowded in like kids asking for sweets.

My sister Josie was married and living in Scotland. That seemed great and I really hoped she was happy. Why shouldn't she get lucky and be contented? Sooner or later she was bound to run into some fella who wanted to end up with eardrums suffering from grievous bodily harm.

My father was working four pm to midnight and he liked the job. That was all she said about him and I noticed that her bed was a single divan under the window, so it wasn't hard to figure that they still didn't sleep together. The lino was polished, but things didn't changed that much.

Ma watched me as I started to devour the fry. In England it would have been called a mixed grill, but the white and black pudding on the plate made all the difference. I'd come across stuff called liver sausage in London that looked like white pudding. That was as far as it went because it tasted like cotton wool dipped in candle grease. And where the sausages I'd eaten in Notting Hill were bread rolls wearing nylons, those lean pork Dublin sausages just blessed the taste buds, and made me realise that much as I loved London, it didn't have everything.

Billy came in from work just after Ma told me he was engaged. I smiled as I bit into a thick slice of white loaf.... The way he used to cover his chopper with the flannel if you walked into the bedroom and he was washing himself in the tin bath. And me, evil little bastard that I was, needling him about it, until I'm sure he was doing novenas that I'd get run over by a truck.

I stood up and Billy shook my hand like he'd just finished reading a self improvement manual which said a firm handshake made people respect you. But knowing Billy, it was probably genuine... he always seemed to do the right thing or at least give the right impression to people outside. And I could feel, by the formality he directed my way, that he no longer thought of me as part of the home scene.

He was a nice looking man, all blond and fresh looking, and he still had that very direct way of looking you in the eye. It was so strong, so bloody definite, that it had to be a front. Not that I minded that... we all had our own way of covering up our insecurity.

I felt no hatred for him, not anything, really. Yet, when we'd been kids, and he used rip into Ma because she'd hauled him out of bed like he'd asked her to because it was Sunday and he had to get Holy Communion, I could willingly have roasted him on a slow spit.

"You're looking well," he said.

I nodded and sat down again. "You too." I drank some tea and he sat down at the table. He was watching me and I put the cup down like a fella who dined at the Ritz every day. His accent was too good, his enunciation too deliberate, that I could only think the muscles in his face must have been in great shape.

"I understand congratulations are in order," I said, glad as a ten year old that he wasn't as tall as me.

"Oh, you heard." He smiled, a bit shy, and I liked him for that.

Ma poured a cup of tea for him and I had a refill. The big day wouldn't be for some time, I learned. He and his girlfriend, Olive, were saving for a house. I saw Ma's expression flash impatience, as she began cooking his meal, and I guessed she'd had to listen to this same verbal since he'd first mentioned the idea. Billy always had to trash things out to a point where he drove everybody nuts. And he asked endlessly for advice which he never paid any attention to. But just then I was glad for him, happy that he wanted whatever was going, that he had no intention of settling for a room or a flat on The Hill. And I knew that if hard work counted, Billy would get whatever mattered. He was like that and you had to admire him, but I know that if I bored him as much as he bugged me that first evening, it was a wonder he didn't wind up with chronic indigestion.

I hadn't given Billy a thought when Ma wrote about me coming for a visit, but he was still living there, and with the old man being home as well, I wondered where the hell I was supposed to sleep. Ma couldn't think I was going to share a bed with either of them. She didn't and she smiled when I let my relief show.

"I have a fold up bed, son," she said, "you can sleep there." She meant the divan, which was typical of her, but I wasn't having that. It took me a few minutes to make it clear that I wouldn't sleep in her bed, that the fold up would do me fine. I hinted that I'd slept on a lot worse but when this brought a small frown of worry to her brow I changed direction and told her I was only kidding.

The next day I helped my father put up the paper chains and the other things that served as Christmas decorations. And I felt so good just doing a small job like that with him, that I forgot the bloody awful night I'd spent trying to get comfortable on what some hustler had had the gall to call a fold up bed.

I hardly knew my father, most of the memories concerning him had faded. Or so I thought until he shook my hand for the first time in something like ten years. It wasn't that I liked or disliked him, he was a stranger to me, a man I'd never really expected to run into again. But when he stood there and I held his hand, when he grinned at me and told me he was glad to see me, I knew that I'd loved him for a thousand years and that no matter what happened it was always going to be like that.

His jaw was still hard and there was some of the fierce, whipcord strength remaining around his mouth, but my God, he'd changed enough for me to have passed him in the street without knowing who he was. I was to learn later that, coming home from Manchester and finding a job right away, he'd worked double shifts heaving coal into a furnace, dropping almost two stones in weight, which, though he was doing an easier job now, hadn't come back. And when he took off his hat I could see that what little hair he'd had had disappeared.

Chapter Nine

During the first World War my father ran away from home and joined the British Army. He was under sixteen years of age but he told them the tale and they didn't argue. Which proves that my ability to bullshit didn't come out of the stones in the road.

Now of all the unlikely places to run into your older brother, a British Army trench in France, must take some beating. But that's just what happened to my father and if it hadn't been for an understanding C.O. my uncle would have been on a charge. Striking the King's uniform, or whatever it is they charge a Paddy with for beating up his young soldier brother, and a battle going on outside.

Well, my father was shipped home under guard, but two weeks after they dumped him in Ringsend where the Grannie Maguire gave him another hammering, his birthday arrived and he was off again.

This time they shipped him home on a stretcher, one of the many soldiers who somehow didn't die from gas poisoning in the trenches of France. He was so ill for months afterwards that the Grannie got over her need to kick the shit out of him, although she did, according to himself, give him a cruel ballocking day after day, for being such a fuckin' eejit.

When the Civil War got under way, Ma didn't see him for weeks at a time, and when it was over he ended up like so many others, out of work with a wife and two children to feed.

He was lost, the dream he'd had turned out to be a nightmare, and for sixteen years he lived on the dole, doing any odd job he could get. So if he was bitter by the time I was old enough to notice such a thing as a black mood, I don't think he can be blamed. Yet, I was twenty-two years old, sharing with himself and Ma the happiest Christmas ever, before I knew this or anything else about him.

After dinner on St. Stephen's Day, Da looked at me in a funny way when I asked him if he'd ever thought of getting a little business of his own. It was a bit stupid, that bald question to a man who'd spent too many years without a pound in his pocket. But it was just my enthusiasm getting in the way.

You see Christmas Eve I'd met a fella in a pub and we'd become instant mates. Eamonn Boyd, his name was, and we spent the evening drinking and talking before we went on to a party that some friend of his was throwing.

It doesn't often happen that you meet somebody you feel you've known forever, but that's the way it was with Eamonn Boyd. And after a couple of hours, before we turned our minds to birds and sinking the log, we knew just about everything there was to know about each other.

Eamonn brought up the thing of me getting a little shop for my father. He knew that I wanted to do something to show the old man that I cared. It wasn't that hard to rent premises and Eamonn, who had his own wholesale tobacco and confectionary business, guaranteed me six months credit on whatever stock was needed to get the thing off the ground in the right way. And the more I thought about it, the more I felt it was a good idea. To give the old man something of his own.

I could earn the money to lease a shop and pay for fixtures and fittings and all that. And I could go on working after it was happening, pumping money into it each week until it was thriving on its own steam.

My father got a charge out of listening to all this over the dinner table and when he nodded his head and said he liked the sound of it, I wanted to get up and hug him. Ma didn't say a lot, she rarely did when my father was around, but she didn't pull any faces knocking the idea. And that was enough for me.

Boxing night, Eamonn Boyd and I went to a dance. But not before we talked the thing out again, and when he shook my hand on it, I knew that everything was going to be all right. I felt so good, so happy, that night, that I wasn't bothered whether I got off with a bird or not. My brain was spinning with this dream, so much so that I was impatient to get back to London.

The following morning I gave Ma a couple of quid before I went into town to get a present for Elsie. It wasn't going to be anything fantastic, but that woman had been so good to me, I couldn't go back to the pub empty handed. I told Ma to get her hair done or something, and she smiled and kissed my face. I tell you, life felt pretty good at that moment.

I was back in town by about four that afternoon with my suitcase in my hand and my goodbyes behind me. My flight was around six and I thought I'd have a few drinks before I got the bus for the airport. I didn't intend to get jarred, I was high enough to fly on my dream for the old man. I'd called Eamonn Boyd to come for a drink before I left but his secretary said he was in the country until the weekend. So I'd just have a few celebration shorts on my own.

I went into Larkin's snug because it was the handiest boozer to the bus station and I was standing by the serving hatch when this tasty bird came in. She might have been looking for someone the way she glanced around but the place was empty except for me. Her face seemed to say "might as well have a drink now that I'm here" and I had to agree with that. Besides which her appearance had done more for that snug than a fresh coat of paint and a new fitted carpet.

There was just the one barman working and though I could see him out in the long bar, he didn't seem to be anxious to see me. When your woman came over and stood by the hatch, her perfume turned me on, as if I wasn't already.

"I suppose if we hang around there's some danger of getting

a drink," I said to her.

She smiled at that, despite its age and she peeped into the long bar. Her face dropped and she pulled her head back.

"Oh, him," she said with a lot of annoyance. "He won't serve me, that fella...."

"Sit over there..." I pointed to the corner at right angles to the hatch. "I'll get you one," I said, thinking I'd sooner give you one, and I don't mean a John Jameson.

She shook her head. "Got a mirror inside... cane see you wherever you sit." I nodded, and if I looked disappointed it's only because I was. And why not? The way her dress was clinging to her was a bigger turn on than if she'd been standing there in the Jeyes Fluid. And if she wasn't what you'd call beautiful, her hot brown eyes and her big sexy mouth more than made up for it.

"We could go somewhere else," she said, after what seemed two years. I nodded, just to show willing to such a friendly suggestion, and I walked over to get my case off the seat, trying desperately to move like a fella who wasn't dying with a hard on.

I never found out what she did that got her barred from Larkin's but it must have been something wild because it kept us out of three other pubs in the neighbourhood as well.

When she said we could have a drink at her place, I gave her money to buy a bottle and I practically ran into a phone box to call Aer Lingus. It took me ages to fix a later flight and I was lucky to land the last seat on the nine thirty-five to London.

Your women hadn't come back by the time I got through with my phone call, so I lit a cigarette and stood waiting for her. The more I thought about her the more I fancied her and I wondered if she wore anything under her dress. She had some form and no gift stamps needed, and her eyes suggested that she was just mad enough to be a raving lunatic in the scratcher. I tried to stop thinking about her then because I was just making things harder for myself.

When I finished the cigarette I felt a bit uneasy and I found myself glancing about, half afraid that somebody was standing watching me, laughing at the idea that "there was one born every minute". I picked up my suitcase, no longer suffering from rheumatism behind the fly buttons and I went and checked it into the bus station. Me? Jesus! Of all the heads in town your woman had pulled a stroke on Jack the Lad himself. I could hardly believe it and I was still shaking my head like a punch drunk fighter when I turned into O'Connell Street.

Ah, well, Head you had it coming... numbers game says you have to come unstuck... averages... can't strike oil all the time.

I pushed that defeatist stuff out of my mind. I didn't think it was funny and I didn't want to be a good loser, either. And if I ever saw that pig again.... This was all bullshit too. What was I going to do? Walk up and slap a summons on her? For Jaysus sake, grow up, Maguire.

In Daly's pub, by the Corinthian cinema, the whiskey practically stuck in my throat, but I stayed there for an hour or so, trying to get my sense of humour back. The upstairs bar was about three parts full and there were a few women I'd seen before. Or if not them, women that looked just like them. You chatted to them and you bought them a few bevys and you gave them something. It wasn't cold and clinical, in no way strictly business as it was in London. Semi professionals I suppose you'd call them, and often enough the drink was your passport to the scratcher if you didn't have any bread left.

Every time I looked around the bar I got signals, and when one of them spoke to me on the way out, I just nodded and passed on, thinking to myself, sweetheart, as far as I'm concerned, you'd be safe in an army billet.

I walked over O'Connell Bridge for the fifth time that day. Jesus, if I did it once more I'd begin to look like a number twelve bus. I stopped and looked down the Liffey which was humming a bit. I could see Butt Bridge, and the reflection of it in the river was so clear that the complete oval was like a huge rugby ball.

When I moved on I thought I saw Ma turn from D'Olier Street onto Eden Quay. I stopped by the end of the bridge. Yes, it was Ma all right. I crossed the road, dodging the traffic, not even thinking of what I was going to say to her. Like, as far as she was concerned I was already on my way to London.

I saw her turn into the amusement arcade and went in after her. It seemed such a funny place to be going. When I caught sight of her again she was sitting down with a lot of other people to take part in a game called Housey Housey, which was a kind of Bingo. I stood back so that she wouldn't see me and in a strange way, I was delighted. It was crazy, unbelievable, but Jesus, it was something she wanted to do. And that made it all right. Anything that helped her keep the emptiness of life away was all right. And let's face it, she could have taken to the booze without anybody being entitled to say one word against her.

I walked back onto Eden Quay feeling I'd been handed a bonus. I thought it was great. I really did. In fact, I felt so good that I thought "shag the bus"! I nipped across the road to the rank and took a cab to the airport. One way or another it had turned out to be a good night.

Chapter Ten

For the first four months of the new year I went from bed to work. And apart from a couple of times when I had to work the steam out of my jockey shorts, I went to bed as I went to work, on my lonesome own.

I packed in my office job by phoning and asking them to send on my cards and within a week I'd left off singing in the pub as well.

Elsie was great, delighted that things had gone so well at home. And when I told her what I had in my mind, she cried, and the night I left she gave me a hug that could have been a turn on if she hadn't been so like a mother to me. Lenny worked me a tenner that I didn't expect, and it goes without saying that I promised to drop in and let them know how I was doing.

In those days in London, a single man was entitled to earn a hundred and twenty to a hundred and forty pounds, tax free. So like a lot of other people who felt about taxation the way some people feel about malaria, I began to change my identity from time to time.

Early in January I went to work night shift in a factory. Now I realise that this admission could get a fella labelled as a masochist, but it was the only way to get your hands on any kind of decent wages. If you were unskilled, I mean, which I was, pretty much.

There were other ways of making money. Like conning or thieving, or pouncing on some bird, be she brass or just some rich raver. But, dumb as it might seem, especially for a guy who'd come up the way I did, that wasn't my way. Whatever I got I had to earn and the great thing about England was that if you were willing to get stuck in, you could earn money. And I was glad I was the way I was... Sometimes when you felt you had little or nothing left, going to work to earn it by the sweat of your brow and all that, reminded you that you still had some small shred of self respect left in the can.

Factory work for unskilled people can't be much worse than labouring in a Siberian timber camp, but I wouldn't like to put any money on that assumption. And if I stuck it, without allowing it to bug me too much, it was only because I knew I wasn't going to be there for long.

The noise is the first thing that slams into you. The pounding and the steaming and sometimes the screaming of man-made machines that seemed to me, within a very short time, to have come up from Hell itself. And somehow I never got used to the damn things. Often when I'd be walking close to one and it excreted its usual racket, I'd jump in the air in fright, as through the Jesus thing was going to eat me up.

The kind of work I did most nights might have taxed the brain power of a retarded mongrel that was a cross between an ass and cart and two policemen. It really might.

One place, my job was to stand at a conveyor belt, making sure that all the cans of beans were upright as they moved along, before they went to another guy who checked that I was doing my job right, before they finally ended up being boxed, so that some time later you could end up eating the farty little fuckers on toast.

I stuck the number for twenty-eight night shifts by which time my nerves were making like a dog with the rabies, while what was left of my mind boggled at the idea that some of my workmates had been there for twenty years or more.

Not that I couldn't have put up with it a while longer, it was just that the time had come for me to go, because I'd earned my tax free allowance. By moving out then and asking the boss to send back my insurance card and my P45 taxation slip, because I was going home to Ireland, I got my tax given back to me. This amounted to thirty quid or more and was a fairly handy way of saving money. All I had to do next day was get a new insurance card under a nice new name, get another job, and do the same thing over again when the time came.

When I was asked at the insurance office for the name of my last employer, I gave them Eamonn Boyd's address in Dublin, so that each time I changed my name, I made out that I'd only just arrived in England. Eamonn knew what to expect and would write back confirming I'd worked for him, and because I moved my address with each job, there was very little chance of coming unstuck.

Each Monday I sent a registered letter off to my father and the fact that he didn't reply at all, didn't bother me. He'd never been much of a letter writer.

I lived on as little as possible and probably did my insides all kinds of damage, by eating the worst kind of stodge just because it was the cheapest and the most filling. Jesus, when I think of some of those steak and kidney pies, with chips that looked and tasted like they had cholera, and the endless plates of bangers and mash followed by steamed sultana roll and custard, it's enough to make me reach for the health salts.

At the time I didn't mind it all that much, because I didn't let it get a grip on my thinking. Any more than the jobs I did. And I had a reason for doing it, a dream that could well come true if I just went on plodding for a few more months. It wasn't hard once you learned to switch off. Which is the only sensible thing to do when you have to live in a vacuum for a period. And doing the kind of soul destroying work that earned you better money than your actual office jobs, made you turn off, so that even this helped you cope with a life that had suddenly become all work and very little play.

My mother used to say you could get used to anything in time, even hanging, and I often smiled as I sat down to my dinner at half past two in the morning. Whatever the meal was called, those factory cooks somehow disguised it enough for it to taste like a plate of hot nothing. I used to empty half a bottle of brown sauce all over it, shut my eyes, and get into it like a novice coming off a three metre springboard for the first time.

At first I looked forward to meal time as an escape for half an hour from the noise of the factory floor, but I soon found that in places like that, the senses get little relief. Fellas get so used to shouting over the noise of the machines that they go on doing it even when they're sitting down to eat.

I noticed this most of all in the last job I had on that night shift scene. It was a rubber factory in Acton, where the noise and the smell together, left you feeling you'd been raped by the Brigade of Guards.

My job there was really the end of the line, and over the years I often knocked myself on the side of the head just to be sure I didn't dream it up. Each night I had to check twelve thousand car battery stoppers to ensure that the two tiny holes, punched into the rubber by machine, were true and clean. I guess, so that the distilled water in the car battery would have some way out when it decided to evaporate, but I haven't really gone into it.

So I stood before a bench holding a yellow card in my left hand. I picked up a stopper and held it over the card. If I could see the two yellow spots, I threw the stopper into a bin. Twelve thousand stoppers a night, so help me God, until I thought I had bells in my head.

Was it any wonder? I mean, in twenty-eight shifts, I checked out three hundred and thirty-six thousand of the fucking things. And to cap it all, just before I left, the foreman, a decent enough creeper from Manchester, came up to me with a tiny plastic bag in his hand, and though he tried for a smile when I said, "No thanks, Ivan, I never use French letters," he didn't quite make it.

The bag contained six stoppers that weren't right. Like the two little holes weren't true and clear the way the two little holes in car battery stoppers have to be. He was supposed to give me a ballocking for letting the black spastics get through.

I gave poor old Ivan a cigarette and he looked at me with the same ox like intensity that he granted to his own stoppers. The poor bastard was numb, which Jesus, he was entitled to be after eight and a half years at the job.

I felt so good that I just wanted to laugh all the time in those last few days, and normally I would have fallen down in hysterics at the idea of what was happening. But Ivan didn't feel good, he never felt anything other than dyspeptic, so I contained the joy that my release at the weekend had induced in me, and I just told him gently that I was leaving to go home to Ireland.

I'd become so used to saying that in the past months at various offices of the Ministry of Labour, that I had to stop and remind myself that I really was going to Dublin, if only for a little while.

Alfie, the one real mate I had in the job, came up to join us for a cigarette. He knew I was going and as he said himself, he was "chuffed to fuck" I was getting "aht" which in English reads "out". His brown eyes were always sparkling with mischief and he got into old Ivan right away.

"Lucky bleeder, in 'e, Ivan?" He winked at me and we both waited while Ivan moved his eyes up to look at us. Not that Ivan said anything, but him reacting in any way was a question in itself.

"Comin' into all that poppy," Alfie said. "Chances are, me old mate, you won't live a bleedin' year..." he warned me... "you'll be nestin' so much you'll just fade away like an old bleedin' soldier...."

"Used to... used to like a bit... a bit of undercut myself." Ivan said in his laborious accidental way. Alfie exploded with shock, screeching wildly and there was no way I could stop myself laughing with him. We must have been at it for a couple of minutes by which time Alfie had to wipe the tears from his face.

"Don't bother me no more." Ivan continued, which blew another fuse in Alfie, and it must have been a further minute before our cackling subsided.

"Sooner have a cup of tea." Ivan got up and walked back down to his bench. Alfie stood looking after the awkward shambling figure of our foreman. He scratched his head and turned to me like a fella who was losing his marbles.

"Six years I bin' 'ere, never 'eard 'im talk like that before... come to fink of it, never 'eard 'im bleedin' talk at all...." I shook my head, admitting my own surprise. Alfie's expression changed. "Couldn't imagine 'im in the saddle though, you?"

"Not even in the cowboy picture," I said.

Alfie went back to work and I chuckled to myself for a while. But I couldn't help feeling sorry for old Ivan. Because he was sort of half head, he wasn't popular, and like everybody else I had thought he didn't care. Yet, his effort a few minutes before to take part, to be associated with me, a fella that he thought had it made, seemed to me an indication that he didn't enjoy being lonely any more than anyone else.

I went back to my yellow card and my bloody rubber stoppers, and for no reason at all it occurred to me that I hadn't been drunk in almost four months.

Chapter Eleven
London/Dublin. April '58

I was pretty checked up when I said goodbye to Alfie and I could see he regretted my leaving. As we walked up to the tube station, I felt like yelling out that I was free. That's just what it was, freedom, and if a fella getting out of prison could possibly feel any better than I did that morning, it'd be worth doing six months just for the experience of getting out. But I kept my mouth shut, went shtuhm, as Alfie would say, remembering that he had to go back there in about fourteen hours time.

It was an easy windless morning with the sun on the job maybe a bit early for the weather to hold up all day. Not that I was bothered one way or the other. I was glowing, fresher than a lot of guys who were just getting up, and whether it rained or snowed, I knew that today I was going to be moving like a pair of well oiled roller skates.

Before I got off the tube, Alfie gave me his address on a piece of paper and I promised to keep in touch. Maybe we meant that we should, but somehow I felt it wouldn't be like that. We'd been mates right off, me liking his cheek and the glorious Cockney verbal he was forever coming out with, while he claimed that my Blarney was strong enough to get the knickers off a reverend mother. But really, we were like tube trains passing at breakfast, and I never did see him again. He was a truly nice bloke and I only hope he finally won the pools.

By noon that Saturday I was standing by the side of the road outside Mill Hill, looking for a lift to Holyhead or any point on the way. I mean, the plane was okay if you were a parcel or a mailbag, but it was expensive and I didn't know how long I'd have to be in Dublin. So the eighty quid in my pocket had to be cosseted as much as possible.

I couldn't see myself ever getting tight... hitching to save the fare on the train from London to Holyhead, which would be a day's walkabout money at home, was just my way of trying to develop an attitude to money that I'd never had before. The bloody stuff had always burned a hole in my hand, but for the first time in my life I'd worked hard and gone without booze and birds just to gather some of the stuff together, and it was going to be used for something worthwhile. Like the dream that my father and I had been nourishing since Christmas.

Getting a lift wasn't hard and I was on the outskirts of Birmingham in the early afternoon. Tommy, my second eldest brother, lived there, so Ma said. Not that she heard from him or got a few quid now and then. He was married but whether he had kids or not, I didn't know. Anymore than I knew Tommy. Or Ben either, for that matter. He was still in Manchester, married too, but different to Tommy in that he dropped Ma the odd line even if he didn't have any bread to send home.

I was in Holyhead by about seven o'clock and once I had my one and only suitcase checked in, I went to the pictures. I hadn't sat in a movie house in months, heavy drinking and sitting still being two things that sat on the stomach like lemonade and milk together. And even though I'd hardly dropped three pints all told, since Christmas, working night after night on a factory floor didn't allow much time for recreation.

Holyhead was all right, I suppose, but I couldn't see myself running to my travel agent to organise a holiday there at any time in the immediate future. I might have been unlucky, the people I spoke with didn't exactly lean over backwards to give me directions or advice, and all in all, when the mail boat pulled out for Dun Laoghaire, I felt that Holyhead was a great place for it to leave from.

The run across to Dublin takes three and a half to four hours, but I got a berth while we were still docked at midnight. I was feeling a bit fragile after my day on the road north, and I didn't want to be all shot when I got back to The Hill. Da and I had a lot to talk about and I wanted him to see that I was on the ball.

I slept until the cabin steward shook me awake and by the time I'd washed my face and given my teeth a rub with the brush, most of the passengers had disembarked. That was all right with me. All that pushing and shoving that people seem to need to suffer after a boat ride or a plane flight... the way they have to get off badly enough to break a leg, well, it never made much sense to me. I combed my hair and the mirror told me I didn't look too bad. My hair was a bit longer than I cared to wear it, but it looked all right over my untidy eyes and my pale face. And if Ma said anything about it, I'd give her a smile and tell her I'd been saving my money.

I resisted taking a taxi and walked up to get the bus into Ballsbridge. It was a long enough walk and carrying a suitcase had never been my favourite form of exercise, but it was a good morning because I was feeling like I was up there on Mount Olympus. This was the morning. One of the big ones, probably the number one up to now, in my life. It was the day when I started something good for my father, and my mother, and for me too. Nothing big, Jesus, how could you start anything big with a few hundred lids and six months credit, but I remembered Jack Smith, a crooner they christened "The Whispering Baritone" and though I blushed for the guy every time I'd heard them call him that, I always liked a line in one of his songs... "Oak trees tall from little acorns grow...."

I was in Ballsbridge in about ten minutes but I had to stand at the bus stop outside the R.D.S. for twenty minutes waiting for the number eighteen to take me up to Charleston Road, which was the nearest stop to home.

Grannie Maguire used to live just five minutes away from the R.D.S. Down the Shelbourne Road, in a cottage where Da had been born. She was a tough character, a down-to-earth, no nonsense Dubliner, who loved a bottle of stout. And she feared nothing, least of all, people. To me she was always the big kind-hearted Grannie, but many a fella had caught a cold by giving her some lip, without having the reflexes to duck before she nailed him with a right hander. And that's not bullshit. More than once she'd beaten the bejaysus out of men who thought of themselves as hardchaws.

I got off the bus and walked up Oxford Road, wanting to run, but managing somehow to hold onto myself. Into Rugby Road and then around into Rugby Villas, tapping our gable end window as I passed it, turning right to bang on the other window before I went into the stinking hallway and waited for Ma to open the door.

She went white, the blood draining out of her face when she saw me. I stepped in and shut the door knowing that something terrible had happened.

"What is it, Ma...? What's wrong?"

"Oh son... Oh Paddy, Paddy love...." That was all she said before she fell into my arms, and all I could do was stand there holding her while she sobbed ten years off her life.

Worlds like "forgive me" poured out, but most of what she mumbled was incoherent. Until finally she calmed down enough to tell me, with her heart cracked open in her breast, that there was no money, not one penny of the money I'd been sending home to Da.

Chapter Twelve
Dublin. April '58

Ma was like someone dying slowly from poisoning and I had to carry her in and put her down on the divan bed which she hadn't had time to make. She twisted and squirmed in the grip of the agony of death, just curling up in her insides, moaning and groaning under the weight and the enormity of her own guilt. And all I could do was wipe the saliva from her mouth with my handkerchief.

I was on my knees beside the bed, allowing her to let it all tumble out, my left hand numbing up in the force of her grip. I felt like someone had turned my guts out with a billhook or at the very least that I'd been hit with a truck. That the world around me had gone fucking mad and that really I wished to be dead.

Oh I know it sounds very dramatic, but I know too well what a kick in the ballocks feels like, and it was being slapped with a feather compared to the pain squatting in my mind at that minute.

I found some hot water and a face flannel and I made her wash her face while I put the kettle on. I wanted to tell Ma to forget it, not to say any more, to just shut up and leave me alone, but I had to play priest and listen to the full confession.

Of course I shouldn't have listened, it would have been best for me to have levelled with her, but she was hurting so badly that it wasn't in me to rub salt into the wound. So I let Ma tell me about it and by doing so, by trying to help her wash it all away, I started to come apart myself.

It started with a game of Housey Housey. Jesus, it was such a sick joke. Even the name of the game seemed to have been nicked from the Brothers Grimm. Loneliness had driven her into town to seek a bit of company and the prizes were good if you were lucky. And the higher your stake the better the prizes.

Still, I let her go on, letting her fill in the colours long after I had the full picture. And I understood, I told Ma I understood, that it was all right. Then my brain snapped, like a strip of elastic when you release both ends at the same moment and I couldn't stop the words, the questions, why, why, why, which really meant why me? Why did this have to happen to me? And I heard a pounding noise, sharp, staccato thumps that didn't mean anything until a pain seemed to sever my arm and I realised that I'd almost broken my hand trying to punch holes in the kitchen door.

Ma held me then and it was something I couldn't bear. I pulled away from her, my anger pouring over again like boiling sugar and I was yelling at her to shut up, to please, please shut up, because I was afraid I might strangle the life out of her.... Not over the money, not the money. And not the time spent night after night... none of that... I could have killed her for the dream... for the way she'd murdered the most beautiful dream I'd ever had.

By the time Da came in from his night shift, I had it together enough to be grateful that he didn't know. And I was truly thankful that he'd been on his way home from the Pigeon House when I arrived. It was pure accident because I had no idea when his shifts changed.

He hugged me and I held him passionately for a few moments. He tapped me on the jaw, swinging his fist gently in a short arc, and there was no way I could ever tell him how badly I needed him to be just the way he was right then.

It got tougher after that. We drank some of the tea that I made and we talked while Ma fixed some breakfast. He was in good form, glad to see me, and I wasn't concerned that he looked a bit grey in the face because that was how I'd felt after every single night shift but the one the morning before.

"Things haven't changed that much in England," he

remarked, his eyes smiling over the rim of his teacup.

"How do you mean?" I asked, waiting for the catch.

"The streets there... they're still only paved with concrete... or is it asphalt now?"

I nodded, smiling a shade. "Oh, I know... the money's stopped growing on trees too." I started to bullshit him, telling him it wasn't easy to find any kind of job with decent readies at the end of the week. But that I hadn't forgotten what we'd talked about, that it was still going to happen, just as soon as I found the right number.

"Ah, I'm more than happy, son, more than happy where I am... and I get a pension and all, y'know, when my time comes to pack it up...."

He sat facing me across the table, spreading a sliver of white pudding onto a slice of bread and butter. His hands were big for a man so slight and they were steady like his peace of mind.

"But try and save a few quid, son... send it on here and I'll keep it safe for you." I blew my nose hard and drank some tea. He finished chewing a piece of bread and pudding.

"Do you need a few quid now?" he asked.

I shook my head. "No, thanks, Da... I've got twenty I want to leave with you... not much...."

"Oh, it's a beginning now... a start... and you never get anywhere till you make a start...."

I knew then that he hadn't cared about opening a shop, that his job meant everything to him. But he'd encouraged me by saying yes in the hope that I would work and save.

"I will save," I promised him...." And one of these days I'll have tons of the stuff."

"I hope so, son," he said quietly, "I hope so... because most of the problems in life, whether at work or at home, they're caused mostly by shortage of money...."

He left the table to go to bed and I watched him close the door. My heart was warm from the contact with him, a balm against the soreness. I looked at my Ma and told her to come and sit down. I poured her a cup of the tea which was beginning to need a fix and I watched her drink some of it.

"Sorry I went mad... doesn't matter, honest," I said it, trying hard to mean it, but what I most wanted was to pick up my bag and get out of there.

"He'd have killed me if you told him." She sniffed and I reached for my hankie. "Not that I could blame him or you."

"Listen," I said, pressing the hankie into her hand... "after what you've been through... for ever and ever... Jesus, you're entitled to take fucking heroin without anybody giving you a hard time."

"I just couldn't help it, son." She was ready to cry again.

"Well if you don't forget it, just forget it, I'm picking up my case and I'm going right now."

"Ah son no!"

"I will, Ma, unless you just drop it. I don't ever want to talk about it again...."

She nodded her head, pushing her grey hair to one side before she wiped her eyes again. "I won't say any more," she promised.

Thank God, I thought. Another half a dozen words and I'll start screaming. I gave her a little smile, trying to make her believe it didn't matter, ignoring myself the truth of what I'd said to her... that she was entitled to do anything without any recriminations... because what she'd done, she'd done to me.

Chapter Thirteen

I might as well have left Dublin on that Sunday for all they saw of me. Ma I had little to say to and my father was going to bed while I slept off the booze on the two nights I got back to the flat.

Monday morning I was dreaming I was being kissed very passionately and my arms were wrapped around a warm soft body. I woke up to find that I wasn't dreaming. Some woman was devouring me and from the way I was holding her there was no way I could claim I was fighting for my honour.

I had no notion of where I was, or how the lady and I happened to be sharing the scratcher. And if I wasn't surprised to find that like me, she was in her pelt, it might have been because I was trying to work out what had happened the night before.

My lady friend rolled over on her back and I was locked in a scissors grip that left me no alternative but to give her one and ask questions afterwards. Well, we did have it away and it was very good for me. But one thing bothered me. I couldn't get my arms out from beneath her. And being a born gentleman, I like to take a weight, or some of it anyway, on my elbows.

When I lit a cigarette... my pocket was right there on the beside table... she took a drag out of it and lay back with her eyes closed, trying to get her breathing back on an even keel.

"Oh you darlin'," she mumbled. "Oh you lovely darlin'..." She opened her eyes and looked at me. She had nice blue eyes and if I say she was clean and decent looking, you might just come to your own conclusion. Like, that she wasn't going to win any beauty contest unless it was a glamorous granny parade.

"That was the best of the lot," she said, letting her eyes rove all over me till I felt like a piece of meat in the window of a butcher's shop.

The best of the lot? Jaysus! We'd been at it before, more than once, by the sound of it. And I couldn't so much as remember meeting her last night, let alone whatever had happened between us in the scratcher. And as if it wasn't bad enough she was at me again with her hand.

I shook my head, trying to get the wrapper off my mind. Where in the name of Jaysus did I get her at all? I mean, I don't want to be unkind, and she was clean, and she knew how to spin the top, but she was fifty years old if she was a day.

She looked disappointed when I moved and sat on the side of the bed. I looked about the room which was tidy and I could see a small kitchenette through an open door. The room was large enough to be a bedroom at one end, while at the top near the window, she'd made a nice sort of dining area. I took another look around, not because I was interested in her furniture, but trying to remember something that I could latch onto. Anything that would help me remember even coming into the place.

Nothing happened... my mind remained a complete blank and I knew if I didn't get out of there and have a few drinks fast, I was going to go clean out of my mind.

"Is there some place I can wash, love?" I said, hoping she didn't think I was being romantic.

"Of course, sweetheart," she purred up at me. "In there, at the bottom of the kitchen, there's a little bathroom."

The way she kept the place made me feel warm about her. It was spotless, and though the bathroom was so small you couldn't swing a cat, it was such a well designed little room that you'd have broken yourself of the habit. With the cat, I mean.

When I came back out to put my clothes on, she gave me a cup of hot tea and a glass of whiskey. I thanked her and you can believe I meant it from the bottom of my hangover, drank some tea, threw the whiskey straight down, topping it off with more tea, before my heart actually exploded on me. She poured me another and while I drank it she started pulling on a black nylon stocking. Then the second one. I killed the whiskey and I felt as though someone had taken a bucket from over my head. She fixed the stocking tops to her suspenders, glancing at me with a little smile. She reached for her uplift, glanced at me again, and left the uplift where it was. And with that little smile still playing around her mouth, she went and lay down on the bed, her eyes on me all the time.

I poured myself another whiskey from the bottle and drank it down, finishing the rest of the tea as a chaser.

"Come here a minute, love." Her voice came across the room and as I looked at her she moved her legs in a delicate way. I shook my head in admiration. And there was no denying her decency in providing me with a cure. Decent bird. And wasn't it only fair to be decent back if it was in your power? I walked over and practically dived into the spot between her knees. I mean, if she wasn't entitled to another one for her decency, she certainly deserved some consideration for her bloody know how.

Monday afternoon I had to go to the hospital and have my right hand strapped up. So much for me taking it out on the kitchen door. I was half cut and I felt fine, but the time between going into town and waking up with Noreen Bawn, the kind-hearted and ever willing heroine of Upper Mount Street, seemed to be lost to me forever.

It was a strange feeling and the more I gave it leg room, the less I liked it, so I had a few drinks and forgot about all the things I couldn't remember anyway.

Eamonn Boyd joined me for a few drinks an Tuesday evening and I had to tell him that when it came to the crunch, the old man was scared. With the steady job going for him and a pension coming up.... I gave Eamonn all the bullshit that was necessary and he more than understood. He wanted me to go with him to the Crystal Ballroom, but I said no, that I'd just have a few drinks and get back to the scratcher. He offered to stay, and I would have been happy to have his company, but I knew he had a bird to meet, and from the way he scraped his shoes in the resin, I could see he was desperate to have a few rounds with the lucky lady. Apparently he'd met her in the Crystal a few weeks before and he'd had no bother in getting her to go over the jumps with him. This surprised me because if there was a place in town where I think even Errol Flynn would have drawn a blank, it had to be The Crystal. I'd been there a couple of times, coming away with a very definite impression that the only thing ever to get laid there was stair carpet.

I left Dublin on Wednesday by plane, which says loud and clear, that I couldn't get out of it quick enough. Pops, as I started to call my father, made me promise I'd try and save some money, and without knowing how, because in no way was I going back to factory night work, I meant to keep that promise to him.

Ma's goodbye eyes were blankets of sadness and regret. I slipped her a couple of quid, just to stay in character, and I put my finger against her lips when she looked like she was going to say "sorry". It was phoney, because I was still raw, but I don't think she knew, so what harm? I could put on a performance for her benefit, make her laugh when I was in bits myself, but I couldn't kid myself about how I really felt.

I tried telling myself that it was only fair. That after all the pain I'd caused Ma in the past, she was more than entitled to level things up. Didn't help much, so I tried vigorously to forget the whole episode.

When I got a drink on the plane I tried to look forward, to think about what I was going to do when I got back to London. Not that I was worried, I mean, I only had my prick to keep, and there was always a job for a fella willing to get dug in.

My father came to mind then and the way he just slipped into my thoughts made me smile to myself. So I was getting pissed, which didn't help me resist feeling the pointless regret I felt when I thought of all the years I'd hated my father, simply because Ma seemed to cry a lot and generally get herself upset, when he was around.

Up to that moment I hadn't copped on to that song about it taking two to tango.

Chapter Fourteen
London. April '58

I left Dublin without giving Pops that twenty quid to mind for me. As it happened, it was just as well, because I was on a skite from the minute I stepped off the plane at London airport. Not what you'd call mad drinking, or anything like that just good steady, long day elbow bending.

For some reason, I'd hated London. I didn't understand it and I couldn't seem to work out what was the matter with me. I'd loved the place from the first hours I'd spent there, but I knew I was going to have to get put off it, for a while, anyway.

I didn't know where I wanted to go, I didn't seem to want to go anywhere. But it figured that if I had to leave the Smoke I'd have to move to some bloody place. Even this amount of thinking made me tired, so morning after morning, I got out of bed feeling cold cocoa, went to a pub and started insulting myself. I guess I was waiting for something to happen. It didn't matter what, just so long as I didn't have to make any decisions, like go out and find myself a job.

When my money amounted to eight quid I began to worry. How could I make it last and me in the grip of a thirst you could photograph? And how was I going to pay my whack at the guest house in Earls Court? The old girl who ran it was all right for an Irishwoman, but I couldn't see her saying any Hail Marys for me when she realised there wouldn't be any bread coming from my direction.

I was walking down Regent Street when the advertisement for Jersey seemed to wave at me. Jersey? That was something I'd worn as a kid though it was mostly called a gansey, until the birds started wearing them skin tight so the tits drove you out of your mind, and then they were called sweaters.

"COME TO SUNNY JERSEY" invited the sign in the travel agency window.

"Where is it?" I said to the man at the counter.

"Jersey, sir? It's a hundred and fourteen miles from Southampton." He was a bright guy with rimless glasses and I liked him for assuming that I knew where Southampton was. Which I didn't.

"In or out?" I said, meaning it.

"In or out, sir?" He looked at me and laughed with the ease of a fella who appreciates a subtle slice of humour.

"In or out...." He shook his head, wishing he'd thought it up for himself. "Very good, sir, very good indeed, yes, I like that, I like that very much."

I picked up a brochure and did a quick grind in geography. He was scribbling away on a ticket for a sun tanned, ageing Jewess who was off to the Bahamas. He looked up at me, still smiling.

"Lovely there, just now sir."

I nodded. "Never been to the Channel Islands - seems like a good idea."

He came back to me in a minute. "There are several flights, sir...." He stopped when he saw my expression. "You don't like flying, sir...."

"It's horrible," I said, "it's the propinquity, y'know...."

He was good, he was very good, because he had no idea what I meant, but in no way did he let it throw him.

"Oh, I understand, sir... and we all have our little idiosyncrasies, don't we...."

"It's that feeling of everybody being, well, in and around and on top of me...."

"Keep talking, sir, you're turning me on," he said and for the first time I thought he might be queer. But he was nice and I was having a bit of fun, so what harm?

"Makes me feel strange...."

"...but wanted," he interjected, delighted with himself.

"I start stripping," I told him, "right there on the plane, all my gear comes off...."

"You have the figure for it," he said, as though he meant it.

"It's some kind of phobia, I suppose," I said, and he nodded agreement.

"I suppose you could call it, clothestrophobia," I said with a straight face. I knew I was drunk - to make jokes like that.

He loved it, repeating it, laughing merrily, and finally writing it down. "I'll dine out on it for a week," he assured me, and I felt like saying "I'll come along with you."

I ended up buying a boat ticket from Southampton to Jersey, thinking I'd hitch down because there was no way I could afford the train ride and have a night's drinking as well.

I picked up a second-hand haversack in Soho and at seven o'clock next morning, I threw it out into the front garden of the guest house with all my worldly possessions in it. Then with the shoes in my hand I crept down the stairs, hoping to Jesus that the landlady was on her knees praying for a busy summer season or something.

As I hit the last step, the very last one, she came out into the hall, and I knew I had to get in fast, if only to stop that dark angry look of suspicion from welding itself to her Mass Card face.

"I was trying not to wake you, Mrs. O'Brien," I said, thinking you'd better fucking well believe it. "Father Coughlan was decent enough to ask me to serve Mass this morning...."

She relaxed then and I went out to the door with her blessing, my shoes already on thanks to mentioning the priest's name. It was always a good stroke finding out what the local P.P. was called, and you knew that if he was a decent man, he'd forgive you, even if it did take a little time, for taking his name in vain.

Mrs. O'Brien stood at the door, admiring my halo, and I went out the gate. I bent down to adjust my shoelace until I heard the front door click shut. Then I nipped into the garden, grabbed my haversack, and was off down the street like a greyhound on a steady diet of goofballs.

There was no trouble hitching a lift to Southampton and I was there by teatime, having stopped off for a few lunchtime pints in Berkshire. God, that was a beautiful county, or shire, or whatever the English call it. I saw a diabolical film while I waited for boat time. The movie was so bad that I felt sorry for Rock Hudson, who looked like he might be a nice enough bloke, but at that time he knew as much about acting as a monkey did about chopping onions. "Captain Lightfoot" the thing was called made in Ireland about fifty one or two, and I could only sit there and wonder how so many talented people could turn out such a load of knickers.

I guess that most people have felt that they could make a better movie than the one which was boring the arse off them. Well, sitting watching that Lightfoot thing, I bloody well knew I could write and direct a movie that couldn't be as bad as that Captain Shitefoot! And I vowed in my own half-pissed fashion that some day I would, some day I'd make a mark, or a stain, leave some kind of imprint that I'd passed this way.

All the way over on the Jersey boat I was picking that movie to pieces, going over it again and again, there I was going to Jersey with buttons in my pocket, not knowing what it was going to be like, and all I was concerned with was telling myself that some day I'd make a decent movie. But then, that was better than worrying about what was ahead of me in St. Helier, and I felt all the better for having another dream to latch on to. Not that it was just a dream - I'd told myself down the line that I was some kind of great talent, which, when you think about it, wasn't a bad thing to have going for you, particularly when you had little or nothing else.

Chapter Fifteen
Jersey. Summer '58

Jersey was a dream all the way. The kind of wishful thinking a fella indulges in when he's flat broke, very horny, but past the hand galloping trick, with his mother bugging him to go to confession and it raining outside.

Now any dream that can insulate you from this kind of situation would be of a very special variety. And that's what Jersey was for me, although my first job on the island would never have got me into the William Hickey column in *The Daily Express*.

Dish washing, would you believe, or as it was called in the trade, pearl diving.

Can you imagine dipping six or seven hundred plates in water, holding them against a revolving brush, rinsing and stacking them, three times a day, not to mention cups and saucers, knives and forks and spoons. Maybe it isn't any kind of big deal, but when you throw in meat dishes and all the other gear used to cook the food, I do think it's worth a mention.

I had a bed to sleep in and because I got along with the second chef, I ate food that wasn't too bad. The food allowed to staff in what was supposed to be a top class hotel, might have been fit for pigs, but I honestly doubt it.

The lady who employed me had all the charm of a skin infection, and despite her money and her power and a very sexy pair of legs, I didn't think I was going to have any trouble disliking Miss Servag. But I needed a base and somewhere to lay the body and, ridiculous though the wages were, I had to earn something.

The cabin steward on the ferry from Southampton had told

me there was only hotel work and potato and tomato picking. Well, I wasn't afraid of work and "The Grapes of Wrath" might be my favourite book, but picking fruit and vegetables wasn't the kind of thing that I felt a fifth generation Dubliner should be caught dead at. And after two days in the plate house, I no longer thought of dish washing as an honourable way to die, so I used my spare time to try and find a job I could have.

I keep coming back to this thing of being lucky, but that's just how I seemed to be. And if I shout about it a bit, it's only with expressing gratitude that my stars were so kind to me. And because I felt lucky, I was happy, so that my boss's thing of treating all of us like shit because that was how she felt inside herself, didn't bother me one bit. Nor the fact that I didn't have a friend, or that screaming Italian and Portuguese waiters gave me a pain in my crotch. Nothing could dampen the good feeling I knew, and without realising it, I spent most of my time singing, while I scrubbed and washed.

It was this, the fact that I could be heard singing away, even when I was out of sight behind a mountain of dirty plates and dishes, that got a couple of Irish fellas in the hotel talking about me. I didn't know this at the time, but later, I learned that their conversation about me went something like this.

"You heard your man above in the kitchen?"

"No... heard about him though."

"Never stops warbling... happy as a pig in shit."

"Happy in that sweatbox... honest to Jaysus, we're exporting more fuckin' nuts than Brazil...."

"We'll go up and have a look at him...?"

"Not me... less bleedin' Paddies I get to know the more money I seem to have...."

"Ah, for the crack, come on will ye?" Paddy Darcy said to Theo Roberts.

Theo Roberts put the *Sporting Life* into his jacket pocket and got up from the canteen table. He was giving in to the persistence of his tough little mate from Monaghan.

"Funny thing about your curiosity," Theo remarked as they left the canteen, "it only gets me into bother."

I was finishing up for the night, wiping down the worktop, and because I had my back to the door and all the waiters were off duty, I didn't expect anyone to come in, so I didn't see the two lads when they arrived. I was singing my head off, fantasising that I was killing them stone dead in the London Palladium. Just as I got to the end of "Dannyboy" I swung around with my arms wide, and though I was surprised to see the two fellas standing there looking at me like a monkey in a cage, I finished the song and took a bow. If I'd learned nothing else during my time on the road, I had managed to grasp that no matter what happens, you keep singing.

The little dark headed one had the look of a half pissed Leprechaun. He looked up at his mate with the brown wavy hair.

"Dublin, would you say?" His Monaghan accent, reminding me of Jimmy Finglas and Belgravia, was very distinct.

"Just because he's got a neck like a jockey's ballocks, he doesn't have to be from Dublin."

In this way opened my relationship with the two lunatics who were to become my biggest buddies for many years to come, and if either of them changed, like, if they were ever polite to me or to each other, well percentages demand that you allow for a certain amount of accidents.

Paddy Darcy bought me a drink and put it down on the bar table. He seemed to remember then that his pal had come along.

"Suppose I better get you one...."

Theo Roberts blew smoke in his face. "Little bollix," he exhaled, causing me to smile. Only a Dubliner can twist the slang word for testicles in that way, and it rates high on my list of "put down" verbal.

We drank and the two Heads spent a good deal of the time slagging each other. Honestly, I might as well have been somewhere else when they got warmed up. But than I'd find them regarding me the way they would a little green man who'd just parked his flying saucer in the corner of the bar. They started discussing me then as though I was somewhere else, and I soon realised that it was me working as a "pearl diver", singing my way through mountains of shitty dishes, that had them baffled.

"Doesn't look like a bleedin' masochist," Theo remarked, while his huge, extra round eyes seemed to comment "but you never know".

"Family's buying him a hotel," Darcy told him... "want him to know the business from the very bottom...."

"Could be resting between the singing engagements," Roberts suggested, nodding his great head like a bloodhound with dreams of getting laid.

"Oh, I'm not a professional singer," I confessed, "I'm a clairvoyant."

They looked at each other again then back to me with an earnestness that suggested I was interviewing them for a place on the board of the Bank of England.

"I only took the job to meet you two."

This stopped both of them and just that once, I knew they weren't playing schtuhmn. "I had to get to know the two guys most likely to help me to get a decent job for the season...."

"Have you any money?" Theo asked me seriously.

"I've got thirty bob... and a couple of quid due for the pot walloping...."

Theo looked at Darcy. "He's got thirty bob..." he said.

Paddy Darcy choked on his whiskey. "Don't forget what he's got coming from the job."

"Told you he was fuckin' nuts. Knew it, knew it when I heard the chanting in the steam bath." He shook his head.

"You eating the hotel slop?" Paddy asked.

"Do I look like a mountain man?" I said. He made no answer. "I bought a second chef a bottle of wine as a mark of respect."

Theo Roberts smiled. "Thanks be to Jaysus," he said fervently, "I thought it was just me against this sod buster for the summer."

Darcy smiled sadly. "Couldn't read the signs when I got to Euston Station... I was shockin' ignorant...."

Theo paid for another drink. "He's managed to hold on to the first shilling he ever earned, just the same."

"Never stops having a go, Maguire, just because I'd no education... couldn't read the signs...."

"On Euston fucking station..." Theo snorted derisively.

"That's one way of ending up in the ladies' room," I said.

"I only hope you get a job in Gorey or somewhere," Paddy said, meaning the other side of the island... "two of you at close quarters could affect my arithmetic...."

"Paralysis might affect your fiddle, Darcy, but I wouldn't bet on it." Theo turned to me. "They're looking for a porter and, I think, a barman at the Courthouse... good hotel..."

"And the manager is not the brightest," Paddy said.

"Once you call him, sir," Theo shrugged. "Something to do with him being insecure... all fucked up on account of being in the lap of luxury...." He shook his head. "It's a true bill... prick is all screwed because his family are loaded.... His mother's a nice old dear... decent...."

"Maybe I can get her to adopt me...."

"Don't forget me if you do."

"And me," Paddy Darcy said. "I have the taste for marshmallows and hot chocolate at night."

"Forget him," Theo warned me... "get yourself in... listen, he's so dumb... you won't believe it... an old slag was jerking him off... back of Kings Cross, y'know... half a sheet and they wind up your stomach.... Anyway, she says to him, "Are you coming, love, are you coming?" Theo looked at me as though he was seeing me from a mile distance. "Do you know what he said?" I shook my head. "You won't believe it, you're just not going to believe it...." He drank some gin and tonic and launched into his punch line. "When she said are you coming love, he said to her, why, where are you going?"

I laughed at the story, at Theo's mock expression of disgust, and I couldn't stop as long as I looked at Darcy, and him sitting there with that "hard done by" look on his face.

"I've an idea," Darcy said mournfully.

Theo looked down at him. "Go on, surprise us...."

"Let's get pissed," he said.

"I'm supposed to work tonight...."

"David can look after things," Paddy assured him.

"David couldn't run a two seater shit house," Theo snorted.

Darcy finished his drink. "Maguire and me'll move then."

Theo looked thoughtful for a few seconds. "Suppose he'll never learn to handle responsibility if I go on 'molly coddling' him." He finished his drink and we all stood up.

"Long as we're not dragging you away from your work," Paddy Darcy sniffed.

Theo winked at me. "Why, where are you going? Where are you fuckin' going?" He started to laugh and I left for the pub with them feeling that somehow I'd got myself involved with a two man circus.

Chapter Sixteen

The dark grey suit looked okay but with the white shirt and the black tie, I felt like a pox doctor's clerk as I walked up the drive to the Courthouse Hotel.

The drive forked when it reached the hotel steps, fresh tarmac that circled the entire building. From the back of the hotel, fruit gardens rolled downhill to several acres of vegetables, the land tumbling further down to meadows that supported fifty or sixty of those fabulous Jersey cows. Honestly, those cows! Always looking so good, like high class meadow ladies, that instead of milk I expected them to produce straight butter, or at the very least, clotted cream.

My head felt all right thanks to Darcy, may God rest his soul, if he can find it. He saved my bacon, by appearing with a long ice cold Gimlet, that must have been half a pint, evenly mixed. It went down smooth as a high class elevator and magically, my head stopped revolving. That was our first early morning drink together, but you can believe it wasn't the last.

"Where was your last job?" Brown, the manager, and by all accounts, son of the owner, asked me.

"The Isle of Man Holiday Camp, sir."

"Your boss's name at the camp?"

I wanted to laugh because I was wondering if the Isle of Man itself, existed. I mean, I'd never seen it.

"Robinson, sir, Mr. Raymond Robinson."

He wrote this down like if he wasn't sure of himself, but that was only because he didn't have a clue. I wouldn't have minded if he'd been in any way a nice man, but he was like a marionette, all pomp and jerk.

"Was that seasonal employment?" Seasonal, smeeasonal, give me a break!

His eyes faltered when I looked straight at him and I felt like asking him how much time he spent each morning working on his ridiculous pencil moustache.

"Yes, sir," I said, "seasonal."

He tapped his fingers on the desk, considering the situation, with the gravity of a hanging judge about to tell some poor head that he was being elected to wear a hemp collar.

"You haven't worked since the end of last season."

I decided to concentrate for a bit, get it over fast, one way or the other.

"I've been at Trinity, sir, Trinity Collage, Dublin." That surprised him enough for me to be glad I'd dreamed it up.

"Doing my finals, sir. English Lit."

Brown was impressed. He nodded deliberately and pushed his chair back.

"Wages are seven pounds ten, living in, with two and half per cent commission. A night off a week until the season gets under way - after that it's doubtful." He stood up and I got off my chair.

"Come along, I'll show you the bar."

I followed him out into the hall needing to laugh at the way he walked, until I saw that the way he sprung upwards, each time he took a step, was to make up for his lack of height. I shook my head - really puzzled how anybody could be that stupid. He was trying to hide the fact that he was a short-arse, and all he did with that affected and ridiculous bloody walk, was to draw attention to himself... and his short-arse.

My first look at the bar scared the hell out of me. I'm not being funny, nor am I telling a lie, though possibly I'm indulging in understatement. It was so fabulous in every way, and what the hell did I know about bars? I mean, even my drinking wasn't what you'd call adventurous. Dangerous maybe, in that I drank more than I should, but I didn't experiment with anything outside of whiskey, brandy, stout, and the odd bottle of cider.

In a nutshell, it was high class, very modern without being in any way cheap or flashy. A long Swedish wood counter, backed by rows and rows of mirror lined shelves, with so many bottles of every colour and description. And not one of the names meant a damn thing to me.

You had to wade through the carpet, and the tables and chairs that lined either side of the long room looked like they'd been made especially to go with the whole layout. Besides this, I took in three cocktail shakers, several mixing glasses, and an automatic glass washer complete with air dryer. And all I could think was, Jesus wept!

I told Brown I'd like to take the job and he grabbed this cue to hit me with the usual bull about rules and regulations. He thought I was interested, which was the main thing, but my ears did move a shade closer to him when he told me that his mother liked to come down and help in the bar sometimes.

"Just to pass the time," he said self consciously, his attitude implying that this was just another trial he had to bear.

He talked a bit more, but fortunately, as I was to realise later, he didn't say anything about stocktaking or ordering, which was a real break, because I just wouldn't have known what to say to him. He was pleased when I said I could start that evening, that I'd move in with my things in the late afternoon. He shook my hand, which was something I liked.

A brown haired girl with flashing, sexy eyes, and the smile of a raver, passed us and went up the stairs. I glanced back as Brown flicked a speck of dust from his pin striped jacket, and she returned my smile before she disappeared around the bend in the stairs. She'd been carrying some towels so it looked like she worked in the hotel. Handy enough. But right then I just wanted to get out of there and get down to see Paddy Darcy. I needed a lot of advice and what you might call a crash course in how to be a cocktail barman.

Before I saw Paddy I went to tell Miss Servag that I was

leaving. Her expression didn't change but then she'd always looked at me as though I belonged under a stone.

"Haven't you people got any principles?" she asked me in a tired voice.

"I don't understand what you mean by 'you people', Mam."

She changed gear. "When people come here for employment in the summer season, when they get work, we expect them to stay for the season."

I told her that dish washing wasn't for me, that had I known how soul destroying it was going to be, I wouldn't have taken the job in the first place. She wasn't impressed but I was. Me coming out with verbal like "soul destroying"... Jesus! Harry Redmond would have given me a round of applause.

"And I tried to work hard and well, Mam, to give you *value* for your money."

She might have smiled at the way I planted that, but she wasn't giving anything away.

"You might save your blarney for some little chambermaid, Mister Maguire, and as far for money, you seriously can't expect me to pay you."

Of course I didn't expect the cow to pay me, but Jesus, you had to try. I mean, knock and the door shall be slammed in your kisser.

"Thank you anyway, Mam," I said respectfully.

She shook her head with something like amazement sitting in her eyes. "You did expect to be paid?"

I shrugged. "Not expect, Mam, not really. Needing to be paid, well, I sort of had to believe I would be." I smiled a shy one at her and tried to look like I was going to leave.

"Emotional, as opposed to logical, Mam."

She became impatient. This bird was queen of the manor and she didn't like anybody talking to her without touching the cap.

"Go and get your things, Mister Maguire, and kindly leave my hotel."

Chapter Seventeen

When I told Darcy how his boss and I had said goodbye, he made no bones about wanting me out of his bar as fast as possible, just in case she saw us together.

"What's her problem anyway?"

"She needs a good seeing to, that's her problem." He handed me a cocktail shaker. "Never mind what's wrong with her, just get on here."

He watched while I poured my first ever cocktail and you could see he thought it was a terrible waste of the ingredients.

"More like a Black Brass than a White Lady."

He drilled me some more, and it was a full half hour before I went back to my stool at the bar to make some notes. Paddy loaned me his book from the Bartenders Guild, and one flick through told me it was going to be a godsend.

Clarence Harvey, the assistant manager, came trotting into the bar. Paddy pursed his lips and waited while poor old Clarence got his breathing under control.

"Maguire? Has he gone?" Clarence asked, and me sitting there on my stool by his right elbow.

Paddy placed a maraschino cherry in his mouth and stood looking at "The Runner" as Clarence was called behind his back.

"Mahoo?" He studied Clarence like a trainer trying to decide whether his horse would stand up to seven furlongs over hard going.

"Maguire, the dishwasher." Clarence turned his head impatiently and when he got over the shock of finding me there he said: "Ah, there you are."

"Special delivery!" Paddy put another cherry into his mouth.

Clarence spoke to me through the side of his mouth. This wasn't affectation of any kind but to do with the fact that his mouth was, what you could call, lopsided.

"You're very fortunate," he advised me, putting a small envelope in my hand. "She told me to pay you."

Even Paddy registered surprise, while I tried not to fall off the stool from the shock.

"What did you say to her?" The Runner didn't even try to hide his curiosity.

He was a nice enough fella, but he was so clueless that it was almost impossible not to be cruel to him.

"Ah, I just told her I'd like to play doggy games with her sometime… the Vaseline trick, y'know…?"

Clarence didn't know and it showed, but neither Paddy or I, laughed.

"What was that?" Clarence looked to Darcy for assistance.

"Forget it, Clarry," Paddy said, putting two glasses of whiskey on the bar. He then held up his own glass. "Remember me," he pleaded… "when you buy the fucking island."

I laughed out loud, double chuffed at getting my money, and not really bothered how or why it had happened. Paddy shook his head like a man denying a bad dream, when we both drank the whiskey, while Clarence stood there like a spare candle on a birthday cake.

By the end of my first week behind the bar at the Courthouse, I had things working nicely and I felt sure I'd be motoring along like a champion by the time the hotel filled up.

At the beginning of May we had about thirty residents, but from early June to mid-October, there were bookings for one hundred and forty, which would make it a full house with all the chimneys stacked.

It was a good hotel and I was happy there. This was hardly

surprising when I compared life to how it had been just ten days before. For a start, it was my bar, and I found myself enjoying the fact that I was responsible for something other than a pregnancy.

When my first customer arrived I gave her a smile and a "good evening madam". She greeted me with gentle dignity that immediately labelled her "lady" to me.

While she decided what to drink, I marked her down for a White Lady... gin, cointreau, lemon, touch of white of egg, but just the merest touch. It was a great favourite with women before dinner, or so Paddy Darcy had told me.

The woman sat up on a bar stool and I could see that her jewellery hadn't come out of any cornflake packet.

"I think a shandy, please, barman," she nodded, "yes, a shandy."

A shandy? Shandy! Darcy hadn't said anything about a shandy. I racked my brain fast, knowing that I couldn't come up with it. And I was bloody certain Darcy hadn't mentioned such a drink.

What in the name of Christ, was it? A shandy? I wanted to reach out for the book, but the old girl was sitting there and she was looking right at me. And she was waiting for some indication from me, that she wasn't going to die from thirst.

"How do you prefer it, Madam?" I heard myself say, feeling, from the bottom of my heart, that somebody was praying for me at that moment.

"In a half pint mug, please barman," she smiled and I wanted to kiss her, "half and half, beer and lemonade."

When she sipped the drink I stood there holding my breath. She nodded then and I could see she was pleased. "Perfect," she smiled graciously, "just the way I like it." She reached for her purse.

"You're my first costumer of the season, Madam," I said, "please have it with me, just for luck."

She lit up like a Christmas tree, so touched by a simple thing.

"How charming," she sighed, "how very charming."

She raised her glass to me. "Thank you so very much."

Before she went in to dinner she worked me a pound note.

"For an off duty drink," she said, "And thank you again."

I was fairly busy just at that moment but I took the time to watch her walk all the way into the dining room. She moved with that security people have when they know, as they always have known, that they're never going to have to worry about where the next meal, or the next mink coat, is coming from.

As far as she was concerned, she'd just given a little gift to a rather nice young man, and the chances were that I'd helped her holiday off to a good start by putting a nice taste in her mouth, the very well made shandy apart. What she had done for me, she'd never know. Why would she ever have reason to consider that her response, to what was a spontaneous gesture of sheer relief on my part, had shown me once again that few people can resist genuine courtesy and consideration. That even people who are tight inside themselves, seldom fail to respond to warmth, and the friendliness of an open, sunny personality.

Well I was a fairly warm character and most of the time I was something of an open book. Personality-wise, I was okay, and I was decent enough, more than prepared to share myself around, pass a little sunshine along to any chick needing to feel special for a little while.

I smiled often during that first evening, thinking of the old lady, who didn't come back to the bar after dinner. Each time a punter appeared for the first time, I found myself giving out the same verbal about it being my opening night and that the first one was on me. And I'll tell you something, it worked wonders for the little brown jug, because I finished the night eight pounds ten to the good. And I hadn't even started to fiddle.

Chapter Eighteen

Brown's mother turned out to be a very tasty woman of about fifty, with auburn hair that looked all right. A bit too all right at times, like, when she returned from a visit to her hairdresser, but I, for one, was in favour of it. I mean, why shouldn't a woman cling on to what nature is trying to take away from her? An awful pity a few more women don't. Taking a bit of trouble could put a lot of them in the way of a little of that sunshine I mentioned earlier, because there are a lot of decent fellas about.

Mrs. Brown had knowing pale green eyes that looked ever so warm when she smiled, but I often noticed a startled look come into them, making her seem vulnerable.

We got along from the first moment she came into the bar, and not just because she made me feel I was the only man on the island. It was her consideration for other people that made me want to hug her at times, though I won't deny that her body, large but well laid out, evoked the same feeling with even greater frequency.

She was big but then I'd never been turned on by featherweights, and a few times during that first week, when she was helping me in the bar, I was glad that she was so well upholstered. A few people might have got the wrong ingredients in a cocktail but there were no complaints. And I'd have changed a drink very willingly for another chance to squeeze past her when she was bending over to pick up a bottle from under the counter.

She stuck out front and back like a cock, a rooster I mean, but everything was so well balanced, that sometimes I wished she'd just fuck off and stop interfering with my arithmetic. I mean I had to keep my fiddle straight.

I liked fiddling even more than thinking about what Mrs. Brown and I were going to do to each other when the right moment presented itself. And by the end of my first week, I just knew that something had to click between us before long.

I'd catch her looking at me with a glow in her eyes that I never saw directed at anyone else. She never looked away at those times, her eyelids would come to the rescue, shielding the fact, that though she was no longer gazing at me, her eyes and her thoughts were attracted to me. More than once I had to take a drink and shake myself out of dreaming I was Bogart or Gable, walking over to her, and saying, as I took her up the stairs, "This thing is bigger than both of us, baby." Might seem crazy when you consider she was fifty years old, but it just didn't matter. I reacted to her so strongly, wanting, desperately at times, to reach out an touch her, to have her hold me, that it made my mind boggle. And there wasn't what you'd call love, like, being in love, behind my need. It was just a fantastic physical longing to get warm, if only for a few moments, with a woman I liked and respected. But I'm prepared to admit, that even if I hadn't cared about her as a human being, I'd still have been just as keen to get her knickers off.

Fiddling was a charge, apart from being a kind of passport to printing your own money. And I latched on to it like spit to a windscreen. Mind you, I had a couple of first class tutors in Darcy and Roberts, and because I was so willing to learn, I turned out to be a pupil they were proud of. Honestly, that Darcy should have been called Houdini, the way he operated, smiling like a tourist board advert, for Leprechaunsville.

I suppose it was dishonest, but then the whole bar business stank to my nose. Owners and their managers, who think of themselves as legitimate businessmen, demanded something like eleven percent over what they were entitled to if the bar was to run according to Hoyle. It was rarely mentioned, being one of the unwritten, unspoken, rules. How you got that extra percentage, they didn't want to know, but you better believe it was expected.

Which meant you had to fiddle the customer. I mean, there was no other way. So you learnt to clip the measure, use half bottles of tonic and ginger ale that were already paid for, and so on and so on. Well, it figured that if you were going bent for the boss, you had to just work a little harder to get a piece of what was going. Let's face it, you weren't going to have the boss's problem about whether to buy a Rolls or a Bentley, but it did make life a little more interesting. So I fiddled while Jersey burned in the sun.

The staff were a mixture of German and Italian, with a couple of English receptionists. The day porter was a Welsh fella with sly eyes and an accent you could cut with a knife, and the night porter was called Eddie and was a kink from St. Helier, who crept around without ever making a sound.

With one thing and another, I was making good money. Fifty or so every week of the season, and sometimes a bit more than that. Mind you, I had to work hard to get it, and I don't think I had more than two nights off between May and the end of September. Still, once I served the lunchtime aperitif I was free until I opened up at six. And in my first weeks I took advantage of the sunshine and the glorious beaches, swimming every single afternoon. But before very long I was using the beach to sleep somewhere, because between them, the ladies weren't letting me sleep in the hotel. Bless them all!

Chapter Nineteen

Because I quit school not long after I changed from nappies to long trousers, it goes without saying that I didn't have any scientific training. But had I been the test tube man, I'd have given some time to studying the female in relation to her environment, specifically, practically all the birds I got to know on the island of Jersey.

Before or since, I've never seen so many cock-happy women in one place. It was like there was something in the air, as if the first lungful blew their tubes, because most of them just seemed to freak out before they'd had time to unpack a suitcase. And it didn't seem to matter what they did for a living, or what sort of a background they came from. As Barbara Cartland might say, "they appeared to hurl themselves with reckless abandon into the spirit of things...."

So I suppose it was just as well there were guys like myself about the place. Fellas who were willing to do anything, even go without sleep, to try to ensure that as few birds as possible ended up doing press-ups in the cucumber patch.

The Italians I worked with were all sex maniacs and a few Austrians I liked, were born hammer men. The Germans might have a bang a couple of times a week, but they seemed more concerned about becoming head waiters. When they were feeling a bit stretchy, they could, whether they'd any time for Adolf's "strength through joy" idea, or not, swing both ways without breaking into any kind of sweat.

The invasion didn't really begin till mid June, so I suppose it was only natural that Mrs. Brown and I should get something going during the long month of May.

Olive wanted me to call her by her Christian name all the time, but I stuck to the Mrs. Bit when anybody else was around. She came to appreciate that, acting as though this decision on my part was some stroke of brilliance. I didn't argue with her. If she needed to believe I was something special, what harm would it do to let her get on with it?

The scene behind the bar had become ridiculous, and once or twice, I was so stretchy from rubbing past her, that I felt like giving her one amongst the empty bottles. And it was *rubbing* past her, because it seemed to take longer each time I had to do it.

Then one night when we were left alone about one o'clock, she suggested I close the bar and go up and join her for a quiet drink and chat. I was halfway through counting the night's take, when she put her hand across mine.

"Come now," she said, as though she wasn't sure I would.

I stuffed the money into the bag. "Come now," she said again, and I thought, "I will, right here, if you don't stop it."

She was a little way ahead of me going up the stairs and I couldn't take my eyes off her fifteen jewel movement. Until I heard Eddie's small phlegmatic cough. Olive hadn't heard it, so I slowed up a bit behind her. I stopped and looked down the narrow corridor to my right, and there he was, his crew-cut head tilted to one side, as he listened outside a bedroom door.

I had to smile at the dirty bastard, at the way his head moved with small appreciative jerks, like a fella listening to a bloody symphony concert. I soft footed my way down to where he stood, thinking that "symphony concert" wasn't a bad analogy. I mean, to Eddie, the sound of some couple having a good bunk up was the sweetest music imaginable.

I touched his arse with my fingers, expecting him to leap up into the air, but all he did was push himself back against my hand. And he whispered, half turning his head away from the door... "Nice and easy kid, nice and easy." I pulled my hand away just about as shocked as I'd expected him to be, while he just went back to full-time listening.

The fella inside the room really was giving his bird an unmerciful seeing to, and was she loving it! Jesus, it was the turn on of the century to hear her calling him names, which if you were to believe her, suggested that he never washed, that he had been born out of wedlock, and that he had a penchant to sodomy, buggery, bestiality, plus a deep desire to perform fellatio on big black men and donkeys from Nagasaki. And all I heard out of him just before he almost nailed her to the mattress, was a fierce, twisted breath plea to his lady, to tell him that he was a better fuck than Burt Lancaster.

I moved back up the corridor, determined not to laugh, because I was trying to work out what your man had meant. I couldn't because I was in no way able to think straight. That verbal I'd just heard had put me into such a state, that I could have got up on a back rasher. And Olive was waiting and I wanted to run up the steps to her suite, but I had to walk slowly, oh God, did I have to walk slowly?

She put her glass down when I closed the door behind me. I put the money bag down on a Chippendale chair, and she held both her hands out to me as I walked across the carpet to where she stood by the fireplace.

"I feel, well, guilty, really for thinking about you as I have." Her voice shook so much that I wished there was some way I could make her see, by just looking at me, how tasty she really was. I kissed her and she pressed her lips into mine. I drew back but I didn't let go of her hands.

"I'm not fifteen years old, Olive, but if I was, I'd still want you take me to bed."

She was beautiful in her love making - controlling herself, and me, so that again and again, when I felt sure I was going to explode, we moved in a gentler way, milking each and every movement, until finally, she shuddered desperately against me while I shattered into a thousand bits.

I felt her tears on my body and I held her till she was ready to dry her eyes. She told me then that it was the first time since she'd lost her husband six years before. I didn't know what to say to that. I couldn't tell her I was glad that she hadn't been laid in six years, and I thought it better to skip saying I was sorry she'd not had a ride in that time. So instead, I asked her if she'd like a drink, knowing that she was going to get up and do the honours.

The money she'd spent to keep in shape had been the best investment she could ever have made, because really, she had the body of a thirty year old health fanatic. As I said, she was big, but there wasn't a wrinkle or any kind of spare flesh, and though I wanted my drink, I felt like asking her to walk up and down a few times.

She came back to bed and we drank together. Her eyes were sparkling and she smelled of velvet musk. I put my glass down and she turned to kiss me. She was all gratitude and I wanted to yell at her that I wasn't doing her any favours, that it was the other way round. But by that time I was too busy fighting for breath.

For a whole week, I slept with Olive every night. Well, I slept a little with Olive, which was fair enough, when staying awake was the whole object of the exercise. We drank a lot, too, which she seemed to need, though I didn't think that like me, she used it for a fast pick me up and the energy for another bunk up. But then Olive wasn't working her knickers off nine hours a night keeping upwards of sixty people supplied with all kinds of high class self abuse in many shaped glasses and tumblers. She gave me a hand all right, but now that there was no need to be rubbing against her perfect arse every time she bent over, she seemed to get in my way more than be a help to me. And something else Olive wasn't doing, was making love to a sexy little Austrian chambermaid almost every afternoon. But then, she wasn't the same kind of insatiable pig I was, or maybe it was just that she was old enough or mature enough, not to be trying to prove something every day of her life.

Chapter Twenty

All I can say about Christina and me, is that I didn't go after her. I might well have done, in fact I'm bloody sure I would have, except I was fairly content getting tucked up with Olive Brown. But when I found my little Austrian friend laying in my bed one afternoon, I just didn't have heart to tell her it was time to get up.

I'd been giving her the chat, but then I seemed to do that with every bird I met. It was a habit, like singing in the bath, and I didn't think that an Austrian would react in any way different to most chicks. But I wasn't making any allowances for her limited English, and the day before I found her in my scratcher, I had laid it on a bit thick.

"Handsome you are," she said, looking very proud of her progress.

"Ah, you're only saying that because it's true."

"You like me?" Her hair hung straight and dark on either side of her face, her brown eyes burning easily, like a blowtorch waiting to blister the paint of a door. And whether she knew it or not, which she probably did, language or no language, the way she leaned on the counter was pushing her boobs up under her lovely chin.

"You nice," I said, "I like you much." Jaysus, I was talking to her in broken English, like Johnnie Weissmuller playing Tarzan.

She was delighted with me and I asked her if she liked to swim. She mimed the breast stroke, and her mouth was open, so that I could see her lovely pink tongue, and I wanted to bite it gently, the way you would a fresh grape or a delicious clitoris.

"I have strong breasts," Christina said.

Shut up for the love of Jaysus, I thought, and again, her reaction told me that my erection was showing.

"Tomorrow," I said carefully. "Two o'clock. We go...." I moved my arms, hands flat out in front of me, in the breast stroke movement, and Christina thanked me with all the bits of English she could get together, before I moved up the bar to serve some guests. A minute later she left with her Hoover and I didn't see her again until I returned to my room after lunch the following day.

It was a decent room at the top of the building, and I hadn't any doubts that Olive was responsible for my move from the staff chalets in the earlier part of the week. When Brown told me he was giving me something a bit better, I meant it when I thanked him. Working with those Europeans was all right, but sharing a huge room with two Italians and a German who was a real Kraut, wasn't my idea of luxury. They were forever screaming at one another and I got a pain in my ballocks listening to them. Those cats could go into the equivalent of an epileptic fit, just talking about music or cycling or football. They were all nuts about cycling, which was a joke to me, though I could still feel the joy and pride I'd known when I'd taken my first bicycle home to The Hill. And poor Noggler Green, taking off his three speed gear, because it had slipped as he negotiated the hump of Charlemont Street Bridge over the canal.

"Nearly smashed my testicles." I could still see his face, and I could hear his pain filled continuance of the complaint after I'd pretended I didn't know what he was talking about.

"Me testicles, me ballocks." Going on then to mumble about "the only bit of pleasure we have left," leaving me badly in danger of falling off my own machine as I laughed my way home.

My room had a big window and sunshine most of the day. There was a good wardrobe, a neat chest of drawers, a wash hand basin under a decent mirror, carpet and a bed.

The bed was a double which I hadn't christened yet on account of sleeping with Olive, but when Christina sat up under the covers when I walked in, when I saw a sheet slip down from about her knockers, I was into the baptism trick without even thinking that I needed holy water.

Christina was fairly slight, which made her breasts seem larger than they were, She was tanned like leather except for a two inch strip across her nipples and her crotch, but she could have been decorated in black and white squares for all I cared.

She knew what it was all about, but I had to slow her down before her enthusiasm had me thinking I was giving one to a rattlesnake. It was good after that, and by the time she left, I knew I was going to have to learn German. Not that I was interested in the language for its own sake. It was just that I couldn't understand one word of all the lovely verbal she'd been groaning into my ear, which was a crime, because whether it was kinky or not, I knew that I was already hung up on "verbalatio", as I'd come to call it. Reversed, it was "verbalingus", and over the years, it helped turn a few latent ravers into the kind of chick they'd always wanted to be. Which gave me great pleasure, plus a good feeling at extending in some small way the ever growing range in the medium of communication.

I never did get into German but it didn't matter. Christina took to English like flies to shit, and pretty soon she was blowing my mind with her grasp of the vernacular. And all those Anglo-Saxon bits sounded even better on account of her guttural Austrian accent.

Well, between my chambermaid with the flair for language, and my employer's mother, I had my beds full, and though there was some lovely stuff staying at the hotel now, I just couldn't cope with any more. Let's face it, I was already increasing my brandy intake at night, as it was, and it wasn't getting any easier to haul myself out of the scratcher and get back to my own room before anybody tumbled that Olive and I weren't playing pontoon.

Christina came to my room a couple of mornings and woke me for a quick one, but I had to give a blank. She didn't like this, but there was no way I could tell her that I'd only been in my own bed for about half an hour. Not that it was any of her business, but she was a nice bird and I didn't want to hurt her if it could be avoided.

When I walked in on Darcy, it was over three weeks since I'd seen him. He was playing spoof with Theo, who seemed to spend most of his duty time sitting at the bar.

Paddy Darcy was a compulsive gambler. He was also fond of booze and he wasn't against a little pussy, provided he didn't have to exert himself too much to get it. Theo liked the birds, but he wouldn't let them interfere with anything he wanted to do.

Over a few rounds of drinks, I told them my news. Theo shook his head, trying to kid me that he was not jealous. Darcy looked like he wanted to spit, and he took back my fresh brandy.

"Do I give it to him?"

"Give it to the pox bottle," Theo snorted, emptying his own glass. "He'll be on bleedin' Bennies if he goes on the way he is...."

I asked him what were "Bennies" and Darcy laughed.

"Ah tell him," he said in his holy water voice. "Be awful if he fucked himself to death before he learned about Benzedrine."

"He's mad enough already," Theo said, "and by the sound of it, he's got a built in high...." He couldn't hold the straight face and his lips split, his mouth opening like a small canoe. "And me sending you up for the Jaysus job...."

Paddy put up fresh drinks, clicking his tongue at Theo.

"Ashamed of yourself you should be, sending this poor lad up there and you thinking it was a graveyard with candles."

"Serves me bleedin' right," Theo admitted... "great bread every week and wall to wall, hot and cold running pussy....

And me scratching in this kip and giving one to that bleedin' old crocodile last night...."

When I stopped laughing, he threw his eyes up to the roof like he was addressing God. "Got to be something... a next life... got to be... just to balance up the bleedin' injustice that goes on...."

"I'll have a word for you with Big Gee," I promised.

"Don't mind him," Darcy said to me...." He left my bar with a very nice lady last night."

"Would you go an' bollix," Theo suggested with what you might call real feeling.

"Got into bed with the same decent woman," Paddy informed me confidentially. "And according to information received from another source, she's very accommodating."

"Another source?" Theo looked at me in amazement. "Did you get that? 'Another source'... from a fella who couldn't read the sign on Euston Station...."

"He's come a long way," I said, "a long way from his family spread."

"He's come a long way from the arsehole of the mountains." Theo agreed. Then he said..."Jaysus! Another fucking source."

Darcy pressed on. "Great in bed, I'm told. A sex machine."

I looked from him to Theo who seemed to have a bad taste in his mouth. "Don't remind me," he pleaded, "I was pissed as a puddin'."

"But not so bad he couldn't enjoy the greatest session he's ever had." Paddy was quick to point out to me.

"The greatest. ...? Ah, turn it up, Darcy, my stomach's a bit fragile today."

"You mean to sit here and tell me that that lovely lady wasn't the best bang you've ever had?"

Theo looked vaguely ill, but he smiled, shaking his head, not wanting to believe that he'd actually given one to the old girl whoever she was. "I'll tell you what it was like, Maguire. It was like having a wank only you'd someone to talk to."

"May God forgive you," Darcy said in a tone of gentle admonition, while I had to grasp the bar rail for support, as I laughed until the tears rolled down onto my shirt.

Chapter Twenty-One

You're only young once, I told myself each time I felt I was being a real pig. It was pretty impossible though, not to get turned on by the endless stream of beautiful chicks, and the way most of them went after hotel staff was ridiculous.

And I don't mean just me. Every barman and waiter that I came to know, could tell you the same thing. But not one of them could ever tell me why a really good looking girl, with fellas who were also staying in the hotel practically fighting to take her out, would sit at a bar all evening, waiting for the barman to close up at maybe three in the morning. All right, most of them wanted to get laid, but they could have been in bed for hours with any of the fellas who chased them night after night.

Even when they'd been out in a party at one of the cabaret spots around the island, I've known girls come back to the hotel to climb into the scratcher with one of the staff. And once I had the strangest time ever with a real swinger who was on her honeymoon.

The first couple of nights she was at the bar with her husband. I wondered why she kept looking at me most of the time. I mean, normally, I'd have known why, but this lady was on her honeymoon and her husband seemed like a nice bloke.

On the third night it was so bloody strong, that it was good that her husband was hitting the Scotch like the supply was running out. And he might be forgiven for not expecting his new missus to be fancying the hired help in his honeymoon hotel.

I didn't need to believe she fancied me. I had more on my hands than I could handle without booze and a couple of Bennies a day. I was attracted to her, but that was all right. A nice safe little private fancy that could never come to anything anyway.

Inside my head an argument was taking place.

"She's definitely showing out to me."

"Bullshit... bird's on her honeymoon for Christ's sake."

"I know that... but just look... look at her now, what's that if it's not the 'come on'?"

"Big headed bastard!"

"Not this time... one thing I know something about it's birds... and she's coming on like the bleedin' Eighth Army."

"Bit pissed...."

"Four drinks? Don't make me laugh!"

All evening, this kind of exchange was bugging me, without helping in any way. But when it came to closing time I was proved right. And all I could think of was: "Does everything have to happen to me?"

Her husband was loaded and Honey told him to go on up to the room, that she didn't feel tired. I watched him go, trying hard not to shake my head in disbelief. She watched me, talking a lot about nothing, while I closed up for the night. I knew then, yet I still couldn't accept it. And even when we walked out of the bar together, while Olive waited for me upstairs, my mind continued to reject the scene as I was reading it.

On the stairs, she took my hand. "I want to see your room."

"What about your husband?"

"He likes his sleep...." Her eyebrows flew up in protest at the doubt in my expression. "It's true, darling, he sleeps ever such a lot."

She followed me into my room, locking the door behind us. I put the money bag in the wardrobe and opened a half bottle of Courvoisier. Olive had introduced me to her favourite brandy some weeks before, and I must admit that I was hooked on it from the first taste. It was no trial, believe me, I loved the fabulous warm glow it painted on the walls of my inferiority complex.

When I turned to hand her her drink, my honeymoon lady was standing there with nothing on but her false eyelashes. I stood there like a cretin, my hands wide apart with a tumbler of brandy in each. She stepped in close against me and I stopped even thinking about it. I mean, I wasn't doing a training course in sainthood, anyway.

I think this backs up my statement that women went crazy when the island got into them. And as I've said, it didn't happen just to me. There was a kind of joke about one big hotel where the night porter had to go around ringing a bell at six in the morning so that the swappers would get back to their own beds before breakfast. And like most stories of that kind, if it was half joking it was half in earnest.

Christina fell out with me because she saw Honey leaving my room one afternoon. I could have put it right, but I was very tired. Honey and her husband were leaving that evening, for which I was truly grateful, but I let Christina stew. I wanted my afternoons back, for Christ's sake!

I was falling apart and I thought it might be a good idea to lay off everybody for a few days. Olive would understand and Christina was doing me a favour without knowing it. But the moment I thought about sex, even when I seriously considered hanging up my gun for a few days, I became priapic again. Which made me glad, just for a change, that I wasn't carrying any kind of double barrelled rod. If I had been, well, I'd have had to wear an icepack or something in my knickers, because as it was, I was half crippled totin' my sawn off job around. But then the hammer was just about permanently cocked.

About this time I started to write long letters that I never posted. I poured out my feelings and my thoughts, filling endless pages day after day. Later, I realised that I'd never intended sending them to anyone. It was just the beginning of trying to write, but even now, it seems a funny way to have begun.

I wrote to my mother about twice a month and I sent her a few pounds each time. I also sent the odd bit of money to my father, more to help him feel easier about me, than because I needed to save. If it made him feel good it was worthwhile.

Each afternoon I slept at least a couple of hours on the beach and I had a swim before I went back to the hotel. I saw a lot of Paddy Darcy and Theo Roberts, and even with the sea lapping at your feet, we would be passing a bottle around.

When those two nuts started to comment on how much I was drinking, I just shrugged it off and tried to act the hard-chaw. What I didn't tell them was that I'd got kind of hooked on Benzedrine, which was bad, but to make things worse, it had suddenly become just about impossible to get any of it. So a bit more booze was needed to keep away the purgatory pains I'd been having. I mean, I had to get on with the job.

I only slept with Olive twice during that first ten days without Benzedrine, and she mentioned that I seemed tired and shaky. She was right and I could only smile because Olive herself looked about ten years younger than she had at the beginning of the season. That night she needed more attention than usual and she soon forgot the concern she'd expressed for me a minute earlier. She had become selfish when it came to sex and, when she started looking for an encore, I had to tell her I was bushed.

"Unless you have some Benzedrine about."

"I'm sorry, pet, I haven't needed any since…" she smiled at me… "I expect you know I'm hooked on you…."

I felt like screaming, my nerves were so edgy. Olive sat up, like she'd remembered something. I watched her nip into the bathroom, but when she reappeared holding an inhaler, I felt like slapping her face I was so disappointed.

"This should be all right, pet." She used a flat heeled shoe to break the plastic tube, tearing the cotton substance from around the supporting stick. "Want to try it?"

She rolled the stuff into little balls and I swallowed a couple of them with a brandy wash down. The charge was near enough immediate and in minutes I was flying again. Flying so well that nothing else mattered. Nothing. Not me, my brain, my health. I wanted to be high, needing so badly to be off the ground, that I couldn't stop for one second to consider how stupid the whole scene had become.

Chapter Twenty-Two

Olive had started giving me a hard time, but though she wasn't getting into me, she'd pulled a couple of bad scenes that added up to another reason why I was looking forward to the end of the season. Theo and I had been talking about going on the boats, but Darcy thought it was all drunken bullshit. It was like he needed to believe this.... He was going back to a good job in London, and I was sure he didn't want to see the trio break up. I tried to talk him into coming along for the crack, but he wanted the London job more than anything else. I couldn't understand it, I mean, all right, he was twenty-five years old, but he was a lunatic, so why the steady job routine?

"He's insecure," Theo informed me, turning his head to spew something out of the car window.

"Keep your drunken eyes on the road," Darcy yelled, as drunk himself as the rest of us.

"Do you know?" Theo sounded like fat Alfred Hitchcock, when he was loaded. "Do you know, he's such a lousy motorist he can't even get insured to be a back seat driver...."

"Listen to who's talking, will you?" Darcy's Monaghan accent slipped further sideways. "I couldn't drive a bleedin' nail through a pound of soap...."

Theo nodded to the windscreen and Darcy screamed drunkenly as we hit the grass verge on the offside of the road. "Insecurity, that's what it is..." Theo had come back to his original point, but he was talking to the windscreen. "Couldn't read the signs on Euston Station, y'know... little bollix!"

Darcy kept complaining about the drunken driving, and I

thought he was going on a bit. Theo's driving seemed all right to me, but when he did land the little Standard in the ditch, as Darcy called it, and I was giving a hand to drag it back onto the road, I realised that I was too drunk to be any kind of judge.

Half an hour later, as I sat in my room listening to Christina, I tried to remember that some days were good days. She was pregnant and she didn't like it when I asked her who the father was. Tears, Jesus, did she cry, and wails that made me glad I'd said it, because she'd been so dumb. I'd asked her right at the beginning about birth control, making it plain as a nun's purity, that I didn't want to make problems for anyone.

I was glad I was stoned because I was nice to her, which she needed me to be just then, and I made her believe that I'd only been joking when I kidded about the baby's father. If she'd hit me with it on a normal morning when my head seemed to be some kind of busy computer, I might have said a lot of things that wouldn't have done anybody any good. All her dialogue about being able to look after herself had been bullshit, and she deserved to be told. Except there was no point. She was six weeks overdue and doing something about that was going to take all the energy and all the patience we could gather between the two of us.

She turned out to be a great bird in the finish. But then we were both lucky that the German housekeeper felt sorry for Christina, and Helga was a woman who got things done when she wasn't in the scratcher with the head waiter.

Helga had always been okay to me, but she only had eyes for Roberto, who was a good head for an Italian. All the staff joked about the pair of them. Every hour off duty they spent in the head waiter's room, taking enormous amounts of food and drink with them even though they ate three or four meals a day just like the rest of us.

Tonio, a crazy Italian, a little guy who was a super waiter, and who really looked like a cannelloni with legs, fractured most of the staff when he described what went on in Roberto's bedroom.

His dark eyes spun like black buttons in his pastry coloured face.

"A little fooda, eh, then a little focka, eh, thena some vino eh, a little focka, eh...." He mimed each piece of action like a spaghetti bender's Danny Kaye, and even Roberto, who could be as temperamental as an opera star, laughed until he had to get up and leave the table.

Helga shrugged philosophically, accepting my word that I'd checked with Christina again and again that she was looking after things. She smiled then, a knowing look in her sleepy eyes.

"The other one, it would be okay, yes?"

I looked at her, not really surprised that she knew about Olive and me. Good housekeepers don't miss much, which is why they're good.

"I'm teaching her Irish," I said.

Her face opened up a bit more and I could tell she liked that one. "How do you make love in Irish?" She smiled and put her hand on my arm. "Everything will be all right, but it takes some money."

I nodded. "I'll fix that, Helga... whatever it is...."

"That's nice, Paddy... many men..." She shook her head... "when it comes to money they forget that one person never made a baby alone, huh?"

What hit me about that scene, and made me appreciate just how realistic those Europeans were, was the total absence of any bull about love and marriage, while the idea that Christina might actually have the baby, never even saw daylight.

When I was alone later, knowing that it would be fixed, I smiled that it hadn't even occurred to me to marry Christina. I mean, I didn't even have to reject the idea, simply because it had never come to life. Marriage? A joke. The longest running bad joke the world had ever known.

"Just a joke," I said aloud.

"You must be talking about marriage," a voice said.

I snapped back into my bar and found I had a new resident waiting for me to serve him a drink. He laughed at the surprise on my face. "I thought so," he said, in a voice that seemed to have trouble suppressing a million bubbles of wicked laughter.

He put out his hand. "Jack Jones, London." I shook his hand and told him my name. He laughed at that. "Oh well," he said, and drank some of his beer. "A bloody Irishman! Well, you chaps make lousy bloody husbands anyway...." He laughed again... "So why the hell bother, that's what I say?" I laughed with him, glad to meet another real live screwball.

"Any man gets married's a bloody head case, that's what I say... said it to my wife just before I came downstairs."

He kept making me laugh, but beneath the giggles, I meant what I said about the marriage bit. Sex on the hire purchase when the world was crawling with beautiful chicks and a lot of them ready, willing and able. And how many chocolate milk shakes could you drink without wanting a little strawberry? Marriage? For the birds! That whole scene was a bad, sad joke.

Jack Jones had another beer and I drank a Mackeson with him. A few new arrivals came into the lounge, a man with a check suit and a lot of mouth, his wife, or so I guessed, from her long-suffering expression, and two pretty girls. The man turned to his wife.

"Where's that Phil got to then?" He asked in a tinny voiced London accent.

His wife started to say something when a third girl came running into the room. She pulled the two other girls aside and mumbled something that sent the three of them into hysterics.

The man ordered drinks and I put them up, giving his wife a lot of attention. He called to the girls and though they were still giggling they came across the carpet to the bar.

The one called Phil smiled pure beautiful innocent wickedness at me and I couldn't believe eyes so brown.

"Hello," she said.

Chapter Twenty-Three

What the hell is it? This thing which makes you feel you've known someone forever, when it's only been a few minutes since you've met.

And how can you feel, knowing that its got to be ridiculous, that "this is what my life has been for". Even worse... you stand looking at a total stranger, wanting to utter what must be the daftest line in any language... "I was born to spend whatever time there is, with you...."

"Love at first sight" is the handiest label, but a fella could be forgiven for wanting to laugh at it. The idea, if you give it any consideration at all, calls to mind those old movies where HE and SHE experience the electric jolt, only to have their flying carpet pulled out from under them by their respective, and often respectable, families into "no daughter of mine is going to marry a son of that mobster, you hear?" and all the rest of it, before love, the love at first sight kind of love, conquers everything. The music is turned up... the two families join hands through glycerine tears, and watch THEM, the eternal lovers, drive off into the sunset, that Buck and Hoppy and Gene and Roy, had to face again and again, but always on the lonesome trail.

Yes, you remember what a load of old ballocks it was, and you feel that the guy who wrote that kind of screenplay, had to be a gin swigging faggot.

She walked into my bar, actually interrupting Jack Jones as he listened to my tirade of abusive comment, on the holy sacrament of marriage.

Hello was all she had said, throwing in a smile that you might get from a Girl Guide who had just slipped a live toad into her patrol leader's knickers. She walked away then to sit with her two friends, creating further giggling with something she said. And I stood there feeling that I'd been hit with a steam shovel. And I loved her just like they seemed to in those crummy movies, and I couldn't laugh it off because, I felt that if I couldn't marry her, my life wouldn't mean a thing.

I promised myself it was daft, stupid, that I was unbalanced from pills and booze and grass, that I was so worried about Christina, and so guilty at the thought of leaving Olive in a few weeks time, that I just wasn't responsible for anything I said or did.

Anyway, I was going on the boats with Theo. We'd shaken on it over a couple of bottles only a couple of nights before. But we had been drunk, it didn't matter. I'd given the head from Terenure my word, and no self respecting Dubliner would break his word. Least of all for a little bird who was some kind of comedienne. It was such a joke, for Christ's sake!

Well, I can say with truth and conviction, that all my efforts changed sweet fuck all. But I did go on trying, fighting against it more and more, it just got worse. And it wasn't my idea of a fun situation. No way

Then I was in agony when I saw her go out with some young resident, a scrawny guy with mousy hair and hardly any arse to call his own. And when she did come into the bar, it was only for a quick aperitif or drink before going out for the evening.

One of her pals, a redhead with lovely boobs and buttocks to match, allowed me a few minutes chat when she came in for change to use the pay telephone to London. The poor kid should have stayed home, because she was so miserable without her boy friend, that her holiday was a waste of money. She wasn't eating and she couldn't sleep, but "don't say anything to the others," she begged me. "Don't want to spoil things for them." I promised to keep our secret, and it didn't help one little bit to know that someone else was suffering from the same disease as me.

Joan, the lovesick redhead, told me they were staying just the one week, which put me in such a panic that I drank a gin and tonic before I realised what I was doing. And you can believe I wouldn't as a rule use that muck to wash the windows down.

I couldn't seem to get off the ground with Phil, even talking to her was some kind of agony. I felt off balance and so bloody shy that I doubted the validity of my own claim to being the biggest bullshitter since Santa Claus. Some bullshit artist! A fella who blushed almost every time a little bird called Phil ordered a drink. Christ! It hit me what was wrong with me. Every time I saw her, I felt like a fella at his first dance without a few drinks in him.

This was what convinced me I was suffering from something I hadn't experienced before. I mean regardless of what labels I'd stuck on my feelings for Maureen and Pauline, and Jenny, too, there hadn't been a time when I couldn't tell the tale, doing with bullshit personality routine all the things I couldn't muster simply by using the plain, flat, pale faced me.

I should never have let that Phil upset my balance. Jesus, all I had to do was give her some crazy verbal to get her interested enough to talk. Once that happened, I could hit her with every card in my stack, after that there was no way she would be able to ignore me. So what if none of it was real? If it got me started, I could straighten things out later on.

When she started to order her drink, I held up my hand like a traffic cop.

"One second," I requested... "I have to have a word with Redmond."

She didn't even blink and I loved her cool. I cocked an eye to the ceiling.

"Okay, Redmond, shoot." I made like I was listening now, nodding my head as I received a report from Redmond. She stood there, determined not to smile.

"I see, yes... right," I looked at the ceiling again. "Good work, Redmond..." I made a gesture of dismissal and gave Phil all my attention.

She waited, receptive, but bloody wary. I smiled, trying to ignore her lovely mouth and those brown eyes.

"This better be good," she warned me.

"A good report on you," I assured her... "in fact, the best you've had since you got here...."

"Whatever you're drinking, I'll have one." Her tone was so offhand that I wanted to hug the breath from her. "And a straight jacket to go with it." she was all innocence.

"Because you've been so good, I'll fix you something very special, all right?" She shrugged, holding down her smile, and sat up on one of the barstools.

"And if you go on playing your cards right... like if you continue to control yourself the way you have been, I'll take a chance and let you talk me into going out with you...." I emptied the Clover Club into a seven ounce glass and placed it before her on the bar.

"Do I fill in the application before I drink this?"

"In your case there's no need," I said, "Redmond spoke so well of you that I accept your invitation here and now."

She sipped the drink. "Do you have houses and shops and things in Ireland?" It came out flat and her eyes backed her up. She might have been a geography student inquiring about how much carboniferous limestone there was in Peru.

"The pictures," I answered, "but none of that back row stuff, right?"

"Ooh, that looks good!" Joan had arrived with the third girl, Leslie, who was a pretty blonde shy beyond belief.

"Celebration," Phil informed her, those brown eyes flicking from me to Joan. "I've managed to talk Paddy into taking me to the movies tomorrow, but he won't come unless you two join us... he's shy, aren't you, Paddy?"

"Pictures? What if the sun is shining like it was today?" Joan's eyes were wide, her expression so ingenuous, that I knew the question was for real.

"We'll buy him an ice cream," Phil replied, her face still deadpan. "He's just been telling me how much he likes ice cream... eats it all the time."

"Tutti Frutti's my favourite...." Laughter replied out of Joan's throat... "You get tutti I'll get frutti, hmmmmmmm."

The three of them screeched at that one, and I realised I was sweating from sheer relief. Phil was coming out with me.

The bar filled up and I coped with one of Brown's tantrums without even having to think about it. Normally I'd have shot his ballocks off but today Brown was okay. I treated him with easy courtesy and it was no problem, because I felt a bit sorry for him. I mean, he didn't know that if I said the word, he'd have me for a stepfather.

Chapter Twenty-Four
Jersey. September '58

When the cab took Phil and her party away from the hotel, I went to my room and lay down on the bed. I had a drink of brandy, wishing I could go to sleep and wake up in three weeks time. Three weeks before I'd see her again. Three whole bloody weeks, which made me sad, while just the thought of seeing her again, filled me with joy.

Joy had become a synonym for Phil, who hadn't laughed when I told her what she'd done to me. Yet how we'd laughed through the afternoon movie with the temperature at something like ninety in the shade. Seven ice creams for me, not counting lemonade and crisps and God knows what other garbage. With just two late night walks after I closed the bar. And one kiss at her bedroom door with my heart pounding enough for her to hear it.

Nonsense I know, and don't think I didn't go on reminding myself about it. It was some kind of dream, the funny ha ha kind that could lead to a nightmare called marriage, if the dream itself was allowed to develop any further. I won't go on about it, but all the thinking, the endless reminders that I had things to do, places to see… all of it and none of it, well, it didn't change a thing. I was all right and I wasn't going to lie weeping into my pillows, but I had an empty, lost feeling that I just couldn't shake off.

Theo still talked about the Merchant Navy and I assured him that I'd be along with him, wherever we were meant to end up. Paddy thought I was mad to be on the island still, and Theo agreed, on the grounds that Christina could have been sleeping with lots of people and that lumbering me with the pregnancy bit. I didn't say too much. Close as the three of us had become, they wouldn't have understood how I felt. Sure it was possible Christina was spoofing me, but there was a chance that the responsibility was mine. It didn't matter if it was evens or a thousand to one, the chance existed, and I couldn't turn my back on the bird when she needed me most.

I was still drinking too much but I'd cut out on the Benzedrine trick because of Phil. She'd been horrified when I told her about that scene and she'd asked me to promise her I wouldn't touch the shit again. I don't know, maybe it was just the fact that she cared enough about me to ask, like, it seemed to matter to her whether I lived or died, but I made the promise and I kept it, though I went through agony for a week afterwards.

My bank book showed about two hundred and fifty pounds, and I had another couple of hundred tucked away in my room. I was afraid to stick it all in one place, just in case anything went wrong. By saving hard I could have saved two hundred or so, but to have the best part of a monkey sitting in a vault was advertising the fact that I had a great fiddle going. Not that I could see anything going wrong, but just in case, I was eliminating possibilities where I could.

Brown scared me badly one morning by knocking me up at ten o'clock for the keys to the bar. He was in a stinking mood and I had a hangover you could have photographed.

When I was in that state, I jumped when somebody walked up to me quickly. Everybody was about to punch me in the head, or so it seemed, and people walking on the street behind me became policeman who wanted my scalp. So that when Brown mentioned taking stock, I really believed he was trying to crucify me.

"This is Thursday?"

His mouth was twitching and he kept blinking at me. "Yes, of course it's Thursday...."

"You take stock each Friday," I reminded him. "So why today?"

"Because it's convenient, today, and it may not be in the morning." He stood stiffly which couldn't have been easy for him the state his nerves were in.

What Brown didn't know was that Thursday night was the most important one in the week for me. Every penny fiddled Thursday, I left in the till, and up to now, it had kept the stock right.

"Do something for me first," I told him.

He didn't like my tone, but I seemed to be standing about three feet behind my own voice, so his baleful eyes didn't bother me too much.

"Do something...?" He was puzzled.

"Get my cards."

"Your cards?" He was shaken some by what I'd said.

"And my wages and my commission...."

"But what on earth...?"

"Listen," I said, as evenly as I could. "The arrangement is that you take stock every Friday - today is Thursday and you want to do it, all right, but as far as I'm concerned you're casting aspersion on my honesty, my integrity."

"But I didn't...."

"And I don't give two fucks what you say to the contrary... you think I've got some kind of fiddle going, right... do your fucking stock take, but not until you pay me my money and give me my insurance cards...."

"Now there's no need to get like that...."

I shook my head, which hurt more than you'd believe. "You must take me for some kind of cunt...." His eyes flipped at my language... "Well, let me tell you something... there's nobody on this island, could have earned you more in that bar than I did... and I've put up with your mother fucking about, getting in my way... so you want to take stock, take the fucking thing, but you don't get the keys from me, until I get what I'm entitled to.... Unless you want to try and take them...."

"I really didn't mean...."

"Well, what does it mean? What would you think in my place?"

He took the trouble to consider this for a few seconds, nodding his head then in an apologetic way. "I'm sorry, Paddy... you're quite right...." His face relaxed a bit...." The strain of the season...."

"I know, Mr. Brown... hits us all about now...."

He seemed grateful. "In the morning then...?"

"I'll have it all ready for you." I promised, thinking, ready and balanced and beautiful. He went away and I shut the door. Jesus! I thought – what little surprise have you got in store for me for next Thursday. Still, it had worked out all right, and seconds later, when I poured a brandy to start the long haul to the point where you just feel ordinary, I realised that my hangover was gone.

Olive was talking about coming to London with me, but it wasn't on. Phil apart, my lovely fifty year old had no place in any plans I might have, though of course, I wasn't going to tell her that. What was the point? She believed I'd send for her, or at least let her know where I was the moment I organised myself a flat, and by the time she realised that this wasn't going to happen, well, she might just be able to accept, without too much breast beating, that Maguire wasn't strong enough to carry any additional luggage.

The time passed very quickly, but then I was willing the days full sail and a friendly wind. Christina had her abortion and Helga handled everything for me. The money meant nothing and the bird was all right, which really made me very grateful.

She was still in bed the day I left the island. I pushed fifty quid under her pillow. She protested, but I made her take it.

She smiled and she drew my fingers to her mouth, and she looked a little bit sad. I had a lump in my throat, and I needed a large brandy in the worst way.

"My good lover, you are good friend...."

"I feel bad leaving, and you still here in bed...."

"Oh, it's just for a few days... have no worry for me... I am well... and a bit wiser...." She went pensive for a couple of seconds. "That is not right, is it? A bit more wiser...? I cannot say it like that, Paddy...."

"It's all right... you've learned something... doesn't matter how you say it." I leaned over and kissed her mouth and when she let me go, I wiped away the few tears that crept out of her eyes.

"No tears, huh?"

"You make me feel beautiful, so I cry a little. Always you made me feel I was the only woman in the world...." She smiled. "When you were with me...." She pressed my hand. "Women will always want you, Paddy...." She moved her shoulders and a sigh escaped her lips... "You make love to a woman the moment you begin talking to her....You are her lover from that moment... bed and sex is only a part of your lovemaking...." She smiled wistfully... "I shall miss my lover... but I wish you happiness...." I kissed her again.

"I'll see you sometime...."

She nodded her head and I opened the door. I raised my hand.

"Ciao." She waved. "Ciao, lovely Irish bastard...."

I stood outside the door and I wiped my own tears out of the way before I went down to meet Theo and say my goodbyes.

Chapter Twenty-Five
London. October '58

"By Jaysus we've done it! We've done it, ye whore ye!" Theo slapped me on the back hard enough to knock me overboard into the King George V dock. He was chortling with excitement, but I couldn't look at him for fear he'd see that I was close to tears.

"New Fuckin' Zealand, here we come!" He was so excited that his phoney brogue had enough life in it to be the real McCoy, and I couldn't help feeling warm for him. About myself, I wasn't so sure. Oh, it was some kind of thrill, all right.... Off to New Zealand, working as an assistant steward, which meant, waiter, on the *Ruatoto*, twenty-two thousand tons of passengers cargo ship, with wages, bed and board, guaranteed, not to mention the free travel. But Christ, we were going to be away four months and I was sick about Phil after five minutes.

The night before, as we sheltered from the rain in a shop doorway in Fulham Palace Road, I told her that she only had to say the word and I wouldn't go.

"I love you enough not to want to stop you, Maguire."

Her words seemed like wisdom to me and I wondered how a girl of twenty could know so much. I believed that she loved me and time was to prove me right, but she knew better than to ask me not to go, regardless of how badly she needed me to stay. And that seemed a very big thing to me.

Theo and I had been three weeks in London, and I'd seen a lot of Phil in that time. Well, in the second and third week anyway... most of the first one was a write off, thanks to a piss-up that could only be described as glorious.

It had started as a bet between Theo and me. It was over

Phil, and though he was only needling me, Theo hit a spot that was raw enough to make me very angry.

"Got you by the ballocks, Maguire...." We were waiting for our luggage at London Airport...." I wouldn't have believed it...."

"She's just a nice bird...." I felt a bit ashamed that I couldn't get my ego out of the way. Just admit you love her, Head, tell him... he won't laugh if he sees it's for real.

"Just a nice bird... for Jaysus sake, you're like a dog in trap one waiting for the bell.... Have you change for the phone?"

"I don't want to ring her right now...."

"I didn't meet her, did I?"

"You know bloody well, you didn't meet her...."

We moved out with the bags. "What's in it, the slow stroll down the isle, a touch of the semi-detached, all that?"

"I've nothing to declare...." I hadn't but the customs fella didn't believe me and went right through the bag. Theo smiled as he waited for me, his bags marked out unopened. I was needled and had trouble closing the case.

"Fitted carpets, wall to wall..." Theo said as I reached him.

"For Christ's sake, I hardly know the bird," I growled, feeling like a traitor and a coward.

"A week on the piss'd cure you, but there's no way you're going to listen...." We got into a cab.

"Cure me of what, for Jesus sake?"

He lay back on the seat blowing smoke rings as big as a halo. "We get on the plane he starts talking about this bird...." He seemed to be addressing a third party... "Not bothered about her, Jaysus no, but talks about nothing else... all the way over, and while we're waiting for the cases...." He turned to look at me as we started into the tunnel. "But you couldn't stay away from her for a week."

"Of course I could...." He laughed at the way my tone dropped to negative on the last two words. And I felt foolish.

"Twenty-five lids says you can't...."

I wanted to protest, to insert a couple of qualifications into my earlier statement, but he had me going by this time, and I agreed to the bet. So we checked into a hotel in Kensington and started drinking. I wasn't unhappy to be drinking but I was miserable about not seeing Phil. Not that I'd let him see it, so I drank more and more to forget her, thinking it wouldn't be a bad idea if I forgot her altogether. Theo had mentioned things that should have bothered me.... All that semi-detached bit and what went with it seemed to me to be a trip to Tombsville. At least it had seemed that way until he mentioned it in relation to Phil. I hadn't even flinched, and worse, the idea seemed good and decent... because I'd be with Phil.

"You can stay away from a chick for a week, you can stay away from a chick, period." Theo paid me the pony without shedding any tears and I put it in my pocket. I really felt like tearing it up, it had come so hard, but those kind of dramatics I left to eccentric millionaires.

"I told you when we got here, she's just a nice bird, and I'd like to see her again."

"Goodbye to the merchant navy," he said to himself in the backing mirror of the bar.

"You wouldn't like to bet another pony on it?"

"Making bets with you is a habit I don't intend to develop, Maguire, cut your bleedin' arm off for twenty five lids. Leave off."

At seven thirty that same evening, Phil walked into the downstairs bar at the Clarendon in Hammersmith. That first sight of her as she came through the door seemed to throttle my breathing and I couldn't move to meet her. She had had her hair cut tight with a razor and her eyes danced with delight when she saw me. And my stupid heart raced as I took her hands.

"Hello, darling...."

"Phil," I said, her name somehow scratching past the fierce obstruction of my constricted breathing.

"I'm so happy to see you...."

I kissed her and I took her in my arms, pressing her gently against me, only to make sure that she was really there, that I wasn't imagining the perfect dream.

"I love you, Phil...." My heart seemed to climb up into my throat, I was so nervous, yet I didn't care that the people in the bar might hear me. God, I couldn't have cared if my voice was being carried to the ears of those people walking by outside on the street. Phil was all at that moment. Phil, Phil, Phil, who right then had the power to crush me like an ant under her foot.

"I love you..." I said again... "that's all I know."

With her body close to mine, Phil leaned back against the cradle of my arms, smiling at me, her huge brown eyes warm as roasted chestnuts.

"I love you..." she said, moving her mouth to mine again, kissing me in a passionate yet desperately innocent way that made my heart want to weep tears of total happiness.

"Ah Lamma Jaysus!" Theo protested... "have yis no shame at all?"

Phil and I laughed out loud, nervous, bordering on hysterical laughter, that poured out like an expression of our gratitude, that the hard part, those first bloody awful and difficult minutes, were over.

From there it was plain sailing... Theo and Phil got along fine, which was a relief. I mean, it makes life that much easier if your girl and your friend happen to hit it off.

He made her laugh, of course, but then Theo had a way with him, that would have made you a millionaire if you could have bottled it for export to the States. And all it was, though it took me some time to work it out, was his ability to be himself. Totally and without any qualifications whatsoever, he was a natural guy, making the best of what he had going for him, but never getting into any kind of sweat to make people accept or like him. He was also a very funny character, able without any obvious effort to simulate a crazy laugh that was infectious enough to turn a room full of mopers into a team of howling head cases in a few seconds flat. And if he'd ever been embarrassed, it must have been while he was still wearing nappies.

It was funny, really, to hear him talk about Phil when I got back to the hotel that first night. In a kind of way, what had happened to me, like my instant change from bachelor of the year to the guy who most wanted to get married, had happened to him as well. Like, only hours before, he'd been going on about a steady bird being a wagon. And there he was going on at me about being luckier than I deserved to have pulled such a great bird.

"Ah, she's all right..." I said quietly.

"All right me ballocks." he snorted. "She's fuckin' smashin' and don't you be so bleedin' smart." He sounded offended by my treachery and I pulled my shirt over my face to hide my grin that split it from ear to ear.

"Don't tell me you've been laying there thinking about my girl...?" I got enough amazement into my voice to make him snort again, and when he looked at me his great eyelids had dropped like pram hoods over his organ stop eyes.

"If you must know I've been laying here planning a wrist job...."

"Whose the lucky bird tonight, Ella Fitzgerald?"

"No, it's the wrong time of the month."

"Did you hear that one about the fella called on the bird when she was in her periods?"

"Everybody bleedin' heard it," Theo informed me, "who do you think I am, Dracula, right?" He pulled a face that told me I needed some new material.

"Bet you didn't hear about the chick with the dirty bust."

He didn't say anything so I pressed on. "She was scared the boyfriend would want a feel, so she made a clean breast of it."

Theo looked at me as though I belonged on a hook. "You just make that up?" I nodded, feeling very pleased with myself. And Theo nodded like an American who'd been left a fortune in Confederate money. "You won't mind if we don't share a cabin in the merchant navy...?"

I smothered my grin and go into bed. "Ah go wind up your stomach..." I said, trying for the last word. He mumbled something that I didn't hear because I was standing at another fork in the road. Suddenly, I wasn't too happy about having to decide whether it was going to be Phil or a job aboard a ship. I knew I loved her but all my life I'd been dreaming about seeing the world.

Chapter Twenty-Six

"I don't want you to go, Maguire," Phil said, "but that's no reason for you not to...."

Her brown eyes were on my face and I felt naked before her frankness, guilty, I guess, for having tried once again to pass the buck. Let Phil make the decision for both of us had been the plan, but it hadn't worked, and I loved her all the more for her honesty.

"If what we have is real... and I hope it is... it'll be there when you come back...."

The way she said it, it made perfect sense, but I was afraid. Afraid that if I did go I'd lose her.

"If it's real we won't lose each other...."

"Mind reader..." I smiled and kissed her.

"Years from now, when we're fighting over something stupid, I wouldn't want you telling me that if it hadn't been for me...."

"We're not going to row or fight...." I said quickly, trying too late, to bite on such a piece of stupidity.

"I'm going to make sure we fight ..." Her eyes were like dark mirrors of mischief... "so that we can make up... mmm-mmm...."

She laughed and I hugged her against me on the seat of the number eleven bus.

"Behave," I warned her, "or I'll tell your father what you're like...."

"Huh," Phil grunted, already aware that I wasn't exactly jumping for joy at the idea of meeting her parents.

"Is he that bad, kid?"

She shook her head, smiling. "He's odd, Maguire, and he's

not the most popular man in London, but I think he's the greatest."

"I'm glad, Phil." I said it and I meant it, feeling a glow of my own when I remembered Pops at home on The Hill. But, at the same time, she had me worried about just what kind of old ballocks her father really was. Her mother sounded like a huge doll lady, but despite what Phil felt for her old man, I had the impression that he was a tough old bastard. Yet I liked the fact that they had insisted on meeting me because it proved that they cared about Phil. And anybody who cared about Phil couldn't be all bad.

Here's where we get back to the word IF. If I'd been a bit brighter, or a little more tolerant. If he'd not been such a bigoted old prick, or if his upbringing hadn't made him so insecure that he had made money his religion, worshipping daily by avidly reading the epistled pink pages of the *Financial Times*. And so on and so on. A joke when I think about it now. Regardless of race, religion, politics, sex or whatever, Phil's father and myself would never have got beyond first base in the friendship series.

Old man Williams thought the Irish were nothing but a bunch of drunken shits. This didn't come out the first time we met but soon enough I could feel it so strong, that I was defensive with him. He was a clever man, much too smart for me, and that night he gave me just enough rope to hang myself. I didn't realise this until many months later, when it had become pretty obvious to Phil's family, that she and I were in love and thinking very seriously about the future.

That first night he poured the booze into me and because I didn't know his form, like how I was supposed to know he was as tight as a duck's arse (which has to be water tight), I didn't think there was anything strange about it. When I stood up to make a move back to the hotel at around midnight, and he insisted that I spend the night under his roof, I was prepared to admit to myself that I'd misjudged him, though, right away, I did think it a bit strange when he told his missus to sleep in the spare room, that he wanted to talk to me further when we were alone. Even Phil thought I'd made the conquest of the century, but in time she too was to realise that her dearly beloved daddy would have made one hell of a chess player.

I lay in Mrs. Williams bed and the old man encouraged me to talk, to tell him all about myself, my background, my hopes and my dreams. It was such an obvious hustle, that it illustrates how pissed I must have been, not to have seen that he was boxing me into a corner.

Naturally enough, I didn't mention Pauline or Jennie, not that my involvement with either would have bothered him, if I'd had money in the bank. To be fair to him, he was a materialist first and a moralist tenth. But when he realised that my claim to being descended from the High Kings of Ireland couldn't be backed up with a few thousand acres handed over by Royal Charter, and that the only thing I'd ever had in a bank was a mate who worked as a porter, it very rapidly became a question of goodnight and goodbye. But like I've said, he gave me no inkling of this until a long time later.

Mrs. Williams was a sweetheart, and through the years that were to follow, though we very often didn't agree about most things, she being a rank Conservative, with me, surely as a natural consequence of my upbringing, some kind of a socialist, she was always kind, and more charitable than most Catholics I'd run into. Her people were Devon and she carried a trace of her West Country accent. She was a decent woman, who loved a laugh and a song and the odd dirty joke, though she would coo and tut tut at the idea of telling racy stories.

The Old Man Williams was slim and wiry, similar in some ways to my own father, both of them being basically ill mannered, uneducated.

He was different to Pops in that he'd made money working sixteen, eighteen, hours a day for twenty odd years, and though he might have been forgiven for the pride he took in being self-made, it became harder and harder to listen to him without wanting to throw up. But then, again, he had provided a good home for his family, and his wife stayed loyal to him, so there had to be more to him than I was willing to admit.

I didn't see him again before I left London. I was busy hustling to get Theo and myself into the Merchant Navy, giving my evenings to Phil. And I was so happy to be alone with her in the little time we had, that it never occurred to me that I hadn't been invited back to the house at Fulham Palace Road.

There's no doubt in my mind that if Theo had been any kind of worrier, any less mad than I was, we'd never have made that shipboard scene, because the very first thing that slapped us in the teeth when we got down to the Navy Pool Office was a sign bearing the information that "Falsification of References could lead to six months imprisonment". And the pair of us about to hand in written, in fact, typewritten, recommendations to the effect that we were first class waiters, clean, honest and industrious. As you may have guessed, I'd given my imagination a walk in the sun.

Theo had thought me a padded cell case when I said we were going to the Savoy Hotel to get a reference. But he came along without too much argument when I bet him a tenner that it was the first step into the Merchant Navy. In quick succession, I took some headed notepaper from the writing room of the Savoy, the Strand Palace and the Regent Palace, before we took a cab up to the Horse Trough, where I knew Elsie had an old typewriter she'd let me use.

"You'll end up in bleedin' nick," Lenny warned me, while Phil fell about us as she read the fantastic blurbs I produced for Theo and me.

It's such a joke when you think about it. As if hotels of that size, where waiters come and go like snowflakes on a river, would hand out typed references. But it seemed like a good idea at the time, and just to cap it all, I did a final one for myself from a non-existent hotel in County Dublin. I used a very deliberate "sure and begorrah" style and finishing the reference off with something like "He leaves here with our prayers and the hope that God will go with him on his journey through life."

Theo thought this was really going over the top and maybe it was, but it was as if I had to get a real gag in there to finish off what was really a bloody musical comedy situation.

The Pool was pretty full of seamen of all kinds, rough and ready people, who didn't go in too much for courtesy or good manners, but as I was to learn, life aboard ship was tough and demanding and to survive it you had to appear to be as good or as bad or as tough as your shipmates. And you never said please or thanks except to your close buddies, because consideration was almost always mistaken for weakness. And to appear weak or unsure at sea was an invitation to trouble of one kind or another.

When we handed in our references, the clerk just gave them a cursory glance, took a quick look at the pair of us, and told us to come back in a week, by which time references would have been checked out.

"What the fuck do we do now?" Theo wasn't worried so much as puzzled. I couldn't answer him at that second. I was concerned over what the clerk had said, and not because of the six months inside bit. I just didn't want to get us barred from the navy for ever, which was bound to happen if there was any check at all on our documentation, as we'd christened the phoney references.

You might wonder why we didn't have real references from Jersey, legitimate stuff that we could present without fear of any comebacks. Well, I had a dream character sketch from Brown but it wasn't any good to me. There was no chance of getting onto a ship as a barman simply because this was a plum job.

Barmen rarely left a ship, but when there was a vacancy, it went to a top side steward, who might have worked his way up from where we were hoping to start, and probably had anything from ten trips upwards, behind him. So, as hopeful first trippers, we could only expect to get on as assistant stewards, which meant that we would be waiters, or so we thought. But there was more to it than that, and not all of it was designed to make you feel that life on the ocean wave was a kind of a floating holiday.

I was trying to come up with some kind of inspired idea, when the clerk was relieved for his lunch. I'd been watching him work and there was no way you could deny the fella earned whatever he was being paid. He never stopped and I reasoned that it would take a real memory man to keep track of everything he had to do. A couple of times his eyes had accidentally drifted my way but there had been no reaction at all. The idea came to life then, that it was all just names on pieces of paper, with numbers thrown in to add a little weight. And I felt in my toe nails that I could probably pull it off right there and then.

The thing about that kind of situation is.... It's all so personal to the fella who is trying to pull the stroke, like he is starring in the movie, and he attaches more importance to his presence than he is entitled to. He has to be so much on the ball that he thinks the people he is dealing with have to be the same way. And this just can't be, when, like the clerk I'd been watching, the man you're scared of is practically snowed under with work. And the longer he's been doing the job the more he moves automatically through the scene, doing all kinds of things without so much as thinking about them. I killed my cigarette and motioned to Theo to follow me up to the grill where the relief clerk was already working his cobblers off.

The great thing about Theo was the way he just trusted me. I mean, with most guys you'd have had to take them outside and explain what you were going to do... with him you just got on with it and he would vamp along like an old busker who had never read music in his life. The clerk looked up at me and now, because I had it together, I could see that it was all so impersonal that he wouldn't have remembered my face five minutes later.

"Maguire and Roberts..." I said, being as offhand as I could... "left references in last week... told to come back today...."

"First trippers?" I nodded and found him a grin. He sucked his teeth and I pulled out my fags. Theo and I, lit up, and then I pushed the packet to the clerk.

"Want one?" He nodded his head and when he had the cigarette going he repeated the names out loud....

"All I can tell you..." I offered... "the man put them in that drawer there...."

He put the cigarette down in a souvenir from Skegness ashtray and opened the drawer. Only half an hour had gone by but your man had to root through a lot of paper before he came up with our documentation. I glanced at Theo and I had to smile as he flicked his eyes, stripped like boiled sweets from so much booze, up to the ceiling and back level again. The clerk looked at the references and took another pull on the cigarette.

"Seem all right," he said, like a fella thinking out loud.

He looked to me. "Ought to be," I assured him, "wrote them myself."

The fella smiled while Theo's expression registered Jesus!

I grinned. We were okay now, although there was still a bit of sweating to be done, just in case the other head came back before we got out of there. But he didn't and about an hour later we were talking to a pompous little bastard at New Zealand and Orient Shipping. He worked hard to make you feel that it was a pleasure and a privilege to be accepted as an employee, and we went into our double act, like a pair of hard done by angels who only wanted the chance to show the world that we were ready, willing and able to genuflect before the altar of the system.

Jesus! When I think of it now. The compliment just to get a job where you had to work like a bloody slave, share cabins with screaming homosexuals, and run the risk of being beaten up, cut up, carved up, or even murdered, by some of the nuts who worked at sea. Like, twenty percent of the guys I ran into were sick or mad or just plain bloody evil. Which is maybe comparable to the way things are ashore. But there is a difference... after a few weeks at sea, a ship, no matter what the tonnage, gets smaller and smaller, while the nuts and the heavies get more and more uptight, and consequently, more bloody dangerous.

Chapter Twenty-Seven
S.S. Ruatoto. October '58

There was no way to post a letter till we docked at Curacao in the Dutch West Indies, but that didn't stop me writing to Phil each evening when the long day's work was finally over. I was really tired when I climbed up into my bunk, but the excitement of the whole trip didn't allow old man weariness to gain any purchase on my sense of well being. I was thrilled and happy and bursting with enthusiasm, and though the physical demands were severe, I seemed to float above the scene. Until I began to realise, as the newness wore off, just how bloody hard I was working.

My day started at five forty five when the second steward, a nice enough bloke of about fifty who came from Reading, and looked like it, woke me up with a mug of hot tea.

"Come on lads and lassies..." he'd yell out, while the kid carrying the tea can cried all the usual rise and shine crap, blasting you awake and making enough of a racket up and down the gangway to ensure that you weren't going to drift back to slumbersville.

I used to smile at first when Colley, the second steward, said "lads and lassies..." but after a few days you just got used to the fact that nearly half the stewards were queer, and anyway, it was becoming that little bit harder to even wake up, so smiling, for whatever reason, was scrubbed off the early morning routine sheet.

Theo was liverish for about an hour after he got out of his bunk. You'll notice I didn't say "after he woke up"... which was something he didn't seem to manage until he was halfway through the first sitting of breakfast. I left him alone in those first days, because the need to be cruel and diabolical to each other hadn't yet developed, like, we hadn't been long enough at sea.

We shared a fourth berth cabin with Big Jim Davis, who lived up to his name, from London, and a sweetheart of a poof, who went by the name of Kitty. She was, of course, a fella, but only in the way she was physically constructed. Inside herself, mentally, spiritually, Kitty thought of herself as a woman, and as you can see, after just a little while on board ship, so did I. It was impossible not to with the way she went on. Even before we left the cabin to go and carry crates of booze topside to the bar, Kitty applied a film of pancake or panstick, or whatever it was called, to her face, and truthfully, she was more feminine than many birds I'd known in my time.

In fact, like most of the fags on the ship, she was too feminine to be real. Everything was overdone, every gesture and characteristic of the ordinary female was magnified, in the same way that a Butch Lesbian walks and talks in a way that few men do. But Kitty was all right once we got it straight that Theo and I weren't interested in the Vaseline trick.

When she'd first come into the cabin, Big Jim had pulled a face without trying to hide his annoyance from Kitty.

"Sorry darling." Kitty sounded considerate despite the lisp. "No choice in this girl's navy...."

Jim smiled despite himself. "Long as you don't turn into a phantom gobbler, we'll be all right...."

Kitty unzipped one of her bags, while I was trying to work out what Jim had meant. They understood each other but I hadn't yet learned how to talk to a fella as though he was a bird.

"Never blow anybody without their permission... eh, what's your name, darling?" Jim told her and she turned to me. "You, pretty one?" I could feel my face blush up but I told her my name.

"What do we call you?" I asked.

"Oh everybody calls me Kitty..." She was hanging a kimono in her wardrobe talking to Jim over her shoulder. "No fun plating somebody if they're asleep, love... sort of necrophilia, I think... just not my movement...."

Jim was going out when Theo came back from the shower. I watched his eyebrows twitch quizzically when Kitty smiled at him.

"Kitty, this is Theo," I said trying a little bit of one-upmanship. "Theo, this is Kitty...."

Theo gave her a very careful hello and Kitty giggled into her hand. "Don't worry, love, won't bite you...." She flicked her eyelashes. "Unless you ask me nicely...."

Later on that day I asked Jim what he'd meant by phantom gobbler and I fell about the cabin while he told me. On one of his earlier trips one of the faggots used to trip around during the night, performing fellatio on guys who were sound asleep.

"Did it happen to you?"

He looked at me, grinning. "Hard to tell, innit? I mean, if I was sleeping I'd have put it down to a wet dream, wouldn't I?"

"No geezer ever got love bites on his chopper in a wet dream..." Theo said, without even taking his eyes off a detective novel he was reading.

Jim laughed. "Here... never thought of that... wondered how these teeth marks got there... coo!"

He was a good guy, gentle for such a giant, and easy to live with regardless of the fact that the cabin was so small that with the four bunks and the built in narrow wardrobes, there just wasn't room for anything else. And as it turned out down in New Zealand, he was a handy fella to have around when the tables and chairs started flying.

Kitty was okay too, and once she got the message, she sort of drifted into a sister relationship with the three of us. Like when she did her transvestite bit after work, she'd ask us if we thought her new frock was all right with this pair of shoes or that piece of jewellery and so on. And I'll tell you straight, when she stood there sometimes, adjusting her nylons before she slipped into her dress, and we'd been about seventeen days at sea, I was hard put not to say "get your laughing gear around this." Especially as she'd offered to do my dhobie, my washing, which was a lot of hard work, if I'd just let her fly down on me now and again. But, as hip as I liked to think I was, I knew I just couldn't get it together with another fella, and even though I tried to be reasonable about it, wondering what difference it would make, it just wasn't for me. And when I told myself that Kitty wasn't really a fella, that she thought, felt and acted, just like a bird, I found that she'd become enough like a sister to me for anything of that kind to be like bloody incest. So there it was... things getting harder all the time, with nothing but one off the wrist to relieve the pressure.

We had to work so hard that I felt I was owned body and soul by the bloody shipping company. The early morning beer carrying trick, was followed by serving two sittings of breakfast, followed by a scrub out of the floor area occupied by my tables. Two sittings of lunch followed by another scrub out, with afternoon tea to be served every other day, followed by two sittings of dinner, followed by another scrub out. Not to mention boat and fire drill about four times a week, which claimed at least two of those "every other" afternoons off.

Fire drill was bad enough. You stood by your station and at a given signal you mimed what you would do if there really was a fire. What a joke! I could just see myself standing there with a stiff upper lip, helping the bloods, the passengers, out, at the risk of my own neck. Some of the bastards I had to serve would have been locked in their cabins if I'd had my way.

Boat drill was another comedy act, although I can't ever remember feeling like laughing, when I had to sit in a long-boat while maybe Kitty and some other fag played around on the winch, slowly lowering the boat over the side down towards the surface of the ocean, while they giggled to themselves about "my unborn child" giggle... "twisting this big handle" giggle... "can't be good for my baby" giggle... with the ship moving at twelve or maybe thirteen knots.

I don't know why the Captain bothered with this bloody nonsense. I mean, it was like training soldiers to shoot blanks at dummies. Like, there's no way you can instruct a shipboard waiter to simulate personal panic, and I'm bloody sure that if there had been a crunch on that ship, the women and children would have found the lifeboats already filled up with members of the crew.

But we had to go through this performance, waiters and bedroom stewards making like they were seamen, just because the Captain was naïve enough to think that his crew members had something to live up to. That's how out of touch he was... coming down from his ivory tower on the bridge only to do inspections, supervise boat and fire drill, and of course to eat at his table in the saloon, with the sycophants and the brown lippers paying homage to his every word as though he was some kind of bright, intelligent human being. Whereas he was just a martinet who ran a tight ship and all that shit, only because he worked by the book. When you remember that a ship is like a town or a city, a country even, and that the Captain really is Jesus Christ, and the judge and the jury, the whole orchestra in fact, you might be forgiven for expecting him to keep his finger on the pulse of his enormous responsibility. Which the guy couldn't do because he was so busy with boat and fire drill, and daily kitchen and saloon inspection. Not to mention crew cabin inspection, which really was like something out of a sad, bad, British comedy film.

Apart from the hard work, which I got used to because there was no point in banging your head against a brick wall just for the exercise, the thing that really bugged me badly, was that you couldn't just tell your superior to get stuffed and to get your cards. And you just couldn't walk out if you got fed up. Well, you could, I suppose, but it's not the kind of habit you'd want to develop when you're a thousand miles or more out in the Atlantic. From the other angle, this meant too, that you couldn't be sacked if you decided you'd had enough and didn't want to work anymore. Alright, you'd signed articles and all that, but this seemed kind of remote in relation to a fella not wanting to get up, say, out of his bunk, and carry beer up to the topside bar. But the bastards had it all worked out and though it rankled a bit, you had to admire them for taking their cue from Captain Bligh.

If you *didn't* do something you were *supposed* to do, you got fined. If you *did* something you *weren't* supposed to do, you got fined. If you *told* the head waiter or his assistant, or the second steward, to fuck off, you got fined. And if you were mad enough to give the Chief Steward any lip, the fine was larger. And the higher up you went with any kind of insubordination, the more money was docked from your pay. And if your record was really bad at the end of a trip your book was stamped D.R. which meant that your Captain declined to report. This was no help when you went to another ship, and if you got a double D.R. you had to just make up your mind that life ashore was going to be permanent.

Still, I was happy to be at sea and even when the first excitement had faded I was already twitching at the prospect of seeing Curacao. Each evening after I'd written my letter to Phi, I scribbled down my thoughts and impressions and if it did nothing else, it kept my mind off Kitty and all the other birds, as they paraded in and out of the cabin, talking about knickers and stockings and all those other things that take up more and more room in your mind, the longer you are at sea.

Chapter Twenty-Eight

The closer we get to Curacao the more I wondered if there'd be a letter from Phil. I'd slipped ashore at Tilbury to post her a mailing list, while we'd been picking up the passengers, so there was a chance her letter, letters, would be waiting for me when we docked.

The arguments inside myself continued but there was no change in how I felt about her. And I wasn't trying to pull any of my lady passengers though there was one French-Canadian chick who was more than friendly. A good body and the air of a bird who knew her way around a scratcher. But Phil kept getting in the way and I just behaved like a perfect steward. It was funny really, but I was good at the waiter trick. Funny? It was a scream... because the only time Theo or myself had served food, was when we'd practiced with Lenny and Elsie's lunch at the Horse Trough, the day before we'd joined the ship. But once I got into my uniform, dark blue jacket and trousers and a white shirt, and the passengers started speaking to me as though I really knew my stuff, I just seemed to land on my feet. Of course, it was a performance, like acting on a stage. And I wasn't short of flannel which made up for a lot. Most of the bloods wanted to talk, and because they assumed you'd been at sea for years they asked your advice and generally seemed to pay a lot of attention to whatever you might say. This helped me become that much more confident and better waiter.

One of my passengers, going home after a long trip to Europe, was particularly friendly, and gave me a fiver the first day out, explaining that he liked to eat a lot. Jesus! Nobody could call that guy a liar. He worked his way through two or three main courses, having already had double entrees, and though he wasn't what you'd call fat, he looked like he was just going to burst out of his skin. Maybe I just imagined that because I knew how much he ate, but I couldn't see him making sixty if he went on the way he did.

His wife was a beauty, with warm eyes behind a permanent film of what seemed to be glycerine. About forty years old with breasts that made my mouth water, and when she stood talking to anyone in the saloon, her feet were always planted wide, like she was just dying for a quick pipe laying job.

She flattered me a lot which her husband didn't seem to mind. At first I glanced his way when she was really overt about how good I looked, or whatever, but he just went on devouring his third helping of crayfish and didn't so much as raise his head.

Almost daily Mrs. McKinnon would ask me not to encourage her to eat anything fattening.

"I'm getting so fat, Paddy," she'd say, pressing her hands flat against her lovely round belly, sucking it in, which sent her boobs up that much closer to my suffering eyeballs. And it was always the low necked dress with Mrs. McKinnon, to a point where I didn't even pretend not to look. Jesus! A woman gets out in a dress like that she has to be asking you to worship her breasts and I made no bones about the fact that I was a daily supplicant before her magnificent shrine. And if she couldn't see that I wanted to lift her out of her chalice and make communion with the twin points of her mammary glands, then she would have been doing a crash course in Braille.

"You must come up to the cabin for a drink, Paddy? Don't you think so, Mike?"

"Mmmm? Oh, oh yes," Mike grunted, through a mouthful of Avocado vinaigrette. "Yes, darling, by all means...."

"I wish I could, Mrs. McKinnon." I'd forgotten him, but did a rapid gear change. "It's nice of you to ask me, Mr. McKinnon, but we're just not allowed."

"Nonsense..." she complained, allowing her disappointment to fill her liquid eyes.

"Bloody ridiculous," Mike agreed, giving his jaws another workout.

"Maybe we can meet for a drink in Curacao..." I spoke to her though I was looking at him. The pig never raised his eyes but she gave me a private smile that nearly blew my barometer.

"She's got some form," Theo yelled, as we stood in the galley, drying our cutlery while we waited for the next course to come up. Momma, a really sweet ageing poof simpered a bit my way, acknowledging the wink I'd given her.

"If he screws like he eats, I don't know why she shows out to me..." I said, really puzzled.

We moved to the counter top as Momma and the other bedroom stewards began serving the food. They had to double as galley hands, but they didn't have to serve afternoon tea. I put two plates on my tray, covered them, set two more on top, and another two to make six. The two vegetable dishes went on top of this again, the whole thing carried flat on the palm of one hand. In keeping with the number one rule, a good waiter always kept one hand free.

"She's got the hots for you, Paddy..." Johnnie Toner grinned at me from behind the counter, laughing out loud when Momma shuddered playfully and said:

"Oh, stoppit, Johnnie, I'll cream my citys...!" She admonished me then with a look of pure chagrin. "Might be a little kinder to a girl...."

"Girl? Girl?" Johnnie Toner erupted into laughter. "Did you hear that? Did you hear it? Bleeding old trout... girl?"

Momma made a swipe at him with her serving cloth and I went into a saloon with Theo at my heels. He carried the tray with both hands and didn't seem to mind being called a cowboy, which meant he wasn't going to win any prizes as a waiter. He stopped me before he split for his tables in the far corner of the saloon.

"What did she mean by that? Momma?"

"Citys? City slickers, knickers - and cream."

"I'm not that bleedin' dumb," he chastised me, splitting then before I could tell him not to put any money on the strength of his I.Q.

That same evening I was talking to Theo and Jim about Curacao, when Johnnie Toner dropped in with some beer. He was a really handsome fella, originally from Cork, but reared in London from the age of three, so that while he might have had what you call "laughing Irish eyes" his accent was a kind of educated cockney.

It was just pure accident that he came into the cabin as I was telling the lads about Mrs. McKinnon.

"Some scene, that...." He passed the beer around and it tasted good, reminding me that I hadn't had a decent drink for nine days.

"Must be if he fucks like he eats..." Theo said.

"But he doesn't... it's the other way around..." Johnnie said, his face where he shaved, blue, in the soft cabin light.

"What's he do then?" Jim Davis asked.

"He takes it..." Johnnie said... "up the Khyber... got a dildo they have and she has to bang him with it...."

Theo looked at me in amazement and I'll bet he thought he was facing a mirror.

"Bird with that form, married to a poof. ...!" Big Jim sounded like a fella who wanted to weep.

"But is he?" Johnnie Toner demanded... "I mean, I don't know... I mean, pooves go with geezers, right? He just takes it from his old lady. I mean, if he was a poof he'd have no bother getting bottled on this tub...."

I didn't say anything because I didn't know what to say.

"He's taking the piss." Theo stood up and took the beer bottle from my hand. "Bleedin' Cork men, all the same they are."

"On my life, Theo..." Johnnie protested... "I saw them at it, this very morning, slipped in with the tea and she was giving it him. He was making such a racket they never heard me...."

Big Jim shook his head in genuine regret. "Anybody giving her one?"

Johnnie said no and Jim looked at me. "Looks like you got lucky, buddy.... If she ain't showed out to old Johnnie here, then she's got to have the hots for you the way she's been showing out...."

"You bastard!" Johnnie Toner grinned and slapped me on the shoulder. "I've been trying to pull her since she came aboard... yes mam, no mam, I'd like to bite your button mam... and all the time she's showing out to you, son of Jack Doyle...." He passed me the beer bottle with a crafty wink. "Still, as long as we keep it among ourselves...."

"Here we go," Jim said to the beer bottle, "bleedin' Irish are at it again...."

"Give her the rosary bead treatment, Paddy..." Johnnie advised as though he didn't want the other two to hear him. "I'll tell you how to do it when we can have a little private discussion...."

"Christ's sake, Theo, give us a song before they get onto nineteen sixteen, will you?"

Theo pointed at me. "He's the singer, I'm just his manager...."

Johnnie laughed and passed Jim a fresh bottle, while Theo stood up with his hand out. "Fee first - my client's a pro."

I began to sing but my mind wasn't really with the lyrics. It was boggling a shade at the matter of fact way we had slipped from our discussion on the hang-ups of Mike and Mrs. McKinnon, to where one minute later, the three heads were listening to me singing a popular song. But that was the way it was with seamen. Nothing really was ever allowed to be a big deal. Which I began to understand when I thought about it. Fella goes to sea at seventeen years of age, he can, by using his head, eat well, save money, learn all the time about every aspect of life. And of course by the time he's in his early twenties, chances are he's been around the world several times. Happy in Hong Kong as he is in London. That's just the way it works out, like one good trip to sea is worth five years ashore.

About ten minutes after we'd started singing, the cabin began to fill up and suddenly we had a party going and Theo was performing as master of ceremonies. Jim Davis sang a great cockney song about a penny worth of winkles, Johnnie Toner did a great Liberace take off, miming his performance at the piano, and Kitty threw everyone into hysterics and several into a state of severe horniness, with her rendering of one of Dick Haymes's old hits "Again".

But the really significant thing for me that night was the response of a Liverpool Irishman called Tommy Clay, to my singing of some Hank Williams numbers. It turned out that Tommy loved, worshipped and adored, the late great King of all country and western singers, and though I didn't give it too much thought at the time, I had made a friend. And it wasn't to be too long before I really appreciated the meaning of the "friend in need is a friend indeed" bit.

Chapter Twenty-Nine

My dearest Phil... From where I sit on my bunk in my knickers... an afternoon off, would you credit? ...I can see through the porthole, the south Atlantic rushing past in great waves, the ridges glittering like frost topped potato drills. The ship is beautiful, but Jesus only knows what she'll be like in rough weather... the slightest swell and she bucks and rolls like a wild horse. First day out I felt a bit ropey... Jim Davis is in charge of the fruit juice locker, and because we're pals, I get all the juice I want... I drank too much that first day... I've got my sea legs by now and I'm eating like a prince... Not that I know how a prince eats, mind you... what I mean is, that the nosh is great... I'm eating things I can't even pronounce, and, would you believe, I've put on weight despite the dog-rough hard work. Sweat, sweat, sweat, and this time next week we'll be on our way through the Panama Canal. I'm told that if the heat doesn't get you the humidity will. And listen kid, I'm doing three scrub outs a day, so don't be surprised if I have housemaids knees when I return. Right now I could do with such a knee provided there was a housemaid to go with it. Boy! Am I randy? I'll tell you, Kitty gets more beautiful by the day. She's got blue pencil on her eyelids today... last night she added a touch of something called Crème Puff, and there was the not so faint whiff of Temptation floating across the cabin. But don't worry, I resisted... just for you. Will post this when we hit Curacao, hoping, with all my heart, that there'll be a note from you waiting for me. I miss you, Phil... you're never far from my thoughts, except when Kitty gets me excited. I love you, just because you are how you are. Don't ever change... wait for me... and think about me some time... no... all the time. All my love....Your Paddy.

This letter and many others like it, I posted in Willemstadt, and I filled up a bit when I read Phil's solitary letter to me. She felt the same way and she was waiting for me to come back, and there'd be another letter waiting for me at Cristobal in the Canal zone. Jesus, my heart sang in those first minutes and Theo smiled happily when he read what Phil had written. But by the time we got ashore for our night out, I was depressed as hell and really ready to get pissed out of my mind. Which nobody could call criminal after being at sea for ten days.

I'd promised to meet the McKinnons at the de Kuyper Hotel, but when I went ashore with my three mates I'd no intention of going there. I wanted to get very drunk and be as sad as I could possibly be. It was late afternoon on a day more beautiful than I'd ever seen before, which had to become a night that was going to be a good backdrop for a little bleeding.

Johnnie Toner and Theo were dancing with a couple of birds they'd pulled. Big Jim was sitting beside me watching them, the pair of us drinking rum. There were a lot of fellas from the ship in the bar and it wasn't hard to work out that there were going to be a lot of sore heads in the morning. Including my own, the way I was dropping that rum. But that was all right... the more jarred I got, the less chance there was of me grabbing some chick. I loved Phil and I didn't want to cheat, even though I was sure she would have understood. Then I wasn't sure if I wanted her to understand... so you can see that the easiest way out of the whole deal was just to tie one on. Which was what I was trying to do when Joy McKinnon walked in with another woman I didn't know.

When Joy started looking around I stood up and waved. She was going to see me anyway, so I thought it as well to show willing. I nudged Jim as she moved towards our table.

I didn't recognise Joy's friend as she slipped into the seat against the wall. Jim had shifted as they reached the table and as I held out a chair for Joy, I saw him smooch by with a big sexy looking coloured girl who started to laugh up a storm at something he whispered to her. I ordered drinks, wondering a bit why Joy wasn't making any introductions. She didn't seem to be drunk, but when she told me I was very kind and kissed me heavily on the mouth, I guessed she was carrying more than I thought. One sip of her drink and she stood up.

"Don't you want to dance with me?"

Maybe I don't, I thought. I took her in my arms and she made no bones about pulling me in hard against her body. I tried to get a better look at her mate, but with the almost non-existent lighting and a mask of heavy make up, I might as well not have bothered.

"Oh God, you're beautiful..." Joy McKinnon said urgently.

I kissed her and she came back at my lips like a suction pump. We came up for air with Joy gyrating wildly against me, her boobs almost popping out of her dress. I saw her friend move by wrapped around a big spade guy and they were kissing fiercely before I lost sight of them in the crowd.

Joy pushed my head down. "Kiss them, Paddy, kiss them...."

"I can't Joy..." I said, expecting her to understand that I wasn't high enough to start the windscreen wiper bit on a public dance floor. She couldn't be blamed for not being able to read my mind. She unzipped the top of her dress leaving her breasts totally exposed.

"Now, Paddy... kiss them now...." She was like a nutcase, her eyes burning in her head, her lips moving around her tongue which seemed to be having a dance on its own. I pressed my lips to the top of her breasts, but I felt ridiculous, and I had to force my head back up on account of the fact that Joy was gripping me like a wrestler just above the back of my neck.

"Where's Mike, anyway?" I managed to say.

"Mike?" She was just plain incredulous. "Fuck Mike... I

want you to kiss my tits...."

"I want to Joy," I said, trying to look obedient, "but not here, not in this joint."

"I'd like to have you here... take me here," she urged me. I kissed her lips to shut her up, wondering what in the name of Christ she'd been drinking. She broke away from my mouth.

"You dirty bastard!" Joy cried into my face, contempt plastered like make up on her mouth. Her right hand rubbed down along my zip. And she broke into a smile that surprised me even further. "But I love you for playing hard to get...!" She told me, waggling her breasts under my chin. She grabbed the front of my slacks. "I want to go down on you, right here."

I could see she wasn't kidding, but I could also see a double D.R. on my book when it came to signing off the ship in London. And thousands of miles away from England or not, I had no intention of giving the local stringer for *The News of the World*, the scoop sex story of the week.

"But what about Mike?" I asked helplessly.

"He's there... right there..." I followed the line indicated by her forefinger. "He's trying to get buggered by that big nigger...." She assured me... "He just loves those spades...."

Her friend with all the make up was doing okay with the big shine and I nearly fell over when I realised it was Mike McKinnon in drag. Jesus!

Joy pulled me around to face her, beginning to laugh hysterically at my expression. I felt a tap on my shoulder and turned around expecting to see Theo or one of the others behind me. But I was looking at the collar button of a red shirt which was being worn by the biggest black man I'd ever seen. I moved my head and by the time my chin was pointing at the button I was looking into the largest pair of burnt brown eyes imaginable, They were deep set in a jet black face that fronted a head the size of a pumpkin and he was built in proportion. What I could see of him anyway, and I thought that if he was hung in the same way, it would definitely be a case of get on the end of it honey and walk slowly towards me.

His eyes left me and planted themselves on Joy's boobs.

"You just got real lucky, lady... you gonna get screwed like tomorrow ain't ever comin'."

Joy stepped back and zipped up the front of her dress. Oh Jesus! I thought... this is no time to develop colour prejudice!

"Go away..." she said, fear and annoyance spitting out of her eyes.

"Sorry, man..." I apologized... "the lady..."

I didn't get any further. "Get lost, kid..." he advised me.

"No Paddy... don't leave me with this animal. ...!

"Joy, don't...."

"I won't tell you again, boy." Words of advice no more. A warning, direct, with me reading it loud and clear, and wishing to Christ, that I was anywhere else but standing right there. And completely at a loss because he wasn't about to listen to any verbal, so that my ability to talk my way out of things wasn't going to be any use. And the idea of hitting him was so funny that I did the only thing left to me. I kicked him straight in the ballocks.

Now if that kick had done its job, I'd probably have had a fair chance of getting Joy out of there, but Snowball was wearing some kind of protective thing and though I didn't feel too much pain when he hit me, I did hurt my head and my back when I finally landed on a table across the room. People are very good about getting out of your way in a situation like that, so I had a trouble free flight until I touched down.

Johnnie Toner and Big Jim weighed into your man, but he didn't seem too perturbed from where I sat. Joy helped me up as Johnnie crashed against the wall. Jim lasted a big longer, by which time I got near enough, despite Joy's attempts to drag me out of there, to throw the glass of rum in the black man's brown eyes. I made a kick at his left knee cap, making some connection before he back-handed me across the room the way you'd swat a fly.

Johnnie Toner was now having a stand up go with another shine who was only about six feet three.

"Picking on fucking midgets..." I yelled at Johnnie, seeing Tommy Clay moved in close to Mighty Shine. I hadn't seen Tommy in the room earlier, and the way the head punched, I didn't think he was going to be in it much longer. I looked around for something that might kill your man. By now Johnnie Toner was jumping on his little coloured friend. Jim Davis was pulling another guy off Johnnie's back... and Tommy Clay was beating the living Jaysus out of Gargantua.

It was incredible to watch. They just stood there slugging it out, Tommy having a slight edge at the beginning because Mighty Shine had been so surprised that he didn't go down when the first torpedo landed. Everything else had stopped. The whole room had its eyes on the fighters in the middle of the dance floor.

Chapter Thirty
Curacao, Dutch West Indies. October '58

They swapped punches, blow for blow, for about fifteen minutes. Incredible, I know, and all the more so because any one of those blows would have marmaladed an ordinary guy. And I could vouch for that on account of my jaw feeling like it was in little chips.

Tommy Clay was just under six feet in height, and around fourteen stone weight. The black man seemed closer to seven feet and Christ knows what he weighed. Yet, finally, Clay knocked him out with a right hand punch that sent shivers around the room. Later I realised that it was his hatred of black people that gave him the edge he needed. The coloured guy had been in the mood for a fight. My first kick proved that he even wore a case of some kind over the crown jewels... but the chances are it wouldn't have happened if Joy McKinnon hadn't been as way out as she thought she was. If she'd fancied him and taken him away somewhere to haul his rocks off, we might have been okay. With Tommy Clay it was different. He hated black people with a venom that could make you feel your blood was being chilled when he talked about it. And it didn't finish when Snowball hit the deck, because by this time the law had arrived.

Two uniformed men, not as dark as the guy on the floor, but brown enough to have Tommy yelling nigger as they tried to get at him with truncheons swinging. I saw him clobber one with a short clubbing right hand, then Jim Davis was beside him and another melee started shaping up. Joy pulled my hand and I let her lead me outside, feeling like a fella on a pass out from a nuthouse.

I turned left just outside the door, lost my balance and fell into a fucking storm drain deep as a small boat, that perimetered the building. Honest to Jesus, I felt like weeping. And I made no attempt to get up, wanting to just lie there and let the world pass me by.

A chair crashed through a window over my head and I moved along the drain on my hands and knees, with Joy, now fully recovered from the whole business, yelping along playfully, like a crazy puppy dog at my heels. Jesus Christ, I thought, she's as nutty as a squirrel's breakfast.

I rolled over on my back, too tired to go any further, and then Joy was kneeling beside me, pressing my face against her breasts, moaning little cries of wild nonsense that started to turn me on. She unzipped her dress again and put her breasts to my mouth. Her right hand undid my belt and then she was sitting on top of me, her hands pressed against my stomach as she moved up and down, practically setting me free each time only to slam back down on me again.

Finally she cried out, shuddering like a train as it hits the buffers. Then she fell down flat on top of me, with me still as erect as when she'd started.

She was lying all over me until I thought I'd smother. And I had to call her name a few times before she reacted at all.

"Yes... yes my darling... what is it?"

"Do you think we could go for a swim?"

"Do you think we could go for a swim?" someone said further up the storm drain. For a second I thought it was an echo, but lying there, looking up at the stars, I knew it was Theo.

"How'd you get on in the fight?" I yelled.

"Took her in the second round..." Theo retorted dryly.

"Inside," I said.

"Inside..." Theo confirmed. "Back and front... smooth as black velvet...."

I was a bit angry with him for not helping out when the skin and hair had been flying.

"We had a punch up, as if you didn't know...."

"Well..." his voice came back... "I had a punch up here... twice I punched this lovely chick up the knickers...."

It was useless, you couldn't get across to him when he had a few drinks, and the black chick had obviously blown his mind.

"You going swimming?"

"Yes we are..." I yelled back... "Help us up will you, Joy?"

We clambered out of the storm drain. I was in bits. And the fight was still happening. We went in search of a cab and Theo produced the remains of a bottle of rum. I took a drink, but Joy refused. Theo grabbed the bottle back, took a gulp and handed it to the coloured girl. She drank from the neck with a kind of practiced movement and laughed as it hit her insides.

"Rum to warm de top of the tum and..." she screeched with laughter... "and you know *what* to make de bottom hot...."

"This is Carmarine..." Theo said formally... "Lustpot, this is Paddy and...?"

"Joy," Joy said, "how do you do?" She shook the dark hand and I could see Carmarine's white teeth flash in a smile. It was all ridiculous, surreal somehow, and yet, was it? And if it was, did it matter?

"What about Mike?" I asked Joy.

She put her mouth close to my ear. "Fuck Mike..." she whispered.

"You fuck Mike," I said. "I'll hold his ears." That made her laugh some and then she whispered something vile. It went on like that quietly and privately, and we were still chuckling when we slipped out of our clothes and into the Caribbean.

"Is this dangerous? The Caribbean? Sharks?" I was lying on my back holding Joy by the hand.

"There are sharks..." Joy said, "but this lagoon has a shark net...."

"No bleedin' shark'd be daft enough to take a bite out of you..." Theo spluttered from close by.

"But I would..." Joy promised, her hands finding my thighs in the water... "I'd bite you to death...." She floated against me.

"Long way from Rathmines," I said for no reason except that it was a long way from Rathmines.

"Who'd ever have thought it? Oi! Floating in the Carib, like bleedin' princes, boozed to the balls, and no shortage of how's your father? Home sweet bleedin' home was never like this." Theo had found his idea of paradise.

"Did you ever know a fella called Redmond?" I asked him... "Harry Redmond?"

"Layabout..." Theo said... "used to hang around Leinster Road, Campions... that ponce?"

"Yeah, That's him..." I was delighted... Theo had brought Redmond right across my mind.

"Why?" Theo asked.

"You reminded me of him, that's all...."

"Thanks a fucking bunch..." Theo snorted...." Like someone saying you remind them of a film star and they mean bleedin' Lassie...."

"Ah he was a great head, Theo...." Where the hell was Harry now? ...great mate to me... the poems to the birds on the Dodder Bank. Shakespeare and Yeats and all the other heads. Harry making out, matter of fact, that he'd scribbled the lines that afternoon. Some of the greatest men in the game helping to open the legs for him. And then his own stuff, mostly bad because he just didn't care, but lots of lines that still lingered because I'd been so receptive to the master who could teach things that he'd only ever experienced in his fantasy world.

Through the Guinness and the sandwich and the cigarette smoke, I could see him like it was yesterday. "I gave her tits a little suck And the cheeks of her arse went Chuck Chuck Chuck." And... "There was a young fella called Dick, Who could stand for hours on his... head... What a trick?" Reams of laughter... memories.

"Let's swim out to the platform," Theo suggested.

"Can you make it?" I asked Joy.

"I was breast stroke champion at school."

Carmarine was already half way there, but the rest of us weren't in any hurry. "Now you're the cock stroke champ!"

She laughed happily. "I'm a sucker for the cock stroke...."

We climbed up on the platform. Carmarine was performing all kinds of incredible dives from the springboard. I lay down flat with my head over the edge. Joy lay beside me. Theo jumped in a few times and I could see that he was mad drunk. Joy couldn't keep her hands easy and it was nice to be touched gently, to slowly come alive, hearing her breathing alter as she felt my readiness.

Her thighs fell apart and I made love to her, fiercely and selfishly taking what I needed. I didn't care whether it might be good for her or not, just using her the way I'd allowed her to impale herself back in the storm trench, but Joy was so hot for it that she blew several times before I finished. Then I dived into the Caribbean, really feeling like king of the castle.

Joy was on the springboard when I climbed up the ladder, her body marked by shadows as she turned around to grab me. I didn't feel like it, but I kissed her and she clung onto me. She was all right, and the fact that she'd enjoyed herself minutes before above on the platform didn't alter the fact that I'd been bloody selfish.

She got so warm so quickly, standing there on the back of the springboard, moving her body so furiously against me, that she began to lose her balance. I held her, preventing her from falling off the board, but Jesus, the next thing, I was toppling awkwardly towards the Caribbean. This was no kind of big deal in itself, but for one second, I thought I was going to land on the outside of the shark net, and to say I was shit-scared, is an understatement as opposed to exaggeration.

I hit the water on the right side of the net, but it had been close. So close that I ripped my left shoulder on the barbed wire, feeling a sharp stinging pain before I hit the water.

The pain when the salt water burst against the wound was probably not as bad as it seemed. I guess it was heightened by that moment of fear when I thought I was going into the open sea. And though there probably wasn't a shark within a thousand bloody miles, I wouldn't have been surprised if one had flashed up, taking my cluster away with one of my hips, before he took off again, picking his teeth with my Hampton.

As I surfaced, Joy hit the water beside me. Christ, I felt like strangling her, accident or not. I yelled that I was bleeding and started crawling for the shore like a fella with an outboard strapped to his belly. Carmarine passed me like I was waiting for a bus, but the stinging in my left shoulder propelled me along on some kind of false energy. I mean, I never moved through water at that speed, before or since.

Carmarine helped me up off the sand. I was exhausted and grinding my teeth from the pain... the air seemed to be hitting it worse than the damned sea water. She helped me into my slacks, and I felt so rough that I couldn't give one second's attention to her fantastic body. So you might believe I wasn't just being dramatic.

Joy arrived and got dressed quickly, by which time, Theo sounding like a diseased porpoise, hit the beach. I started to leave - mercifully the ship wasn't far away. I yelled at Theo that I was all right, to look after Carmarine. I wished Joy was some place else. She meant well, but I needed to be on my own. She was mumbling about getting me to her cabin, which just the kind of nonsense I expected. Christ! To be seen coming aboard with a passenger could land me on the carpet, let alone running the risk of going near the passenger deck.

I made her leave me and stood in the shadow of the ship while she went aboard. She kept looking down at me, her face quilted in worry. I waved her on, wanting to yell at her to move her arse a bit faster. The pain in my shoulder was murdering me. And by the time I hit C deck, I knew that I had to take a rest if I wasn't going to collapse on the spot. There was no way I could get down to the crew quarters without breaking my neck.

My legs started to wobble as I moved along towards the prow. I sat down on a for'ard hold. Well, it wasn't the first mistake I'd made in my life and it wasn't the last, but the moment my behind hit the canvas cover of the hold, I passed out. It was about six o'clock when I woke up... an incredibly warm and beautiful morning. My head was clear enough though my face ached, especially where the old black magic had hit me on the left jaw. I was lying on my back looking up at the sky, wondering what in Christ's name I was going to do. It was some kind of sick joke I know, but my own blood had me stuck tight to the canvas beneath my back. And I had to get up and serve thirty four passengers wanting their breakfast.

Chapter Thirty-One
S.S. Ruatoto. '58

Almost three weeks later I had some stitches put into my shoulder at a hospital in Auckland. The doctor told me the wound should have been stitched immediately, and all I could do was smile to myself, acknowledging the fact that when it came to any kind of crunch, the English stiff upper lip, took some beating.

"Mmmm, quite a bad scratch," the ship's doctor had mumbled, with me too weak to take him up on it.

He dressed the wound, telling me to come back in a couple of days. I was going to ask him about stitching it but I was afraid that if he put me down, I'd just lash out and punch him right in his supercilious puss.

So for the next three weeks I worked with a cotton pad taped to my shoulder blade. Through the tropics where I broke out in prickly heat, and all the way down to Auckland I nearly went nuts trying to keep my white jackets clean. Apart from all the sweating, blood kept on seeping through the cotton pad.

Joy came down to lunch, all eyes for me, and all concern about my shoulder. I told her it wasn't too bad, making it sound as though I was getting through a sheer hell of bloody agony. Big Jim went by whistling "I Only Have Eyes for You..." his shiner toned down with a touch of Vaseline covered in talcum powder.

"Where's Mike today?" I asked her. He hadn't appeared for breakfast, no more than she had.

"He's a bit sore," she said, her eyes smiling. "He's sleeping it off...."

"Somebody punch him?"

She laughed. "If that's what you call it."

I went to pick up her order, and about half a ton of various food for the other gannets. Johnnie Toner was ribbing Theo about the punch up.

"Bleedin' nutcases the lotta you." Theo turned to me then and said,"And you, you're bleedin' worse."

I looked at Momma. "You letting him talk to me like that?"

Johnnie Toner fell backwards laughing. Momma turned her head quarter profile, gave Theo a cold look with her left eye and said, "He's so uncouth, so painfully straight, he's a bore."

We were loading our trays when I noticed that Johnnie had a swollen ear. He nodded when he knew I'd seen it.

"Good job Scouse was about..." he said.

"Maybe it wasn't! ..." I said.

"Black bastard," Tommy Clay said at my right ear, "head like bleedin' concrete...."

Jim Davis moved up beside me. "Hurry up with that Sexton, Harry... geezers eating the tablecloth...."

"And what about my two roast beef?" Kitty complained "God... the service around here...."

"Belt up Ass," Tommy Clay hissed.

"Get you, Twinkle toes," Kitty purred. "All the charm of an open grave."

"Bleedin' puff..." Tommy spat at her. "Should be fucked over the side...."

"Don't mind duckie, where I get fucked, just so long as you're not giving me one...."

Kitty said it all without so much as looking at Tommy Clay. He didn't know what to do. He couldn't very well hit her, and there was a kind of grudging admiration in him for the fact that she was fearless.

"Got some bottle, ain't she Scouse?"

Tommy nodded to Johnnie Toner, conceding the point to Kitty's guts. "Just hate ass..." he said and moved up the line to pick up his veg.

Theo rushed back into the galley. "Have you had any of my forks?" he asked me.

"Have I fuck?"

He shook his great head, "Some bastard nicked three of my forks...."

"Well, nick someone else's, love..." Momma said sweetly, "and stop bothering my lovely Paddy...."

I picked up my tray. Theo looked from Momma back to me. Johnnie Toner chortled away behind the counter. Momma reached over the flat top and touched my arm. "If he bothers you love, just tell Momma...."

"What'll you do?" Theo enquired, "hit me with your handbag?"

"My new crocodile skin?" Momma gasped, horrified. "You must be joking!"

Theo shook his head and rushed away cowboy fashion to the saloon.

"Never make a winger, that one..." Momma observed without any kind of malice. "Two hands to carry a tray-"

"Used to be a truck driver," Johnnie said.

"Don't tell *me* about truck drivers," Momma warned him. "I've had more truck drivers than you've had wet dreams...."

I went back to the saloon, wanting to just sit down and belly laugh.

"Will I see you in Panama?" Joy asked me seriously.

"Depends on how the shoulder is," I said, smiling, "But no swimming."

She smiled, running her tongue across her bottom lip.

"Whatever you say, Paddy."

Chapter Thirty-Two
Panama Canal Zone. October '58

I had a list of all the people I hated in my pocket as Theo and I followed the doctor ashore. He smiled as he got into his taxi and I gave him a salute. But it didn't occur to me then that the bastard was smiling because he hadn't stitched my shoulder, just to teach me not to be so snotty in the future. And the shoulder still bothered me every time I changed the dressing or strained it in any way.

"You're mad wasting bleedin' money," Theo told me as I addressed another postcard.

"These people have to know I've got this far..." I said. "These people laughed at me when I talked about things I wanted to do."

"I just don't understand you, Maguire."

"You're not supposed to," I grinned, "not till I understand myself."

The cards to my mother and Pops and a few mates, were already in the post box. But I was getting an almighty bang from the ones I was sending, with real American stamps, to the people I really didn't like. Just to drive the bastards mad with envy. Just to show them that even if it took a bit longer than a guy intended, he really could do the things he wanted, just as long as he wanted to do them badly enough.

There was no letter from Phil.

"Maybe the post get held up, head."

I nodded and Theo put his hand on my shoulder. "A few gargles, a bit of music and a nice piece of ass... how does that sound?"

It sounded good and I didn't give him any bullshit.

He grinned at me and tapped me on the jaw. "That's more

like it...." He stopped. "Jaysus, I never sent a card to Darcy."

"I sent one for both of us."

"Wouldn't want that little ballocks to get too comfortable," he said affectionately. "He'll cut his bleedin' throat for not coming with us."

We left the Post Office and went to meet Jim and Johnnie. It was late afternoon and Panama City seemed like a good place to be. Apart from the humidity, which was really chronic. Just like the driving. Christ! I've never seen such lunatic behaviour behind the wheel, not even later in Italy, where it's hair rising enough. Those Panamanian cats gave you a grin as they drove over your foot, and the taxi drivers that we met never stopped touting for whorehouses and bars. And all kinds of places, which, they assured us, they wouldn't mention, "except to very special nice people".

We ended up with a driver called Tony, who danced along the street beside us, when we finally left the first bar we'd hit with Johnnie and Jim Davis. It was about ten o'clock and time to be organising something in the way of pussy. Which didn't seem like a bad idea, though I did have a date with Joy McKinnon.

The city was big on prostitution. Tarts just sat in their windows, half naked. All kinds of kinky poses, swearing then, getting obscene and pretty abusive, when they were sure you were just passing by.

Tony was a long way from his taxi when he found us, and though we didn't need any telling, he warned us off the whores we'd been looking at. He'd come to rescue us, he said, at great risk to himself and his taxi.

He was a little guy. Like my idea of an organ grinder. Dark eyes in narrow brown face, with a pencil moustache, that got more attention than his broken down teeth. But his foul teeth didn't stop him smiling all the time. And he just ignored completely the fact that we were ignoring him.

"You like to see the woman focka donkey?"

"No, but I'd like to see him focka the donkey." Johnnie

Toner pointed to Theo.

"That'd be a real piece of ass, wouldn't it?" Theo screeched at his own joke. And Tony was still with us dancing about like a fella with a hot poker up his arse.

"Lovely girls... virgins," Tony stopped, smiled at our sudden interest and moved his hands up apologetically. "Well, nearly virgin... fresh... not too much jigga jig...." We moved on.

"Two girls together... exhibition...." He mimed what could have been a fella eating an ice cream, only I didn't think so.

"Two young birds...?" Jim Davis let his interest show.

"Two... more if you want..." Tony promised.

"Sounds good..." I said.

"How much?" Theo asked. "And no old ballocks 'cause we didn't come up on the last fucking load."

Tony gaped at Theo. "Can't understand you, prick," Jim said... "Just cut all the Paddy chatter, for Jesus sake."

"How much?" he said to Tony.

"One dollar each for me... I take you long way... maybe over the border... wait for you, bring you back to ship...."

"What about the girls... girls how much?" Jim asked.

"Three, maybe four dollars each... not more...."

We looked at one another. It seemed all right.

"What about your date with McKinnon?" Theo reminded me.

"Oh, he's not gone and given one to *him*?" Johnnie winked at me.

I smiled. Theo snorted. "Jesus! All this way to get lumbered wit a bleedin' Cork man...."

I wondered what to do about Joy McKinnon.

"She gave him a fiver today..." Theo said... "and there might be more that came from...."

"In that case bring her, a fiver's a fiver," Jim Davis said.

"I don't mind..." Johnnie said.

"Ah, you're the soul of kindness..." I said.

"Go get her then... don't say fuck all..." Theo urged... "and

- 174 -

bring her old man too if he's there...."

"What if he's in drag...?"

"So what?' Jim said... "we'll find him a spade along the way."

"They're both mad, you know that?" I advised.

"They're mad!" Theo complained. "Talk about the pot calling the kettle black arse...."

Tony went silent through all this, his dark eyes moving about like dancers.

"All right," I said. "Let's go and see what happens."

Tony lit up. "Jigga jig," he said, dancing up and down – "everybody jigga jig."

Johnnie knew the Eldorado and Tony waited while I went inside. It was a rough looking place, so I went back to the taxi.

"Come on in with us..." I said, "it's a bit dog-rough...."

Johnnie and Jim got out of the cab. "I'll mind the taxi...." Theo promised... "just in case he decides to piss off on us...."

"You're all fucking heart..." I told him.

Joy was at the bar in a skin tight dress cut so low that her navel was peeping out. The white material against her body made her tan seem even deeper than it was, and when she kissed me, I felt the heat of her through the lightweight fabric.

She ordered a drink and seemed perfectly at ease with my two buddies. They were happy enough and not just because they wanted to give her one. She was a cool, intelligent bird, until she started raving, and even then it was no hardship to be in her company.

"Are you alone?" I asked.

She smiled, moving her head, and in the strip lighting above the bar, I noticed some grey in her dark brown hair.

"Michelle is in the ladies...." She shrugged and we both laughed. The barman put up fresh drinks and I found I was getting a taste for Bacardi.

"We were going to have a bit of fun..." I said carefully to

Joy. "Taxi driver says it's worth seeing... cabaret... a bit kinky by all accounts."

"Sounds interesting, Paddy."

"I hoped you'd come along...."

"We'd love to," Joy said gratefully... "thank you for asking...." She waved at the barman and I could see the drink beginning to reach her. "Another drink, please barman...."

The booze was beginning to find me too. The Eldorado was stuffy and hot, and I thought I'd be all right once we got outside in the fresh petrol fumes that served as air. Joy raised her glass to me and the boys, and I kissed her. I liked the way she was, and I wondered if I'd ever learn to be that cool. Like, the way she didn't need to ask if it was all right for her old man to come along and him in drag. Making no excuse about his kinkiness with no bullshit routine to try and explain it or justify it.

When Mike did appear, Joy introduced him as "my friend, Michelle" knowing enough about people to be sure that nobody was going to start getting coy or stupid. Mike nodded, giving Jim and Johnnie, a lace gloved hand to shake. And he was unrecognisable under the ginger wig and several layers of make up.

We were moving towards the door when this tasty coloured sort started doing a pretty lively strip act under a single spotlight. I stopped beside Joy because the others had paused automatically when the stripper started getting provocative. Joy took my hand and I could feel her turn on as she watched the girl move. I could see the bird, and I thought she was pretty well built, but I couldn't be sure. That last Bacardi was giving me a bit of bother.

"She's beautiful," Joy said, her voice very dry.

"You want her, do you?" The question was an effort to be really cool.

"I want everything," Joy admitted, moving on behind the other three, pulling me after her, pissed enough herself, not to realise just how drunk I was.

The air helped me all right. It helped me lose control of my legs, so that I fell into the bloody taxi. Joy tumbled in on top of me, and I was conscious of a lot of laughing going on, and that Michelle, as we called Mike, was sitting on Big Jim's lap. Tony started off, driving like a fella with a death wish, and he didn't go short of encouraging verbal. Joy wanted to kiss me but I couldn't breathe, so I started mumbling something about getting her a girl, two girls if she wanted. The same shit that Tony had given us earlier. She started yelling, excited at the prospect... telling us just what she wanted, then she was kissing Johnnie and Theo, and just before I passed out, I heard Jim moaning about missing out on a blow job or something.

We were moving through the Panama Canal. Slowly hitting one lock after another, before I remembered this. There was nothing else, not from that moment in the taxi, though according to my mates, I'd been the life and soul of the party at some wild club across the border.

At first I just took it for granted they were having me on. That was the way we were - always kidding, trying to put the other fella on some kind of spot. What made me believe them finally, was the way they admired my cool. They thought I was acting dumb, taking the mickey out of them. And this was genuine applause from guys who didn't hand out any flowers.

It was a strange feeling, to do something and not remember it... I didn't understand it, but I thought it had something to do with all the hard work, and my torn shoulder, which was still bleeding.

Chapter Thirty-Three
S.S. Ruatoto. October '58

I wasn't bugged for long over my loss of memory. At first I resented it, not liking the fact that I'd lost control, but when I discovered that this kind of thing had happened to most fellas on the ship at one time or another, I just shrugged and accepted the fact that I was one of the boys. I was excited that I qualified as a hard man where drink was concerned and I was happy to be regarded as "a right nutter" when the story of my behaviour at Panama had circulated around the ship. And though I hadn't thrown one decent punch in the Curacao brawl, I took some pride in being pointed out as the cat who had started what Tommy Clay had finished.

I didn't go ashore at Balboa because I'd said I wouldn't drink until we got to Auckland. Just to prove to myself that I could do it. Really, wanting my mates to see that I had iron will power when I put my mind to something.

The ship was quiet as a pancake and I wallowed in my aloneness. Phil loved me and I wanted to eat the pages of her letters as I read them over and found myself wishing that we were on the way home instead of hitting the Pacific, for the long haul down past Pitcairn Island to New Zealand.

It really was some boat ride for a first tripper. Thirty one days from London to Auckland, with just three nights ashore. Big Jim Davis and Johnnie Toner had been just about everywhere and they reckoned the Union Castle run to South Africa was the perfect first trip. The voyage was six weeks round trip with something like thirteen ports including Tenerife, Aden, Laurenco, Marques in Portuguese East Africa. Plus the run of ports in South Africa itself, which meant people embarking and disembarking, so that the wingers, the stewards, made more tips. Whereas, on the run to New Zealand, you had the same shower all the way, and as it turned out, those Kiwis really thought that a pound note for thirty-one days of three meals a day was some kind of big deal.

Tommy Clay had been to New Zealand before and said it was a terrible kip altogether. The booze and cigarettes were cheap but there was a chronic shortage of birds. And he wasn't mad about this.

"And they're all bleedin' nutters... like them horrible fuckin' Abos in Aussie.... Straight up, they look more like savages than them black enamel bastards in Africa."

"They're just people like the rest of us..." I said.

"What? People? Leave off, Whack! ...They're bleedin' animals...."

"You can't say a thing like that..." I objected, knowing that he could say what he liked. But I was banking on my Hank Williams appeal, knowing that if it hadn't been for that, he would have just whacked me.

"I mean, there's no way you can just label a whole race of people like that, Tommy...."

"Here, Jim Boy...." He appealed to Big Jim. "You've been on the Castle boats right? Right...." He smirked a bit at my innocence. "Tell this Irish twit what they're like... I mean, really... would you want to live amongst them?"

"Leave off..." Jim answered, as though Clay had to be joking... "I'm not saying I haven't had a bunk up in the mud huts at Mombasa, but live with them... coo! The William those people make...!"

"Right," Tommy agreed vehemently. "Stink like shit... bleedin' coconut oil in their hair, never bleedin' wash...."

"Never mind about South Africa and Kiwi," Jim said, "they're spilling out of Brixton... be in Thornton Health by Friday we don't watch it...."

"Right..." Tommy said, turning to me. "You don't have

spades in Ireland, do you?"

"Students," I said, knowing I had no argument from this angle.

"You want to try living in the Pool then, or Brixton or Brum... Jesus! What they've done to Brum...."

And so it went on, leaving me frustrated. And having to admit to myself that I hadn't lived around coloured people, so I couldn't be sure, as I had claimed in my argument, that I'd treat each man individually. Yet I knew for sure that I was against any form of racial prejudice.

Joy McKinnon seemed to fancy me more than ever, which made me scour my mind trying to remember what had happened back at Panama. And Mike was as good as gold, hitting me with another five which had me hoping to Christ I hadn't been out of my mind enough to...? No! I wouldn't so much as give the thought waiting room. Anyway, I had no memory, and I couldn't get anything out of my mates because they thought I was having a long distance spoof, that I knew exactly what had taken place.

When we dropped anchor off Pitcairn Island, all I could think of was Gable and Charles Laughton. "Mr. Christian, anyone here seen Mr. Christian...and I'll hang you from the highest yardarm in His Majesty's Navy...." In the Stella Cinema, Rathmines and me looking for my grip in one of the back rows at the same time with a girl I didn't know.

The island looked like a long rock that McAlpine might have ditched at some stage. That was it, and it was hardly surprising that Christian and the rest of them found it hard going, before they started killing each other. Standing there looking at the place from the deck of the ship, I couldn't help feeling it was probably for something to pass the time that they'd started shooting.

That was Pitcairn Island, so I went below to freshen up, thinking it was no place to live. One serious tidal wave and it'd be goodnight and goodbye.

I was shaving, and Kitty was washing her nylons in the

basin next to mine, when one of the Islanders came into washroom. He was a nice looking fella, dark but a long way from black, and the only thing about him that looked odd, were his feet. They were twice the width of mine and they looked as tough as leather. He never wore shoes, so he said, but he liked the jeans I was wearing. So right there on the spot we did a trade - he gave me a couple of hand carved, wooden flying fish and a tortoise, throwing in a couple of what you might call grass skirts, except they were made from wood shavings or something like that. I took my jeans off and once he was sure that the brassy looking zips on the back pockets worked, he went off as happy as Larry.

Back on deck we bought some bananas and pineapples, the best I'd tasted, while the women from the Island practically bought the shop out of Tampax and sanitary towels. Then it was over: We were pulling away while the Islanders bobbed up and down in their long boats, squeezeboxes going full blast, as they sang in their glorious Welsh accents... "We shall meet on that wonderful shore." And that, though it hardly seems worth it to mention, was as close as I got to Pitcairn Island. When you thought about it, remembering that the Bounty was a sailing ship, it was a hell of a long way from Bristol, which was where she sailed from under Captain Bligh. Christ alone knows what those seamen were made of. And there wasn't a bloody vitamin pill to be had!

From there we sailed, though really, I suppose, I should say engined, down to Auckland. The work didn't get any easier and although I was glad of the time change, because we got a bit of extra sleep each night, I knew that by the time we crossed the line on the way back, I'd be cursing the loss of the nightly half hour or whatever it was. Anyway, we crossed the date line without any kind of obvious bump.

I was writing quite a bit each evening and I got a great charge out of not needing to drink my beer ration. The others shared it, and I tried not to look superior. All the fuss about a few bottles of ale. Who needed it?

Dearest Phil... We hit Auckland yesterday and if you could just see this weather, like, believe me, November was never like this. Great to sit here with your letters close to my hand... I love you so much that I don't know anyway to tell you about it. I'd like to spend the rest of my life with you, if you'll have me... now, I can't say much more than that, can I? The last day... on the way in here... you'd have laughed at the speculation among the wingers... about tips... how much would the tall geezer, with the corduroy walking stick, leave? ...Or the fat old bird with lumpy corsets, or the gummy doctor with the bedraggled look? Well, I ended up with twenty four pounds. Jesus! When you think about that, it's like tuppence a meal for the trip. One little shit gave me ten shillings, but the look of terror in his beady eyes when I slammed the note back into his mangy little paw, well, it was worth a tenner in pounds. Some of my mates ended up with as little as seven quid, which is sickening after all that work. Never mind, ay! Auckland looks all right... Queen Street runs from the dock road straight through the town, stretching for a lot further than I felt like walking today. Place is full of old tramcars, which did a lot for me. I used to love the Dublin trams when I was a kid. I also saw a locomotive. I nearly died... like, your real live bloody steam engine, and it full steam ahead down the centre of the bloody street at the end of Queens. Somehow, there's a Yankee air about the place... bit like San Francisco, though I've never been there... the trams, I guess, and the up and down streets. A glass of beer costs sixpence... the pubs are lousy, impersonal places, not a bit like at home or London. And they shut at six o'clock, which seems bloody odd. But I don't see that stopping us getting tanked up tonight. I feel we've earned a drink... I mean, resisting that lovely Kitty all those weeks at sea plays on a fella's nerves, let me tell you. Now, will you do me a favour? Tell the lovely and adorable Miss Phil Williams that Paddy Maguire loves her more than she'll ever know... that he is missing her all the time and that he can't wait to see her again. Oh, by the way, I had some stitches put in my shoulder this morning... doctor at the hospital said it should have been stitched when I first got hurt. So, I guess the ship's doctor got his own back on me for cheeking him. Fair enough, but it's a long ride back to Blighty, and boy, is he going to know it. Write to me when you can Phil. Your letters mean everything... goodnight my darling... I love you, I love you, I love you, you you you you you you you you you, I love... you... Your own Irish Leprechaun, Maguire Rex II.

Perhaps two hours later, three parts drunk, I was on my way into a dance hall with Theo, Jim, and Johnnie Toner. We each had a bottle and I was close to the end of mine, feeling that anything that might happen would be a good idea. And that's bad, dangerous way to be thinking.

We'd only just paid our admittance money when this big black girl came storming down the passage. She has some form and she's angry as hell, and you didn't need any degree in mind reading to see she was on the way out of there. I reached out and held her arm... she spun around to face me, her big dark wild eyes, frightened, softening a shade as I smiled and made a half bow from the waist. She didn't smile, but the filter that had slipped over the anger and the fear in her eyes did something to offset the hard line of her heavy mouth.

"Just arrived from Ireland, Macushla, and I insist on tearing up this ticket just for the honour of being seen walking out of here with such a lovely young lady...."

What bullshit! A touch of Rodgers and Hammerstein. The corn is as high as elephant's eye. Honestly, only the booze which had me red in the face, stopped me from blushing. But her face relaxed, the skin no longer so tight over the high, wide cheekbones, and you could see some of the tension slip out of her shoulders. Thing is, when you get that corny, they've just got to believe you're sincere. Like, nobody in his right mind is going to hand out shit like that and expect to be believed. Although, maybe they don't have to think you're sincere - just out of your mind.

"I don't mind..." she said pleasantly, the Maori accent, again that touch of the Rhondda Valley, thick and strong. I took her arm, my palm resting against her triceps. I looked at my three mates; they looked a bit surprised, though Johnnie Toner was grinning the words "dirty bastard" at me. I shoved my admission ticket in my pocket - no sense carrying out that dramatic "I'll tear it up" bit. I mean, I might need to get back in if she turned out to be a wagon. And it wasn't going to take long to find out.

We moved down the street from the dance hall and I stopped her. She grinned when she saw me take the whiskey bottle from my pocket, and she took a slug out of it that was *some* kind of drinking for a twenty year old bird. I took a belt myself and handed it back to her. When she gave it to me again there was just one drink left in it. I threw the empty bottle into a bin on the side of the street and we moved along, arms about each others waist. It was poorly lit... some old warehouses facing neglected hoardings with old posters peeling off.

"I enjoyed that, thanks." She turned her head, easy enough now, and I kissed her mouth. Her arms went around me like elastic. Christ, she had the strength of a bloody python, and within seconds we were like a couple of inexperienced wrestlers practicing some kind of backbreaker. She was some bird, and I could only think that if all the Maori chicks were like this one, New Zealand was going to be very demanding.

When we stopped for a breather, I looked around. There was no place to lie down, so it would have to be standing up. The first one, anyway, because this was no time to go walkabout looking for a cab or a hotel, or anything else. Some loose boards in the hoarding moved in the breeze coming down the narrow street, then I was ripping them loose of the supports, and she was clambering in ahead of me, neither of us bothered about being seen. The way I was feeling they could come along with the net and she seemed just as nutty as me!

The next thing I was back on the ship. It was the morning after the trip to the dance hall. I really wasn't sure, but Big Jim pulled a face, convinced I was spoofing again, that I was enjoying myself at their expense, and I couldn't make him believe that I remembered nothing from the moment I'd torn the old boards from the hoarding, minutes after I left them.

I gathered that I'd gone back to the dance with the bird, and that we'd been all over each other, on and off the dance floor. We'd been gone for about an hour and a half, Theo said, and I could see that for the first time, he was beginning to accept the fact that I was having some kind of bother with my memory bag. Jim wouldn't have it - he scoffed at the very idea.

That was how it happened almost every time I got drunk in New Zealand. At a certain time my brain seemed to switch off, though, apparently, I behaved as normally as my buddies had ever seen me. The only snag was that I couldn't recall one single thing that happened, which wasn't funny.

"This is a volcanic island..." Theo said one day, as the four of us sat in a little beer joint in Lyttleton, the port for Christchurch.

He waited until the three of us had finished looking at each other in surprise, every eyebrow flicker, indicative of our collected opinion - that he'd lost his marbles.

"That could be your problem with the gargle," he said seriously.

"I drink whiskey, brandy, sometimes rum. I never touch volcanoes... just don't like cocktails...."

"Give you the burps.." Jim added, "erupts a bit, see."

"Flash bastard..." Theo dismissed him with a glance.

"What're you on about then, Theo?"

Theo turned and gave Johnnie his attention. He was grateful that someone was taking him seriously and it showed in his great gob stopper eyes.

"The bleedin' water, that's what I'm on about... could be screwing his metabolism...." He worked hard not to look condescending, but he didn't make it. "It's not unheard of, y'know...."

"Go on..." Jim said sarcastically... "that a fact? Coo!"

"The whiskey comes from Ireland or Scotland, the brandy from Christ knows where... so how do you work that out?" I knew I sounded a bit belligerent, and I didn't mean to, not really. It's just that it was such a laugh, Theo turning into some kind of bloody head shrinker.

"That's not the point..." Theo said, kicking for touch like a rugby player out of wind.

"Ballocks," Jim said, just beating me to it.

An argument started, but some birds arrived, which had an amazing effect on the gents who were shouting and screaming at each other as they tried to sort out what was wrong with the inside of my head. At this point, I found that I was willing to accept what Theo said. One second I was yelling at him that he was talking through his arse, then for no reason that I could finger, I accepted that there was something in his theory. Not that I was going to admit it.

For once, the four of us together seemed to have touched for a bird we each fancied. Mine was a lovely little egg of a Maori, with evil eyes and a smile that lit the room up. There was no bullshit, no playing hard to get. If they fancied you, those Maori chicks wanted you in the scratcher. So we bought some hooch and went to a hotel. The owner was a little Scotsman, miserable as sin, like a walking advert for piles, and if he used water in his tea, that was about as close as he got to the stuff. The gaff was in a terrible state, but he didn't look like he'd be too disappointed if he didn't get that three star rating he hadn't applied for.

Four of us piled into each of the two bedrooms. My bird, Claire, stripped off without any claims to modesty, and I passed her the bottle, while I climbed out of my gear. Johnnie Toner was already humping his bird and the verbal he was giving her had me bursting out of my skin. I egged him on as I hopped about on one leg trying to get my Jesus trousers off too fast. Toner was going like a fiddler's elbow and Claire was urging me to hurry up. I finally got the slacks off and threw them against the wall. I turned to the bed.

"Come on baby...." She held her arms up to me.

Next thing, I was back on the ship serving lunch to some of the younger officers and though I worked up a sweat trying to remember what had happened, my mind was blank from the second I lay down on top of the little Maori chick called Claire.

Chapter Thirty-Four
Wellington, New Zealand. December '58

The self pity trick did what it liked with me after we got to Wellington, and I was practically doing novenas to hurry up the day when we started for England. I didn't have any interest in New Zealand. As far as I was concerned they could give it back to the Maoris, with apologies. It was too far away from home and far too far away from Phil.

I felt lost, even though I had three friends and a few acquaintances that I cared about. I was miserably lonely for England, for Phil, and I seemed incapable of enjoying my self pity. Something to do with the fact that I hadn't induced it in my own kinky way... it happened whether I wanted it or not, and I resented losing another bit of control.

Believe me, I tried hard not to let it show. I hated people who bled in public, but keeping up this performance became the cause of my acting like a real prick to Theo, who was, I suppose, the closest person to me after Phil. I didn't know I was being a pig until Jim Davis told me, and I won't pretend it didn't hurt. I was conceited to a point where I hardly bothered listening to anything I didn't say myself. I made all kinds of rash judgements, and I was on Theo's back all the time about stupid things that really couldn't have mattered less.

"And it's no good old buddy. You go on like that and you end up on your own... being witty and a bit of a singer, whatever... don't make up for piggery to your mates."

"Maybe it's this... cooped up," I was just making excuses. "Don't think I'm cut out for the seagoing bit?"

He shrugged, unable, or maybe just unwilling, to help me kid myself.

"If I didn't care about you, I wouldn't say fuck all."

I was surprisingly close to tears. "I know that...."

Theo appeared from the shower room, looking like an unmade bed in his towelled dressing gown. I told him I was sorry for getting on his back. He looked at Jim as though he wished he hadn't said anything to me.

"You should have told me..." I said...."Given me a whack."

"It's all right, Head..." Theo said, affected by the emotion in my voice.

"But it's not all right..." I said...."You should have told me."

"There' you go again..." Jim reminded me...."He's only just come in the fucking door and you're telling him what he should have done.'

Theo looked at him, trying to silence him. "It's okay."

"I don't want to be a prick, Theo... it's just that... well, I don't know... it's just that...."

I cried then, wept like it was going out of fashion. And I sobbed, great tearing bubbles of pain that burst out of me until I was aching all over. Theo held me like a baby. Jim stood there waiting for it to pass, and when it was finally ended, he handed me a white linen hankie.

"Don't say I gave you nothing for Christmas...."

He smiled down at me, his eyes gentle, and I found a lop-sided grin from Christ knows where.

"It's been a long time..." I said, "glad it was you and Theo." He nodded and I pointed to his head. "You've some grey hairs."

He put his right hand on his hip and did a fair take off of Kitty.

"Whatever am I going to do about it," he lisped.

"All right now, Head?" A weary smile made Theo's chin move upwards a little bit.

I nodded. "Right as I'll ever fuckin' be...."

Jim and I got a job ashore working on the docks. We were supposed to be on duty a day about, but Theo stood in for me, Johnnie for Jim, and what we earned ashore we split down the middle. It was all right, the work wasn't that hard and the money was very good. And when I came away for the last time, I kept my billhook, a reminder of my fantasy that I was the Brando character Terry, or was it just plain Brando, in "On the Waterfront".

I watched my drinking a little more now. Trying to stick to beer, but it didn't go down too easily. I was born to drink spirits, using beer only when I was beginning to feel a bit dehydrated from too much whiskey.

The McKinnons I stayed away from.... What was the pointing seeing them? I didn't want to behave the way they would have expected me to. I loved Phil, and square though the thought might be, I believed in one man for one woman. And the only woman I really wanted was my little brown eyes with the cheeky face and the leprechaun's smile. God, I was longing to see her? ...hold her in my arms... meet at the tube when she came from work in the city... take her to a movie... hold her hand... kiss her sweet goodnights without sex coming into it, for a while anyway.

Doubts creeping in... four months is a long time to be away - a long time to leave a cute bird with brown eyes and a wicked smile. Especially with her old man getting into her all the time about the Irish being a bunch of nothing people. Judging a whole race by the behaviour of a sad few on Hammersmith Broadway. Guys who were too shy to do anything but get pissed out of their minds, by which time, all they could do was only have a punch up. And they fought because you can wank only so much.

How could old man Williams understand that so many Irish fellas were crippled with shyness, hardly able to breathe due to an inherent belief in their own inferiority. Country men, fighting dead generations, forced to accept that they were second class citizens. Oh. There were the chosen few with the gift of the gab, blessed with enough bullshit to hide how they were really feeling.

Did you kiss the Blarney Stone? No sweetheart, I took a bite out of it. Allowing the world and his wife to believe that Paddy the Irishman, had done just that.... That he could talk the apples off a tree, sing the birds off the bushes, laugh the long day through and drink the knobs off a coffin.

While the many, the common herd men, left home because they had to. Most of them never seeing much more than ten bob on a Friday night for working fourteen hours a day on some bit of scratch land that would break the heart of a plough.

Becoming a Wimpey human cement mixer or a shovel soldier in McAlpine's Brigade. Working desperately hard by normal standards, but feeling it was money for nothing compared to how things had been back home.

Tough, hard, strong men, with built in thirsts, lacking among other things, even basic training in social intercourse. How else could it be, coming from a land where stupid, small minded, ignorant little demi-gods roamed the countryside in dark suits and white collars, discouraging anything even approximating to contact with the opposite sex, putting little but the fear of Christ into innocent neglected hearts, rarely mentioning the word love, even in relation to God. The word love might connote physical contact, which was the way nature designed that love should be consummated. It's a wonder they allowed you love your mother, for Christ's sake!

The day came to go because there wasn't anything for which to hang around, and they went without tears or too much in the way of embraces. They moved into the ghettos of Hammersmith and Shepherds Bush and Camden Town, because they didn't know what else they could do. The window remained closed tight for so many and not a lot of people cared enough to even try to understand. Give a man twenty-five pounds for working half as hard as he worked at home for ten shillings or a pound from his father on a Friday... might you not expect him to turn into some kind of obnoxious drunk.

Paddy the Irishman knew little other than to take a drink.

So he drank and when he needed to fight, he fought with his own, even though they were strangers just like himself. The Church had taken the pleasure out of masturbation... "self abuse will drive you to the madhouse"... say little ejaculations to Mary the Mother of God. Did you ever hear the like of it?

So frustrations had to burst the sausage skin. And it would be many years before Paddy realised that every priest wasn't right. That the good cloth of the dark uniform didn't guarantee the calibre of the man inside it. Would he ever realise that some people laughed at some of the teachings of the Catholic Church? Surely he'd come to know that any number of people even went so far as to deny the existence of God. Not bad people necessarily, just people who had worked things out for themselves. But meanwhile, people would be surprised to see Paddy blush if a woman smiled openly at him, or if for any reason he became the centre of the smallest amount of attention.

I remembered Phil's father, talking to me early in that evening I'd spent at his home. Trying to be nice, kind, to make me feel welcome, talking about the increase in coloured people in England. Calling them lazy and feckless and dirty, not succeeding in his efforts to keep contempt from contaminating the saliva in his mouth.

"The Irish do work, I'll grant them that... give a Paddy a job anytime before a nigger."

I hadn't looked at Phil; my heart had been like a bastard file rasping away at my breathing. I had wanted to do something really violent, needing at the same time to cry for the poor nigger and the poor Paddy, and poor me. Wishing then for a sick moment that my skin would change to black before the old bastard's eyes.

Chapter Thirty-Five
S.S. Ruatoto. January '58

The Atlantic was what Harry Redmond would have called a whore's melt, but I'm sure I improved on that during the five days the ocean kept us battened down. When you curse and swear from the pit of your gut, it's just got to smell foul.

I wasn't sick like a lot of the guys and, like an answer to a prayer, most of the passengers, but I had a pain in my arse, picking myself up off the deck. Jesus only knows how many times I was thrown out of the bunk, until I just gave up, scared I'd break my neck. But the mattress on the floor trick wasn't all that hot because I had Theo and Big Jim: Jesus, he was even bigger than I thought: tumbling on top of me as regular as diarrhoea, though Kitty somehow managed to sleep each night without falling out of her bunk, even once.

"Her bottle's like a bleedin' suction pump," Jim said,"such a change for her to lay on her back, glues her to the mattress, long as she doesn't apple tart and break the vacuum holding her."

Kitty's appetite over Christmas guaranteed that she wouldn't have much peace for the rest of the trip. But her carry on as the New Year ticked in had really put the tin hat on things.

Christ, they must have been in a queue down the gangway: dropping in to wish her the compliments of the season... between the sheets.

"Oh, not another, Kitty, for fucks sake," Jim had complained all night, while Theo and I, pissed out of our minds on rum, howled at the genuine pain in his voice.

"All right for you lot," he slagged us. "I'm lying under the stinkin' whore. Her and some bleedin' chocolate speedway merchant is going to land on top of me, If I don't watch out."

"Won't be long, pal...." One of the comics promised as he climbed in beside our ever ready sister.

"But long enough, love, bless you..." Kitty murmured.

"Why don't you sing him a bleedin' love song?" Jim sighed from the bottom bunk.

"Oh shut up down there, sexy kecks...!" Kitty had laughed, "Easy, love, easy... let's use the one that's there, no sense trying to bore a new one now, is there? There... now...."

And New Year's morning in the galley. Waiting for the coffee to come up, Kitty pained with me for mentioning that she was a pig, with no consideration for the rest of us in the cabin. One weary flick of the lashes, and a long weary sigh.

"Don't go on, Paddy, there's a love...." Accompanying this with some kind of shy little smile...." Not just my head's sore this morning...."

I liked Kitty... you couldn't help liking her... she was honest and she could be very kind. And though I wouldn't have wished it on anybody, she seemed to be even more desperate for love or affection, or whatever name you give it, than I was myself. And being queer couldn't have made her life any easier for her. At least, I didn't think so. It was hard to be sure how she felt.... We'd never had any kind of serious conversation. Nobody's fault - that was just the way it was.

Tommy Clay hated fags of any description. And it was a waste of time trying to talk to him about it; his conversations about poofs was a duplication, word for word, of how he felt about black people, regardless of where they were born.

In Wellington, Kitty and some of her team had come into a bar we were using, and along with them was a fella who worked in the galley. A quiet guy who didn't say much. I mean, I said hello to him ten times a day for nearly four months and I never knew his name, any more than he knew mine. But he was all right, and the fact that he liked queers was his own business. But on that afternoon in Wellington, Tommy Clay got up on your man's back and he wouldn't get off. When you remember that Tommy was what you could call heavy company, it seemed almost funny that this slim blonde guy was pleading with him to just leave it, to have his drink and mind his own business.

"You're ass." Tommy spat at him for the tenth time.

"I don't want any bother, Scouse, leave it out." Your man's eyes were clear blue under a hanging shock of blonde hair and he looked about nineteen years old. Tommy wouldn't let it go.... I said nothing, what was the point? Big Jim shrugged at me to stay quiet. Johnnie and Theo sipped their drinks like fellas listening to something on the radio.

"I've nothing against you, Scouse, I don't want to fight you...."

"Fight me? Ah c'mon, for fuck's sake - a bleedin' poof." The Scouse accent was so like parts of the adenoidal Dublin brogue that at times he might have been born up around Gardiner Street.

Finally, and only because Tommy wouldn't forget it, we all trooped out of there, into the alley behind the pub. They were going to fight. It seemed like a bad joke, everybody on the ship knew what Tommy had done to the black guys in Curacao, but there was something about the blonde guy, something I couldn't understand, that stopped me suggesting he shouldn't fight Tommy.

As it turned out, it wasn't really a fight. And it was all over in about three minutes. Three minutes that I'll never forget as long as I live.

The blonde guy moved so fast that I swear I couldn't see his hands go. They were just blurs, like pale feathers maybe, flashing so fast across my vision, like some kind of subliminal happening. Tommy never hit him, though you've never seen a guy trying harder, and within that few minutes, he had his nose busted open, the top lip line of his glorious teeth smashed from his mouth, and his two eyes so badly bruised that he wouldn't see out of them for two weeks.

He was confined to his cabin and I used to go and talk to

him, sing a few Hank Williams numbers. When he could see again, he sent for the blonde guy. He wanted, he demanded a return fight. He had to show us, all of us, that he had courage. As if any of us could ever have doubted that after Curacao. The blonde kid didn't want to fight, but he did something that would have warmed an igloo. He came into the cabin, agreeing to have a go. He let Tommy catch him with a good right hander under the left eye, then he moved aside and said: "I swallow." He walked out of the cabin then, big enough to have given Tommy back his pride. Big? So big... so bloody generous, that I could hardly breathe.

There were other things to remember. And there were things best forgotten. Like the way the booze had been getting to me... my shitty behaviour to Theo... But thank God, he was still my buddy, and I knew that Johnnie Toner and Jim Davis were going to be friends of mine for a long time.

When we hit Victoria Dock, I ran up to the phone box to call Phil. It was a cold and miserable January morning, but I felt warm just for being so close to hearing her voice.

The phone rang for ages before Phil came on the line. It was eleven o'clock on a Sunday but she made me feel that I'd got her up in the middle of the night.

I had to repeat my name four or five times before she realised who it was. Then little or nothing. No laugh, no sob, no shout of joy. A quiet hello, like I'd been down in Clapham for two or three days. I was in tears in the phone box, wanting to tear the fucking instrument off the wall.

"Could you call later?" were the last words I heard before I slammed the phone into its cradle. I stumbled back down the dock, blind with misery and I was inconsolable, despite the efforts of Theo and Jim to reason with me. I got down on my knees in the cabin and thumped the floor, swearing I'd never speak to her again.

The three of us hit the bottle, but me worst of all. I drank dangerously, like a fella trying to turn out the light once and for all. I didn't care... I wanted to just insulate myself from the pain. But of course it didn't work. Finally, just helpless for the sound of her voice, I called Phil.

"Maguire!" she screamed my name down the phone. "Where are you, I love you, when did you get back, God, I love you, and I dreamed about you last Sunday, love you, that you'd phoned, love you love you, where are you, I want to see you, I'm bursting with the way I feel, love you so much."

I couldn't get a word in, so I just stood there with the tears running down my face, warmth melting the cold anger stifling my heart, practically wishing I could just die there and then, because no matter how good things might be in the future, no moment in time could ever be so kind to me again.

BOOK TWO

Chapter One
London. April '70

My wife is dying, I wanted to yell. She may even be dead This morning she was in a head-on collision. Five hours in surgery, for Jesus sake! But I couldn't tell them. There's no way you can talk like that to a cab driver at London Airport. Bastards! Not one of them wanted to go to Fulham. And short of whacking somebody, getting myself into a punch up, there wasn't anything I could think of doing. My mind was in too many bits.

So much so that even traffic outside the Arrivals building seemed to be moving in and out of my head. And the lights and the screaming and shouting and the pushing and shoving, all thrown together, like a representative painting of the word cacophony.... A noise from hell bouncing through my eyes and ears into my brain in a kind of visual onomatopoeia.

I had to go back inside the building because, truly, I was close to screaming. It was always the same at Heathrow. I'd never managed to get a cab from there without some kind of bloody argument. And I made more allowances than the ordinary cab rider because I'd driven a London taxi for six years. But I had tried to be some kind of decent taximan, and it was an accepted fact in the trade that the regulars at the airport numbered few sweethearts among them. The easy money merchants, the spielers and the hardchaws. The turnover boys, waiting patiently for hours for the Yanks to arrive, often earning a days pay and more from one ride into the West End. You see, most visitors were dumb enough not to have studied the basic rate of exchange.

I went to a hire car desk and asked for a chauffeur driven

job to take me home to Fulham. Home? I still think of Fulham as home. I didn't live there anymore, and the odds weren't good that I ever would again. Still, it had been home to me for eight years and you don't wipe that out by flicking a little switch inside your head.

I was sore inside. Some of it was self pity but I couldn't help it. I was tired and weary, reacting a bit now to the shock of the phone call, from Phil's mate Betty, earlier in the day.

I was in my Dublin living room on Anglesea Road, listening to Phil Lynott and his mates working good sounds, when the phone rang. When I picked it up, the first words I heard were: "It's Betty, Paddy...."

"How is she?" My first words to her as I motioned to Phil and the other "Thin Lizzie" heads to hold it for a minute. I could still hear Betty gasp in surprise and I could see the group put down their instruments and take a break for a cigarette.

"Is she dead?"

"She's been in surgery for five hours," Betty explained.

"Jesus Almighty God! The poor little bitch! ...That much life, that much love... and dear sweet God could think of snuffing it out."

"How did you know?" Betty asked,

"I've been phoning her... didn't she tell you I've been asking her to go and see Dolly?"

It was a bad dream of some kind. It had to be. This was the kind of thing you read about in the papers. It never happened, not really, not to me. Not to Phil, Jesus, not to Phil.

Three times in the previous fortnight, I had seen Phil involved in a collision, an impact of some sort. And I'd been getting the name, Tom, each time. I knew who Tom was and that he'd always been special to Phil. And because I didn't know how to read what I'd been seeing, I couldn't come right out and talk to Phil about it. Besides which, I had no right to tell her what to do with her life. Not after all I had done to her. But I cared, loved her still, no matter what, and I didn't know whether the crash was a car accident, or just that she was maybe hurling herself into some kind of emotional cul-de-sac. I'd asked to go and see Dolly, just for me, having no idea whether she had done so or not.

Dolly was a clairvoyant, a medium, a spiritualist, and Phil believed implicitly in whatever Dolly told her. Though I'd been sceptical, sneering openly at the very idea when I'd first gone to see the old girl, I'd come to believe that there was something in spiritualism. I didn't understand it, nor was I going to pretend I did, but Dolly had told me things not even Phil knew about. More than once, certainly enough for her to have stopped me being so high and mighty sceptical.

Betty said several things I didn't hear. The kids? What about the kids? They were all right... Betty was there to look after them... Phil had been going to a wedding in Bristol, so the kids knew Mammy was going to be away for a few days.

"I'll get the first flight out of here... be over today, tonight, soon as I can...."

I put the phone down. Jesus! What time was it? Phil Lynott was standing beside me.

"Anything I can do, man?" His long dark fingers scratched at his head, his eyes still and silent, seeing something terrible in my face. Phil was like that - receptive to a point where he was like an advert for osmosis.

"My missus... she's been nearly killed in a car crash... I'll have to leave for 'the Smoke'...."

"Sure...." he nodded. "We'll split...."

I shook my head. "I'll be out of here in fifteen minutes... use the pad... go on with the rehearsal... no need to leave...."

He nodded. "You got my number... if there's anything...."

Anything? Something? Everything? Nothing! Nothing anybody could do. Oh Phil! Not even me, I couldn't do anything. Doctors, surgeons, they were the only hope Phil had. No! Her guts could pull her through if she was meant to live. A fraction of a chance was all she needed. If she had that, Phil Maguire, nee Williams, would be all right. All right? What's all right? Being alive? That wouldn't be enough... not for Phil... she'd have to be the way she'd been... those eyes would have to sparkle as only they could... a candle flicker would be no good where those dark brown dynamos had been.. ...

I got into a hire car and told the driver where to go. He was a well dressed, clean cut guy, and he could be bothered to be polite. And to think I had stood there like a bloody fool pleading with one bloody cab driver after another to just drive me home. A laugh really, but that was the way those Airport regulars were - out for any fiver, with no interest in the bread and butter trade, if you could call fifty shillings or three quid to Fulham, bread and butter.

Most London cabbies were decent blokes, who worked hard for a living, having to take a lot of stick from passengers, police and Public Carriage Officers, alike.

The Public Carriage Office. Jesus! That fucking snake pit. Retired fuzz pissing all over guys who just wanted a taxi badge so they could go out and drive a hundred miles or more, six days a week, through London's traffic for a week's wages.

I knew all about the cab trade and the Carriage Office, and though it was probably the best job I'd ever had, six years of it had just about driven me gaga. And to think of what I'd gone through along with every other holder of the Green Badge.... All right, London had the best taxi system in the world... the passengers were guaranteed more protection in London than any other city, but Jesus, had I known what it was like to be a driver there, I'd have told someone where to shove his Green Badge.

Chapter Two
London. '59

It sounds crazy I know, but the day I decided I was going to be a writer, was the day I signed on to study "The Knowledge of London" which meant I wasn't going to have enough spare time to write my name for the next year or thereabouts.

In the cab trade, studying for your Green Badge, your taxi driver's licence, is known as "doing the knowledge" - acquiring a knowledge of London - its streets, hotels, etc., etc., to enable you to pass something like eighteen oral examinations set for you by ex-fuzz type civil servants at The Public Carriage Office, Lambeth Road, London S.E.1.

Thinking in terms of a year marked me down as a right optimist. A lot of guys, many of them born and reared in London, took two and sometimes three years to complete the bloody demanding course.

It wouldn't be too hard to learn parrot fashion, the name of streets, avenues, crescents or whatever. A lot of bad actors learn lines this way, but this wouldn't be good enough for those carriage officers at Lambeth Road. And though I hate to admit it, it wouldn't be good enough for the cab driver, either. You really have to go out and see London. You have to see it to see it, if you see what I mean.

At the Carriage Office you were given a book listing four hundred and fifty taxi rides. Starting and finishing point was all you got. You then had to use a large scale map to work out for yourself a route as near as possible to the one a crow might fly if was sober and in the best of health.

I threaded two sewing needles with a length of cotton...

you stuck in a needle at starting and finishing points, writing down the name of each street along the straight line of the thread. You did this four hundred and fifty times, and then you had something to go to work on. And you went to work, in my case on a bicycle.

I shake my head now in disbelief... but much as I'd like to say it's bullshit, I have to confess that it's for real. Jesus, at one time I had the haemorrhoids to prove it from those little pain-filled badges, which represented hundreds of hours spent with a busted bicycle saddle sticking up my arse.

The only way to get through the "Knowledge" was on a bicycle. If you happened to have a car, you missed lots of points on the run, like, you had to give a certain amount of attention to the driving trick. Well, those points along the way were terribly important, because no way were you likely to be asked, when you went for your monthly examination at the Carriage Office, for something as simple as one of the four hundred and fifty runs in the "Blue Book".

This was the name given to the *white* pamphlet you had been given, which means that somewhere along the line there must have been an Irishman involved. So your four hundred and fifty taxi runs were just the beginning. I mean, if you took one that began at say Kensington Palace Hotel and ended at Leicester Square... you should be so lucky... but you've picked a simple journey just to show how difficult it could become when one of those Carriage Officers got through with it.

Instead of a hotel, you would be asked to go from Kensington Square (not to be confused with Kensington Gardens Square in Bayswater) or Gloucester Gate, which is a street and not a gate to Hyde Park, or any other of a dozen points around the Kensington Palace Hotel. Then instead of asking you to go to Leicester Square, at the other end, you would be asked for "The Kismet Club" or "The Arts Theatre Club", or Endell Street, or St. Peter's Hospital (the best place in London for a blood test) or Seven Dials, or a dozen others.

So you can see where the bicycle came in. Not only did it get you about, you were moving slowly enough to make notes of major and minor points at each end of each taxi run. And as those runs started and ended all over the town, you had to see and try to remember just about everything, with the exception of a Mews.

Another reason for using the bike as opposed to sitting over your map in the comfort of an armchair, was that maps didn't always show you which streets were "one way" and which way that one way pointed. And good luck to you if you said "forward Piccadilly" and you going the wrong way. The examiner turned the lighter shade of purple before he told you to get out and come back in twenty-eight days. Nothing else... no word of encouragement, no explanation, just get out.

I worked at the knowledge for eight and ten hours each day, which wasn't all that easy when you consider that I had to earn a living at the same time. Yes, that was something else, I didn't get any financial help while developing my calf muscles... not unless you were entitled to a grant from the British Legion, which I wasn't. So I had to find a job which would allow me some time to get out and about on my bike each day.

For a time I worked in a club in Clifford Street as a waiter, but the money was a joke for a split shift, lunch and evening. Evening lasted till three in the morning and except on your one day off, you had to be back in the restaurant for twelve noon. Well if the money was a joke, the food wasn't in any way funny. I ate warmed up spaghetti every evening for two months, if I hadn't been such a clever thief, keeping back a little of whatever order I fancied, I might have ended up in the Mafia. The club was well laid out and the people who ran it tried to keep it right. But it was on of those places that seemed to attract the heavies and the real villains, and there were more fights than I could be bothered to count.

The manager got very mad at me one morning about two

o'clock. A joker wouldn't pay his bill because he claimed he'd been refused a drink. This was true enough but as he'd ordered it the bar had closed, I wasn't working up a sweat over it. And I refused to keep the guy on the premises while the manager called the police. Not because I liked the fella, nor was I worried about him getting himself in trouble with the law. It was more to do with the fact that he was built on the lines of the Sherman Tank, and I reasoned that if the manager was so blind he couldn't see the fella was spoiling for a row of the "walk all over you" variety, then he should go and see an optician. For fourteen quid a week and warmed up spaghetti, I didn't feel obliged to give our heavy customer a workout.

I left the club next day… the hours were making it murderous for me to push the bike around, and at times my brain was so beat, I couldn't remember things that were essential if I was going to do well at my monthly exam at The Public Carriage Office in Lambeth Road.

The Automobile Association ran an emergency service at Fanum House, Leicester Square, and I heard it wasn't a bad job from a fella who drank in a pub in West Kensington where I was filling in as barmen while I looked around.

I had a room in Barons Court with a decent landlady who told me straight I was the first clean Irishman she'd ever met.

It wasn't far from where Phil lived up on the other side of Fulham Palace Road, so I accepted the old girl's questionable compliment, and in time, I grew to like her.

The pub was run by an Irish guy with a "put on" English accent and a genteel English wife with a fat body, who talked about breaking wind like she was saying fart. I couldn't stand either of them, although he made me smile when he talked about his pub being "fiddle proof". He hadn't made it any easier by eliminating the obvious ways of getting a few shillings on the side, but a few times, as I handed Theo a ham sandwich across the counter, I felt like opening it up under your man's nose just to let him see how the odd fiver could go

AWOL, if a fella was really interested in fiddling. But the way it was, your man knew it all, and I didn't want to disturb his sense of security.

I did well at Fanum House. Not so much for the Automobile Association, as for my knowledge of London study. I worked shifts, which suited me fine; two days nine to five; two days five to ten thirty; two days ten thirty to nine the next morning, with a few hours sleep thrown in. Two whole days off followed the six days on, and apart from all the maps and reference books at my hand in the office, I was able to spend a lot of time out on the bicycle.

By this time I was developing a fair grasp of London, but if you think of a six mile radius of Charing X, you'll realise that there was some ground to be covered. The fact that I answered some questions on my second monthly appearance at the Carriage Office was more luck than anything else, but it gave me a lift. And that evening, Phil and I went out for dinner to celebrate my first score.

It was nothing grand, I can promise you. I was earning eight pounds a week from the A.A. which was paid fortnightly in advance. Don't ask me who worked that one out. All I know is that by the end of the first week I was moving onto brown bread and cheese, and more than grateful for whatever food Phil could bring home from the lunch club where she worked as a cashier.

Phil had become the centrepiece of my existence. All I wanted to do, to be, stemmed from the point where she created whatever warmth I knew. I loved her more each time I saw her, and I didn't care who saw me run down the street when Phil was coming along to meet me.

My room measured ten feet by seven at the top of the house in Barons Court. It contained a wardrobe, a chest of drawers, a single bed, one tiny table with one chair tucked underneath it, and I cooked on an electric ring the size of a dinner plate. There was a slim cupboard on the wall over the table... my few bits of delf and my food lodged in this, and I had to go downstairs to the bathroom to wash my dishes. But I was happier in that little box of a room than I'd ever been in my life before.

Phil came there about four evenings each week, arriving about six thirty, helping me to call over my runs, and then when the work was over, we'd talk about our dreams and hold each other close on the narrow bed, with the ceiling slanting down under the roof, so that lying together, we could touch it with our fingertips.

We made love all the time without ever having sexual intercourse, and I thought I wanted her very much, my heart wanted to keep her the way she was until we could get married. So that on an evening when I took her home early with chronic stomach pains, and her father looked at me as though he could kill me, I looked innocent only because I was.

Chapter Three

Theo Was working on the Union Castle Boats with Johnnie Toner and Big Jim Davis, and after Phil came out of hospital and went away to convalesce, more than once I cursed myself for not going with them. But this was bullshit. They had taken off on the very day Phil had gone into hospital, and I wouldn't have left London then if the Castle line had made me Chief Steward.

Phil had a pretty ripe appendix but she didn't make any drama out of it, and in a couple of days she was scratching to get out of hospital. We laughed over what her father had been thinking when I'd taken her home with the stomach ache, and if we both stopped laughing at the same instant, it seemed that her throat was as dry as mine from just thinking about how she would have become pregnant. And I don't mean for one second that she didn't know about the birds and the bees.

Her mother was okay to me when I met her at the hospital but the old man didn't really take the trouble to be polite, so I just ignored him and tried, unsuccessfully, not to hate him too much. He thought I was a fortune hunter, which annoyed me on several counts. Not only did it make me out to be some kind of ponce, it also seemed to suggest that I couldn't love Phil, the most adorable girl I'd met, for herself. I'd made it clear when he and I had talked, that I wanted nothing apart from what I earned for myself. And though I'd told my share of lies in my time, it made me wild that he didn't believe me when I was telling the bloody truth.

I walked Mrs. Williams home from the hospital just before Phil left for the country, and she was decent to me. Dad was a very stubborn man, she admitted, and he was funny about money, but give it time, she urged me, give it time and work hard, and he'll come around.

"And if he didn't..." she smiled, a believer in love for love's sake... "if he doesn't, that shouldn't stop you and Phil, not if you really love one another."

I was grateful to Mrs. Williams for that and I walked home that night feeling better than I'd expected to. The old man was self-made, I knew all that. He'd worked eighteen hours a day for twenty odd years - I knew that too - he'd made sure to tell me on that one and only evening, but what he didn't see or know, was that money is good only as long as you control it... as soon as it gets a grip on you, like it had with him, it is a kind of prison. He was serving a life sentence as far as I could see, and I wanted none of it. I just wanted enough to live on from the cab while I got myself off the ground as a writer. I'd work and work and work, to keep Phil happy. I wasn't afraid to graft hard, and though he didn't know it, that's what I'd been doing since I first went out on the bike. And something else the old bastard didn't know... I hadn't had a decent drink in bloody months. So fuck him and his cocktail cabinet bursting at the seams. He wasn't going to keep me awake, I decided as I got into bed. Not bloody much, he wasn't.

Life suddenly seemed very hard. My room wasn't the same any day I knew Phil wouldn't be coming. And my bicycle started to fall apart on me. Which is bad enough in itself, but when it happens at the end of your day's work, at say, Victoria Park, in East London, and you have to get back home to Barons Court on the West side, it's inclined to make you feel hard done by.

The joke became even less funny when I got to thinking about all the money I'd spent after Phil and I got together a week after my return from New Zealand. Jesus, with the tips I'd given to barmen and waiters I could have bought two new bicycles. But there I'd be, sitting on the side of Mile End Road or somewhere, wielding a spanner with all the skill of an unfortunate spastic, covered in grease and muck and trying for all I was worth not to think that Phil hadn't written to me for over a fortnight.

When she did write, I was very conscious of the name, Tommy. Phil and he used to play together when they were kids. *Please don't play with him now, Phil, I love you and I miss you and... oh Jesus!*

Her father wanted her to go abroad for a long rest after her operation. And she *was* feeling a bit run down still. It was something that surprised her, because, as I knew, he wasn't the kind to throw money around. But she wasn't sure if she wanted to go... maybe a few more weeks in the country would put her right. It was fun watching Tommy practice for the trials at Blagden or some place with a name like that. He was a fantastic horseman... and he had his own farm now...

I tried to dream a picture of a country yokel, a sodbuster, an English bogman, with the cap on the side of the head, straw sticking out of his mouth, and a pair of rubber boots with patches on. Christ Almighty, what did I have to fear from a character like that? I mean, Phil had to know that his mouth would drop open if he stood in Piccadilly for two minutes and watched the crumpet and the traffic float by.

I buried myself in the knowledge, falling asleep sometimes at the little table in my room, and I made sure of getting out on the bike every day. Even after finishing at five in the afternoon, I'd get three or four hours before it got dark. And I was glad to be so brutally tired when I got back to Barons Court. At least I could sleep fiercely, which helped me to keep at bay the insistent nagging for a good piss-up. Which I really didn't want and which I definitely couldn't afford.

There were a couple of guys in the office that I got along with because I made them laugh. They were all right and they thought they knew me, but all they got was the "always leave them laughing" bit. How could I talk to them about how I felt? And what could I say to them about studying to be a taxi driver? I wasn't about to give them a real belly laugh by telling them that I had dreams of being a writer. They saw me as a comic, yes, but a writer never!

John Denham was a tall, gangling character, who might have stepped straight out of a story about public schoolboys in "The Wizard" or one of the other comic papers for fourteen year olds. He was either a genius or a lunatic, or both, and he talked loudly enough to embarrass me when we were in a café, or riding on a tube on the very rare occasions when I didn't have a bike with me. But because he didn't give a damn about anyone I liked him, and though he earned the same money as I did, I was forever buying him cups of tea. Which probably had something to do with his seeming to like me.

The other fella was a nice enough phoney, a grammar school boy who needed everybody to assume that he was upper crust. Which was a shame because he was a good enough person in himself, and though he was married to a very tasty bird, he was making other chicks all the time, which seemed to me be part of the same insecurity thing.

He was stocky with that sort of brylcreem look, and you could see he was going to run to weight if he ever got a decent job with real wages. His name was Barry Taylor.

He'd been on at me to go to a party with him somewhere in Hampstead. A Friday night after we finished at ten thirty. He kept on about how good it would be, with tons of booze and all kinds of wild crumpet. Actresses, he assured me, and lots of arty types who only went to parties to get stuffed. I shook my head and I told him I had work to do when I got home. But home, my ten by seven, in Barons Court, was getting harder to take the longer Phil was away.

I was sitting at my little switchboard, wishing to Jesus I was in South Africa with my three mates. All the lights were flashing, so lots of people were in trouble, needing help from Emergency Service. Good! Let them all be broken down or out of petrol, and if the rain was soaking them to the skin, so much the better. I had nobody to ring when the bike let me down, and those chalk bullets from the doctor weren't doing much to relieve the ache up the khyber.

"Call for you, Maguire." I looked over at Barry. "A bird, old man, sounds rather super... on ten."

I pressed down the ten button, hoping he wasn't just passing a dodgy call onto me. He sometimes did that when he had a sticky costumer on the line. Only a few days before I'd stopped another guy from belting him in the mouth for lumbering him with a right bastard.

"Maguire?" It was Phil, surprising me so much I almost dropped the phone.

"Phil, kiddo, where are you?"

She was still in the country. "Sorry for not writing more...."

"That's all right..." I said, trying not to sound like it was anything but all right. "Any sign of you coming home?"

Not right away. Her father was still on about her taking a trip abroad. He'd even driven down to the West Country to see her and repeat his offer. The bastard!

"Might do you good..." I said casually, feeling some of my hairs turn grey at the thought of her being away for maybe months. But still, at least bloody Tommy wouldn't be blowing her mind with his Roy Rogers bit.

"How are you?" Phil asked.

"Well to be truthful, I'm like a sore thumb. I'm lousy and there's no sense in telling you lies."

"You working hard on the knowledge?"

"Every day... I've been buried apart from the hours on the bike...."

"It's worth it, Pads. You want to write, cabbing is the perfect job - work when you like, earn what you need, write the rest of the time."

What was she giving me, for Christ's sake? I was doing "The Knowledge" so that I could marry her. Once we were together, in our own place, I'd be able to write.

"The bestseller can wait. Phil. I want to marry you first."

Phil didn't say anything, for a fraction of a second too long.

"How's Tommy?" I asked, "and how is he shaping up for the trials?"

"Oh, he's fine." She sounded relieved, grateful almost, "still the same old Tommy."

Did you play together when you were grown up, too? Oh God! I felt as if I was being strangled in slow motion.

"I'll write to you soon. Maguire."

Dear John, I sent your saddle home. Don't feel too bad... out there somewhere in this big wild world, there's somebody who will love you as you deserve to be loved.

"It's over, Phil, isn't it?"

"I'm just trying to get well, Pads. I am trying to sort myself out. Don't let's talk about it now."

"Why not now? I mean, I'd sooner know - between your old man and his money and Tommy and his farm and him being so fantastic in the saddle...."

"Maguire, don't, please."

"I'm only fucking human, Phil, and that kind of competition is too much, even for me."

"I've got to go now," she said coldly, then in a softer tone... "it's difficult to talk, Pads. I'll call again."

"Give Tommy my love, and tell him I hope he breaks his fucking neck."

I sat there, holding the dead phone in my hand, wondering what sort of animal I was. But she had been giving me a load of bullshit. Not one word of love... no answer when I talked about marriage... after all the hours spent dreaming together. I put the phone down, ignoring the flashing lights in front of my eyes. I looked up at the ceiling. "Bastards!" I cursed, hating the Gods who were making me pay the bill for all I'd done wrong in the past. Why did they have to take it all at once? Couldn't they let me work it off a bit at a time? I felt like spitting upwards because I was sure I could hear them go laughing away, as they worked out the next step along the way in my destruction.

Barry Taylor took me to the party at Hampstead, and though he wasn't all that pleased, he had to take Denham, who'd worked himself into the group. I was glad of this because John was mad enough to be sure that the night would be lively, if nothing else.

Inside, I was brutally sad, sort of dangerously so, and if ever a fella needed an excuse to drink himself out of his mind, well, Phil had given me mine. And at the party I behaved like a lunatic, but all those phoneys put up with it, treating me with decency when they should have been kicking me up the arse.

Barry had told them, strictly for a laugh, that I was a writer, and with me being Irish, well, before I knew where I was, I was up to my ears in bullshit chat about literature and Joyce, and all the rest of it. Until I gave a couple of yells and threw myself on a bird who'd been showing out to me from the moment I arrived. She had copper coloured hair and a firm body and she made no bones at all about getting into the scratcher. She seemed to love the pounding I gave her, but then she wasn't to know I was just trying to hurt her the way I was hurting myself.

Chapter Four

For Two weeks after that party I didn't go out on the bicycle and if I looked at the map it was to find a location for some guy who was in trouble. As Barry Taylor remarked, it was odd to see me doing some work for A.A.

Rusty, the girl with the copper coloured hair, was some kind of heiress, but despite this, she wasn't short of a few quid. That's right, I mean, despite being an heiress. It takes time and a lot of knocking about before you learn never to pull an heiress, just go for a bird with money.

She drove her own car with a kind of enthusiasm that was Italian flavoured, and she fed me and wined me, and did all kinds of things for me that I couldn't do for myself. And I wallowed in her, trying to forget a girl named Phil Williams, and find whatever it was that would take me down to "The Pool" and onto a ship going anywhere.

There was nothing wrong with going back in the merchant navy. The money was all right and if I was serious about writing, I could get something done each evening when work was over and there were still a lot of places I'd wanted to visit. But it seemed a waste after all the work I'd put in on the knowledge. And there was no denying that a cab badge could be very handy. Once I had it, there wasn't a thing in the world to stop me doing trips to sea as well. So I could have the best of both scenes if I stuck things out for another six or seven months.

Beside which, Rusty always had too much booze about her flat and I was drinking it simply because it was available. I didn't want to, even though the loss of memory act hadn't happened since I'd been drinking again. I smiled. Theo and his volcanic speech down in New Zealand, with me believing it because it suited me. Here I was back in England, having been drinking my loaf off for a fortnight and no loss of memory. He wouldn't believe it when I told him.

I started going out on the bike again, determined to get that taxi badge, even if I was to throw it into a canal the minute they put it into my hand. I borrowed a tape recorder from Lenny and Elsie. I didn't go into the pub much, but they always welcomed me when I did, and they both thought it was a great idea that I was going to be a cab driver.

The only way to get those streets burned into my mind, was to ride over them, go back home and call the runs over to yourself until you had them off pat. Most fellas worked with somebody else, which was ideal, but I was something of a loner, except when I'd had Phil to hold my book and check the runs as I called them out.

The first day out on the bike, I did three runs. Called them over till I knew them. And three runs each day after that, but always going back to the first three before getting onto the others. So that, even accounting for my two week lay off, after five months or so, I was calling over the four hundred and fifty runs in the Blue Book, which was really white.

From that position, I just had to go on calling over the runs, which I did with the tape, listening to my own voice until even I got sick of it. But this was a very important part of the operation. And of course, I went out on the bike still to look for the locations, points for which I might be asked when the next examination came around.

Suddenly I knew London like the inside of my mouth. Or so I thought till I stood on the mat before the examiner's desk and he showed me just how far I had to go. But one day I answered most of the questions. It was my sixth monthly appearance, and when I'd finished, he told me to come back in three weeks.

"Three weeks, sir?" I asked, checking it out, because I was

so desperate that I could have been kidding myself.

"Yes, three weeks. And call Linden up on your way out."

I floated out of the office. I was over the halfway mark. I leaned over the banister and called the name Linden into "the snake pit", which is what we called the basement room where we sat, sometimes for five hours, waiting for our names to be called out. All kinds of fellas, all nationalities, with Jews about the most predominant. There were a few coloured guys and one or two Irish besides me, and I thought it was sad that the Jewish cats, who had been the whipping boys for so long, made it bloody clear they didn't think it right to have black cab drivers.

The only guy I ever really got to know in the snake pit was a Jewish guy called Ronnie Millar. He was a happy little character, who could make a cat laugh, and he donated all the spare time he could to sharing himself around between the girls. But he was just like all the rest when it came to coloured people. I'd mentioned to Ronnie that one of the Hampstead party chicks, a well bred English girl was badly hung up on a coloured musician and that she was pregnant for him, and his first reaction had been to laugh, because he was sure I was kidding him. Believing me then he said: "White bird who goes with a schvartzer is only a scumbag..." He was filled with disgust.

"But you'd lay a coloured chick! Or maybe you wouldn't."

"That's different, Irish, entirely different. Geezer dips his cherry, walks away - bird takes it - different."

"Ah, bollocks!" was all I could say.

"Would you let your daughter marry one?" I looked at him and I could see he was serious. His blade of a nose hid part of his upper mouth from a certain angle, and he was like some kind of belligerent bird behind the horn-rimmed shades.

"I don't have a daughter," I said. "But old man Williams does and her name is Phil and I love her, but I'm a black man to her daddy, so there!"

I'd really considered cabbing seriously from the moment I

realised there were so many Jews doing the job. I'd always admired the way Jews were willing to work, but because there weren't too many of them sweeping the streets, you could bet that there wasn't much money to be earned pushing a brush. So the cab trade had to be favourite, regardless of how many drivers gave you the poor mouth and told you what a hardship it was to make a decent living.

I was over Lambeth Bridge, gliding by the roundabout into Horseferry Road, when I thought of calling Phil. No matter what, she'd be glad to know that I'd been moved forward at the Carriage Office. She had been born and reared and steeped in cabbing, so she would know exactly what it meant to me.

She no longer worked in the same job. She'd given that up when she'd gone off to the country. Jesus! Maybe she was still down there. Maybe she was married to Tommy.

I had to stop the bike and light a cigarette. Just the thought of it: Phil married to anybody except me. Good Jesus! And I used to laugh at stories of fellas who went nuts over some woman. Second-hand eejits, I called them. And there I was fighting for breath in Victoria Street. I got back on the bike and I rode like the hammers of hell. Through South Kensington along Old Brompton Road, over Lillie Bridge, and along up to Fulham Palace Road, my legs going like pistons. What sort of gobshite are you? Letting your stupidity screw up the one thing that can help you grow into some kind of human being? For Jesus Sake! When I knocked at the door of the house, I was nervous, bloody nervous, and I won't deny it. But I was going to have a go, and if her old man gave me a hard time, I was going to take it. If it choked me, I was going to swallow it. He was her father and whether I liked him or not, he was doing what he thought was best for Phil. Oh Christ, open the door, somebody please open the door.

Mrs. Williams was standing there. "Hello Paddy," she said.

"I'm sorry to bother you, Mrs. Williams. I was wondering, er, ehm, is Phil... is she at home?"

"She left about fifteen minutes ago, to walk around to your place," Phil's mother said.

I don't know what I said to the poor woman. I don't remember a yard of the ride to Barons Court. I took the stairs three at a time, all the way up to where my box room sat so close to the roof. I burst in the door, almost collapsing - Phil wasn't there.

Oh Jesus! Oh Jesus God! I fell on the bed and I couldn't stop the tears that seemed to be pumping out of my heart! My spirit just seemed to cave in, and I was so helpless, so lost in the grip of my own loss, that my head seemed to be about to explode.

Then I felt her hands on my face and my neck and her tears falling into my own. I could hardly see her for my fucking tears …then her lips pressing me, loving me.

Later, the pain had washed itself away, to be replaced by the sure and true knowledge that nothing would ever come between us again. Not Tommy, father, money. Nothing!

"But where were you? I didn't pass you on the street?"

She shook her head, her eyes as bruised as my own from the tears. "I was having a cup of tea with Mrs. Bell."

The tears slipped out of me again. "When you weren't here…I thought, oh God, I thought I was just going to die…"

Phil sat up, found a tissue and wiped my eyes. "I'm going to make some tea." She stopped by the door, the small tin kettle in her hand, on her way to the bathroom for water.

"By the way, Maguire, I told my father this morning, that if you still wanted me, I was going to marry you. You and nobody else."

"I'll try and get along with him, Phil. I really will."

She smiled. "Mum thinks you're alright."

"And so she should. Didn't I walk her home one night?"

"Did you give her all the old Blarney you gave me when I first met you?" Her eyes shone wickedly and an edge of laughter had slipped into her voice.

"Ah, go make the tea," I said.

Chapter Five
London '60

Twelve months isn't a long time, though it might seem forever if you were marooned on a desert island without a record player or a copy of the Karma Sutra. As I stood waiting for my taxi licence and my Green Badge, I felt that the year out and about on my bicycle had just slipped by.

Which of course it hadn't. It had been the longest fifty-two weeks of my life, full of sweat-hard work, endless sickening bile swallowing days of work for buttons, and having to take a lot of shit from examiners, employers and Phil's father.

More than once I really was so close to blowing up in the worst way, particularly in the Carriage Office, that I was blinking back the tears, tears of frustration and anger, as the effort to stay cool became demanding enough to be just bloody unbearable.

It wasn't really to do with answering questions in the seemingly endless line of oral exams... most times after my sixth appearance, I answered well, but when they started to break my balls, testing my temperament, my suitability as cab driver material. For Christ's sake! You'd think you wanted to be Prime Minister, or something.... It was doubly hard for me because I didn't realise that this was what the bastards were doing. And because I didn't put myself about too much, I didn't have anyone to mark my card, put me wise to this sadistic little ploy, designed to send the examiner off to lunch in near hysterics, as he remembered poor Joe Soap, standing there in a lather of sweat, silently pleading for the chance to go out and work his knickers off in London's traffic for the privilege of just earning a living.

When you first heard the guy tell you that such and such a

street wasn't where you said it was, you really did think you had heard him wrong. You insisted, mildly, but with an effort at firmness. He looked at you with eyes that belonged in the head of a dead halibut, and told you to go out and see it for yourself. He was so certain, so quietly adamant, that bits of electrified elastic seemed to have taken out a lease on the inside of your head. And you came out of there really feeling that you were going mad. You had to be. To have told him you were positive. How could you be positive about something that was so obviously wrong? It *was* wrong ... he had told you so, and if there was anybody who knew more about London than a "knowledge boy" in the final stages of his suffering, it was those men who asked the questions on behalf of the Public Carriage Office.

So you got back upon your bike, wondering what in the name of God? And you rode up to the place you'd disagreed about. Then, finding that you were right, totally one hundred per cent right, you wanted to ride back down to Lambeth Road and punch the bastard in the head for taking the piss out of you. But you didn't. You didn't because you couldn't... not then... not after all the work, and all the nerve-racking minutes you'd stood while the guy made you eat humble pie. You stood there nervous, only because it was so desperately important not to be so nervous, and you fluffed answers to simple questions because you'd been "set up" to fluff by having to sit in "the snake pit" for four or five or even six hours, and further pressured towards failure by the attitude of the man in the chair, who somehow made you feel that you belonged in the skirting board with the other termites.

But it was over, thank God! You were about to get your badge and then you could walk out of there and go to work and just forget the whole thing the way you would a bad dream.

The window came up and the clerk looked over his glasses at me. He seemed to hate me, but how could he? He didn't know me from a hole in the wall. His eyes fell back to the sheaf of papers on the ledge desk inside the window. Then back up to my face with an expression that suggested he would sooner be cleaning lavatory seats.

"You made one appearance in court... fined a pound for non-payment of fare on the public transport system...."

He went on but I couldn't hear him. I didn't dare let him get to me... I had to shut out his voice and yet appear to be listening to what he said. I was suddenly aware that he was waiting for me to say something. I didn't know what to say but I knew I was delighted that the little bastard had no hair.

"I'm sorry, sir..." I said, then, pathetically, "It was very unfortunate...."

I thought the ghoul was going to hit the roof. His mottled, purple grey face lit up like a neon and he whipped his glasses off as though they'd given him an electric shock.

"Unfortunate? Did you say unfortunate?"

Yes, yes, yes. I said unfortunate, scumpig, unfortunate, sad, miserable, stupid, ridiculous, petty, unfortunate.

"I'm sorry, sir..." I said, giving God the right look, the correct tone, the perfect note of capitulation. "I didn't mean to...."

I stopped. Deliberately. I didn't know the next word, let alone the reminder of the sentence.

"You're Irish?" he said, with deliberate distaste.

"Yes, sir, I am..." Paddy was touching his cap, accepting his position in the second class compartment.

"We take a very, very dim view of this kind of thing... I hope you understand that...."

I was drunk and I was broke and the bus conductor was a turd. No excuse, I know, but sometimes we have a reason for the odd things we do.

"It won't happen again, sir...."

Does your wife call you sir? When you're gargling your throat passionately while she lies waiting for the gynomin to dissolve.

Finally, after a lifetime of turning me slowly on the spit, his magnanimity got the better of him and he granted me my licence, like someone doing a favour against his better judgement.

I staggered out into Lambeth Road. I was so relieved that I hadn't flipped, hadn't let loose all the invective that had been building up in me from the time I'd first walked up those steps to ask for a copy of the Blue Book, which was really white.

Looking back, it seems unbelievable that the situation could have grabbed me the way it had. Yet I wasn't alone. I'd seen many guys who were close to "getting out" suffer just as much as I did. And they weren't necessarily sick or insecure, nor did they have to be Irish or any other nationality. Some of them were really heavy people... ex-boxers, footballers, fellas who'd been commandos in the war... all kinds of people. And it seemed all the more crazy because being a cab driver couldn't be anything special. Like you were going to be a working guy and you'd never get rich from what you were going to earn on the cab.

You could earn real money within the wages structure, but it was hard work, tough, nerve racking, demanding work, pushing a cab around for ten hours. But unless you worked you got nothing... no sick pay, no holiday pay worth the mention, and you had no bonus schemes, no holiday or pension funds. I mention those things to illustrate that it wasn't any easy number.

For me it meant a kind of freedom. I had a job that proved I was highly skilled at something, I could earn good money, and I could work or not, when I liked. I wouldn't be working for somebody else, in the strict sense of the term. I would take out a cab from a garage, paying them a percentage of what appeared on the clock, the taxi meter. If I wasn't going to show up on a certain day, I just phoned and said I wouldn't be in. Nobody gave me a hard time and I could work day or night or both, to suit myself. And that was worth an awful lot in money and bloody pension schemes.

I won't go into a job by job description of my first days behind the wheel of the old FX3 diesel job that my future brother-in-law, Jackie Williams supplied for me. But two things stick in my mind. "The Knowledge", as I'd studied it, was very little use when you ran into a traffic jam. And while a lot of things in London might have been scarce, traffic pile ups, weren't. So much so, that sometimes it was practical to shoot across the Thames, coming back over it by a bridge further down. Now if a fella was to suggest such a thing when he was on appearance at The Carriage Office, he might well have ended being hurled out of the room by the examiner.

The other thing was that for all the months of sweat and the rest of it, nobody had given you any idea of how to handle the people who were going to pay your wages. Not that this bothered me; I could get along with most people and I'd been lucky to work in catering but a lot of fellas weren't as fortunate as I'd been, and this was an added burden in the first weeks of finding the way.

The most marvellous thing was that every time you dropped a fare, you had money placed in your hand. So that after an hour or five hours or whatever, you could stop and have a count up, knowing within a few shillings how much you'd earned for your time on the road. And this could be a great incentive to work, whether you were doing well or not. Obviously if you were running into it, you pressed on until you dropped. But if it was going bad, your count up told you that you needed Mr. Right to come along with a long job and a good tip.

It was exciting work in the first few weeks. I was earning real money, fifty and sixty pounds, when I punched in, I could work as many hours as I wanted, and I was meeting all kinds of people. Which was almost as important as earning wages, because I knew I was going to write, and for a story teller, the basic raw material necessary to his craft were actually getting into the cab and tipping me for good measure.

Chapter Six

When Phil showed her father her engagement ring, he sniffed a bit, like a tired bloodhound, which seemed to be as close as he could get to being pleased, or happy or enthusiastic about us. You could see the guy was trying, and probably trying hard, to mean it when he mumbled his congratulations. But he just didn't make it.

This went right up my nose, and I had to remind myself that he couldn't help it, that this was the way he was. I wasn't happy with him, but then I'd never understood parents who wanted to live their children's lives for them. Like, he'd had his share of time, and he'd done with it what he wanted. Which was to make a lot of money. And good luck to him.

I knew he'd had his dreams about Phil marrying into money. Ideally she should have married Tommy, who not only had money but owned hundreds of acres of land. The old man had a hang-up on land and the whole country bit, which I *could* understand, because although I was a city hound, this love of the earth was deep rooted inside me.

Not that the old man bugged me all the time. He didn't because I was too busy. Working twelve and sometimes fourteen hours a day on the cab, saving every penny I could. I gave the bread to Phil and she added it to her own savings account. My lovely girl was a natural with money, whereas I could part with it before it even got acquainted with the inside of my pocket.

My needs were few. It was very much a case of going from bed to work, and happily so. Often I'd finish at three in the morning and be up and out, back behind the wheel, eight hours later. I was enjoying the work because I had something to work for, and I could see Phil every morning. Most times it was just for an hour or so, and we laughed a great deal about the romantic way I was itching to get back out on the cab. I couldn't help it - there was money to be earned and I was greedy to get my hands on some of it. Even on nights when I took Phil to the movies or the theatre, I usually did another few hours work after I'd taken her home.

Ma was thrilled to hear I was engaged and she told me in her letter that Pops thought it was about time I settled down. Which made me feel a little easier... like, for once I seemed to be doing the right thing all round. If you could ignore the novenas Old Man Williams was doing that I might be eaten by a shark.

By Christmas, Phil and I saved enough for a deposit on a house. So without consulting anybody we set a date for our wedding, towards the end of the following March. This would give us time to get a pad together, find the money for some furniture, and not send her family in a flap with last minute arrangements. Which brought us to the point of deciding where we were going to get married.

"I'd marry you in a Turkish mosque..." Phil said.

I knew this to be true, and we both felt that if it wasn't for the parents, we'd just start living together and not to be too worried about pieces of paper. But we were getting married, so we had to talk about it. I had no problem inside myself, I mean, I'd never been a voluntary member of the Catholic Church, and as soon as I could think for myself I found that in no way could I accept what it was all about. But the idea of telling Ma and Pops that I wasn't going to get married in a Catholic Church wasn't something I was going to enjoy. And yet I knew I had to do it, to be straight about it.

"I'll marry you in a Catholic Church, Pads, if that's what you think best."

"I couldn't ask you to do that. I haven't been inside a church, well hardly, since I was a kid. I've no time for it, never did have. We can't start out our married life with me being a hypocrite."

"I just want you to know...."

I stopped her lips with my hand. Kissing her then, smiling in the hope of easing any concern she felt.

"I know. Forget it." I held her face between my hands. "Will you give me a straight answer to a straight question."

Phil nodded and I kissed her nose, making her smile.

"Would you like to get married in a church... as opposed to a registry office, I mean?"

"Well, I know Mum would like it to be in a church."

"Sexy devil, isn't she?"

"The wedding, Maguire!"

"Well, let's do it then...." She seemed surprised. "I can go into your church and get married. I couldn't go into a Catholic one - all that stuff about kids being brought up as R.C. I mean, how could I promise that, when I don't believe in the religion in any way?"

"What about your parents? Won't they mind?"

"I don't know," I said, honestly. "I'll go over in the New Year and talk to them. It's not something I want to write to them about."

"You may not always make it, Pads, but you try to do things right."

"You just wait till we're in bed together. I'll make it."

She hugged me. "Oh, don't thing about it, Pads. Don't start me! I'll end up raping you." She pulled her head back and I grinned at the lust in her eyes.

"Horny bitch!"

She nodded, a broad grin on her mouth. "You're absolutely right."

"Love you, Phil."

"Oh Pads, I love you so much."

"Don't ever stop...."

"Never." She rolled her eyes in mock agony. "Oh Jesus!" she sighed, "roll on March."

"You'll be Mrs. Maguire."

"I'll be full of you. Oh God! I want you to pump children into me."

"Go on," I said, my throat like sandpaper, "you mightn't even like it."

Her eyes opened wide, her expression admonishing me, whether I was kidding or not. "I'll love it, Pads, I just know I will."

"If we don't stop talking about it, you'll be finding out a lot sooner than you think."

This wasn't all banter. It was becoming more and more difficult not to jump into the scratcher with Phil, particularly as I wasn't sinking the log anywhere else. But it was the way I wanted it, and as far I could make out, the celibate bit wasn't actually killing me, even though I was suffering a fair bit of arthritis behind the zip.

The only booze I had over Christmas was a glass of beer with the turkey and ham dinner Mrs. Williams served. I worked right through the holiday, earning fantastic money, and I was as happy as a dyke in Holloway.

The only rough spot was the Christmas meal. I was there because it was what Phil wanted, but it would have been better had I stayed away. The old man couldn't even make an effort and if I hadn't been so busy hating him, I might have managed to feel sorry for him.

Jackie took some of the edge off it. I liked him, and felt grateful to him, from that moment. He wasn't a gusher, I suppose you could have called him taciturn, but he went out of his way to make me feel at home, and he seemed to be saying "don't mind the old man, he can't help being a miserable old prick".

Mrs. Williams was all right; she was kind, and in a tough position. She wanted me there because it was good for Phil, and she was decent enough to have thought it ridiculous for me to sit in my room eating from a tin of something, when all she had to do was set another place at the table. She couldn't come on too strong without her husband getting the needle.

I tried very hard to be there without intruding, but I found it hard to be silent without appearing rude, and almost impossible to be light hearted without it sounding flippant. God, I was so self conscious that I was afraid to blink, just in case it was the wrong thing to do.

Jackie came to the rescue as soon as the dishes had been cleared away. He suggested a game of cards, winking my way, and I smiled my appreciation. I hated playing cards but as the old man was now glued to the television set, I was more than willing to make an effort to be part of the scene, without bugging him.

The whole family were cards fanatics, and I saw a tough, almost ruthless streak in Phil, as she hammered her cards down to win. Jackie was the same, his oval face set like granite as he waited for someone to let him in with a trump card. And when he did top somebody easily, he got as much joy out of the game as he might have had if he been playing for hundreds of pounds, instead of just pennies.

His girl, Val, played well, and if we liked each other right away, I guess it was because we were both sort of outside things. She was an attractive bird, blonde with fine boobs and a tiny waist. And I could see she was crazy about Jackie, who was so easy with her that they might have been married for ten years.

Susan was Phil's only sister, a sizeable fourteen year old, with a cupid's bow mouth and large bright eyes. She was her father's pet and already she talked to him as only a spoiled child can. I couldn't help enjoying it when she told him to shut up, or when she reminded him that he was being silly and old fashioned, while her mother just sat and chuckled at the very idea of anybody talking to the old man in that way.

I left the house at seven to go to work. As I held Phil in the hallway, I knew she was just as relieved as I was. She kissed me fiercely and I made myself a promise that next Christmas would be a happier one, because we'd spend it in our own home.

Just before the end of the year, we found a small terraced house off Fulham Palace Road, and once we'd set the deal in motion by paying a small deposit, I flew home to Dublin to talk to my parents about the marriage and the fact that I wasn't getting married in any Catholic Church.

Several times on the flight over, I wondered why I was bothering. I mean, I'd done so many things without consulting them, even marrying Pauline, and finally having the marriage annulled on the grounds that it had never been consummated.

I knew, by the time I got to The Hill, that I wanted to start out as near as possible on the right foot. The fact that Phil wasn't a Catholic was going to be handicap enough and her relationship with my parents, and if it ever came out afterwards that I married her in a Protestant church, well, Jesus, it would have been the end altogether.

They took it a lot better than I'd hoped. Ma warned me that she would pray every day that I'd see the light, and while I could see that Pops didn't approve, he didn't go on about it. The fact that I had a good job was the all important thing, and he just hoped that things would work out the way I wanted.

He didn't look too well, and Ma told me he had to take pills several times a day. A weak valve in his heart had placed a strain on his health, but as long as he did what the doctor told him, there wasn't any reason why he shouldn't go on for years.

Ma was in good shape, smoking more than I'd ever been aware of before, her hair just about white now. This made her look older than she was, but her eyes retained the vitality that had kept her going through so much, although the built-in sadness was still there. Her mouth could still become a granite hard line, and there was enough venom left in her speech to clearly establish that her batteries were still full of juice.

I saw Billy only once while I was in Dublin. He was married now and his wife, Olive, seemed like a nice girl. I mean, she was no Miss Ireland, but she had kind eyes and a high voltage smile, and one of the best pair of legs I'd ever seen. She also had what the Irish call "child bearing hips" and I only hoped Billy was giving her the time of her life in the scratcher.

I mentioned this to him in a vague kind of way. His eyes flashed in and out of annoyance, as though he wanted to tell me to shut my mouth, but felt that wasn't the right thing to do. Instead of which he said, matter of factly:

"Oh we're not very keen on that sort of thing."

I wanted to pursue it, because I didn't believe him for one second. But I didn't know how or where to begin. Billy and me, well, we'd never been that close, and though it was just possible I could have helped him, I couldn't see him talking to me in an intimate way, so I let it go.

Dublin left me so cold that it became another reason for getting out as fast as I decently could. Eamonn Boyd was in good form, making a bundle out of sweets and chocolate, and if he was a bit surprised at the idea of me getting married, he didn't seem to think it was a bad idea. And he promised that if I told him when, he'd come over to London for the wedding.

When I was on the plane back to London, I realised that I'd had little or nothing to drink in Dublin. And what was more, I hadn't given much thought to the gargle. I'd been too busy building up to what I had to say to Ma and Pops, and then when it was over, I was high enough on the relief I felt, not to need any booze.

Phil was at the airport to meet me, and just seeing her standing there, I knew that I wanted to spend the rest of my life married to her. And from the way she held me, clinging to me like a second skin, I knew that any plans she had for the future were centred around me.

It was so good, so huge, compared to how it had been when I first told her how I loved her, that it seemed impossible I'd been telling her the truth back then. It was some feeling.

Chapter Seven
London. '61

I was drunk the morning I got married. Not falling down drunk, but carrying enough brandy for Theo to have to stop me from dancing up the pathway to the church.

Fortunately I could carry my booze, so that nobody but Theo knew, and he looked after me like a stand-in for W.C. Fields in his morning suit. So that I felt like hugging the lovely nut.

I didn't set out to get high, but when Theo had suggested a few belts to steady the nerves, I didn't give him an argument. To steady the nerves *was* the idea, but by the time this had happened, we were both getting a taste for the stuff and I was feeling more and more pleased I'd asked Theo to be my best man.

I couldn't believe my nerves. Straight! I'd have laughed at somebody else behaving in the same way. Really terrified of the whole scene, and when you remember that this was no shotgun affair, and that I loved Phil and wanted to live with her, it just seemed all the more ridiculous.

Theo had stayed the night with me at the flat in Gordon Avenue. It was the upper half of the small house Phil and I had bought, and it was more than ready to be lived in, if you ignored the lack of carpets and proper curtains. Such things didn't bother me, but Phil considered putting the wedding back until we'd earned the bread to get them. I talked her out of it, gently and with surprising skill, but to be honest, I really felt like laughing at her. This lovely girl who had been willing to marry me "in a Turkish Mosque" or anywhere else that suited me, being bothered about things that didn't matter, was something of a bad joke. But I wasn't honest enough to tell her how bloody stupid I thought it was. I knew it was wrong not to have it out with her, but I didn't think arguing about it was going to cover the floors in Wilton or put curtains on the windows, so I shut up, telling myself that everything would be all right once we settled in, with the world and his wife shut out beyond our front door.

My nervousness did help me understand, suddenly, those fellas who'd split on the bride at the last second. And I could believe that some of them anyway, loved the lady at the moment they shot off for the hills, but that they just hadn't been able to get it together enough to sign on the dotted line.

Up to that morning at the church in Hammersmith, I'd always thought it crazy for a guy to do a thing like that, but without Theo and the heavy brandies he poured, I'm not sure I'd have made it to the altar myself.

The church itself was cold, and running a bad second to any Catholic church, when it came to colour and laying on the statue and the holy picture bit. I liked it better, which didn't mean much and I fell in love with a Psalm about "The Lord is my shepherd". I felt Theo twitching a bit and smiled sideways at him.

"This bothering you, Head?"

"It's all right, just can't stand fucking churches."

"Don't let it get to you. It's all a joke."

He looked back at me, surprise pushing his face out of shape.

"Not me and Phil. This… the mumbo jumbo stroke, and the bits of paper. All ballocks."

"Ah, Holy Jaysus!" Theo protested, looking about furtively in case we were being overheard.

"Just think of it like a lavatory."

His surprise tripped into amazement and he laughed despite himself. "You're pissed," he said.

" If you need to piss you use a jax, right? I need to marry Phil. Here we are, no big deal, just using this place, giving the head a workout with the marriage service… that's all."

Theo shook his head, leaning forward, his arms resting on the seat. "I always thought you were a lunatic," he whispered, "but Jaysus! Now I'm fuckin' certain of it."

The booze also helped soothe my feelings, which were roughed up from the brunt of Old Man Williams' behaviour of the night before. Which had to be a good thing, because I was going to have to see him, and talk to him, and shake his hand, phoney as it had to be, and I would have been hard put to do it without some bevy inside me.

The night before I'd worked the cab until nine o'clock. I'd been putting in something like sixteen hours a day since coming back from Dublin, even refusing to go out on a tear with Theo when he got back from a trip. I'd gone into the house to see Phil, and reassure her that it was going to be all right. She was in a pretty nervous state herself, acting as a kind of buffer between her father and me.

There were a few people in... friends, one or two neighbours, plus Phil's Uncle David and his wife, Sal; two people I was glad to see because they went their own way and didn't give a damn about what the rest of the family thought about them.

Phil took me into a living room, and for a minute as the congratulations rolled out, I was the centre of attention. David shook my hand heartily, and Sal, who was a fine woman, about forty with sexy blonde good looks, kissed me, and told me with meaning, that with Phil I had every chance of leading a charmed and happy life. She and David loved Phil dearly and that guaranteed them a round of applause from me.

The old man was handing drinks out all round, but he made no effort to offer me a glass. Sal's eyes flicked to mine when the slight became obvious. I shrugged casually, trying to show that it didn't matter, that the old boy could go and screw himself for all I cared, when really, I wanted to tell him what a boring uncivilised peasant he was.

"Aren't you drinking, old chap?" David asked me, loud

enough to be heard, without it appearing to be anything other than casual concern that I'd been accidentally overlooked.

The old man looked at me and I hoped my face showed that it didn't matter, that it was all right. I really tried the full Stanislavsky bit, having surrendered my World Heavyweight Title on a bad decision, so bad, that the winner was standing before me, apologising for something that wasn't his fault. "It's all right," I told him, knowing that magnanimity would never be dead while I was alive.

Whether it worked or not, I wasn't doing it for the old man, nor for myself, but for Phil, and for her mother, and the other people in the room. Phil's father and I didn't have to bother kidding around any more. We knew where we were at, and that was it. But I told myself that he was going to have to learn to play the game... he had to start putting up with me as I was willing to endure him, when most of the time I wanted to piss down his shirt front.

You know, people can laugh at the English "upper crust", call them "chinless wonders" and all that bullshit, but when it comes down to good manners, and just being bloody civilised , you have to take your hat off to the sheer sophistication of those people, which most of the time, if you give the thing its proper name, is simply consideration for other people. And that was something that Old Man Williams could have used a crash course in.

"There's beer out in the hall if you want one," he said directly to me with all the charm of a prolapsed rectum.

The break in the "rhubarb" buzz in the room was like an explosion, and I saw Phil go through hell in that fraction of a second. And she couldn't be blamed for thinking I was going to lash back at him. Her mother didn't look too happy either, so I said, as casually as I could: "Thanks, Mr. Williams, but my almost wife has already promised me a cup of tea...."

David, who was Mrs. Williams' younger brother, gave me a "good for you" smile, and out in the kitchen, Phil hugged me with so much gratitude that my ribs complained.

"Oh I love you, I love you, I love you."

I held her at arms length. "And why wouldn't you, girl?" I grinned, delighted that for once I'd kept my big mouth shut... "and me a direct descendent of the Royal Kings of Ireland, the land of saints and scholars... for God's sake, girl!"

Phil kissed me very passionately, and then with her eyes liquid brown and overflowing with relief and love and the sheer shine of wanting, she blessed my face.

"Just tonight, darling." Her breasts rose high, slipping back to normal then on the sigh that escaped her lips.

"Tomorrow night." She shook her head. "Oh Jesus! I mustn't think about it.." She broke away and held the kettle under the tap. My hand shook as I lit my cigarette, but things were all right now.

Phil was excited enough to have forgotten her father for a minute, and I'd had time to get it together. He could do what he liked now and he wouldn't get into me. I had all my routines on the cuff and no one was going to spoil this night for lovely Phil and her mother. But I knew that if I loved forever, I'd never be able to wipe out the memory of how my tomorrow father-in-law had made me feel just a few minutes earlier.

Inside the church, Theo seemed a bit uncomfortable as we waited in the front seat for the Vicar to get his production going. He was a bit fuzzy although he didn't seem to be getting anywhere. There was something nice about him, but I found that anybody who qualified as "a white collar worker" just got up my nose, regardless of his church or denomination.

I meant every word I said to Theo, but I also put my heart behind my promises to cherish Phil. That was something I wanted very badly to be allowed to do and I felt so close to her, as I slipped the gold band onto her finger that I wanted to weep. And I thought my chest was going to explode on me, bellowing my joy, this wondrous, magical will to love the whole world, out and upwards, so that even the birds would hear how my spirit sang.

I was full of splendid sentiment and noble ideas, and determined to love lovely Phil to death. But by the time we got back to the flat, finally alone, the booze was practically spilling out of my ears and my virgin bride found me snoring like a pig when she approached her marriage bed.

Chapter Eight
London. Early '60's

What is this thing called love? Or, nearer the mark, what was the thing I felt for Phil that I called love? How much of it was accounted for by the sheer physical attraction of the glory days of our early married life? When bed was the main course, and the couch and the bath snacks to keep us going until it was time for another full meal?

I don't know for sure, but I feel that if our sex life hadn't been so easy... so natural that we seemed to fly together, from the very first time we made love, returning to this earth spiritually entwined, well, I don't see how our marriage could have lasted longer than it took for the gilt to wear off the gingerbread.

I loved Phil, in that I made love to Phil, and for close on to three years I hardly noticed another woman. I loved Phil by constantly reassuring her that I belonged with her, and around, inside and on top of, and underneath, her. In the way I could hold her so willingly when she was low, when she was ill. I loved her by placing a hot water bottle on her stomach, trying to massage away the agony when menstrual pain sucked her dry, until she was a grey, faded print of the laughing girl who supplied the ribbons of happiness on which my precarious well-being was so infirmly erected.

I loved Phil by appearing with a painting I'd bought from a real live artist in Piccadilly, an impressionistic street scene in Marseilles, executed with a palate knife, and so alive, so warm with colours that would never creak or groan, that she just had to fall in love with it.

I saw wonder glide like a bird across her face, wheeling for a fleeting second into perplexity when her birthday gift turned out to be a pair of opera glasses. I loved her then, by "magic wanding" away her protest that she'd never been to the opera, with the production of two tickets to Covent Garden and "The Tales Of Hoffman", which happily, thanks to the luck of the Irish going full blast for me, we both loved.

But was I loving Phil when I let her father walk all over me verbally, adding to the long list of liberties he'd always taken with me. If it wasn't for Phil and the way I love her, believe me, you old prick, you'd get a roasting that'd blister that asbestos coat you use for a skin.

At the time I felt noble, doing what I did, not saying all I wanted to say, because I wouldn't risk hurting Phil, or her mother, who continued to be kind and decent to me. It just didn't occur to me that I might have been building up a store of ammunition, for use when I would have to go on the defensive, to cloud the issue of a legitimate attack on the same area of my behaviour.

Anyway, regardless of why I didn't attack the old man, I kept on hoping that he would come around, that with time and the obvious signs that I was a hard worker, he'd break down a bit, and if nothing else, wish me well. I couldn't bring myself to like him, but the clear realisation that he couldn't stand my guts, made me need all the more, to make him love me.

I was working hard; we both were, Phil doing a good secretarial job where she was virtually her own boss. I drove the cab days, beginning when I dropped Phil to work at nine, finishing, without having stopped for a lunch break, at about six each weekday.

Weekends, I worked Saturday night, from six until three or four on Sunday morning. Everybody wanted a taxi Saturday night, and people could be very generous when they were in their cups, and you reminded them that they could have a lie in the morning. Sunday, I went out about nine thirty, carrying on until about two o'clock Monday morning, because again, people had to get home after drinking and dancing.

Day work was murder during the week. Honestly, the traffic seemed to increase in density, week by week, so that even when there was plenty of work about, it was ten times harder than it need have been. Ideally, the day should have come on to rain about ten thirty. By this time people were out and about, and the blessed rain drove them to taxis. Whereas if the rain appeared at say, eight o'clock, most people put off their trip into town. Except for those out of town motorists, who came mostly by public transport. Early rain forced them to use the motor, and this helped the traffic jams no end. But, all in all, you could earn top wages for any eight hour shift, starting at any single hour in the twenty-four and regardless of the moans and the complaints, which gradually I was becoming more and more adept at using, you could do this seven days a week, three hundred and sixty-five days a year. If, that is, you wanted to be a cab driver.

About four evenings a week I wrote on a portable typewriter. Phil would sit reading or watching television, while I spent five or six hours in the corner of the huge lounge, trying to find some kind of magic formula to stop the never ending flow of rejection slips.

Within three years I had over one hundred and fifty. Slips of every size, shape and colour.... From the high and mighty publications, all the way to *Reveille* with *The Star* and *The Evening News* turning me down, while they printed stories and articles that were often so bad, I couldn't have got down to such a level, even if I'd been working at it.

I admit that I hadn't studied my market. Which meant that a lot of my rejections could have been avoided. I mean, it was just plain stupid to send *The Sunday Times* something that was suitable for *Titbits* and vice versa. But that was something I didn't get wise to for quite a while.

My all-time personal low, was a letter from Raphael Tuck & Sons Ltd., for some Christmas card verse I'd submitted, but the fact that even something as horrific as this didn't stop me, helped me realise that if nothing else, I was a compulsive writer. Which made things easier, because I no longer had any choice about giving up my dreams of being a writer, and making a real go of the taxi business.

I wasn't too happy writing in longhand. The words seemed to come alive easier when I typed them. So, with some tips from Phil and a marvellous book "Teach Yourself Typing", I learned to touch type in one long sitting of ten hours. I know it sounds like bullshit, but it was something I badly wanted to do and I discovered in myself a sense of application I wouldn't have thought possible in the sort of mercurial character I was. But I was forgetting the year of riding the bicycle "on the knowledge", and let's face it, if you can come through that scene without loosing your marbles, you can do just about anything.

Phil and I didn't go out very much so that most of my drinking was done at home. Beer as a rule, carried home from the off-licence on Fulham Palace Road, with only the odd party or late night poker session, when we did go through a fair amount of whiskey.

Paddy Darcy was married and living in Putney. His wife, Mary, was some kind of angel. A beautiful, raven haired, Irish girl, with a keen and often wicked, sense of humour, and the patience of Methuselah. Darcy hadn't changed one little bit... still loving a gamble, and shifting more than his share of booze, and with Theo now permanently shoreside you can see we had the makings of a card school for lunatics with nobody likely to object to a drop of the hard tack. Provided it was a drop in the bottom of a bucket.

Darcy was still the best cocktail barman I'd ever seen and regardless of what he was like outside his work, he took his job very seriously. Even after an all night session of poker and whiskey, he'd shave with my razor, borrow a clean shirt, and get into town in time to open his bar. And he was something to observe when he worked. Drinks appeared as though out of his sleeve and the bullshit flowed from his Blarney Stone heart, yet without even having to think about it, he knew when to play things cool. He had built in traffic lights... some kind of reliable warning system that never allowed him to stray over the top. Except when he was off duty and drinking, and then, my Jesus, he could go from sweet to mean, without pausing for breath, and Theo had me agreeing with him when he said: "That crotchety little bastard could start a row in a confession box."

Darcy's heart may have been "Black Irish" a lot of the time, but whenever Phil or I needed him, it was then that we saw what the word "friend" was all about. He could give of himself with a generosity that startled you, but you could never let him see that you were grateful, or that you cared for him. When he was embarrassed, his evil and often sadistic sense of humour would whip around on you, and he'd have you believing that you were after money or something. Which, he'd warn you, he wouldn't give. I used to smile when he got like that. Darcy wouldn't give you anything, except his life's blood.

Theo was land-based and living in Fulham, down off North End Road. He was more of a loner than before, and though he had a steady job in a club in St. James Street, he somehow seemed to be still drifting. He didn't do anything except drink and go to the movies, and have a slice off the legs when he needed to. And I mean when he needed to, because Theo was too lazy to go after a chick just for the exercise or the fun. Phil often said he was just more adult than we'd all been, over in Jersey, and I disagreed with her about this. I tried not to let her see that I was actually hot under the collar about it, not wanting her to know that I resented Theo not using his freedom the way I would have done, if I'd been free.

But Phil and I didn't disagree very much about anything, most of the time she went along with what I thought, which was easy and convenient. But after a time this began to bug me badly. I didn't like Phil burying her ballsy personality, but that was pretty much what seemed to be happening.

One thing we did have some words about was her father's Freemasonry. My reaction to his bullshit about how marvellous it was was predictable. I said nothing to him, but to Phil I scoffed at the whole idea. Jackie, who in my eyes was a great guy, was also a "Mason", but it never got between him and me.

His father preached a bit, to me anyway, going on so much that I wanted to tell him they were nothing but a bunch of boy scouts in long trousers, whereas Jackie appreciated his "Mason" connection and what they could do for him, apart from which I don't think he ever mentioned it in my company.

Again, my emotional bit was responsible for most of the disdain in my attitude to Freemasonry. I hated going to their lodge dinners, occasions at the end of each year to give thanks to "their ladies" for allowing them so much time to attend meetings and a lot of other functions that were a good excuse for a stag night out.

I thought the whole thing was a joke and right or wrong, I let some of my feelings show. But I went to their boring dinners, listened to a lot of bullshit that meant nothing to me, having eaten a meal that was usually pretty rough by London standards. I mean, in Ireland I expected the food to be lousy most of the time. Which is fair enough when you consider that the Irish don't know how to cook vegetables, particularly the "national fruit": potatoes, and that they have a hang-up about serving good beef unless they have first of all burned it to a frazzle. But in London I expected good nosh and usually got it, though never in my experience at those Masonic dinners. It was card service, waitress dealing out plates of this and that with the kind of chronic boredom that practically guaranteed you the wrong kind of start to any evening.

I tried, and really mean it, to be easy and just have a good time. I was attentive to Phil, wanting them all to see that I loved her, and that she was everything to me.

Fuck it! If I had to be there let the peasants appreciate me.

A lousy attitude, I know, especially as most of those people were good and kind and more than decent. But there were a lot of fuzz in Freemasonry, the kind of social climbing policeman who made me want to vomit if we got within three feet of each other. And I gave them no time at all, though a lot of them wanted to know me simply because Old Man Williams was my father in law, and he was a big deal in one way or another.

I always drank too much at those affairs, and though I could carry my booze, things were getting worse each function I attended. But Christ, the fawning that went on, nice people practically genuflecting before some guy who just happened to be in a position of power. I've seen men, some men, Christ! ...stand by smiling self-consciously, while another prick was pawing his wife, like, insulting both parties and practically getting a round of applause for doing so.

So for one reason or another, it became more difficult for me to go along. If I mentioned that to Phil, she'd point out that she didn't make many demands on my time. Which was fair enough. She didn't make any demands on my time because she didn't have to... when I wasn't out on the cab, I was with her, even if several evenings I was working in the far corner of the room. She was upset by even the merest objection to going... we'd kick the thing back and forth and I would finally capitulate, but not before I'd taken the edge off her evening's enjoyment. On the other hand, when I didn't mention it, I had to go into an act. I resented having to do this with my own wife, so I'd just award myself a medal for good behaviour, which entitled me to get well and truly pissed, and dance with any stray bird I fancied. This humiliated Phil and probably guaranteed for all time that I'd never feature on her father's Christmas cards list.

It was all right, legal even, for me to dance with Jackie's wife, Val. Which I enjoyed doing... she could dance and she had no hang-ups about pressing her lovely body nice and close. But because I was going to enjoy dancing with Val, I used to go through my "guilt routine" which involved dancing with Phil's mother, who was incredibly light on her feet for such a big woman, and just about every other woman at the table.

Jackie used to make me smile. I mean, he might do this "last waltz" chore with his wife, but he never volunteered for anything more than this, though occasionally he would yield to Phil's persistent request for a dance. No matter what, those two people loved each other, and it never failed to do my heart good to see it.

Val and I got along, and I know a lot of the good feeling between us was caused by our common position of being outside the scene. She liked my sense of humour and I was a good dancer. She was crazy about Jackie, and I was often glad of this, because she turned me on in a way that could have created all kinds of problems. Like, the way she felt about Jackie, prevented me making any serious passes at her, but I knew that despite my liking for Phil's brother, I'd have loved to give her one. Which, I regret to say, I never did.

Val then was the first woman I'd wanted, apart from my wife, and though the thought didn't lead to anything, it wasn't long before the ideas of the same kind were flashing in and out of my mind. And still I did nothing about them. Phil was everything to me... no matter how stupid I could be. I loved her, and though many a day I resented being so tied down, I kept it to myself, and made vow after vow, that I'd never pull another bird.

I remember discussing the whole "bird thing" with a big cabbie I'd got to know in the Bell and Horn's Shelter facing Brompton Oratory. This was a cabbies' resting place, a pull in, quick service eaterie, where the food was good and the prices not over the odds. And I can still see O'Casey, with his bland Irish face, nodding his head, like a fella thinking, "give it time, old son, give it time."

"All I'd say to you, Paddy, is, well, when it does happen...."

"It won't," I assured him, with the kind of vehemence

peculiar to the insecure.

"When it does happen..." he insisted... "just forget it... don't let it get into you... it's just a piece of pussy, after all."

"No way," I protested. "I've done it all. My bird is too good. I... Jesus, I just couldn't do it."

"I believe you," he smiled, "but what I'm saying is, just in case, all right?"

I let it go at that and I went with Herb O'Casey for a drink. It was a Saturday night, but things were quiet, and a few drinks weren't going to hurt anybody.

Chapter Nine

I enjoyed Phil's pregnancy long before she did, but then I wasn't tearing my insides out with chronic morning sickness. Which is how it was for the first few months, with me feeling pretty helpless, holding her over the sink when she needed me, making tea and trying not to hear what she was going through when she wanted to be left alone.

Once she got over "the early morning retch", as I called it, Phil started to bloom like a flower opening itself up to the first sun of Spring. And I was so proud of my laughing girl, and of me. She was as big as a house; but I took her everywhere, and made more fuss of her than I'd ever done before.

Phil was what you might call a late starter, like she didn't really come alive until about noon, whereas I woke up singing, bouncing out onto the floor, sorry, the fitted carpet, and I always made the first cup of tea. It wasn't any kind of big deal to me, but as I came to realise what a cup of tea in bed meant to Phil, I began to feel noble about the whole thing.

I thought of Jennie many times in those days, remembering how she floated through the pregnancy scene, happier than she'd ever been, and wanting to make love all the time. I tried not to wonder how she was. What was the use? Had she got another fella? I didn't want to even think about that... but I did hope that the show was going well and that she didn't think too badly of me. What a joke. Walk all over them and expect them to carry a torch till the day they die.

Phil's mother was up in the air about the baby. She was already a grandmother (Jackie and Val had a three month old girl, Lisa, who was something of a doll baby). They planned to have lots more children and Mrs. Williams loved the big family trick. Phil and I were thinking in terms of two or three children, but it remained to be seen how she was going to feel after our son was born.

Mrs. Williams was convinced we would have a girl. I didn't pay her much heed. Our first baby would be a son! It was the way I wanted it and that was the way it was going to be. But as the Grannie Maguire used to say: "Whatever it is yiz won't be sendin' it back..." and nothing was more certain than that.

One thing I couldn't make up my mind about was whether Cassidy – my son was going to have Sean O'Casey's surname as his Christian name – was going to be the Heavyweight Champion of the World, or the greatest soccer centre forward since Tommy Lawton. It was some problem, I'll tell you.

I was having other problems too. Like, not saying "it was a real pleasure" when Phil's father finally condescended to congratulate me about the baby. And in fighting not to eat my typewriter as the rejection slips continued to stink out the mailbox. Apart from which my tenant on the ground floor was turning into a real ball breaker.

I'd bought the house with the "sitting tenant" firmly entrenched, and I'd never, in any way, tried to give her a hard time. Had she not lived there, the house would have cost me twice what it did, in which case I wouldn't have been living there. Her rent was minimal, like, under two pounds a week, but it paid the rates, which was a help, and seeing how apprehensive she was when I first met her... the previous owners had, according to herself, given her a very hard time... this wasn't my way, particularly as she was a widow, and I told her so. Going on to say that I would be decorating the hallway which we both used to get in and out, and that I would be painting the house front and back just as soon as I could make time. All of which I meant, and had carried out within a year. By which time she was starting to make demands, which though they were legal enough, were an imposition in relation to how the place had been before I'd moved in. But that seems to be the way people are... You try and give a fair crack of the whip, for no reason other than you want to be fair, and before long you know that those same people have made the age old error of mistaking consideration for weakness. So I began to be told that this was wrong and that something else wasn't right, until I had a pain in my face.

I did many jobs that she could have done herself, and as her boyfriend was a tradesman and not just a willing amateur like me, I felt I was being cheated even though she was within her rights. And the next thing I knew she was expecting me to put in a bathroom, or at least a shower closet.

Remembering that my writing was being rejected at a rate fierce enough to give Orson Wells an inferiority complex, that I was sick and tired of pushing the cab around, that my wife was pregnant, that my father-in-law bugged me almost out of my mind, and that I was drinking more than I should. Also I was feeling even more guilty for being deceitful about it to Phil. Well, I think it might have been forgiven for hitting the lady tenant with some extra heavy verbal. But I didn't. I kept my mouth shut and went to the council offices to see exactly where I stood.

In just a few minutes I discovered that if I put in a bath or shower for my tenant, Mrs. King, and I got her to agree to pay a two or three shillings a week increase in rent to help pay something towards the cost, that this arrangement constituted a new agreement, which meant that the lady would no longer be protected by the rent act, and that I could ask her to leave any time I liked. Which wouldn't have crossed my mind if she hadn't been bugging me with her constant petty demands on my slender reserve of patience.

I wasn't obliged to do anything about the bathroom, and I told Mrs. King this, but I said I'd think about it, that if I ran into any money I'd do what I could, warning her that it might mean a slight increase in the rent. She nodded, accepting this as being fair, and I felt like a prize shit as I walked upstairs to my own place.

When I told Phil the score, she was silent for about a minute. I watched her draw smoke deep into her lungs, exhaling before she shrugged and said: "It's up to you Maguire, whether you decide."

I felt like slapping her face. Not for putting the ball into my court, but because she hadn't just rejected out of hand even the suggestion of what was in my mind. I hear myself laugh, nervous, shaken at discovering something I didn't like.

"You wouldn't mind if I conned the old girl - give her a bath, to get her out."

"She's not our responsibility," Phil said, in such a matter of fact way, that I went cold.

"But she would be out of her home...."

"Let the council find her somewhere...."

"But supposing they wouldn't?"

"They always do, when they have to...." She got up and took another cigarette. I lit one up myself. I was in need of something.

"These people, Pads... they're all the same...." She smiled a little kindness my way...." They never think about tomorrow...."

"These people?" I needed to yell at her but I kept my voice under control. "What's that supposed to mean? She's the same as us... well, me, anyway.... "I stood up and walked to the window. She works for her living, just like me."

Phil sat down as I turned to look at her. "I'm getting heavy as a pig." She rubbed her leg. "You're not going all Socialist on me, are you?"

"Come on now," I grinned. "You know bloody well I'm a Socialist at heart."

"Never mind your heart for a minute." She stopped. "You don't like me very much, do you?"

"I love you out of my fucking mind, you bitch," I said.

"But you don't like me. It's all right... Socialism can't work, you know that?" I didn't say anything, more than half afraid she was right, but unwilling to admit it.

"The idea's good, Pads, but England falls apart under a Socialist government, just look at public transport when they nationalized it."

"So a few tubes arrived late. Come on."

"As we are now, we're encouraging layabouts to stay home... with enough kids and national assistance, they get more money for staying in bed... I mean, it's sick joke."

"That's ridiculous bloody example, Phil, I'm sorry."

"Well, you know what I mean and there's a lot of other things - just go into any of the new council estates... see the new cars. All kinds, belonging to people living in council flats...."

"They pay rent."

"Not the point. I know some of them pay as much rent as we pay mortgage on this house. The point is, they don't want the responsibility of the house - rates, repairs, anything... like Mrs. King...."

"I'm not with you."

"Well, don't you think she could have bought this house?"

"Maybe she didn't have any money."

"She would have got it cheaper than we did, as a sitting tenant. She could have got help from the council. The money involved wasn't a lot."

"It'd be a lot to somebody without any money."

"She's got a few hundred, that's all she'd have needed. The point is, she didn't want the responsibility... none of them do... they want a free ride if they can get it."

"That's a pretty wild generalization."

"Which means, and I'm not ignoring your remark, which means, that she is not your responsibility, so if you want to get her out, do it any way you can."

"And if I don't?"

"Well, you brought it up, I just assumed."

"Forget it," I said.

"You're mad at me."

I didn't speak.

"I'm sorry if I've disappointed you, Pads... I can't help believing in man mind thyself...." She smiled, lovely to look at even if her politics were right wing enough to hurt...."Man mind thyself, and thy wife who loves you, and thy unborn baby."

"Fuck it!" I said, tasting the disgust of my own lousy luck... I mean, why did a thing like that have to come up? Who needed to have to consider whether she should behave like ... Oh Christ, who wanted to make decisions?

I walked over and knelt down before Phil, laying my head on her stomach.

"If he's punching, Pads, you'll get your boxing champion, but if those are kicks, he'll be another Johnnie Haynes."

I looked up at her, moving up then to kiss her mouth.

"Tommy Lawton..." I said. "And by the way, I love you so much, I have kicks and punches inside my stomach, too."

"Coming out in sympathy... all you men are the same...."

We cuddled gently together... I was so afraid of hurting Phil that she had to keep reminding me she wouldn't break. And when I worried about making love to her she said very calmly: "If I weren't suppose to, the doctor would have said... beside which, nature would have made it impossible...."

"You have it all worked out, haven't you?"

"I'm just brighter than I look, that's all."

The doorbell rang and I went to get it, hoping we weren't having visitors. It was Mrs. King, with a registered letter for me.... She'd taken it in earlier. I thanked her and said goodnight, and I went back upstairs trying not to feel too grateful to her.

Chapter Ten

Parnassus Publications, Paris, France, were offering me six hundred dollars advance royalty, for a story of mine called "Hell Gets Warmer". Jesus! Phil and me... we danced around the room, leaping and howling like a couple of lunatics with hot chestnuts in their knickers.

Six hundred dollars. How much was that? I couldn't think, and Phil, who was a wizard with the adding and subtracting touch, had to sit down before she could work it out. It was near enough two hundred and twenty pounds, and it was only an advance against sales. God! I might make a fortune if the book took off. I mean, look what happened to Peyton Place!

What can I tell you about the book? If you could call it a book. Well, with the title like "Hell Gets Warmer" you could obviously forget shades of Joyce, and you might be forgiven for expressing the opinion that Steinbeck and the likes of Graham Greene hadn't got too much to start sweating about.

But it was a book all the same, and even though I'd used a pen name I got a terrific charge that somebody was willing to pay me real bread to publish it. Not any kind of fortune, but enough to suggest that the guy thought I could write, or that I could sell... something!

I'd written the thing, start to finish, in ten days. About fifty thousand words of pure, unadulterated bullshit. It had a strong enough plot line though, with some colourful characters, and more bad jokes than Max Miller could have used in two years.

It happened because of a letter I'd read in one of those literary magazines. The guy who ran Parnassus had written that he'd be happy to consider manuscripts from young English writers, so I decided to have a go, despite being Irish.

The head's name was Jammet, and he made it clear that he preferred material on the risqué side. So, like entering a talent contest, I sat down and pounded out my two hundred pages, without making so much as one character sketch, and it never occurred to me to rewrite one line. Not very professional, right? But somehow I wasn't bothered. Expecting another rejection anyway, and really trying to think about it as a good exercise in discipline.

When you thought about it, it had to be like a talent contest, because London is always full of guys trying to write. And they all read the kind of paper the letter appeared in. Well maybe they don't read it, but they buy it the way they do the Sunday Times and the Observer, and they walk on home with one or the other wrapped around the News of the World or the Sunday Mirror, or whichever paper they buy for the hand gallop material.

I always thought that those great newspapers, the Sunday Times and the Observer, were doing more damage to the book trade and the theatre, not to mention the cinema, than the entertainment world could stand.

I mean, think of all those pseudo-intellectual types, and the way they rush home to read the reviews, never, or very rarely, buying the bloody books. And how often did I hear them bullshitting about a certain play, when every word; appreciation of criticism; was a direct steal from a review by Hobson or Kenneth Tynan. Not that I had any time for critics. I know I wouldn't pay too much attention to a fella who couldn't get a hard on, were he to start telling me how to go about getting laid.

Anyway, Jammet and his Parnassus Publications had taken on an enormous responsibility, because whether the book was good or bad, whether it sold or it didn't, they had given me enough encouragement to ensure that I'd go on scourging editors and publishers and what have you, for the rest of my life. For which in time they may be forgiven. But I wouldn't give any long odds on that.

When I sent the contract back, I mentioned to Jammet that I had another book featuring the same hero, if he was interested in reading it. Back came his reply saying "send it on". But not quite so long as "Hell Gets Warmer". I dropped him a note I'd be through in about two weeks, and then with Phil's full agreement, I took eight days off the cab and hammered out another purple-piece called "The Corps Just Stood There".

It ran to one eighty pages on the same lines as previous joke and again, any sex that was in it somehow ended up comically. I wasn't under the impression that I'd just pulled this out of space, after some guy had chased the bird around the room and he finally threw her on the bed and hurled himself down on top of her, the bed collapsed or the floor caved in, so that if the guy did ever get laid, well, he deserved one of Audie Murphy's cast-off Purple Hearst.

The contract came back within a few weeks, exactly the same as before, and I signed it, keeping my copy, and posted it back fast, just in case Jammet changed his mind. The first one was close to being published and my lovely Phil was getting nearer delivery time. And I was finding it impossible to push the cab around. My heart was at home on the typewriter and to say that life was just unbearable was sad, but true.

It's crazy, I know, but that was just how I felt, and hard though I tried, I just couldn't seem to snap out of my depression. I acted desperately okay around Phil, not wanting my mood to rub off on her. She had her own problems and I didn't want to add to them. Apart from which, I was scared white that I'd alienate some little part of her affection. I couldn't risk that happening, because I seemed to need Phil more and more, and I had no hang-up about admitting it.

I wanted to talk to her about how I was feeling, maybe get her to help me sort myself out, but I felt so bloody stupid, ridiculous, that I couldn't bring it up. She was within a week of her confinement, naturally enough she was a bit scared, and though I felt like a yellow-headed pimple, I wasn't about to plant myself on her backside. Besides, I'd no reason to be moaning and feeling hard done by.

Sure I had rejection slips coming in, but I was about to be paid over four hundred pounds for under a months work, which after years of constant rejection slips, could hardly be a bad thing.

The main trouble was cabbing. yet when I asked myself in all honesty, what the hell was wrong with the job, I could only come up with shit like, the traffic, and it can get a bit lonely, or, I'm just a bloody delivery boy, except that instead of delivering groceries, I deliver people.

All bullshit when you weighed it up against the fact that I could work, or not work, when I liked, that I could earn in two full long days more than most men could in a week, and that I was learning something about life and about people, every time I took a cab out on the streets of London.

I'd met Ted Connor in the cab, and he'd been good to me from the first time I'd taken him up on his offer to have a drink in the pub he ran on Fulham Road. And it wasn't just for the fact that he never stopped reminding me how lucky I was to have a taxi badge, with the kind of freedom that a cabbie could enjoy. I mean, I could stop any time I liked - go for a meal or a drink or whatever, and if things were bugging me badly, I could just pack up for the day without getting a hard time from anybody.

Ted Connor wanted to be a writer, but his job was too demanding for a fella who wanted to be part of the Chelsea scene, and keep a wife and kids fed and happy at the same time. But Ted encouraged me like nobody else ever had, and I was only glad whenever I got the chance to show him that I was a real friend to him too.

Mind you, while he was good for me, going into his pub was probably the biggest mistake I ever made up to that time in my life. It was an Irish pub, really, but it attracted all sorts and all nationalities, with a lot of artists using it as their local. And I mean artists, not the phoneys who got down around the Kings Road, making like they were artists just to impress the upper crust ravers who went looking for a bit of bohemianism and a tear up in a glorious, flea-ridden scratcher. "It's so quaint dahling, fucking amongst the paintpots." Yak!

The trouble with Connor's pub was that it attracted too many tasty birds. The real and hard working artists I came to know were warm, colourful people who went for a pint or a glass of Schluck, without having bothered to change out of their working clothes, and the birds were around them like flies around a fartcake. The odd one started coming on to me and remembering the state I was in, I was put to the seam of my Y-Fronts to remember I was a married man with a strong urge to remain so.

I began dropping into Ted's pub at lunch time, just for one drink with a sandwich. A bottle of Guinness was the idea, but, Christ, how many afternoons did I stay there through closing time, talking and laughing, and kidding myself that I was having a good time, when inside I was blistered with guilt for drinking during my cabbing day, and for not having the guts to mention it to Phil.

I switched to night work then, and for the first few hours, I'd push the cab around brilliantly, and if I ran into a real streak of luck I'd work non-stop for seven or eight hours. But most evenings I'd drop into the pub for one, and still be there at closing time. Not pissed, because I did watch my intake, I had to. With a few hours of work time still left to me, the easy time for a cabdriver, the traffic is not heavy, apart from the odd bunch up in Soho, but those hours were murderous.

Murderous because I had to try and make up for the time I'd spent in the pub, and this wasn't taking into account the money I'd spent on the booze. Often I'd go through two pounds and if I was there three hours, this left me five or six hours behind, I mean, if you weren't taking a pound an hour, you might as well have driven the cab up your arse.

The upkeep of a London taxi is high and apart from what you needed to earn, you had to make some kind of decent return to the owner if you wanted to go on driving a decent cab. You could always get an old banger, but doing a night's work on something that wasn't in the best of shape was too hard for somebody who wasn't an active masochist.

Of course, regardless of the many guys I came to like in Ted's pub, it was the birds that drew me back there again and again, and its only jazz to say otherwise. But I wasn't making any time with any of them, which, as it often does, made some of them come on to me like I was the only man on the island.

As I felt more and more the need to get tucked up with one of them, I drank a bit more to drive it from my mind. Which often resulted in me not going out on the cab at all. But I'd go home, telling myself that I was a good guy not to have given one to that blonde, or that redhead with the long legs, and every other variation on this kind of bullshit. But next evening I'd be back in the pub, talking to the same birds, indulging in the same word games, fencing against the same equivocal chatter, basking in the same egotistical bell sound that had cost me my night's work, and a shred of my self-respect, the night before.

I was helpless, like a kid in a toy store, knowing I wasn't allowed every toy in the shop, but hanging around in the hope that somehow I could have my cake and eat it.

Chapter Eleven

My son turned out to be a daughter, coming into my life in September, sixty three, the time nine o'clock in the morning of the twenty first, and if I ever forget how I felt when I first saw Kate, my brain will have turned wet and I'll spend the rest of my life looking at the wall.

Kate was just over twenty inches long, brown as a nut, with a fine, soft down covering her from head to toes. Her tiny head was perfect, symmetrical to an unbelievable degree, and it was difficult to accept that this little dome had withstood something like ninety pounds of pressure per square inch when just a few hours before, Phil had pushed her first born out into the Princess Beatrice Hospital.

I went to Phil and kissed her again. She looked pale, and under her eyes she had dark, grey pouches, but the eyes themselves were smiling, and all in all, Phil looked just a bit like the cat who'd got the cream.

"She's something else, kid, beautiful."

Phil's eyebrows jerked fractionally and she smiled.

"What about me?" she asked.

"You?" I pursed my lips and slipped into my Harley Street voice. "Yes... well, Mrs. Maguire, in view of your prompt delivery I want you back in the labour room ten months from today...."

Phil started to say something, stopped herself, then hooked the index finger of her right hand to draw me closer.

"Get stuffed, Maguire," she whispered.

I drew my head back, playing surprised. "Why, Mrs. Maguire..." I stopped, half choking and just not able to fool around. "I love you."

"No tears are allowed to visitors," Phil warned me, dead pan voice, touching my face with her hand. I sniffed.

"Are you all right?" she said, wife-mother that she was.

"Course I'm all right... me? The descendant of the Royal Kings of Ireland?"

As it happened, I was far from being all right. I had a hangover you could have painted if you got it to stand still long enough, and I felt lousy, crippled with guilt for pissing our money away while Phil was in the labour ward.

"Been drinking, Pads?" She made it sound like a question but the knowledge in her eyes turned it into a statement.

"Have I been drinking? Maybe I haven't... God, gallons of the bloody stuff...." I grinned down at Phil, trying to confuse her, make her believe that I was bullshitting, that I'd just had a few, when the amount I mentioned wasn't all that far from the truth.

"I could do it with a gin and tonic myself..." Phil said.

"Could I go out and bring one in?"

"Better not, Maguire, much as I'd like it, fussy people running this place... kind, capable, but Jesus, fussy fuss fuss."

I nodded. "I'll have a couple for you, later on."

"Bastard!" Phil hissed, changing gear then as she got my meaning. "You're not working tonight?"

"Believe it," I promised, "tonight I'm going to get twisted."

"Jesus!" Phil pretended to complain, happy somehow, by just knowing what I was going to be up to. "What it must be, being a man."

"Keep in touch," I suggested. "If I ever make it, I'll let you know what it's like."

She smiled, well aware I wasn't the most mature fella in West London, but I knew she preferred not to think about it.

"Jennifer is with me, kid... all right for her to come in?"

Phil hesitated and I said. "She's been very good, means well."

Phil nodded. "She's all right. I'm just a bit fractured, that's all."

"It'll just be for a minute," I promised.

Jennifer was my brother Tommy's wife. Tommy and Billy were both in London now, and thanks to me striking oil, like decent wages, they were both cab drivers. Tommy wasn't my kind of people, though we looked just a bit alike, and Billy was turning out to be a real toothache. His wife, Olive, was okay, kind and considerate to everybody except Billy. Jennifer was a sweetheart, warm and tolerant to a point where I often felt like shaking her. We got along well, and if I was her favourite brother-in-law, it wasn't any kind of big deal, though it seemed to travel up brother Tommy's nose.

What really drove the wedge between Tommy and me, at least as far as I could make out, was a little more than his missus thinking I was a good guy. I'd helped him get started on the long haul out of the financial hole in which he'd been floundering forever. He resented me, his younger brother, for being in a position to help him… It wasn't his fault, he wanted to be grateful, but Tommy just couldn't bring himself to do something as simple as express a word of thanks. And it's no lie to say he felt the world owed him something. So, he had his scars just like the rest of us.

Billy was something else again, and somehow incapable of taking half a look inside himself. He was sincere, hard working and filled with a determination to get on, but he hadn't grown one inch in his mind.

He had a surface intelligence that could have been developed, but he was too self-centred to notice that he was standing still, too busy talking about his problems, most of them nonexistent. A well meant word was so often taken as criticism, and Billy was paranoid about anything even close to this. Though he was forever asking advice, what he really wanted was approval. This led to a bad row between us a few days before, which in itself would have been worthwhile if it had helped him change in any small way. But it didn't change anything…. It never had, and I was telling myself that I was no longer interested enough to wonder if it ever would.

It was terrible, but I continually found myself feeling sorry for Billy, and if he'd known that, Christ, it would have been punch up time. But I loved him, even if his "death warmed up" expression got on my wick, while the drawn-out sigh that slithered out of him on the tail of every sentence left me boiling with frustration. Like, Billy could make "Oh, all right" sound like the prelude to the wave of goodbye from an octogenarian whose new overcoat was going to be tailored in pine.

Tommy was less successful at "The brotherly love" stroke than I was, because mates of mine who had never met him before would say to me after we'd left Tommy, "Christ, does that guy hate you, brother or not." I didn't worry too much about it. Tommy didn't like many people, and right from the sale of my first book, he was kind of green with envy, and usually managed to make my little bits of success sound like the luck of a fella who'd won the pools without even sending in a coupon.

The night Kate was born, I ended up at a party in Redcliffe Road and I drank enough to blister my stomach. I was trying to knock myself out, because I needed to pull a bird but I didn't want to be unfaithful to Phil.

The booze didn't help me out. At midnight I was flying happily instead of being stretched, and I got such a show from a lovely and really nubile art student called Sue something, that I just couldn't keep my hands off her.

She didn't care at all that I was married, and she thought it was perfectly natural that we should end up in bed on the night my first child was born. I didn't want her talking like that... I couldn't get used to it... like, she was reminding me of what I was doing, when all I wanted to do was do it and not think about it or talk about it. So I worked harder than I'd intended, and after a little while any words she gave me were just signposts of encouragement to help me out as I took her with me over the jumps.

I loved what happened between that Sue and me, wallowing in every second of the glorious time she handed me, once I stopped her talking. But in the morning I couldn't so much as look at myself in the bathroom mirror. And it was hard work to talk to Sue who had that rare gift of being a sweetheart in the mornings. The truth was that. I needed a few bevys to give me a lift and help me get rid of the guilt and the remorse and the shakes, mental and physical, that were giving me a very hard time.

So I was drinking to get over the shakes, pissed or high enough to be insulated from guilt, by the time this happened, then hungry for another bit of *romance*; Jesus! And telling myself all the time that I should be working, that I had to earn bread to keep the scene going at home, that I would, I would get out to work, just one more for the road and I'd be off. Of God, the ability I had to kid myself blind.

Not feeling so bad about it at the christening of Kate, simply because I didn't believe in all that water on the head bit, didn't want it for my daughter, but, sure, wasn't I a real sweetheart, to go along with it for my wife's sake, she not wanting to hurt her mother and father. Her mother believed in the whole bit, and if her father didn't give a damn, he had to be seen to go along with his wife, allowing this little bit of leeway, just to show that he wasn't as hard as people made him out to be.

Somehow working the cab then for a few weeks. Staying out of Connor's pub, a bit like a fella off the booze for the seven weeks of Lent, then feeling that I deserved a present in the shape of a large brandy and a nice pair of legs or boobs, for the heroic effort of the few weeks before. And all I'd been doing was what normal people, with their feet on the ground, did every week of the year.

My daughter Kate clung like a magnetic blanket to part of my heart, keeping an area of me warm, regardless of how I was feeling in general. And again luck walked arm in arm with me, because lousy husband though I might have been; I couldn't help being, a full-time father.

The reason I harp on about luck, well, Christ, what else could it be, when I could use my upbringing on The Hill to help me be a better father, remember the screaming and the fighting; would I ever forget it? See Ma's eyes, wild with fury as she hurled a teapot of boiling water at Pops, hear the grunt of pain tear out of him as he hurled a small axe at her, destroying one side of the old wardrobe, as Ma, with a fleet footed movement surprising in a women of her size, easily avoided his effort to kill one half of the source of the malignant antipathy that coughed its way up out of frustration, to destroy whatever modicum of peace the world in which we lived might allow us, if we stepped carefully along the path designated to us by fate and made certain to remember our place.

Because of this, all of this, and more that need never be said, I had a hang-up about ever hurting or frightening a child, in even the smallest way. Children had to be protected from the self indulgence of adults, or children who called themselves adults, simply because they had the size and the years usually associated with the full grown muscle. Children had to be loved, and warmed, and cosseted, spoiled even, and they had to be handled gently, tenderly with love and devotion, guided with sensitive, willing hands, encouraged to rise, rather than be lifted up when they fell down. Made to feel secure at all times. And in this I felt I succeeded, though I wasn't any great shakes in a lot of other ways.

The first book had arrived, six copies of it, from Paris, and the initial bang at seeing something I'd written in print, was only slightly soured by the fact that my name wasn't on the cover. And I found myself wondering why I'd put a pen name on the thing? Again, valid or not, I put the responsibility on Ma... not wanting to hurt her by sticking the moniker on a sexy book... but was it that? I don't know... it hardly matters.

I was working hard at the typewriter and being hurt more than ever by the rejection slips. I had a book. Good or bad, I had a book, two hundred odd pages, to my credit, and I was having my balls broken still by every bloody outlet I tried. Surely they weren't reading the damn stuff... they couldn't have been, they were sending it back so rapidly and so consistently. Christ, they couldn't have been reading it.

My cabbing was going from bad to worse, and I was suffering badly... from the night I snapped alive, sitting behind the wheel of the cab outside my house. It was dark, three in the morning according to my strap watch. And I had no memory of driving the cab home. I checked the figures on the clock... I'd got twenty-six jobs on there, and something like eighty-four miles travelled since I'd gone out at six... I remembered going into Connor's pub at a quarter to nine... I'd been chatting to Ken Johnson, a painter I cared about from Canada. I remember a couple of birds, they'd been in the bar a few times. We'd had a few jars, but it ended right there. So whatever had happened was a blank... bad enough if it had been just a question of drink some more and maybe going back to Ken's place with the chicks.... But it wasn't that simple. I'd only done twelve jobs on the cab before I stopped for that quarter to nine break, so that after I'd left the boozer, I'd somehow driven fourteen different fares to wherever they wanted to go.... And I couldn't have picked any one of them out of a line up, not if my life had depended upon it. Jesus God! What was happening to me? Was I losing my mind?

I got out of the cab, shaky and cold. There wasn't a dent anywhere on the great, square, beetled, black body. So I hadn't hit anything, or, good Jesus! anybody. I broke into a cold sweat at the thought. I could have had a bad crash, killed some poor bastard trying to cross the road even, and I wouldn't have been able to confirm or deny it... I closed my front door quietly behind me and padded up the stairs as quietly as I could... I was sick to the pit of my stomach, terrified to the roots of my hair at the loss of control over my life. I wanted to weep, be held firmly, made to feel I wasn't all bad... I needed my wife, wanted her in every way. But I went into the lounge and flopped on the couch. I felt sick and sad and dirty, and I couldn't hold her when I was that way. She was good and pure and I just wouldn't risk contaminating her. I loved her too much to let her hear my heart cry out. God help me!

Chapter Twelve

Phil had started fighting with me about money. I usually earned enough to keep the scene ticking over, but rarely was there anything left for the things you don't plan for. Like, new clothes, additional bits of furniture, replacement of breakages, wedding and birthday presents, not to mention the Christmas gift trick, which really could hurt you in the folding money.

She also thought I drank too much, but she was the first to admit that I scarcely ever got drunk. At which I would grin and point out that if I was overdoing it, wouldn't I be pissed out of my mind as a result?

"I didn't say you're drunk all the time," Phil would apologise, checking herself then. "You bastard! You always end up making me apologise."

Which was true enough. I could twist things enough to throw most of her arguments out of gear, and I was more than willing to do it to get off the hook.

I'd bought my own cab with the advances from the two books, and though I wondered more than once about the wisdom of the move, it did mean that my earnings were my own business. Not that Jackie, who really was a good fella, would ever have said how much I was taking home, which he could judge easily enough by the cash I paid in to him at the garage…but there was the odd time, just before I'd struck out on my own, when Phil's dad had taken over the 'Paying In' window, so that Jackie could have some time off. Jackie worked sixteen hours a day, most of the running of the gigantic garage was handled by employees, but the money was always taken by a member of the family... Well, wouldn't you know that when dad was sitting there at the window nodding happily as cab after cab pulled in, each and every driver about to walk up to him and hit him with some bread, wouldn't you just know it was always at the end of a shift that hadn't earned me a fortune? And if I paid in say, two pounds which was about my average for times Dad was one duty, he could tell I hadn't earned anything more than two pounds ten, which was something of a joke, only neither of us seemed to do much laughing over it.

Old Man Williams had a way of whistling tunelessly as he took the money for a shift that hadn't been good. He was a man obsessed with money, and the power he knew it could bring. It is no lie to say his respect for another was based entirely on how much the man was worth, or how much he could earn in a given week if he wasn't afraid to go out and graft. This word 'graft!' usually part of a double act with 'corruption', simply meant 'hard work' to Phil's father. It was a hint to me...intended to be oblique...but coming from a man possessing all the subtlety of an Aberdeen Angus Bull with a hard on...Well, you can judge that my father-in-law's contempt for my earning ability hit me as obliquely as a truck might have done if it had run into me head on.

The strange thing was that up to a point I respected Old Man Williams. I couldn't help it, even though I couldn't stand the old bastard. He wasn't popular, and like most successful, self-made men, he was the target for a lot of envy from all kinds of wankers whose only claim to fame was the 'I knew 'em when when 'e 'ad nuffin' but one bleedin' banger of a cab'. It was those guys, with their endless stories, most of them intended to put Dad down, make him into a joke, tales of his guts and his single mindedness and his unbelievable capacity for work, plus his gift for thinking in a dodgy situation, that turned me on to Dad, despite all the bitterness that he'd helped me find inside myself through his pig-headed behaviour, from the first moment he convinced himself that

I was a hustler and only interested in Phil because I wanted to get my hands on some of his hard earned money.

You had to hand it to a man who drove through the Blitz of London with headlamps cut down to a one inch circumference of light. A fella who found a formula in his own marble bag, an uneducated man coming up with a recipe of petrol, paraffin oil and camphor balls, which stretched his severely rationed fuel allowance giving him the chance to get his hands on some of the easy money that was floating around. Which he used to buy one cab after another until he had eight altogether. Eight cabs that he turned into twenty-four, by having them worked for three separate eight hour shifts, seven days a week, by drivers who, though they complained about the stink of the shit fuel, were only too happy to earn a week's wages.

Dad worked ten and sometimes twelve hours each day in the garage, maintaining his small fleet of cabs, using his skills with a spanner to save paying the wages to a mechanic, even fixing punctures himself. Going home in the evening to eat, resting for an hour before taking a cab out to get his night's wages and anything that he could earn over the top.

So that when I said easy money a moment ago, I meant only that there was a ton of it about, because people were desperate to spend it today, tonight Jerry might drop something your way, like the direct hit on the London Underground Station where thousands had gone for safety from the bombs. Enjoy it today was the name of the game, because tomorrow you mightn't be here.

According to some of the older cabbies who hadn't lost the desire to talk about sex, pussy was thought of in the same way as the bread. Women parted the hairs simply because 'why not?' They were being deprived, a lot of them with husbands and lovers off fighting overseas, and with little else in the way of comfort who could blame anybody for wanting to be wanted, even in the most basic way, when tomorrow might not arrive.

During that time, a London cab driver could use his motor like a mini bus. Doubling up on fares, dropping people off and picking up, as they wished. All things so strictly taboo today were allowed to happen when the country was at war. And Dad went out and earned, the hard way large bundles of that easy money I mentioned.

Phil's memory of that time was clouded by the predictably emotional reactions of a very small girl who thought, many nights, that she was going to die - be killed with her mother by one of Jerry's bombs.

During most of the heavy bombings of London, Phil was alone with her mother. Dad was out driving his cab, Jackie was part of the exodus of evacuee children to all parts of rural England, and Susan, who made my day every time she told the old man how soppy he was, hadn't yet been born.

Mrs. Williams emerged as a quietly courageous woman doing all she could to help Phil not be frightened, and again I found that I envied her this quality of stoicism, handed down to so many English people, I suppose it came from the yeoman ancestry and all that; leaving out the upper crust; and worth so much more in any kind of crunch, than all the bullshit and verbal artistry that people like me seem to possess in abundance.

In the small back garden behind the Williams' house the remains of the air raid shelter, where my wife Phil and her mother had prayed for survival, was now being used as a coal bunker.

"Mum and I - can you see us in pyjamas, dressing gowns, gas masks slung around our necks - me with my favourite Teddy…and old Mum, worrying more about her china tea set wedding present than she was about the chance of being blown to smithereens…I used to see Dad most evenings…he ruined me, taking me out of bed, and more times, when he came home in after his night's cabbing, three or four in the morning, he'd come and get me…wrap me up and rock me on his knee. Old Mum would be moaning about his disturbing my sleep. Dad never listened, just rocked me away until I went back to sleep...He was funny like that..."

The Old Man was a cheapskate, and as I got to know Mrs. Williams better, she was forever telling me how tight he was. She needed to know this the odd time, but you knew she didn't want any comment against dad, except from herself. Which was fair enough...But Jackie was becoming more and more outspoken about his father...He was fed up with the Old Man's reactionary attitude in a day and age where expansion was the scene, and though he knew he would get this and that willed to him when his father died, Jackie said, "I want it now."

Trying hard not to be emotional about it, I though his attitude was reasonable, even if, once or twice, he did go in a bit strong. I'd have been on Jackie's side anyway, but as Dad realised that the pressure was on, and that unless he did what Jackie wanted, his son was going to take his obvious talent and make his own money. I actually felt just a little bit sorry for Phil's father.

A couple of times when Phil and I dropped in to see her parents of an evening, the Old Man tried to beat my ear about it. A shame that Jackie was so impatient to be overall boss, and lots more of this kind of crap. I drank my Guinness, and I mean *my* Guinness, because I took several pints in with me just to be sure I would get a drink. But I refused to be drawn into any discussion. I'd been outside the family for long enough not to need admittance any more. I went along with Phil for her sake, playing the game of social intercourse with my in-laws...I joined them at their 'Ladies Night' Masonic dinners, and once I even agreed to a holiday in Cornwall with her mother and father. when Kate was a year old, I was thrilled to live in the same world with my little girl. She meant everything to me, of course, I loved Phil, like a man convinced he was going to lose her, and at the same time I wanted to fuck every good looking bird I laid eyes on. But I wasn't about to side with Dad against Jackie, who had always been all right to me.

It was during one of those evenings that Dad mentioned my sitting tenant ...Phil threw me a glance of apology, as I reacted badly to her father interfering in my business when I was so willing to keep my nose out of his affairs. But, with his usual effrontery – and his wife wasn't guiltless here, often taking it on herself to make statements as to what I should do about this and that – the old man told me I should work that bit harder, get the money for a bathroom for my tenant, and when she paid her first week's rent at the agreed new rates serve her with a month's notice to get out.

"But she's lived here for years," I explained.

"Hmmph." Though he wouldn't have known it, Old Man Williams' grunt suggested that my explanation was something of a *non sequiter*. "Should have owned it by now then, shouldn't she?"

I really don't know," I said, "maybe she just couldn't get the money together."

"Get the money together! Not your problem anyway, is it!" He looked over his glasses at me, his eyes flat above a beak of a nose, giving him an owlish look, and the distinct impression that my lack of interest was ruffling his feathers.

"It could be my problem if she was to suffer."

"Suffer? How suffer? The council would have to look after her. That's what they're there for." He sounded as though he had to bite on the exclamation, "For Christ's sake!" which had it come out, would have been a total condemnation of my belief, my feelings, and he wasn't dumb enough to be that overt.

"See what happens," I said, "she's been very good recently...."

"Very good?" he said, irritating me with his habit of taking some statement of mine and turning it into a rhetorical question. "She's a tenant, paying less than two quid a week for a flat that could earn you ten or twelve pounds... I should think she would be very good...."

I got up and poured another Guinness for Phil's mother. Phil shook her head when I glanced at the sherry bottle. She'd had two already, and I could see that she hadn't enjoyed them too much. I drank some more Guinness. As usual the television was switched on, so whatever conversation there was happened while the adverts were being shown. I nodded to Phil and she got up to get her streetcoat. Kate was asleep in the pram in the hall and I envied her being sealed off by her age, from those times with her grandparents.

"You can't do nothing without the money, Paddy," Mrs. Williams assured me, as I moved to the door.

I smiled, trying not to patronise her. She meant well, and I had no need to tell her that I could think and dream, and do a lot of other things that she wouldn't have understood.

"Goodnight, Mum," I said.

"Goodnight." She always drew it out so that without her mentioning your name, it was included in the one word.

Phil kissed her mother, and I nodded goodbye to her father. I'd given up saying goodnight when most of the time he didn't answer me.

I pushed the pram down along Fulham Palace Road, and Phil told me she was sorry she'd mentioned the bath bit to her father.

"It doesn't matter," I said. "I'm not going to do it anyway."

I felt her go tense, her fingers tightening on the handle of the pram.

"Because of Dad, is that it?"

"I'm not sure," I admitted, "something to do with him, I suppose, but not all."

"We could use the money."

"I know... but it'll have to come from somewhere else... I'm not stroking that old girl just to pay a few bills...."

"Maybe you'll work a bit harder then, earn the kind of money Eddie Gage does."

"I'll try, Phil," I promised, knowing that despite her tone, and the edge on her voice, she was entitled to be concerned about the way our finances were drifting the wrong way. I would try. I wanted to. And I needed to. Christ! I had to.

Chapter Thirteen
London. '65

I got a lot of encouragement with my writing from Ted Connor and from people like Ken Johnson, who used the pub in Fulham Road, as their local. But it was a little prick by the name of Teddy Lomax, who really drove me to it.

He was a pathetic little guy, and like most intellectual snobs, he was pseudo in this and just about every other department of his life. I had to admit he was a good designer of ladies' clothes, and I knew for a fact that he could pull a bird. But then he worked so hard at it, spending so much time and money impressing chicks, that he just had to make out a lot of the time.

Trying to put me down over the Parnassus books, he made me angry - angry enough for me to promise him – as opposed to belting him in the teeth, which I was tempted to do - that before very long, I'd have a novel published in England.

Up to that moment, I'd never thought of writing a novel. I recognised the Parnassus things as books, and they had proved that I could sit down long enough to write fifty thousand words, but I wasn't expecting anybody to come up to me and tell me that I was the greatest thing since Donleavy.

Lomax helped me decide to go to work a lot faster than the nice guys and their encouragement ever had. And this is true, like, those people who make you mad, touch you so that you get the bit between your teeth, they are often responsible for the drive that an immature individual can't find for himself. Not that it matters a tinker's damn where your motivation comes from when you've got the finished manuscript in your hand. It might be of interest to a student headshrinker, but I can't think of anybody else who'd be concerned.

I'd said goodbye to Parnassus Publications a few months before. The sex in my books was funny, Jammet told me, so would I write a book, a very sexy one, that didn't play for laughs. I thought about it for a few days, and began a book called "You're Never Too Young".

In the first day at the typewriter, a long day of some fourteen hours, I typed nearly forty pages, quarto size, of pornographic rubbish. I wasn't happy about it, feeling just a bit like I'd been down to a guy who would help me sell a TV script.... Not that I'd ever crash dived, but it wasn't hard to work out how a normal fella would feel after doing something like that.

When Kate cried out, I left her for a minute or so, but when she didn't stop I went to get her from the crib. She was a good baby, who slept the long night through, so something was bothering her.

We'd been very strict about lifting her up, suffering like bloody hell during the "try on" period when Kate was just looking for attention. And we hadn't altered our way of moving about or anything like that. Kate had come to live with us, and the only valuable piece of advice my brother Tommy had ever given me, was to play the radio at normal volume, and make the usual household noises, so that right off the baby was learning how to live with us.

I could handle myself around Kate, thanks to helping Phil, and eventually leaning how to fix a nappy properly. I wanted to be able to look after my daughter should Phil be sick for a few days. I didn't want in-laws, on either side, doing me any favours.... Most of them wash a cup for you and go away giving the impression they've spring cleaned the flat after they've finished decorating it.

There was another reason... I believed that a child, even a baby of a few months old, derived some benefit when it's father became involved in its welfare. By osmosis, or whatever, I didn't know, and I didn't care... I just felt that this was so, and I applied myself sincerely to learning all I could about looking after my daughter. So that when I changed Kate's night nappy - Phil was at a whist drive with her mother. I knew what I was doing, and before long Kate was all tucked up again, sleeping the way I'd have loved to sleep.

She was a doll of a kid... running about at a year old, clean shortly afterwards, and already saying a few words that were music to our ears. Like Phil really, but a live wire like me in the mornings.

I went back to the typewriter, but I didn't sit down. I just stood looking at the heap of manuscript I'd banged out that day - pages that included little else but descriptions of the sex act with many variations. As a matter of fact, the only stroke I hadn't pulled so far was to have a couple doing it standing up in a hammock.

It was a load of crap, and I knew it, and suddenly I didn't want to be responsible for deliberately releasing such garbage into a bookshelf anywhere. It was as easy as that... no big deal - no major decision. It was a load of crap and I didn't even want my pseudonym on it. So I stood there, methodically tearing it all into bits, small enough for a curious dustman not to be able to read it. And when I was done, the task over and done with for good, I sat down, smoked a cigarette, and turned on the goggle box.

Most of the television I saw seemed to me to be very slipshod. Good or bad, it just appeared loose... under rehearsed, with sound booms, production assistants, and actors who were supposed to be out of vision often being caught in the camera frame, plus quite a bit of bad continuity and so on. And I thought I could write scripts that would be as good as most of the stuff that went out week after week.

One of the birds in Ted Connors' pub worked in television, I remembered, and I made up my mind to ask her to get me a script, an old one, just so that I could see how the thing had to be laid out to look professional. You never know, and if you didn't try, you never would.

I'd given up the booze again, but I still dropped in the pub.

I say *again* about the booze, because I'd given it up a few months before, and hadn't touched a drop for several weeks. And when I did drink it was with Phil's encouragement... we were going to a party and we both thought it would be easier all round if I was drinking a little and not standing there like an eejit trying to explain why I was off it. Which, when I thought about it, was because Phil had asked me to cut it down, and I had responded to this by saying that I wasn't bothered about drink. In fact, I felt so easy about the idea, that instead of just easing off, I'd give it up altogether.

But still I dropped into Connors' pub to pay him a few quid off what I owed. He'd let me open an account, which was a godsend in one way, and at the same time, a curse. It meant that I could drink a bit without dipping into what little I was earning on the cab, so that when Phil commented on the consistency, if not enormity, of my earnings for a few weeks on the trot, I lied to her, telling her that I only stopped for the odd bottle of beer, and not very often at that. But then, every few weeks I had to work like a maniac for the bread to keep the account in the pub from getting out of hand.

One way or another, I stayed out of financial trouble at this time. As I've said, there was no need for me to be short of money. By working a steady seventy hour week I could have been paying my way, getting the extras that Phil seemed to need, and even saving a few pounds a week.

My trouble was that I knew I could write and I'd become very bitter about not getting anywhere. No longer was I philosophical about rejection slips. Each one was hurting more than the one before, and when I had three television plays, admittedly written like stage jobs, returned to me without a solitary word of encouragement, I went on a piss-up that caused all kinds of aggravation between Phil and me.

I was in Connor's pub drinking heavily, letting myself slide into a situation with a crazy bird who talked so much about getting laid that I thought she must turn out to be nothing but a prick teaser. But I couldn't back off because her body fascinated me, which she knew, and I was determined to stay sober enough to be able to perform.

But I needed a bit more booze to help me forget Phil, and my baby daughter, Kate, and my vows not to have sex except with my wife, and all the other things that were driving me out of my Jesus mind.

My head was spinning between thoughts of what the bird, Emma, was going to have granted to her if I got her into the scratcher, guilt over all the reasons for which I was entitled to feel guilty, worry about not earning bread on the cab, and the pain, self induced, I'll admit, at having been turned down again, and this time with three plays that had taken a lot of time and energy. So that when one of the barmen tapped me on the shoulder and told me there was a phone call, I picked up the receiver without really thinking.

It was Phil. "Are you coming home?"

"I'll be home...."

"Now? Are you coming home now?" She didn't sound too pleased, but I didn't seem to care how she felt.

"Not long."

"How long is that?"

Somebody brushed past me, yelling something in my ear.

"What? Sorry, " I said to Phil, "not long...."

"Oh for Christ's sake, Maguire. What is it?"

"Look, kid, listen, I'm just having a drink. Jesus!"

"And I'm the nagging wife." She laughed. "Sounds funny when you say it, doesn't it?"

"Yeah," I said, "all right?"

"You won't be too long...."

"Why, Phil? I mean, is it something important? Is Kate all right?"

"Kate's fine. No, just wanted you home."

"Well I need a few hours out, kid. Spend nearly all my time at home... a break for a few hours... that's all."

"Well have your bloody break.... Sorry I disturbed you...."

"Come on... don't get like that...."

"I'm not being like anything...."

"Jesus!" I said.

"Look. Forget I phoned," Phil said bitterly, "go back to your booze companions... let them tell you what a lousy time you're having...."

"Phil listen...."

"Oh fuck off. Grow up for Christ's sake, Maguire, before it's too bloody late."

She slammed the phone down so that my ear rang with it. I stood there frightened. Really, for a split second I was cold with fear. But, Emma, appearing at my side, holding my glass to my lips, helped me then by kissing me on the mouth.

"You haven't got another date?"

"Wonder if I'll ever get to like this tack?" I threw the rest of my drink down, wanting it to hurt, and beckoned for a refill.

"You don't believe I want you, do you?"

I turned my head to look into her earnest brown eyes. She had what you called a Jewish schnook of a nose, but her mouth was really beautiful, the lips large and fleshy enough to provoke a wooden Indian.

"You birds... the ones who talk about it all the time...."

"Where's your cab?" She stopped me answering her with her hand on my mouth.

"Take me to it now," she said, looking very fierce, like a bad actress making sexy, "right now, please...."

"What for?" I said, sipping the fresh drink from Ted, who was grinning behind the bird's back.

"I want to," she lowered her eyes for a second and then looked back at me. "You'll see," she promised.

"We'll have another drink first," I said, "I'm shy."

My cab had a diesel engine and I bought my Derv, the stinking fuel on which the thing ran, from a mate, Chesney Haynes, who had a little cab garage in a mews just off Fulham Road. The fuel pump was inside the door and when you'd taken what you wanted, you signed for it on the honour system, so it was some kind of good character reference when Chez let you open an account.

But as I pulled up outside the garage door with this lustpot, Emma, practically melting the leather on the back seat, I can tell you that Derv was about the furthest thing from my mind. You see, often enough there was just one motor parked in the garage, and I was going to drive the cab in there. Just to know I wasn't going to be disturbed by some nosey copper with an unromantic heart.

A cabbie caught putting some down in the back of the jammer could really get himself in trouble at the Carriage Office. Let's face it, a cabbie sneezing the wrong way could find himself on the carpet at Lambeth Road.... So you'll understand me wanting to eliminate the kind of possibility that could cause suspension of my licence, and the volcanic eruptions that being caught with my knickers down would surely guarantee. Like, in no way did I want to break things up at home, and crazy enough though I was to get into dearest Emma, I wasn't that crazy. At least, I didn't think so, until I found two fucking motors parked in the garage.

I got in the back of the cab to try and explain to the bird what had happened, but Christ! I didn't get a chance to open my mouth. Well, that's not quite true. I got my mouth open all right, but Emma rammed her tongue into it like a hamburger in a sandpaper wrapper, and before I could even consider holding my horses, we were both starkers, and in no way suffering from the cold.

It's ridiculous... like, it's bullshit, to say I couldn't help myself, but, I couldn't help myself. She had so much form, and it was in such good shape, that I knew I was a gonner, coppers or no coppers. Jesus, if they were to come for me with a net I wasn't going to pass this one up. Let's face it, if we'd been in Selfridge's front window at noon on Christmas Eve it wouldn't have made a bit of a difference.

I lost myself in that lovely nutty bird, and I had no more idea of time than if I'd been out sleeping in space. So that when the knocking happened, when I heard the tapping at the window, it took a few seconds to come up out of the warm wrapper that enveloped me in every way, before I felt that fear filled and bloody urgent need to empty my jittering bowels.

The cab was steamed up like a Turkish bath, and I bit into my bottom lip as I tried, hopelessly, to think of something to do... something to say. Christ! What could I say? The fuzzman was going to know what was going on... I mean, it mightn't have been spelled out for him in his little handbook, or whatever they gave him to work to, but I knew, and, you could be bloody sure, he knew, that my place was behind the wheel, and not between the long supple.... Oh forget it!

I could see myself in the divorce court, after they got through with me at the Carriage Office. Oh Christ! I couldn't even bear thinking about all that was going to happen, so I decided, Screw it! And I pulled down the window in the off-side door of the old FX3.

There was a face peering in at me, and when I realised there was no chinstrap, meaning no helmet, meaning no big black boots and pocket book, I nearly fouled up the floor of the cab out of sheer relief.

"Sorry mate," the pale face said. "Could you move up a bit so I can get some Derv?"

"Can I" I couldn't speak. A bloody cab driver! And all he wanted was some of Chesney's fuel. Jesus! I almost fell out of the cab, the sweat going cold on my body.

It was this... the cold sweat, that made me realise I was naked, but I was getting out from behind the wheel by this time and I'll say this for the other guy... he took it all in like a fella who didn't surprise easily. It must have hit him a bit later on though, because within days, I was like a marked man.

Cabbies I didn't know.... How many could you know out of five thousand or more? ...suddenly, they knew me... All kinds of obscene gestures came my way... smiles and nods of encouragement from complete strangers who wore a green badge, having happened to hear the story in one cab shelter or another. Not to mention the crap I had to put up with from Darcy and Theo, and Herb O'Casey, and the other guys I knew from the shelter at Brompton Oratory.

With the exception of Paddy Darcy, who lived for horses and the booze, though he did seem to keep Mary very happy, those guys would get up on a back rasher. So that for me to have pulled a stroke like the one in the mews, and to have got away with it, well, it gave me a kind of gloss I didn't deserve.

Phil didn't talk to me for days afterwards, annoyed that I'd been out half the night, with no wages to show for it. But I worked hard for a week, making up for the loss of the money, and she came around. The effort to keep her happy, the work I had to do to make things tick over, well, it was knocking the guts out of me. My own fault, I know, particularly as I wanted to be straight and good, and above all, true to Phil, but I seemed to have moved into a priapic stage in my life.

It was nothing to brag about, it was like some kind of success but I was randy eighty per cent of my waking time, and I wanted to lay every decent looking chick that got into a cab.

Somehow I was getting some writing done, and I was earning some kind of money from the taxi. But every chance I got to climb into some bird's knickers, well, I took it, and it wasn't long before I stopped thinking altogether about what a shit I'd become.

Chapter Fourteen

The more you drink the less you sleep. Fact. Well, by midsummer, I was making out on about four hours in twenty-four and more often than not, I was tired when I woke up. It didn't make sense - I needed more sleep than four hours. It was like I was being prodded awake but I didn't give it much thought. I was too busy trying to knock out as many pages as I could on the typewriter before I took the cab out to look for a living.

I hadn't yet started to drink in the early morning though I often felt the need for a few belts to put some life into me. That was one of the great things about booze, it gave me a lift whether I was tired, unhappy, or just plain nervous. And I often used it in that way, thinking that whatever it took to keep going, well, it had to done.

I'd had drinks in the morning to cure myself when those lovely, reckless holiday makers in Jersey made sleep impossible except for the hours grabbed on the beach in the afternoons. But then everybody had been doing the same thing, not to mention the Benzedrine touch, so it hadn't bothered me.

Things were different now... I was a married man with a baby daughter and another child on the way. And I was behaving badly enough, indulging my hang-up on sex, so that for any number of reasons, I could hardly afford to let the booze really get to me.

I was enjoying a lot of my drinking, and unlike Phil, I wasn't worried by how much I put away. I knew that if talking had been banned in pubs I'd have stopped going into them, and as long as I wasn't pubbing strictly for the booze, I felt I was all right. And it's no lie to say that regardless of how much I drank, I didn't fall down, and I didn't get mean and obstreperous, like a lot of drunks I knew.

I just needed people and the kind I liked were all drinkers. Cabbing was a lonely job. Oh, I was pulling a lot of birds on the cab, but this was strictly a sex thing, with the minimum of conversation... and I had to have voices, words and thoughts that would, hopefully, stimulate my brain. In Ted Connor's Pub I got what I needed, and I could usually wheel a bird out of there, if I put my mind to it.

Not that I bothered all that much. I'd put together a way of pulling a lot of my female fares that seemed to me to be a stroke of genius. Mind you, it meant that an awful lot of guys got left standing in the streets at night, waving their arms and swearing my life away, as I drove on past them with my FOR HIRE sign blazing.

I ignored men because my pulling system had to do with the numbers game and there was no percentage in picking up fellas. I mean, I was no queer, so after about ten o'clock at night, I only picked up women. You can take it or leave it, but working at it, you could nail two out of ten, so the more birds you picked up the more notches you got on your butt. And this was before I came up with my master stroke. This bumped the figures up to a point where I had to leave it out the odd night, just so that I could earn *some* much needed wages.

I've already told you that my singing didn't start any bush fires in the Irish countryside, but it did put some heat into a lot of panties in the back of the old cab. Not because I'd suddenly found a new voice. It was more to do with surprise. Like, most people tended to think of the cab driver as an extension of the steering wheel. An automaton without life or personality. Even when they were paying you off, most of them didn't look at your face. It was like they didn't bother because they didn't think you might have one.

So the singing bit hit them hard, really making them sit up, and it became a passport to success with enough chicks to make me realize how Sinatra had blown so many minds. Again I'm not saying I could sing like Old God, as I think of Francis Albert, but then again, I didn't have Tommy Dorsey or Nelson Riddle to help me out either.

What I did have going for me was the element of surprise, and the confines of the driving cabin. Honestly, if the makers of the cab had known just how helpful, acoustic-wise, that little cabin was, they would have added twenty per cent to the price. But they didn't know, any more than the makers of "Three In One" oil knew how important a small can of their product was in the business of a cab driver getting laid.

Each evening before I started work, I oiled the channel that housed the sliding glass pane in the partition between the passenger and me. When a tasty bird got into the cab, I made sure she saw me shut the window tight. I knew that when I made the first left turn it would slide across in its bed of lubricating oil, leaving the regulation six inch aperture.

Then I'd launch into one of our songs. The word *our* indicates that at least two people were connected with whatever I sang. Right. Myself and Frank Sinatra. You see, I found that his kind of number was right up my street, and while he sang to make bread, I wasn't that good, so I sang to make time... with my tastier lady passengers.

When things were going my way, the first thing that happened was the perfume coming closer. Meaning that my fare had moved onto the pull down directly behind me. You couldn't always hear that seat come down. Between the racket from the engine and my controlled cacophony, the ears might be forgiven for not being a hundred per cent reliable. The fact that the nose was on the bell was something cool, and you'd know if you've ever been around an ancient, overworked, and severely overheated diesel engine.

The chat would start soon after the seat came down... I didn't stop the crooning touch till the opener had been elicited from the lady.... And this could vary from a word of surprise, to en exclamation of admiration, sometimes for the singing, sometimes for the driver, me, for managing to warble at all under such trying conditions.

Occasionally, the song itself would be the springboard, but however the opening gambit was served, I weighed in right away with an apology for intruding on her privacy.

"I was sure I closed the window, sorry."

"Oh no, fine, really. Most enjoyable in fact."

I took it from there, and within minutes you could tell whether you'd struck oil or not. But making out or not, I felt I was really doing something positive to bring people together, spread a little sunshine, and as I had no hang-ups about race, creed, or colour, I regarded myself as a sort of unpaid trouble-shooter for the United Nations. And if I wasn't exactly happy in my work, I have to admit that it did bring me a certain amount of pleasure.

I'd always liked the English as a race. Oh, I'd run into the odd Fascist, and one or two coppers who gave me a hard time, and of course, I wasn't ever going to include those Public Carriage Officers on my Christmas card list, but, all in all, the English had been good to me. And the women, well to me, they were the most attractive females alive. Not necessarily the prettiest, or the most beautiful, but through effort and know-how, with clothes, make up, and hair dos, they turned me on like a light switch.

And as the whole country moved closer to being a classless society, the women seemed to get better and better. They took to the emancipation bit, and they wallowed in the lifting of so many of the social barriers, and I found that most of them took you just because of how you were. Who you were and what you did seemed secondary to whether you were an all right fella, like, were you fun? And I must say, I found it just as easy to pull a bus conductress or an actress, as I did to make out with one of those titled chicks, who talked like she'd cut her mouth on a sharp slice of melon.

A lot of the time, I had to join the fare in the back of the cab. A cigarette was the usual excuse for getting in there, unless of course I touched for a complete raver like that Emma, and then I didn't even get a chance to ditch the preliminaries, on account of them never even showing up for me to sling out of the way.

The back of the cab wasn't ideal, but when a bird was married, or living with her parents, I hadn't much choice. And anyway, I couldn't very well slag the lady for having nowhere to take me, when I didn't know her name, and I didn't want to draw attention to the fact that I hadn't any little love nest of my own.

After a few months of really scoring touchdowns, I'd become cool enough to try and take time out to think about my behaviour. I mean, it wasn't what you could call normal... not for a married man who believed that he loved and was in love with his wife. But a few drinks knocked any idea of taking self inventory right out of my head.... It didn't stop me shaking my head, grinning at my own incorrigibility, as I accepted the thought that I got a bigger charge performing in the back of the cab than I did in the most comfortable bed.

Something to do with the risk, the danger of being caught, and I went on doing it, being less and less careful, pushing my luck a lot of the time, screwing in select residential areas, as opposed to driving up to Hampstead Heath, or creeping around the back of any of the railway stations, where I had a fair chance of being left alone. It got so bad, that one night, after this raver had given *me* a pull, without me having to chant so much as one bar of schmaltz, I bet her a pound note that she wouldn't have the nerve to strip off with me in the back of the cab, if I parked the thing in Curzon Street.

I couldn't assess how drunk your woman was because of the load I was carrying myself, but there was no doubting her qualifications for the first vacant padded cell. And she was only about half as crazy as I was.

How does a guy get away with that kind of carry on? I don't know.... Maybe the Patron Saint of lunatics puts a little more into his work. Or is it that people, even if they were to see us at it.... Is it that they wouldn't, that they couldn't believe, imagine, comprehend even the idea of a cab driver, ballock naked, with his female passenger, in the back of the jammer, in Curzon Street, Mayfair, London, W.1?

Surely that's got to be it? Like, if some fella walked up to the cab thinking it was on rank and FOR HIRE... if he glanced in the back and saw the driver's arse moving like a fiddler's elbow, could he be blamed for doing a double take, before he walked away, knocking himself gently on the side of the head?

Anyway, however it happened, I came through any number of mad moments. Scenes that make my hair curl now when I think of them. And what makes the thing even more horrifying is the fact that I wasn't in any way trying to be out of the ordinary. Like, I wasn't trying to impress anybody. It was perfectly normal to do whatever seemed like a good idea at the time. And some of my ideas? God! My skin bursts into a field of goose pimples just remembering the odd one.

Obviously, all the action didn't happen in the back of the cab. And where it was going to take place was another branch of the situation that had to be weighed up as the cards were dealt out. A lot of women who badly wanted to have a bit of stray with a cabbie, would have been shocked out of their lovely knickers at the thought of parting the hairs in the cab. So I followed many a pair of nylon clad legs into one pad or another. And here again I was lucky.

Regardless of where I ended up, not once did I get caught by an angry boy friend or a husband who didn't approve of his wife parting with a slice, no matter how well cut the loaf might be. And I hit some fancy pads, from top class apartments in Ennismore Gardens, to houses in Hampstead, and back down west to one very special session in Arlington House.

More than once while I was in bed with the lady of the house, the master was asleep in his own room along the hall, and one guy, who was fairly pissed, asked my pardon for staggering into his wife's room, and she with her pelvis welded to mine. Talk about being civilised,

One night I was giving one to a women out in Ealing, and she after telling me for an hour what a fabulous man her husband was. She'd been playing with me right through this verbal picture of the saint she was married to, and I hadn't said much on account of fighting for breath. Anyway, there we were, right in the middle of this late, late performance when the head himself came into the room.

Your man rushed across the room as I tried to disengage myself from his missus without hurting her feelings. Not that she was sensitive... not with that scissors grip she had me in... honestly, it was worthy of Jackie Pallo... not that I've ever been scissored by that marvellous wrestler. Anyway, I just couldn't budge, so I lay there, waiting for the first punch to go crash against the side of my head.

There was no blow, no bone crunching fist smashing into my haircut.... Instead, your man's hand on my shoulder, and his voice, lisping a shade, urging me not to move, not to disturb myself, that everything was perfectly all right.

I looked from his to his missus... she was smiling like a reverend mother presenting you with a prize for top marks in religious knowledge. Then she came at my mouth again. I broke the kiss fairly quickly. This was one movie I wasn't keen to star in. I mean, how could I be sure your man didn't fancy himself as The Chocolate Soldier? Or as the top slice of bread in a sandwich, with me as the rare roast beef... I mean, you never know. A guy who let his old lady bang the cabbie, was more than capable of slipping a sneaky one up the cabbie's cocoa. And that was one scene I hadn't any desire to make.

He sat across the room and once I felt he was just a piker, a voyeur, and I got on with things, even though I did feel a bit strange. Later on, when I was leaving, he paid me over the odds for his wife's cab fare and he shook my hand gratefully as he bid me good night. I found myself smiling as I started up the old FX3, thinking that I must have been some kind of natural actor to have made a scene like that without so much as blushing.

The one hang-up about going into a place for a few hours, was that when the fun was finished, you still had to come out and push the cab around to get your money.... And to make-up for three or four hours in the scratcher you needed some kind of miracle at that time of the night.

Most times, as I poked the cab around the West End, praying that some guy would rush out and ask for London Airport or some other double fare ride, I'd be cursing myself for having indulged for so long... I mean, to be holding peanuts at one o'clock in the morning gave you little chance of going home with any decent wages.

Once, and only once, in probably hundreds of times, did a woman save me that afterwards aggravation... I was sitting on the rank at Hammersmith, reading by torchlight, when this fantastic perfume stopped by my right ear and started polishing my hormones. I looked up and there she was.... Blonde and soft and very lovely. About forty-two years old built like a slender cockerel, her fur coat and her jewellery, her make up and her hair do, all screaming *class* and her soft, well modulated voice filled with more sex appeal than ten fully loaded size forty brassieres.

"Arlington House, if you please, driver."

I can't remember which of my stock replies I used. I was too busy with my wishful thinking bit, trying to will into her a desperate need to hold onto me. And I made sure she saw me slide the parting window shut. As I reached the Clarendon I realised that, if I went along Hammersmith Road, past Olympia, and on into Kensington High Street, I wouldn't be able to help the little window slip across because it was a straight run all the way, so I did a right turn just beyond the Clarendon and then a sharp left onto West Cromwell Road. I was already singing, having decided that the right song for this lovely lady was the very great "As Times Go By". Let's face it, it had been good enough for Ingrid Bergman in "Casablanca".

This was the way it had become with the singing trick.... Not only did I work it on all women under fifty who got into the cab... now I tried to pick the exact number for the right woman..... It was a bit like a fella getting good at draughts or checkers, moving then on to chess. A little more demanding and a lot more fun.

The perfume came that much closer and then she said.

"Surely that song is more my time than yours."

I gave her my apology bullshit. She dismissed this as totally unnecessary.

"It's one of my favourites, and you sing it so well."

"Mine too, a favourite, and ageless, timeless, I think."

She agreed with this, which was what I'd been leading her into.

"So that statement about your time as opposed to mine, it really, well, it's just hay, isn't it?"

She laughed. "Hay? Is that what it is?"

"Well, men, women... time... age... where does it come in unless the gap is so wide that it's a joke."

"You like older women then, I take it." She laughed a little bit, and I felt she was delighted with her own daring.

"Do you really want me to be honest?"

"Of course," she said, "please."

"Just to talk to you, someone so lovely, well it's such a charge that I wish I were dead."

"Come on," she pleaded, "whatever makes you say that?"

"I take you to Arlington House, you pay me off, and I drive away, with your perfume driving me out of my mind for the rest of the night.... is that reason enough?"

"I'm sure I've never met a cab driver quite like you before...." She lit a cigarette and I accepted her offer. Our fingers touched for a second, and I really did wish I was dead. Christ! To be so close to someone so lovely. The way my thoughts echoed the line I'd just given her, made me wonder whether I was kidding her or myself. And I dreaded the thought of watching her walk into the building with me sitting behind the wheel and my tongue hanging out.

"Would you like to come in for a drink?" She looked at me with such frankness in her eyes that I nodded. All right, she'd give me a drink, but we both knew it was for something else that I was being invited. I followed her into the elevator. The doors closed silently and it was then she shoved the fiver into my pocket.

"Your fare and something to buy yourself a present." She said it in a way that made it absolutely all right for me to take it. As though she was thinking, if the situation was reversed, I'd take it from you without any bullshit or hang-ups about being patronised. And being an easy going fella, I took it in the spirit in which it was given.

Now I've never claimed to be any kind of hammer man. I know that some of us can be good in the scratcher some of the time, that you'll get a turn on with one person that will give you an edge you wouldn't have with somebody else.... And though I've always tried to make love, even when it appeared to be just another screw, I make no claims to being successful beyond average. Enthusiasm I had, but that's not always the answer. But that evening in Arlington House, that lady with her fiver stuffed in my top pocket. Well, without knowing it, or maybe she did, she had given me a few hours of freedom... from concern about whether or not I'd be lucky when I left her. Would I run into a good show of work, pick up some fast rides that would boost my take? She had put me ahead and I relaxed in her bed. And though we said goodnight after some hours of holding each other, both of us knowing that it was just a one night lay. I think that she got the best out of me, the best that I could give. And wasn't it only right? I mean, an open handed woman like that, didn't she deserve to be treated like a queen?

Chapter Fifteen

I don't know how I managed to see that my marriage was heading into trouble. I was so busy cursing readers and editors, wallowing in self pity, and then most nights of the week scouring the streets looking for any easy lay. My idea of a bit of solace, a few minutes of comfort or warmth.... And feeling so sick with guilt over my behaviour that I was banging down more and more booze to insulate myself from inconvenience of what little bit of conscience I had left. Feeling like death then the next day, trying to write, working harder than ever because it was harder to sit and make the words come, and almost slaving to appear all right to Phil, not wanting her to see just how terrible I was feeling. And convincing myself that she didn't, that I was a good enough actor to kid her anytime I needed to. When all the time the poor cow was so desperately aware of what I was doing to myself and to her and to our marriage.

God, I had every reason in the world to be happy.... Happy? Yes, happy. I had a wife who somehow seemed to love me still. I had a lovely daughter and you can believe that Kate was the sun, moon and stars to me.... And I now had a son two weeks old. Oh Dan, Dan. Beautiful blonde boy, son of mine, with the blue eyes to come, though as yet I'd not seen his eyes for long enough to see that the colour hadn't yet established itself. Dan was a good baby too, a sleeper, and he seemed to grow, to expand with every meal he took from Phil's breast.

The sad, ridiculous thing about the situation was that I was crazy about Phil.... And there hadn't been one single time when she didn't respond to my need for her.... A touch from my hand and she would melt against me, blessing me, pouring the contents of her constant heart all over me.

Physically, we were like a nut and bolt. Fitting together as though we'd been specifically designed for each other - taking off together, flying, flying, flying like Siamese clouds, buffeting along, up, down and around, in a fierce, demanding wind that somehow broke evenly, always at the right second for us to land again exactly on the beat, with music, glorious, fine, bitter sweet, indigo strains, caressing nerve ends that had been extended drastically in the violence of a love so gentle.

Yet I could fight with Phil over Dan's name... I wanted to call him Cassidy for O'Casey, for our own great suffering Sean Cassidy, who was everything of a hero to me. But Phil thought it ridiculous. The kids in school would end up calling him Hopalong, she said. After William Boyd, who had moped through all those bloody awful creaky movies that looked like they'd been made in three days, when in fact, they'd taken six.

I didn't agree with Phil on this, I mean, while my generation knew who Hoppy was - knew that his pal Lucky was played by Russell Hayden, while the comic of the trio was usually Andy Clyde, with George "Gabby" Hayes, standing in the odd time, when he wasn't working with Roy Rogers and Dale Evans. Memories are made of this. And my generation had loved those characters a lot more than they did most of their relatives, but a boy who was going to be ten years old in 1975, well, neither himself or his schoolmates, would be able to tell Hopalong Cassidy from a loaf of bread. But Phil insisted, which was something she didn't often do, and though I fought with her about it, and used it as an excuse to go out and get locked, I gave in... Dan it would be... Dan, not Daniel, or Danny or Dannyboy... I loved the name and I loved my lovely son, and in a way I wished he could have known those old cowboy movies as I'd done.... That I might have shared with him some of those golden moments from my own childhood... queuing up for the Prinner and later the Stella... two cinemas on Rathmines Road, graduating into town, into Dublin proper, where at the Corinthian, you could see, week after week, nothing but cowboy pictures.... So many Westerns that we christened the place The Ranch, and joked that instead of seats they had saddled installed, and that they kept a barn full of hay out back for the horses....

Another bad bout of boozing. I drank for days and just couldn't seem to get enough.... What a bloody shame it had to happen this way.... Up to Dan's arrival, I'd been good for a few weeks.... No booze, no birds, just hard work and a good few quid to show for it.... And I looked after Kate through Phil's confinement, delighted that I'd always been involved, that I could see to her with skill, and then dive into this time with my tiny lady, filling her days with happiness and laughter, singing all the little songs she had come to love.... Dreaming up stories that made her dark eyes glow with excitement and wonder.... Thinking that sometime I would have to write a book for kiddies. And fucking it all up by hitting the juice so badly that I ended up on my knees before Phil, begging her to bear with me, once more with feeling.

"I'll stop," I pressed her reluctant hand against my tears. "I'll beat it, Phil, I swear... just don't give up on me... don't stop loving, caring... God, I'll just die if I loose you...."

"Come on." She pulled me carefully to my feet. I ached all over and my stomach felt like someone had run a blow torch around it. "Come on, Maguire, it'll be all right, don't cry."

"I'll stop it... Jesus God! It's ridiculous... I mean, I don't want to drink like that... hurt you... you know I wouldn't do anything to hurt you... not deliberately...."

"I know...." The smile, wan though it was, bathed me in a ray of absolution... Phil looked tired, worn, but her vitality was there under the sad surface....

"I won't have another one till Christmas... how's that?"

She nodded, smiling another kind of smile and I had to

check my anger.... She seemed to be smiling at a naughty child, allowing me to say what I needed to say but not really paying too much attention to it.... Not allowing it to get into her... taking not the slightest chance of being disappointed again.

Well, she wasn't going to be let down.... Not this time... this time I was going to do what I said... and I began by serving all the drinks at Dan's christening party, without touching a solitary drop myself.

I took a terrible verbal hiding from Theo and Paddy Darcy, but Mary took my part, telling her leprechaun of a husband that it was more than he could do.

Paddy grinned like a self-conscious elf, shrugging off the gentle admonitory tones of his marvellous missus.

"Sure I only drink stout... that baboon puts whiskey away till the cows go out again...."

You lying bastard, I thought.... Bullshitting Mary like that... face of an altar boy, eyes like a tired saint, and a tongue that could charm the mitre off a bishop. Jesus, what a liar... a bloke who'd drink whiskey off a dead soldier's arse... I stopped.... Didn't I do the same thing to Phil? Kid her about how much I drank, usually halving whatever the amount was... this, apart from almost always lying that I'd had beer when I'd been lowering nothing but whiskey and water.

Old Man Williams didn't say much, but his attitude suggested that I was a fool... A few drinks never hurt anybody, he informed me... so why give it up? I lied to him about this... saving up for Christmas, or some such bull... wanting to spend all my time off the cab at the typewriter.... A sniff of disdain at this.... Writing.... Didn't you need a University education for that? And wasn't it true to say I wasn't educated? That my formal schooling had finished at fourteen or thereabouts? What could I say to him? He didn't understand and he didn't want to.... He had no desire to discuss anything other than ways of making money.... But I sent Phil a silent kiss – all I had put her through and the old man didn't even know I drank too much.

Just for that I had to keep my word to my wife. When she might have been forgiven for running to her parents with tales of my behaviour, she had held on with pride, keeping it all to herself, or at least away from the ears of her family. Which made her shine even more in my eyes. I loved her dignity, her strength of character, and I brushed away any thought of the things I could find wrong with her. Her right wing attitudes, the selfish streak that made her think of number one, except in my case – and the other little things that I could build up to all kinds of proportions when it suited me. They were all just so much hogwash in relation to how good she could be, and she was so worth being good for, asking very little in return for all that he was so openly prepared to give. Well, I was going to make it up to her, she was going to reap the benefit of her own goodness. Somehow, somewhere, I'd find the guts to be man enough to keep her happy and contented, I wasn't going to lose my wife and my family.

Ma was thrilled about Dan, but when her parcel of knitwear arrived for him, she hadn't forgotten Kate who was the apple of her Irish grannie's eye. Pops wasn't all that well, Ma wrote – something wrong with a heart valve... not serious if it was looked after. I wasn't sure about that. Anything wrong with the heart was serious – and I said so in my next letter, learning in reply that he was attending hospital, but wouldn't take any time off work apart from the hours for his visits as an out patient.

I wrote to him, which was something I had done only rarely in the past – and to my amazement I got a note back. He said that Ma was exaggerating, that he was just a bit run down. I didn't believe him for one second but he wasn't the kind of man you could say that to. And his hang-up on work had to be a scar that burned itself bitterly into his self-respect during all the years there was no work for him So what could I do? He was entitled to tread his own path. As he might have said himself, every cripple had his own way of walking.

Anyway I was busy. Busy writing a book that had started out as short story. I was to finish it in six weeks of very hard work – though weeks with endless hours of application and concentration. But a fine time for me... a kind of glowing time as page after page rolled off the machine. A selfish time with me finding I had little to give to anybody, but simulating warmth, love, call it what you will, for Phil and Kate.

That sounds awful I know, but that's how it was, being involved with either my wife or my daughter just didn't come all that easily during those weeks, so I acted a bit and from somewhere deep inside myself found something akin to what Phil thought I was giving her. Not that she asked for anything. She was shining in the shadow of her reformed lunatic husband, and so involved with the kids that she didn't seem to notice much of the time when I was too preoccupied to talk.

The strange thing was that I wasn't missing the booze at all. Truly, and I was glad to be able to stop, just as I had told Phil I would. And what made me feel even better was that I didn't mind other people drinking, although I felt like punching Darcy one Sunday evening when Phil and I were at a party in his house in Putney.

Paddy was jarred and as always he was pouring whiskey like a fella who believed in empty bottles. He was always the same, and to give him his due, he'd pour your whiskey with the same degree of intensity that he would his own. And he was insisting that I have a drink – insisting as only he could, ignoring my determination to stay on the wagon.

I'd been singing and telling a few jokes. In other words, doing what I always did at his parties. I was a little bit nervous admittedly but there was some consolation in the fact that I could hear a bum note if I hit one.

"I don't want it, Head," I told him for about the tenth time.

He stood above me. My eyes flicked to Phil who was sitting opposite me. She smiled with just a hint of worry in her eyes. I winked at her and looked back up at Darcy who was swaying a bit. He held the empty glass out to me, the bottle in his right hand.

"You're a little ballocks, d'ye know that?"

He smiled, beaming drunkenly. "Ah, just a wee drop for the rheumatics, darlin'."

"Paddy, stop it for heaven's sake." Mary had moved over to stand beside him. "Maguire doesn't want it."

She was frowning seriously, bothered that Phil might be upset by her husband's utter bloody wickedness. And she went so far as to try and take the bottle away from him. I smiled at her, loving the way she always called me Maguire.... It was the easy way to avoid confusion when Darcy and I were together.

"He's all right now," Darcy assured her, not moving an inch, but hanging onto the bottle.

"All right," I said finally, "you can pour me a drink."

I held the glass and he filled it. He stepped back a pace then and waited for me to drink it. His expression changed when I put the tumbler down on the table. I grinned sweetly at the little bastard.... He was puzzled, so I stood up.

"Time we were making tracks, love," I said to Phil.

She stood up and Mary winked her eyes at me, delighted that I hadn't given in.

"Drink the Jesus whiskey," Darcy said.

"Christmas," I promised...." Leave it where it is till then... all right?"

Phil put her streetcoat on. Darcy was annoyed, his eyes like specks in his whiskey flushed face.

"Wanker," he said, with his own brand of alcoholic venom.

I kissed Mary goodnight, said goodbye with a general wave, but made a point of shaking Gerry Hall's hand. He was Mary's young brother, a tall, innocent Irish kid with the sort of well washed good looks that guaranteed him a busy sex life in the not too distant future.

"Goodnight Mr. Maguire." He smiled shyly as we locked hands.

"Paddy," I said, "and not so much of the mister."

He grinned, blushing red. "Right so, Paddy...."

"And the long suffering lady is Phil, all right?"

He nodded and shook Phil's hand with some kind of gentleness that most people reserve for children.

Darcy looked at me as though he was about to spit right in my eye. Then he hymned a bit, nodding his head with a certain amount of reluctant appreciation. He lifted the glass of whiskey he'd poured for me. He smiled at Phil, his warm heart and the affection he genuinely felt for my precious girl showing in the great wide smile and the inclination of his head, before he said. "You're much too good for this prick, y'know that, don't you, darlin'?"

"But how could I be, Paddy?" Phil's eyes opened in a mockery of amazement. "Sure, he's one of the Royal Kings of Ireland, didn't you know?"

"And I have the fuckin' Blarney Stone in my pocket..." Darcy sniffed..."Would you like to kiss it for a shillin'?"

He looked to me. "Here goes nothing," he said, and lowered the glass of whiskey with one flick of his wrist and the slightest twitch in his throat. I watched his eyes explode as the spirit hit him. He smiled at me for a second just before he collapsed on the floor.

"He's all right," Mary insisted...." Do him good to sleep on the lino for a change...."

She wouldn't let me help lift him up. There were enough people to help her.... "Get Phil on home... she looks tired."

"All right so..." I kissed her face. "If you need anything," I nodded towards Darcy. "Just ring."

"I will, and see you both, soon."

We didn't talk much on the way home, it was too much effort over the noise of the engine. But as I took her up the stairs she stopped me and kissed me on the mouth.

"I was very proud of you back there...."

"I love you, Phil, love you more than I ever did."

She looked at me for a doubtful second, seeming about to

speak, stopping then, her expression moving into another gear.

"Will you give Kit a run home? It's late."

I nodded. "You go on to bed. I won't be long."

Kit was seventeen, like a young Egyptian, built on lines older than her years, with the heavy black hair over the low forehead, and a Semitic nose overshadowing her sensual mouth. Her mother was an acquaintance of Phil's and by all accounts Kit was a bit wild, at the very least undisciplined and self-willed. And she looked like she was more than ready for a rub of the relic.

She sat on the bucket seat as I drove over to Rosehampton.

"I think you're marvellous, not drinking like that strong man...." She spoke the last two words like someone who wanted to believe what she said.

I thought I was getting a show from her – in fact, I knew bloody well she was coming on strong. And the thought of it, of this young girl finding me attractive, left me short of breath for a few moments.

"You're not talking much, Paddy." Her accent might have been working class Cockney, but she had a way of saying things in such a loaded fashion that I was sure she knew what she'd succeeded in doing to me.

"Strong and silent." This was all I could find to say to a seventeen year old girl.

"Go on," she chided me, like a nanny cuffing one of her charges. "And me thinking you were a swinger."

What was I to say to that? Whether she knew it or not she had planted something there, as though she'd designed the sentence to make it impossible for anyone with ego to resist the implied criticism.

I didn't say anything.... With her perceptive thing going for her, she knew she had me sweating a bit. And I was damned if I was going to be manipulated by a seventeen year old....

"Go up Priory," she told me, like a fare paying passenger. "It's quicker."

Going up Priory Lane made no difference and we both knew it, but I didn't argue. Suddenly I wanted her and if she was looking for it, she was going to get it.

"Are you in hurry, Kit?"

"You know I'm not," She said offhand, "you know I want to stay with you for a while."

I pulled off the lane into a crescent of houses, finding a place at the end of the line of dwellings, under some trees. I got out of the cab, noticing how quiet the night was with one star sitting majestically close, like the fairy on top of the Christmas tree.

She was all over me the minute I got into the back of the cab and I didn't have to work at forgetting I was a married man and that she was a seventeen year old who baby sat when my wife and I wanted to go out. The warmth and the strength and the desire in Kit just blew my mind, and I made love to her without any concessions to her age. Which was how she wanted it – coming back at me like experienced woman of thirty, urging me on to greater effort, bucking beneath me with all kinds of natural flair.

My orgasm brought a long low whimpering from her lips, and she continued to hold me longer after her own orgasm was done.

When it occurred to me that I might have made her pregnant, she reacted to the sudden stiffening in my shoulders.

"There's no need to sweat, Paddy. I used a Gynamin."

I didn't understand. "But they take five minutes or something to dissolve, or whatever they do?"

Her teeth flashed in a smile. "I put it up when I got into the cab."

I resented that, the sureness of the bitch, but she made me smile none the less.

"You bloody cow."

She stopped my words with a kiss that was a demand for further attention. I broke off and her arms relaxed about me.

"You have to go."

"Phil is waiting for me...."

"I like Phil," she said, calmly, "but I love you."

"Me and everything else in trousers..." I said, in an attempt to shift the direction of the chat.

"Don't worry... I won't make any trouble for you...."

She kissed me with gentle lips, easy now in her acceptance of what had to be. "I did screw a few people, Paddy, but nobody since I met you...."

"I'm a married man, Kit." I was trying hard even if my voice didn't carry too much conviction.

"I just want to be your girl... one of your girls."

"You're crazy, you know that, don't you?"

"You don't have to love me," she said calmly.

"That's where you wrong, nit...!" I kissed her for a long time. "It's going to be bloody impossible not to love you and you know it...."

"Well love me then, mate..." I could hear the happiness in her...." Love me then and don't be bleedin' worrying about everything...."

"I couldn't hurt Phil, Kit. I love her.

"So you bloody should. She's a great bird... one of the nicest women I've met.... And you don't meet many...."

I drove back to Fulham, reeling just a bit from what had happened. Trying not to think about it, wiping my mouth with a tissue before throwing the rolled up paper hankie out of the window. I used the lavatory and brushed my teeth, making sure that I didn't smell of Kit. Jesus Christ! Seventeen.

Phil turned to me when I slipped into bed. Her arms encircled my waist and she kissed my mouth.

"You were a long time..." she mumbled, and I helped her out of her nightdress.

"You told me to pay the babysitter..." I groaned...." Why didn't you just tell me to give her money ...I'm worn out...."

"You may be..." Phil sighed, "but my friend is in good shape...."

The sheath of her good and decent love closed about me and I went to work to give her the best time she had ever had. And I mean, went to work, because with the nagging fingers of conscience poking into my peace of mind, and more than a slight area of concern about whether or not Kit could have given me the pox, there was no way in which I could just relax and enjoy making love to my lovely wife.

There was something else bothering me too. Up to that night I'd been able to excuse a lot of my promiscuity by blaming my behaviour on the booze.... Well, I hadn't had a drink in weeks, but my sobriety hadn't helped me walk away from the demands of my ego. Not when a seventeen year old typist cum baby sitter had made me feel that her life wouldn't be the same if I... ME... the great Paddy Maguire, was to turn down her offer of a bunk-up in the back of my overworked taxicab.

Chapter Sixteen
London. Winter '65

I wrote "Butcher Boy" in six weeks, and when I typed "The End" on the manuscript, I knew what writers meant when they said that those two words were just the sweetest pair in the English language.

The first novel... the only novel... the miracle book. God, but everybody should know, just once, what it feels like to sit there with the finished manuscript like a great golden weight in your hands.

You feel that some kind of miracle has happened. And I suppose it is a kind of miracle, at least to a guy who has dreamed for most of his life about being a writer. A fella who knows little or nothing abut the literary bit. And he's sitting there with sixty-five thousand words of a story that seems to have something in it that makes it special.

Obviously it's special to the fella who did the writing.... It should be, has to be, ought to be, even if it's the biggest load of knickers ever typed onto a bundle of paper. As I sat there I wondered how much of my own good feeling was just gratitude that I managed to write the book at all. And that kind of gratitude which borders on suppressed hysteria, leaving you feeling that you're just going to pop right out of you skin, well, if it didn't cloud your judgement, Christ, you'd have to be some kind of superhuman being.

"Butcher Boy" was a very simple story told in the first person singular. It was about a boy growing up in Dublin, and of course a lot of it was me and my life and my own background. Part of the boy was me, but then I discovered that most of the characters had a bit of me in them somewhere.

The good people were endowed with my better qualities and the shits were decked out in my bad habits. They seemed, to me at any rate, to come off the pages just like real people. And the narrative line was easy, ruthlessly pruned, so that I believed there wasn't one word that didn't earn its place. But then I was biased about the whole thing.

What was there though, and on this I was prepared to stick my neck out, was a kind of innocent ring in the voice of the storyteller who thought he knew it all. And paradoxically, the things that should have screwed him up, like the boozing and the hand galloping and the endless pursuit of one bird after another, instead those ingredients helped him cope with living in circumstances that seemed to be forever bordering on depravation of one kind or another.

His inherent hatred of his neighbourhood, his built-in resistance to the Catholic bullshit, as he saw it, just increased his determination not to go under, not to put some mot in the family way and marry her just because that was what the other fellas did. And he was sure of one thing. There had to be something better than this... so, much as he felt he loved one girl, he just walked away from it all, sad that he left little or nothing on leaving his girl, his home and family, for the first time. And that was it. That was my simple little novel, but to me it was a combination of the Bible and the Book of Kells, with a smattering of Frank Harris thrown in to keep the pot boiling.

When I thought about trying to get it published, I didn't really know how to go about it. I asked a few people in Ted Connor's pub, and all the waffling was finished, with me more confused than I'd been before I opened my mouth, a Dublin guy. A Dubliner who was a fine painter by the name of Will Kenny, took me to one side and told me to send it to Harrisons. I knew the name all right... a big publisher in the West End, but I wondered why he mentioned them.

"They seem to go for Paddy scribblers," he said

I thought this was about the best reason he could have

given me and I made up my mind to get the pages off to Harrisons the very next week. Will Kenny warned me not to be expecting any instant replies from them. Publishers were slow to send out acknowledgement slips, let alone give a decision about a book. Six months, he reckoned, before I'd know, one way or the other.

"Try to forget it, once you've given it to them, otherwise you could go nuts sitting around waiting."

I nodded. That's what I'd do, just send it off and forget about it. FORGET ABOUT IT! Sweet Jesus! Who was I kidding? I wasn't going to be able to sleep till I heard that somebody thought I'd written something special – and Christ only knew what I'd be like if it really was just a load of old cobblers.

I'd been doing some day work on the cab, with long nights at weekends. Working something like office hours I couldn't earn any big money, but at least I wasn't out hunting pussy, which hadn't helped the wage packet either. By really grafting Friday, Saturday and Sunday nights, I could make the week a good one financially. And it meant that I could see Kit for a few hours without anybody being any the wiser, and without running the risk of hurting Phil.

I was certain Phil had no idea about Kit and me, but something was there, like a wedge between us. Nothing that I could put my finger on. She was still a good wife and a superb mother and we were lovers in the same way that we'd always been. But something had gone out of our marriage.

It didn't have anything to do with my thing with Kit. She was good for me... I liked her a great deal - loved her I suppose, and I felt good when I was with her. Ego, sure, but what was the good in denying that to myself? It was there, needing to be fed, and Kit went a long way towards keeping it happy. And because I was doing a line with her, I wasn't putting myself out to go after other women. I loved making love to her, losing myself completely, forgetting all my responsibilities for the time we could spend in bed in the room I'd taken at Worlds End on New Kings Road.

Kit was remarkably mature for her age – a damn sight more so than I was, and she hadn't reneged in any way on her promise not to bug or make any trouble for me. She also cared about Phil and my children, and she still came to baby sit when we needed her. This was something that took some getting used to. We'd be undressing to get into the scratcher and she'd be discussing Kate and how much she loved her, and how happy Phil seemed that I was off the drink.

Phil didn't know it, but she did derive some benefit from my affair with Kit. Every time I came home from my seventeen year old, I took some kind of present to my lovely wife; flowers, chocolates, a magazine she wanted, something. And on the nights when Phil wanted me, I could always make love to her, regardless of how many times it had happened with Kit earlier in the evening. It was no hardship at all to try and give Phil a trip to end all journeys to love.

Phil had changed. She was quieter than she'd ever been, and it seemed to me she was getting more so as the year wore on towards the last furlong.

At first I put it down to habit. After all, it was for me that she stayed quiet when I was writing. But after a while I didn't think that this was the reason. And she had developed a taste for lying on her side when we made love. Again, this didn't bother me at first. What married couple didn't experiment, indulge in a little variation on the theme? But as it became more and more important to her, I had the bloody terrifying feeling that she just didn't want me on top of her. That she didn't want my face, my lips, close to her mouth. And I bled to think that this could be true. That during all those times when I stank of whiskey, when I thought I was King Fucking Kong as I took her, God, was it possible that I'd been turning her stomach with my whiskey stanched presence had to be something akin to violation? Oh Jesus God! Had she tolerated me when she didn't really want me? Had she let me use her when the sight of me drunk or close to it had made her want to run screaming from the room? I didn't know, but in the pit of my stomach I experienced a feeling of dread. A sickening, crab apple coating of bile seemed to be creeping around the walls of my gut, choking up and into my throat, so that I couldn't breathe. And so my screams of pain, my tortured ego-sick protest, tore through me silently, a cacophony with the power of a plague of locusts, eating up with ease whatever little bit of security I'd had where Phil was concerned.

My kids were a delight, with Dan, two months old now, was very much a sleeper. But just to stand over his crib and look down at the contentment in him – it seemed to be wrapped around him like a blanket. Well, just knowing, feeling his presence in the flat, was enough to fill me with the odd moments of joy.

Kate of course was Queen of the May. Tiny and truly beautiful, running about from the time she was ten months old, and sharp as a new razor. Cheeky, I suppose, but that was how I wanted her. I wanted her to be able to fend for herself, hold her own in any company, and once she could be bothered to excuse herself, I permitted her the right to throw her two pennor'th into any conversation that aroused her interest.

She was only two years old, but she could talk like a child, an intelligent child, of eight years. But then I'd been a chatterbox at a very early age, and Phil had a record of precociousness that made her recent passive, retreating inward behaviour, even more desperately sad.

Kate was a very loveable child. Many's the time Phil and I howled with laughter at the way our two year old sprite would request, would you believe, demand, a cuddle.

Phil and I, were great cuddlers. Well, we had been, and to know that Kate wasn't going to be tight with herself, to see the openness of her nature revealed in that, to us, special way, was very good for the heart.

I tried to teach her to be independent of me, to let her

breathe her own air, enjoy her own laughter, collect her own bruises. It was hard for surely she was made to be loved and cherished, to be cuddled all the time and to have warmth and love and affection brim filling her daily bath.

But I loved her that much: enough not to selfishly touch her and caress her silken hair, which I wanted to do every time she came into vision. I cared enough about her life for herself not to try and turn her into an extension of my own personality. She had to walk her own road and I believed in an early start. Not that I was ever callous or unyielding to her, it was just that by trying to rear her as a mate of mine, I felt she was less likely to have any filial hang-ups later on.

Phil disagreed with me when I encouraged Kate to call me by my Christian name, but Kate didn't grab this idea anyway, so it never became a major issue. But her swearing was something that did make Phil really mad, and I got the blame for it only because it was my fault.

I tried to placate Phil. "She'll grow out of it."

"You're talking about a two year old girl, for Christ's sake..." Phil was fuming, her eyes broken with anger, seeming to have as many separate areas as a diamond.

"It's sickening, for God's sake. She said fuck to Mum only yesterday."

"What did Mum think?" I managed not to smile, relishing the picture of Mrs. Williams chortling at the very idea.... A nice woman who wouldn't be mad about a thing like that....

"You make me sick." Phil spun on me and I regretted the tone of my voice when I'd asked the question.

"I didn't mean to annoy."

"You never mean to annoy me or to offend me, or to hurt me." She stood with her feet apart and I could see that she didn't want to go on, that she felt it better not to say any more. But she couldn't suppress her anger and I tried to believe that whatever she said, it was only hot temper.

"I've had about as much of you as I can take."

"Oh, come on now."

"No. No I won't bloody well come on now.... And this time I'm not going to end up apologizing.... This is one time you're not going to beat me with words...."

Kate was watching a kid's show on television and so far Phil's anger hadn't penetrated into her contentment.

"Can we leave it for now..." I flicked my eyes at Kate's back.

Phil looked as though she was going to strike me. "You bastard...." She shook her head in disbelief, her nostrils dilating as she fought to control her anger. "I can't talk to you in front of Kate about your swearing in front of Kate... God, dear Christ, but there's no end to your gall...."

"We made a deal..." I reminded her as easily as I could....

"Oh yes... yes, I forgot... your childhood... it was littered with broken teapots and plates and saucers that your parents threw at each other.... And you don't want your daughter to grow up in that kind of atmosphere...."

"That's right..." I nodded, grinding my teeth, to stop myself ripping into her "I'm sorry about swearing...."

"Sorry!" Phil made it sound like a foul swearword "Almighty Maguire has to say he's sorry.... Sorry I got pissed again... sorry I didn't get home for the dinner you cooked... sorry I didn't earn enough money for us to have a decent holiday... sorry sorry sorry... the King of Ireland is sorry.... Which fixes everything.... Just one little word and everything is all right... the instant panacea for all ills... sorry from High King Maguire...."

"Look Phil, if we must, can we go down to the kitchen?"

"Don't worry yourself. I've finished." She was holding back bitter tears and I stood there looking at her, drowning in my own emptiness.

"But just before I shut up, do one thing for me... use your magic word... say sorry about fucking up my life...."

The tears disappeared from her eyes and the veil of resignation slipped back indoors. Phil bent down to pick up some toys of Kate's.

"Kate?"

"Yes Mama..." Kate turned obediently to face Phil.

"Is it fair that I have to pick up your toys...?"

Kate jumped to her feet "I'll do it darling...." She rushed to Phil and threw her arms about her neck. "I'm dreadfully untidy for such a small person, aren't I, Mama?"

I bit my lip, praying that the child wouldn't look my way. Phil buried her face in the dark brown hair. And she began to cry.

"Why are you crying, Mama?"

I stood there helplessly, my heart in splinters. Did I ever do anything but hurt people, cause pain? Phil told Kate it was all right... that she was crying with happiness and love for her.

"And Dada? Aren't some of the tears for Dada?"

Phil looked up at me and all I could think of was a broken fireplace in a cabin in Northern Ireland, a broken fireplace filled with dead grey ash. Ash that represented the total remaining sum of a dream.

Chapter Seventeen

My book "Butcher Boy" was accepted by Harrisons, and I signed a contract without even reading it. This all happened within six weeks of me posting the manuscript off, which I'd done because I hadn't the guts or whatever it is you need to just walk into the publishers and offer them the thing myself.

But there had been a few seconds, three or four days before I got the first call from the publishers, when it didn't matter whether the book was accepted or not.

A stranger on the other end of the phone connection, a reader for Harrisons, had phoned me to say that I'd written a bloody marvellous little novel.

"I've no right to call you. In fact, it's probably against the rules, but I simply had to. It's a lovely book and you should be very proud of it."

Fire engines raced through my head and I prayed that somebody wasn't pulling a gag on me. I asked my caller his name again – if I'd heard it at all, I couldn't remember it.

"Devlin, David Devlin... I write a bit myself...."

"Mr. Devlin, listen... I don't know how to thank you. I can't believe, it's, well, oh God! Where are the fucking words? Thanks. Jesus Jesus thank you. Mr. Devlin."

I embarrassed the poor guy, which I hadn't meant to do.... And I worried him a bit as well.... Making him wonder if he hadn't been unwise to call me at all.

"It's just my opinion, you understand, and though obviously I intend to recommend the book for publication, it might very well not happen...."

"It doesn't matter," I heard myself say... "I don't give a

damn.... Somebody, you, Mr. Devlin... telling me I can write... that's enough for now...."

After I put the phone down I knew that I hadn't been kidding him. I'd meant it.... Somebody believed I could write.... Me, writing, Jesus! The Head with the complex about not being educated... forever beating the breast about no schooling and with hardly a good word to say about what schooling I'd got... I turned to Phil... "He likes the book. ..."

She nodded, her eyes misty. "I'm glad, Maguire... and... well, I'm sorry for those things I said...."

We'd been having almost daily arguments, so much so that I'd come to regard them as a kind of safety valve for Phil. A release of the tension that my presence seemed to create. I nodded my thanks, but I felt that she really should have said she was sorry things had got to a point where she had to say the things she said.

When I signed the contract, the fella who was to become my editor at Harrisons told me he thought the book was a piece of straight autobiography. I laughed out loud, telling him that I'd made it up. That the background was authentic enough, but that the characters and the story line had come out of my head.

"Really?" He seemed genuinely surprised, which was, I suppose, a compliment.

"Like, what's the most autobiographical part to you?"

He gave it a few moments thought, pursing his lips. He seemed like an all right bloke, but a bit pompous for such a young man. All waistcoats and horn rimmed glasses that made him look overdressed. But nice with it.

"The moment when your young brother dies...." He nodded... "Yes.. that bit... that was it for me...."

"But I didn't have a young brother who died," I said. "Call my mother and ask her right now if you like."

The idea of Ma being on the phone made me smile and of course he wasn't about to make the call. After that we talked about a few points and I came away feeling happier than I can describe. My book was going to be published. My book....

Christmas arrived, with my promise about not drinking still intact. We had a good few quid too, thanks to some very hard work on the cab and little or no spending. Phil was easier with me than she'd been in a long time, but the fact that she hardly ever seemed to need me, rarely making any advance towards love making was the barometer reading cloudy depression overhanging all points of the compass.

I had always loved Christmas, ignoring the chat about it being for kids and shopkeepers, that it was the annual take-on by big business. Christmas to me was a good thing, a time when people seemed to take the trouble to wish each other well. I'd heard it called ridiculous, out of date, and all the rest of it. That it was a joke for people who didn't see each other from one end of the year to the next to be sending each other greetings cards. To me, this made the festival even more valid, more important. God, if people couldn't say hello to each other once a year.

Unfortunately, Christmas hadn't been the same since I'd married Phil. We'd had the big day dinner with her family every year, and I'd come to dread even the thought of sitting down at the same table as Old Man Williams.

Phil's mother I loved in a strange way; Jackie was a great guy as far as I was concerned, and I liked his wife, Val. Susan, who was growing into a very tasty bird, was a real pal of mine, and though herself and Phil didn't look much alike, a blind man could have seen they were sisters.

But Phil's father I couldn't take at any price, and, to give him his due, he was equally consistent in his total lack of regard for me. He continued to refuse to even try and play the game, which was something I'd been willing to do for everybody else's sake.

The acceptance of my book hadn't caused the slightest ripple of excitement to creep into his attitude. Mrs. Williams was so surprised that her reaction was practically an insult, but I took it in the way she meant it. She was a good and kind woman, devoid of any desire to hurt a living soul. Jackie thought it was cool, and I knew he wanted me to make a million out of it. Val was impressed enough to make me aware that she hadn't taken me very seriously up until then and Susan was as proud of me as she could have been, demanding a signed copy for her bookshelf when it was published. But the father of my lovely wife, hearing that I hadn't expected to make any kind of money from the book, sniffed his only comment, which was one of utter disdain and went back to remembering that I'd turned down a chance to be a part of his firm just a few weeks before.

Jackie had offered me a job. He wanted me to run a new cab garage he was buying and his proposition had been so attractive that I'd had to sweat a bit more I could bring myself to turn it down.

I would be me my own boss. The wages were as much as I could have earned in a very good week on the cab and I would get commission for each new driver I lured on to the work sheet. There was a car supplied, plus perks like free insurance, bonuses, any number of nights out during the year, not forgetting a directorship of the firm within two years and a certain number of shares with my name on them.

When Jack had first mentioned the job I had just submitted my book to Harrisons, and despite all my bullshit about forgetting it for six months, I was sweating my way towards a nervous breakdown, wondering how long it would take and if it would be accepted. So that I could have lived without the added responsibility of having to decide if I should go into business and make myself some real money and lay the foundations for a secure future for myself and my family.

Phil didn't say much, but she made it fairly clear that she thought it was a golden opportunity for both of us. And it would help things between her father and me. But her words were flat and I knew she was thinking that regardless of what she felt, I would do my own thing.

I was oscillating like a bloody pendulum, and a couple of

nights I lay awake trying to decide what in hell I should do. That guaranteed a monthly income was a bloody great temptation to guy who didn't earn a shilling for any hour he wasn't behind the wheel of the droshki. Droshki. It's an aberration of the Russian / Yiddish word for cart, but meaning to me, shitcart, which was how I thought of the old FX3 from which I earned my living. And a good living at that.

Old Man Williams called me on the phone, trying not to tell me I should take Jackie's offer, but pointing out that it was a chance to better myself. He made it sound as though I was being adopted by a magnanimous family who had seen me lying drunk in a local gutter. I didn't shoot him down because I knew he couldn't help the feeling that I wasn't good enough for Phil, which I was prepared to accept as the truth. But I did want to yell at him that he should have spent the bread to finish her education, sent her off to Switzerland to a school for young ladies, if he wanted her to have any chance of marrying the kind of person he thought of as a gentleman. I said nothing. Not until he informed me that if I did go into the business, he would pull whatever strings necessary to get me into the Freemasonry. That did it. Freemasonry and me? No way. Christ! After my experience with Irish Catholicism, I wanted to be a "Mason" about as desperately as I wanted to be a bloody Scoutmaster.

I talked to Jackie that same evening. It was funny, really... the nights without sleep looking for a decision from inside myself, then a few days later, having that elusive bloody decision made for me by Old Man Williams.

"I'm hung upon the idea of being a writer...."

"Fair enough," Jackie said. "I can get plenty of people to do the job." He grinned. "Trouble is you can't trust the bastards."

"How do you know you could trust me?"

"What? My own brother-in-law. Come off it... you wouldn't turn me over." He gave that a fraction of a second's thought... "Would you?"

"No, but I'd steal the old man blind for the charge...."

"Oh, dad's all right... the odd time... he just can't stand the Irish." He smiled, relaxed as always, his oval face free of any line of concern. "Some Mick shoved a rifle in his face in nineteen twenty-two I think it was. He was delivering a truck of something. Left him shit scared and anti-Irish ever since."

"I'd love the job, really, Jackie, but it wouldn't be fair to you." He looked at me quizzically and I went on: "I've dreamed for too long about being a writer. If you got half of my interest you'd be doing well."

"If it's something you want," he said.

"Oh, it's crazy, I know... I mean, how many times have I stopped to ask myself what have I got to offer. The Old Man is right about no education and the rest of it....But I can put words down on paper.... And I know that in time, with any kind of encouragement, the words will be good... I just know it...."

"You did the right thing then." Jackie emptied his glass. "Want another of those?"

I shook my head. "Another bleedin' orange juice and I'll begin to look like Max Jaffa."

He grinned: "You can make up for it at Christmas."

"Believe it," I said. "I'm like a dog in the trap one. Waiting for the bell."

And that was it. A straight talk with Jackie and not one shred of hard feeling as we left the pub. I was grateful to him, but then he was always the same, and in the years to come he wasn't to change, not to me, anyway, and before too long he was going to prove just how good a friend he could be.

Chapter Eighteen
London. Christmas '65

While Phil put the finishing touches to the children, I went down to the local to have my first drink in what seemed like a lifetime. And I swear I was licking my lips at the thoughts of what I was going to do to a fair amount of Scotch whiskey.

It was a late lunchtime and I felt very good. I'd done my duty to my wife. A nice watch that had cost me twenty lids, loads of presents for the kids, my in-laws, and a letter long gone off to Ma with a fiver in it for herself and Pops. Not that Pops would spend the money. It would go into his drawer, the second one down in a chest of drawers, which had a clasp lock on it, now that it contained his life savings.

When I walked into the pub, Darcy was at the bar with Theo and Gerry Hall. There were a few other heads in the company, but I didn't know them, apart from nodding the odd hello.

Darcy leapt into the air, and young Gerry, Mary's tall, gentle brother, laughed in embarrassment. Theo nodded my way, as much as to say "he's pissed already".

"Oh, we'll see some drinking now," Darcy cried, so that the whole pub seemed to turn and look at me. "Jesus God, when Romeo gets a taste of it, lock up your missus."

He clapped me on the back, hugging me a happy Christmas, and I loved Darcy at that moment, though a moment later he had me so mad that I wanted to punch him in the head.

"Pissed tonight, Maguire. All of us. Langers, the lot. Even Gerry here, waiting to see you drop the balls of malt...."

"I never drink Irish, you know that."

"Ah... shit, you'd drink whiskey out of a pauper's pisspot...

Irish, Schmirish, will you listen to him?" He turned to Theo... "Remember Jersey?"

Theo looked just a shade fed up. "No, can't remember a bit of it... tell us about it?"

Darcy smiled at the sarcasm. "Go pull yourself." He turned to the barman. "Harry, will you stick four of them miserable little measures into a glass... mister Maguire has a hole on his tooth...."

Harry looked at me, I shook my head. He waited for me to tell him what I wanted. Darcy turned back to him and repeated the order. Harry didn't move.

"I don't want your whiskey." For some reason I was really angry. Christ! All I'd wanted was a drink, not a bloody grandstand performance. But that was Darcy all over, meaning well, but nagging people to do things his way when it came to drinking.

"I'll have an orange juice, please Harry."

Darcy almost fell over, Harry smiled, delighted, while Theo looked at me without trying to conceal his own surprise. He didn't comment, Theo rarely did in situations like that. He went his own way absolutely, and he allowed that other people were entitled to do the same thing.

"What is this?" Theo turned away from Darcy's appeal for guidance. "He's taking the piss, right?.." He turned to Harry as he put the glass on the counter. "Give him whiskey, Harry, he's acting the maggot."

Harry reacted to my headshake by taking the money for the orange juice and ringing it up on the cash register. I held up the glass of juice. "Happy Christmas, everybody."

"Missed you in the shelter the other night." Theo said, when all the greetings had been seen to.

"Only popped in to see if you were there, grafting like a slave the past month."

"Maguire, come on now, a joke's a joke," Darcy pleaded.

"Can't you see we're in conversation you little ferret?" Theo growled at Paddy, winking then at Gerry who looked just a bit uneasy at his tone. It was understandable... the kid hadn't been around us long enough, to know that this was how the script was read all the time.

"You're doing well with the sauce." Theo made no bones about the fact that he was impressed. "Never thought you'd last."

"You were nearly right about every other day...." I shook my head... "Especially when I got word about the novel."

Darcy just stood there looking at me. His face was sad and his eyes were those of a man who'd been badly let down.

"Surprised you came in at all," he moaned, a glint of annoyance pushing the hurt out of his eyes. "I mean, with all your literature friends."

Theo flicked his eyes to the ceiling in annoyance. "Don't start for Jaysus sake. It's only bleedin' lunchtime."

"How's the job, Gerry?" I wanted to steer the verbal in another direction. Once Darcy got the bit between his teeth there was no stopping him.

"Oh, it's great, Paddy, great altogether."

"Screwing that barmaid with the big knockers, are you?"

He smiled, blushing deeply at this. "If he's built in proportion, she's in for a right roasting," Theo commented.

"Won't be seeing you tonight, I suppose. Be off down to Chelsea.... Or is it Knightsbridge this Christmas?"

"Well, fuck me gently," Theo sighed. "Happy days are here again...."

"Mary ruin the turkey or something?" I said to Darcy.

"Fuck the turkey... won't get out of it that way.... We're just cab drivers and barmen... you're the big writer."

I looked at Theo. "It's a toss up between him and Phil's old man.... My Christmas double, right?"

Theo nodded, spitting a long stream of imaginary tobacco juice in Darcy's direction. "A spittoon with legs," he said. He looked at the glass in my hand. "You sure?"

I nodded and he told Harry to set them up again. "How's Phil?" He knew what had been happening between Phil and me, and he was concerned as much about my wife as he was about me.

"All right," I said. "It's not great, not right, but I don't seem to be able to sort it out now."

"The four year scratch?"

"What's that?" Darcy asked him.

"Well, it's ten times worse than the seven year itch, but don't worry, you're too much of a pisspot ever to get involved with another bird."

Darcy was very drunk. "Don't mind that, don't mind it. We can't all be good looking, can't all have the bullshit to charm the knickers off. Can't all be big writers like Mister Maguire."

I put my glass down. I wasn't angry any more, I was bored. Jesus, was I bored? I winked at Theo and he made an almost imperceptible nod with his head. I moved my left hand an inch towards Gerry, a short and sweet gesture of goodbye. He seemed surprised but he nodded and gave me a wink. He was young and he was green, but he wasn't slow on the uptake. I moved on to the door before Darcy could give me another argument. "Happy New Year, Heads," I said and slipped out, relief like sweat, filling the pores of my mind.

I walked back to the house and picked up Phil, Kate and Dan. Phil didn't have much to say but then she had a fairly tough day ahead, stuck between the two men in her life like someone waiting for a dynamite keg to blow.

I couldn't help her. I'd tried by assuring her I'd never really get stuck into her father, but she'd seen me lose my temper elsewhere and she didn't put too much faith in my control if I was really pushed to the wall.

Mrs. Williams fussed around the kids, and for me the meaning of Christmas was illustrated by the warmth and the joy in her, as she welcomed her children and her children's children to her dinner table. She practically skipped into the parlour, Dan in her arms, Kate at her heels like a little terrier, to find their presents at the tree. Phil smiled at her mother's excitement, which was considerable. I mean, to see that woman skipping along like a two year old, well, it was no easy task for a woman her size.

"Happy Christmas, Head, I said to Phil. She nodded, but she just wasn't able to hide the wish in her eyes, a wish that we were really happy and not just mumbling words at each other because it was the thing to do today. I kissed her gently on the lips. She didn't back off or anything like that, but she didn't come back at me and if she was in any way surprised that my breath didn't smell of whiskey, she managed to hide it pretty well.

Old Man Williams was pouring drinks all round when I followed Phil into the dining room. For a few seconds there was much kissing and hugging. Val looked lovely in a tight fitting orange dress, her second pregnancy not showing yet. Lisa ran to kiss me, three years old and a sweetheart, with legs so long that she had the awkward look of a foal. She was my god-daughter and I loved her very much. Jackie was sitting there nodding his head at something his father was saying. Then Phil was in her father's arms, hugging him with love, while he sort of waited for her to finish so that he could pour the rest of the drinks. But, as always where he was concerned, Phil didn't notice, or if she did, she didn't allow it to show.

Maybe I was feeling a bit superior after my dry trip to the boozer. I don't know, I mean, Darcy taking me for granted like that, well, it had just gone right up my nose. To hell with it, I wasn't going to be that predictable, not even for someone as close to me as Paddy. I watched the old man hand Phil a glass of sherry: he turned to me then, and I thought I'd have a drop of Scotch.

"There's beer out in the hall if you want one," he told me, charming as a crocodile with halitosis.

It's funny how you can feel you're reeling backwards, when you know that in fact you're not moving. And I wonder if it showed in my face just then, if the others in the room could see that I felt I'd been kicked very hard in the ballbag.

I knew that Phil would be willing me to think the old man didn't mean it, and I was aware of the tension that had crashed into that Christmas Day. It quivered like an arrow, the silence it created being a noise of its own.

I hope I mumbled "forgive me" but I just don't know... I left the room as casually as I could. I pulled the door gently after myself, hoping they would assume I'd gone to get my bottle of beer, my happy day drink from my father-in-law.

The violence inside me had made me weak with terror. As it had done so often in the past. And I knew if I didn't get out of the house, my self-control, which was spinning away from me anyway, would desert me completely.

Better to go, to get out, than to stay. The risk was too great for me to remain. My spirit was shaking with rage and I was sore inside, hurt to a ridiculous degree by the old man's attitude. If I didn't go I just knew I'd crack up completely. I'd swallowed too much venom to come out, all of it with his name written on it.

I got into my cab and drove up to the Greyhound on Fulham Palace Road. Phil and the kids were safe and sound. My splitting out of the house wasn't going to help her in any way, but this was one time, when regardless of what she or her family thought of me, I was doing her a favour. And what I did with myself didn't seem to matter very much. I wanted a drink, many drinks. Enough anyway, to help me lose the smell that was lousing up my stomach.

Theo was in the pub. He'd left Darcy and the others to join a cabbie called Tony Marsh and his family. They'd asked him to spend the day with them, and I was never so glad to see a bunch of people in my life before. Theo put a large whiskey in my hand. He didn't say anything, but he knew somehow that I wouldn't be eating any turkey with my wife and her people.

Tony Marsh was a Cockney who loved the world and his missus, Beryl, was a jolly bird who enjoyed life without bothering two fucks about anybody else. They had two children,

Eddie who was about twenty-two, a rangy, tough looking fella, who worked in the fruit market his mother ran, and a daughter, Eileen, who was tall and sexy looking, but shy to a point, that practically made her invisible.

I spent the afternoon and early evening, dancing and drinking, with everybody, except Eileen, doing their party piece, while Theo and I took turns at keeping the party going. I sang my heart out. Every love song I could remember, pouring out my misery through the lyrics of Rodgers and Hart, Porter, Gershwin, and all those other great purveyors of the indigo mood.

Just before I left – and I was carrying a load, Theo who was ossified out of his mind, began eating a dozen red carnations for a bet of ten shillings. And within thirty seconds he had each and every one of us rolling about the carpet, pleading with him to stop before some of us burst a gut laughing. He sprinkled imaginary salt on the petals, rejected some as being not quite ripe, picked his teeth with the stalks before chewing them with avidity, ending up by putting the vase on his head, draining every drop of the water, before he had to rush out into the front garden to shower the flowers beds with the whole lot. I left him semi-conscious with the Mash mob, shaking my head at his lunacy, before I tried pulling myself together enough to go back and pick up Phil and my children.

I waited outside the house while Phil dressed Kate. Dan was already asleep and I put his carrycoat on the floor of the cab. Phil didn't have anything to say to me, and yet I didn't feel she was blaming me too much. Not that I was feeling anything at all now that the night air had reached me. Luckily I didn't have far to drive and I was able to carry Dan upstairs to the flat, before the very definite need to sit down hit me hard.

I slept on the couch that night, feeling very sorry for myself, as some fella in the street staggered by singing "I'll Be Home For Christmas"... "If Only In My Dreams...."

Chapter Nineteen
London. '66

I finished my days and nights as a London Cab Driver in June. This should have happened about two years earlier. A professional driver who had to drink the way I did, just to keep going, well, his behaviour is criminal, and there is no point in pretending otherwise. But I didn't think about that. I was in an almighty bind. I hated the job, I wanted to write full time, but I had a family to support, and I needed desperately to be the bread winner.

My standards began to slip as the going got tougher. For the first time I wished my wife had some money, something that would have bugged me when we first got married. I just loved Phil and the fact that her people had bread, well, if it meant anything to me, it was that I had to try all the harder to show I wanted none of it. More than one cab driver congratulated me on landing "the boss's daughter".

My first year on the cabs, I drove for Jackie, moving on then when I got my own motor. I resented those guys patting me on the back. They were the kind of men who would have jumped three feet in the air to get into the Freemasonry or the like - it would have lifted them above their mates, just like marrying into money. Well, it wasn't my way and I had such a hang-up about it that people might have been forgiven for thinking I protested too much. This shouldn't have bothered me, but it did. I wanted everybody to think I was a great guy, and great guys didn't think about marrying for money.

Phil had some shares in the family business, given to her to avoid death duties so that it was less a personal thing on Old Man Williams' part than a matter of principle. He hated paying taxes of any kind, and I'm not sure I blamed him.

Each year there was a dividend of a few hundred pounds and though I felt bad about allowing Phil to use it for any reason other than personal things, it began to happen, and I didn't bring it up, unless she mentioned it.

When my cabbing became pointless because of my boozing – I seemed to be working only to get money for drink – I thought about stopping, but I couldn't bring myself to think about doing another job. And anyway, I told myself, I'm going to stop drinking and earn some decent money for a change. Jesus! Talk about kidding.

I was still involved with Kit, and to be fair to her, she settled for what she could get off me. Secret meetings, sex together a few times a week, without so much as a trip to a cinema, theatre, restaurant or anywhere else in all the time we were together. In her place I wouldn't have stood for it, but I didn't twist her arm and each time she showed up to meet me I was surprised. Despite her words of love, I expected her just not to show one night... and never again after that.

In the previous nine months I'd been involved in two accidents with the cab. Both, strangely enough, on nights when I hadn't yet stopped to have a few drinks. Neither accident was my fault, though in both of them the other guy was injured, one of them badly. I was steeped in luck, having about fourteen witnesses to the first one, and nothing less than an off duty copper backing me up on the second. I didn't even have to go to court either time.

Then during a filthy night in May, a bitterly cold rain-filled night that seemed to have slipped out of November, I was driving over Waterloo Bridge with a bird I'd pulled, and both of us langers, when somehow I saw a woman start to climb up onto the parapet of the bridge.

It was crazy that I could see her at all. The windscreen was filthy despite the wipers, I was full of booze, and most of my attention was being directed to the raver on the pull down seat behind me. But I did see the woman on the bridge.

I pulled the cab into the kerb, breaking, turning off the engine, telling my passenger to stay put, opening the door and jumping out, all without a single thought. I ran back along the footpath, drenched to the skin before I reached the poor cow who wanted to kill herself.

She was just standing up on the thing when I got to her. It was something to witness. The way she pulled her shoulders back, drawing her chin up, as though finding a shred of dignity with which to turn out the light.

I grabbed her skirt and just yanked her backwards as fiercely as I could. She tumbled towards me, yelling obscenities, clattering down on top of me, punching and spitting and trying to get up and away from me. But I held onto her, shaking her like an old sack, slapping her a sharp whack across the face, when this didn't work.

Then there were coppers all over us – three of them – the crew of a passing squad car, and because I'd forgotten how much I'd been drinking, I was bloody glad to see them.

I got up with the help of one of them.... My face was bleeding where the bird had caught me with a sharp right hander. The rain was still pumping down but I could see the wild eyes of the woman. She was being held by two of the coppers – and I hope never again to be the object of such malevolence.

"Fuck you. Bastard! Interfering swine." She spat at me, but the wind gave it to the river. The fuzz took her away to the car and I felt beaten.

"What happens to her now?" I said.

"Don't you concern yourself, mate. You did enough."

Suddenly I was hysterical. "But what happens to her for fuck's sake.... What's to stop her doing it tomorrow? Tell me, just tell me that?"

The big policeman took me by the arm and led me to the edge of the footpath. Thanks to the weather there weren't any curiosity merchants about.

"You've been drinking, son, right?"

"Of course I've been fucking drinking. Oh God!"

He touched my cab badge. I'd forgotten it was in my lapel. "You're a London cabbie, son. Get yourself in bother, y'know. Now why don't you go on home. Get into some dry clothes."

He cooled my hysterics with those few words. A man who was entitled to nick me for being pissed in charge of a motor vehicle. The fact that it was a London Taxicab meant that the book would have been thrown at me. I got the message fairly fast.

"Thanks, Sergeant."

He nodded, rain dripping off the edge of his cap. "You go on home now, son, and watch out in the future."

Moments like that, fractions of time which seemed to be designed specifically to help me realise what I was doing somehow didn't reach me....All the luck I'd had in two accidents, that scene on the bridge.... Surely I should have realised that somebody was praying for me.... That I was being spared injury, prison, death, for some reason. But next night I was out cabbing again, with enough booze to help me try and earn a night's wages.

It was another accident that made me quit, in this scene I was a witness, a helper, but probably the fella who suffered most.

I'd come out of the Bell and Horns Shelter at Brompton, I was tired and going home. It was about two thirty in the morning and I'd had a decent enough night. Theo was still in the shelter but I'd listened to enough chat, some of it very funny, and anyway I needed some sleep.

I went towards Cromwell Road taking it easy and I had the green light at Exhibition Road. I moved into the junction but the cab seemed to freeze on me as I heard this screech of brakes on my right. This huge American car was burning up rubber – obviously the driver hadn't seen the red light facing him till he saw me across from the main road on his left. He came onto the junction, broadside, so that the rear bumper of his car barely missed the back of my cab. He hadn't hit me but it was so close that I'd made a move in the driving cabin, as though I could help the cab out of his way by jerking my body forward. The bang that followed was so loud, like some kind of heavy gun going off close to my ear, that I'd stopped and ran back without taking the time to work out that it really wasn't any of my business, but then of course that would have been the sensible thing to do and I wasn't too hot in that particular area.

The American car was a write off – practically wrapped around the remains of the traffic island and the traffic light pole. As I got to it, I couldn't see the driver anywhere. Mind you, I was making the mistake of looking for him inside the car. There were bottles of brandy and champagne all over the floor of the motor. Then I found myself looking at the soles of the driver's shoes, heels up, against the dashboard. He had been thrown through the windscreen, so that he was now lying across the right hand bonnet, with the toes of his shoes keeping him from rolling onto the ground. As I moved to lift him out of the broken glass, his blood was dripping down by the front wheel which, like the back one, had twisted in half. He was a tall man, but slim, so he wasn't too heavy. I lifted him off the bonnet, bending sideways to get as much of my right side as possible under his chest and head. All kinds of do's and don'ts were running in and out of my head but I ignored them. All I could think of was getting him out of that broken glass, get him covered up while we waited for an ambulance to arrive.

He looked like an Arab but his suit and shoes were Saville Row and Bond Street. I turned him gently in my arms. Surely he was dead. As I did so part of the side of his head flopped a little bit, some tissues almost covering his badly damaged ear. For a fraction of a second, I seemed to be looking inside his head. My legs started to buckle, so I shut my eyes, got it together and staggered away from the car, only to fall down on my knees in the middle of the junction. Cars were stopping and someone yelled that the ambulance was on the way. I held your man and somehow I got my jacket off to cover him. He was semi-conscious for a few moments, and he was trying to touch the torn side of his head. I wanted to weep, to scream at him to lie still. A woman bent over me and held a cigarette to my lips. She slipped her coat off then and wrapped it about him. The cigarette helped me steady up. I saw a taxi stop and three birds get out. They ran across, hostesses from one of the clubs in the West End. I knew them only because many nights I'd dropped them in to their work, and a few times I'd taken them home again.

"There goes the party," one of them said looking down at the Arab, while I remembered all the booze in the car.

A tall man, who looked like an Equerry, but only because the cat in my arms seemed to me be some kind of Prince, started rabbiting in some foreign language – and it was angry stuff directed at the young Arab. I started to scream at the man, telling him to fuck off, shut up. Jesus! The fella had to be dying in my arms and somebody was trying to read him the riot act.

When the ambulance men took him away a couple of cabbies helped me to my feet. I was numb with cold and my legs were dodgy for a few minutes. A copper asked me a few questions.... Just witness stuff.... One of the cabbies, an oldish man I didn't know told me I shouldn't have got involved.

"Bleedin' piss artist... car's fulla booze.... You should have kept goin' mate, not your affair."

If I'd had the energy, I would probably have hit him, or at least given him a mouthful that would have curled his grey hair. And yet he was right. I should have ignored the bang and driven on home.

Home. In the bathroom I realised for the first time that I was drenched in claret.... Right through my shirt, right down the front of me, I was covered in blood. I tore my clothes off, ripping them away from my body. I ran water into the bath, but my legs deserted me again and I remained huddled on the floor, all my helplessness streaming out of me through my eyes, and I'd swear it was an hour before I was able to get up and climb into the bath.

For a week after that the cab never left the street outside the house. I couldn't even look at it and by the time I got back each night I couldn't even see it, I was so drunk. And I was so confused inside my head that I didn't even think that I should stop... I needed to drink.... And worse, I didn't want to do anything *but* drink.

Chapter Twenty
London. Summer '66

My brother Billy bought the cab from me. Not that I cared whether anybody did or not. I felt nutty enough to just go out one morning, pouring petrol over it before I put a match to the whole thing.

Phil flipped when I told her the cab was going. I couldn't blame her.... She had every reason to worry where the grocery money was coming from. I told her things would work out but she wasn't having it. She was sick to the teeth with me.

"And what's worse, I've lost my respect for you." She paced the room like a caged animal. "I've tried, tried to hold on to it... I believed you... every time.... Every time I said to myself, this time he'll do it.... Every stupid fucking time...."

Five times in the previous week, morning after morning, I'd been on my knees in desperation, begging her not to leave, not to tell me to go. If she did that.... If her life became totally unbearable because of my presence, I felt I'd just walk out and kill myself. Oh God! It sounds so dramatic, and yet it was such a simple thing to consider.... She was the norm, the good, the decent, the ordinary human being, growing to womanhood without a single hang-up.... Confucius might have been her teacher, for she practiced tolerance in such an easy, matter of fact way that she never had to stop and think about it.... She made tolerance the highest virtue, without ever appearing virtuous.... And if I drove her to tell me to get out, I knew I had nowhere that I wanted to turn.

"Don't say it," Phil pleaded. "Don't say it again.... No more promises."

"Phil, for God's sake, listen, I'll beat it...."

"You're hurting my hand."

I let go of her hand and she pulled back from me. She looked worn and beaten, desperately lost. And God knows what I must have looked like from where she stood.

I was shaking visibly, badly in need of drink just to lose the jigs. I'd stopped trying to remember where I'd ended up the night before.... It was pointless. The wrapper that booze tea-cozied over my mind was too thick to be penetrated, except by accident. But there was one moment of relief. That second when my eyes opened in the bed and I realised I was at home. It had got so bad that regardless of where I might be when I opened my eyes, I'd be praying please, please let me be home, with my knees pulled up to my chest in the foetal position. When my words were heard, my request granted, a slither of thanks escaped my lips, and if ever a prayer was meant that was the one.

"I can't take much more Maguire." Phil lit herself a cigarette and I could see she had shakes of her own.

"I'm not having a go at you." She shrugged, missing badly with an effort to smile... "What's the use of having a go? Doesn't change anything."

"Phil, I swear...."

"Please Maguire, don't ask me to believe, don't say it... no, please, let me finish." She waited, to be sure I was listening. "I'm taking a job."

The wheel had moved a bit further towards the full circle. Phil was taking a job. And she wasn't asking me if it was all right. She was just letting me know. What could I say? Hit her with some verbal about sorting it all out? She'd heard all of that a thousand times.

"I've tried not to let Mum and Dad know the position... I'm not going to broadcast that I'll be working.... But, sooner or later, they're going to find out. It won't be my fault."

"I don't want you to work, Phil...."

"For fuck's sake somebody has to work." She checked her anger, her voice dropping the octave. "If you can't, if you've *had* cabbing, well, for God's sake, we have to get money from somewhere...."

"I'll get money... we've got to click soon...."

She shook her head. "You ought to click, we both know that...." She looked at me as though the wounds were too deep to bare. Then her expression changed and her eyes were flat, cold, when she said: "I'm taking a job."

"Just like that?"

She shrugged. "I don't know what's happened... I've done everything I know how..." I moved to touch her but the alarm that flashed into her eyes stopped me dead. She shook her head: "I'm sorry, don't... don't touch me."

I stumbled out of the room with my heart choking me to death. My body was screaming for drink, a few shots to get rid of the pain and the twitches.... And my mind needed insulation, fast, and so desperately that I knew I would have sunk a pill that granted me oblivion, even if it was the total final touch.

Phil went to work nights as a cashier in a club and somehow I stopped drinking for six weeks. Six weeks that didn't see any change in Phil's attitude to me. She wouldn't sleep with me, and I stopped even trying to make love to her. I gave up because I knew it was more serious than it had seemed at first.... It wasn't just that Phil wouldn't make love to me. She couldn't – couldn't even bear for me to touch her. And though she was normal around the kids, asking no help from me, the withdrawal thing was so strong that I feared she was going to lose her mind entirely.

By August I was beginning to hold my head up. Six weeks is a long time, and this time I was sure, certain I had the thing licked. And not just till Christmas or St. Patrick's Day, or any other "excuse" day. This time I was off the booze for good, for the rest of my life. Jesus! Just the thought of never being able to take a drink again, it hit me so hard my brain went numb for a minute. Jesus!

I was working on a second book called "Roads" which was

going to be a sequel to "Butcher Boy", but I found I was trying to write and I had to keep reminding myself to forget about writing and just tell the story. Maybe part of my difficulty was being off the drink. I don't know, but I went on sitting at the machine, often thinking about all the people who want to write. Who think it's glamorous and arty and all that bullshit, when really it's just so much hard and lonely work, with say ten per cent talent, ninety per cent application, concentration, and sheer bloody sweat.

Phil didn't have to say but she did admit that she was enjoying work. I was baby sitting and I kept the place clean, even doing the simple bits of ironing. She was looking for an au pair girl, and I didn't argue. If she felt I couldn't really be trusted for very long, how could I get up on my high horse?

I enjoyed my early evenings with Kate, reading to her before we sang her to sleep with her favourite songs. All the kiddy songs, but especially the one Burl Ives sang about "The Big Rock Candy Mountain" and her number one favourite "Scarlet Ribbons".

Kate was a fantastic child, full of wit and love, bright as a new penny, and wicked like Phil had been when I'd first known her in Jersey. And I watched over herself and Dan, taking my night's work very seriously, trying not to hope that everything would come right between Phil and me. I didn't have any right to set my sights that high.

I didn't see much of Darcy or Theo. Paddy was bugged by me being off booze and Theo was just working bloody hard. He had a steady girl and he was so non-committal about her that I felt it was a serious courtship.

Herb O'Casey dropped in for a cup of coffee a couple of times a week and he helped me more than he'll ever know. Just to talk with him, that big gentle guy, listening to his dreams of returning to Ireland, to the West where he was born, to have his own land, to be a real Irishman again.

O'Casey was the first friend I'd made in a long time. Oh, I had Theo and Darcy; and Johnnie Toner and Big Jim Davies were out somewhere on the seven seas, but realising how close Herb and I had become, brought it home to me that I was something of a loner. That I'd been like this for most of my life. And yet I loved people. It seemed crazy until it hit me that I didn't really allow people to get close to me.... Not really close, although a lot of them, because of one or another of the performances I gave, might have been pardoned for thinking that I was their friend. Not that this was of paramount importance, or anything like that. It just illustrated that I was starting to think again, that my brain was beginning to function now that the whiskey fumes were evaporating off the machinery that made it all happen.

I was living in a vacuum that was becoming less uncomfortable, having just made up my mind that time was the only pal I had where Phil was concerned. But life had other plans for me. The design wasn't couched in pleasant colours, and the fabrics to be used weren't to be ease and peace, or happiness....

Life is no respecter of fiction, and all the study given to construction, form, balance, whether it is in the book or a play or whatever, mean nothing, have no place, if you need to tell the story the way it really happened.

This has always been my way, to tell it how it really is. And I know that life, coming off the presses the way it does, doesn't make it easy. I mean, every day is filled with stories most writers would shy away from if they happened to dream them up. Too improbable. But that's just it... that's life.... And I press on with my story knowing that having got to this point, I couldn't have got here any other way.

The morning the postman brought me two proof copies of my book "Butcher Boy" I sat at the end of the stairs and wept. All the years of dreaming and working, all the mental burning up, the endless stream of excuse to the few mates who still asked how things were going.... It had all been worth this solitary moment or as I told myself.

A fella shouldn't be alone at a time like that.... And I don't just mean alone because he doesn't have somebody standing by his side.... Like those books should have reached me before Phil had been buffeted away to a point where our voices were whispered across a canyon ten miles wide. Oh God, how I wanted to run up the stairs and wake her up, show her the books, share my excitement with her. But she needed the sleep she had earned, and anyway mornings were murder for her, even if she hadn't been working till two or three am.

I walked upstairs into the lounge. Dan was in his play pen with Kate pushing toys into him. The pair of then were laughing hysterically, he pushing the toys out as fast as he could, both of them trying to prevent the other getting the toys across the line of wooden bars. Kate's pleasure bubbled through the high pitched stream, Dan's laugh being deep, while his blue eyes were perfect glass buttons sparkling in sunlight.

The proofs bore the usual brown paper cover, but I sat turning them over in my hands as though they were the most precious and priceless volumes that had ever been known to man. When the phone rang and I stood to pick it up, I was pressing them against my breast, feeling warm where they touched me.

Ma was calling me from Dublin. Pops was in hospital. He didn't want any fuss but the doctor had told her it would be as well to notify his family. She was upset, but still she was apologising for worrying me.... I listened to her and I seemed to grunt or say the right thing without knowing or remembering any part of my contribution to the conversation.

Phil came in as I put the phone down. She knelt down by the play pen, still half asleep, but showering love upon the kids.

"Sorry about the phone. I got it as quick as I could."

She stood up. "I was awake." She looked at me for the first time that morning.. And the sleep seemed to roll off her like water off a duck. "What is it, Maguire? What's happened?"

"Pops is in hospital."

"It's bad, isn't it?"

I told her what Ma had said, keeping my voice low. The kids went on playing and I walked down to the kitchen with Phil shuffling in her slippers behind me.

"Let me get a cup of tea. I'll call the airport."

I stood looking out the window, knowing that a good healthy spit, if there is such a thing, would have hit the back window of the house at the end of my tiny yard.

"You are going?" Phil stood watching the kettle.

"A watched pot never boils," I said.

"It's not a pot, it's a kettle." She looked up at me. "What is it?"

"Where the fuck do I find the bread? I'm not working the cab, remember?"

She smiled quietly. "Do you remember how I hate making the first cup of tea?" I nodded and she shuffled to the door. "Just run a bath, find some knickers...."

I made the tea, let it draw, fixing it just as she liked it. I was in bits, so close to weeping that I wanted to tear my eyes out. I was fed up with being such a bundle of shameless, pointless, emotion. I was supposed to be some kind of a man for Christ's sake. Phil came back into the kitchen.

"Phone for you..." I handed her the tea and she sipped it. "Thanks pal...." She smiled but I didn't dare try to take advantage of her kindness.... Blind as I was, I could see the pity for me in her eyes.

"Phil told me about your father," Jackie said, "I'm sorry, Paddy."

"Thanks Jack," I said, not able to go on.

"Look, Paddy, no shit now, I know things are a bit rough. Don't let bread stop you going. You can have whatever you want."

I didn't give Jackie any rubbish... I was broke and I needed very badly to go and see Pops.

And that was it. Two hours later, with just under two hundred pounds in my pocket, I was on a plane home to Dublin. Jackie had picked me up and hit me with the money – and he made it clear that it wasn't important, that it could be paid back in one year or ten. He was like me about money. With the way things were going for him, the two ton was the equivalent of twenty that I might hand somebody else.

As I left the house, I pressed one of the books proofs, signed, with all my love, into Phil's hand. And after telling her I wouldn't drink, I ran out to climb into Jackie's Bentley. I hated goodbyes and I was scared shitless about weeping in front of the children.

My father was dying. It was so clear that I could feel it.... Death seemed to be slipping her shroud about him as I sat holding his hand. We talked, well, I did most of it.... His breathing was low gear stuff, and his head seemed little bigger than a goose egg on the hospital pillow. Ma sat across from me, stoic, but deeply grieved, and I wondered if like me, she was remembering Larry.... She and I had shared that time too.... That cheeky little bastard with the flaxen hair, like a butterfly he'd been just before death, coughing away what life was left in him, doing a first class demolition job on Ma.

"I've got that money now, Chief..." I lied, and he gave a flick on his eyelashes in response...." When you get out of this kip, we'll do something about getting you into the country... fresh air, that's all you need...."

"Me mother... she'd turn in her grave..." Pops murmured... "born and reared in Shelbourne Road... country, huh... me?"

I couldn't bear it... looking at him like that.... And I couldn't show him the proof of my book.... This was no time to be demanding his attention, his applause.... He was on the way out, but if he knew it, he wasn't letting it show. And I loved him more than ever for that.

I kissed his face when I left, wanting to just get on the plane and go home to my children. I don't know what I expected of myself... he was in good hands, and I wasn't in any way equipped to put new life into worn heart valves, but that didn't do anything to alleviate the feeling of helplessness. It was stuck in my craw like a lump of apple, the indigestible acceptance that for most of my life I'd been helpless about most things.

Next day I went again to the hospital, and he was in such discomfort that I left in a few minutes. I couldn't even pretend to hide my tears as the barman stood and watched me drink whiskey in the pub opposite the hospital. He didn't say anything.... You could tell he'd seen more than his share of pain in the faces of those customers who came in once, maybe twice, needing a drink as an anaesthetic against the kind of grief that visits all of us at some time or another.

I didn't go back to the hospital and I left Dublin as my brothers and my sisters were about due to arrive home. I'd given Ma some money, and I was drinking heavily enough for her to express her concern. I just looked at her, and I must have looked as rough as I was feeling, because Ma just nodded her head and said: "Ah, don't mind me, son."

I had to buy presents for the children at London Airport, thanking my stars they were young enough not to know they hadn't come from Ireland. Phil listened while I told her what things were like, how Pops was, or wasn't. She cried a little bit, having loved him from the word go. And then my phone rang and it was my brother, Billy, telling me from Dublin that Pops was dead.

I put the phone down and I gave Phil a stiff shot of brandy from the half bottle I'd brought in with me. She took it and drank deeply, pointedly ignoring the large one I put into my own glass.

"You know how sorry I am, about Pops."

I nodded: "It was awful seeing him that way, better off dead." This was the truth and I knew it, but the way the words came out, forced, made me sound like a fella acting the heavy, the tough guy... and it just didn't work. It didn't work because just then what I needed most in the world was to be held by my wife, pressed against the breasts that had once been mine to love. It was no longer new, this feeling of being deprived, but today my loss was double the usual, because Pops, to talk to, to touch, to love, was no longer available to me either.

Chapter Twenty-One
London. Winter '66

Probably the most overworked situations ever used in movies and television is that moment when MAN finds himself staring at a large pair of black boots. The ANGLE is reversed quickly a couple of times, with one CLOSE UP on MAN'S FACE to establish his reaction.... Another change of ANGLE, as the CAMERA becomes his POINT OF VIEW.... The CAMERA PANS UPWARDS, slowly up the dark blue trousers. Featuring the buttons of the blue tunic, revealing then the chin strap and the helmet which appears to sit on the bridge of the policeman's nose.

It was funny when it was first used, but like most good things, it was flogged to forget-it-land, old and tired and no longer funny. Yet it made me laugh out loud, when I found myself playing MAN, hearing the deep, not unkind voice of the copper, predictably utter that old line of script: "What've got here then?"

The scene had opened with me looking down at my bare feet. My expression must have registered bewilderment.... My bloody feet were sore and painful, even in the Mickey Mouse light from the street lamp I could see that they were bleeding. And I felt like falling down in the road.

"You couldn't make it up," I mumbled, receiving neither confirmation nor denial from the man in blue. I wasn't aware I had a bottle in my right hand until I threw it between his feet in annoyance. That was when he seemed to doubt my word when I gave my address as the Hill of Tara.

"Where else would you expect the Royal High King of Ireland to sit?" God, I was amazed at the ignorance of a fella in such a responsible position.

He was cool.... I'll give him that. He pushed the broken bottle to one side, moving his left foot gently in the task, but keeping his eyes riveted on me.

"Why did you take your boots off?" he asked me, with the patience of a man who no longer believed in Santa Claus.

I had one boot in both side pockets of my tweed jacket and I heard myself wonder out loud: "How in hell did they get there?"

My legs clocked out at the moment but the big copper held me easily, practically carrying me the few yards to the police box, I mumbled something about the hazard of coincidence.

"I heard you singing," he said. "Came out to have a look... nothing coincidental about that."

I started to agree with him, but the most vile smell stopped me. I turned on the stool, wondering what's in God's name he kept in the place that'd smell like that. He puffed at a cigarette and in answer to my silent plea, passed one, already lit to me.

"Jaysus! What is it?" I stopped, puzzled for a second by his expression.... Then I realised it was me. Me! Jesus! I could smell myself.

"It's me," I said, feeling like a fund of useless information. "God," I puffed at the cigarette. "Sorry."

He smiled and took his helmet off.... A nice looking man if you ignored the short back and sides haircut. I took the cap of his flask filled with hot coffee.

"You've been having something of a piss-up."

I sipped the coffee, wondering how he could bear the stench of me. And I felt glad that there was always one copper to prove the rule that they were nearly all bastards.

"What time is it, please?"

"Four thirty." He had an accent I couldn't place.

"Look, Constable, you're not going to believe this, but I don't know where..."

"Brighton," he said. "You're in Brighton."

"Brighton? Brighton in ... Sussex?"

He nodded smiling a bit. "Is there any other?"

I tried to think. Brighton... Sweet Jesus! What was I doing in Brighton? Some hope... I couldn't have answered that one for a thousand pounds.

"I've got to get to London. I have a book being published today.... Monday is my big day... October the...."

Again his expression cut me off in mid sentence.

"This is Tuesday," he informed me, genuine regret showing in his face.

"Tuesday? Tuesday? But it can't...." I was beginning to sound like a bleedin' parrot.... "But Monday... the cocktail party...for my book..." I tried to stand up, painfully aware then, that walking, the ability to walk easily, was a gift I'd always taken for granted.

"Are you...? Is there a charge?"

He shook his head. "You haven't done anything, apart from half killing yourself with booze...."

I didn't say anything to that. If only you knew, mate, I was thinking, trying at the same time to remember where I'd been, what I'd been doing. Nothing was coming through.... I searched my pockets... I had no money.... Money....That struck a bell.... I remembered Saturday night, well, Sunday morning... and I'd had about eighteen quid in my pocket....

The policeman called me a cab, loaning me ten shillings to get to the railway station.... I wrote down his name and address.... He'd get his money back.... And a copy of my book.... A souvenir of a lunatic....

In the cab, I knew I wasn't going to sit around waiting for any train. I was sick with cold again, my feet were working full time to aggravate me further, and on top of this I needed a drink, knowing that I'd never be able to hold one down.... My guts were scattered like buckshot from a gun.

Mercifully the cab driver didn't talk much, which was something I was scared of when we started off. After about a minute, despite how rough I was feeling, I noticed him rolling down the window at his side, as surreptitiously as he could. My nerve ends seemed to have blistered from a run in with a blow torch, but I chuckled insanely at the idea that I stank enough to be giving the driver a bad time.

Saturday lunchtime came back to me then.... Walking down to the local for one... just one drink.... On the way, developing a pain in my right knee....Working out that whiskey wouldn't help get rid of it... I liked whiskey too much for it to do me any good. So, rum.... Rum, which I hadn't enjoyed since the trip home from New Zealand. If I drank that, hating it as I did, well, it might do something for the knee.

Suffering all kinds of agonies, I worked my way through a bottle of navy black rum during the lunchtime opening, but I seemed even more depressed then when I'd started drinking. And it's no lie to say that the rum tasted like liquid cellophane to my whiskey weaned tongue. But this didn't stop me accepting an invitation back to a pad with some of the people in the pub. I didn't know who they were, nor did I care, I was going to go on drinking and it seemed like a good crowd for an afternoon piss-up.

By five thirty I'd finished the bottle of rum I'd bought, somebody had been playing piano, and though it was all a bit civilised, I was sitting there trying not to get maudlin. A fella walked over to me. I'd seen him on the phone, which he'd put down to come and talk to me.

"What's your name, man?" He was smiling, a tubby guy with a poofy smile, and yet he didn't seem queer. Not that I cared... he'd been playing good piano. At least I thought he was the one....

"Paddy Maguire," I replied, wondering why in hell I was so sober.

"Thanks." He nodded and went back to the phone. "Hello... hello darling," I heard him saying in a smoother tone than he used around me. "Yes, I know, love, sorry. Yes, got a bit involved with some Irish writer. Maguire, Paddy

Maguire, bit of a party for his book which comes out Monday.... Yes, I know love...." He turned and winked at me... "Couldn't get away from him... mad Irish, y'know.... No, he's not queer...." He pulled a face and I felt sorry for a bird whoever she was.... "Yes, of course I do... you know I do...." He hesitated and his voice dropped to a drunken whisper... "I love you... yes... bye."

He put the phone down and looked at me, lifting his glass. "You didn't mind?" He had moved over to where I was sitting.

"You're full of shit, man... but at least, you know it."

"That's what I say." He nodded enthusiastically. "You have to bullshit them or they curl up in pain. And she's such a great bird, honestly, nobody else would put up with me for a week."

I remembered being in a pub and drinking pints of Flowers Keg. Your man was still with me, telling me jokes I'd heard before... I was feeling dehydrated after all the rum.... The beer was just liquid to help me lose that blotting paper feeling... I said something about feeling depressed.... All the booze and nothing... not a glow of any description....

He threw down a couple of pills.

"Try a couple of these... give you a buzz, guaranteed."

I swallowed the pills, washing them down with beer.... The next thing I could recall was standing on top of a piano in a Territorial Army Barracks.... Don't ask me which one... I was singing, with tears streaming down my face... "Oh My Papa" had replaced "Mother Machree".... I was still wallowing over Pops... Drinking out on it, the way some fellas dine out for a week on a couple of good stories.... And that was it.... That was the complete picture until I came out of it in Brighton. And I knew from experience that it was a waste of time to try and make the rest appear.... If it didn't just happen to slide onto the screen... forget it.

Two days in bed, grinding my teeth ends to powder in the throes of withdrawal.... Jabs in the arse from my doctor,

Oscar Lewis.... Loving that big Jewish G.P.

But Phil said little or nothing, offering me soup which I couldn't swallow, keeping the publishers off my back, when they asked to talk to me. They had been irate at first, but my disappearance had got some little bit of coverage that the cocktail party wouldn't have warranted. I didn't seem to care, one way or the other. It's not easy to care, when your brain seems to have left town.

Kit came to baby-sit when Phil went to work. After the kids went to sleep she came to the room and sat on the bed. I asked her to go away, to just leave me alone. I didn't mean to be unkind, I was so consumed with self pity that I wanted her to believe me when I told her she would be better off if she just forgot all about me. She fell apart right there on the bed, weeping in what seemed like real anguish, before finally running from the room to storm out of the house, almost taking the front door out into the garden after her. If Phil saw her again, I don't know, but she didn't come back to the house at any time.

I was up and about in three days and it was amazing to me that once I had a good tight shave and had bathed enough to shake the smell of me out my nostrils, I looked all right. I mean, for nearly seventy-two hours, I'd been pulled through a self-made wringer – and I didn't think I could get away free. Nothing came for nothing. There was always a tab to be picked up. Like, lying around somewhere, there had to be the equivalent of The Picture of Dorian Gray.

Chapter Twenty-Two
London. '67

A bad review is not a review at all. And the only bad publicity would be your death notice in a newspaper. As long as no man writes your epitaph there's a chance you're still around some place, alive and sweating. So, this extreme apart, all you ask of the mass media is that they spell your name correctly.

I was lucky. I had the gift of the gab and my honest opinions about most things made the odd person sit up and take notice. Here again, it doesn't really matter whether they like you or not, just as long as they remember your name and the name of the book.

The other thing I had going for me was this thing of being an ordinary working fella. The cab driving bit came in handy. In the same way that Humphrey Bogart opened the door for actors who weren't all teeth and beefcake, Brendan Behan had blasted through a few portals, blazing a trail for fellas like myself. The very talented Frank Norman broke a few barriers too and many of us who were to follow owe a lot to both men.

Back when I was sixteen, I was drinking stout in the Dawson Lounge in Dublin, when a big dark haired, heavy jowled man, informed me in a low, gravel based voice, that the nutter who was singing in Irish was Brendan Behan. The name meant nothing to me, but the gentle giant, Sean O'Sullivan, the painter, assured me that despite "this gurrier act... he is truly talented." The singer stopped and told O'Sullivan that he was "some class of a dilapidated bollix". After which Sean whispered to me, whispered so that they could only hear him in Nassau Street, four hundred yards or so from where we stood: "But his manners are equal to his humility, in that they are non existent."

Another year, a hundred years later, myself, Brendan, and two or three other "characters", all of us of course taking seconds to Brendan – you did, whether you wanted to or not - falling out of a taxi in Soho, heading for the Kismet or some other afternoon drinking club. Brendan staggering up to two bowler hats who were deep in conversation. He poked the taller one in the arm, at a moment when the fella was emphasizing some point by using his index finger like a baton.

"Hey Wire," says Behan. "You leave my fucking Aunt alone."

And Frank Norman, always a decent fella, proving to the knockers when the first wave of success had long since hit the beach, that he had the real stuff of writing in him: that he could come up with "the makey uppers" when they all thought his real life material had run out of steam.

My book "Butcher Boy" moved very well. I had two thousand leaflets printed, advertising it as "the publishing event of the year...." This brought me a sticky phone call from my editor at Harrisons. They liked my book a great deal, says he, but to call it the publishing event of the year?

"Listen," I said, as politely as my hangover would allow."As far as I'm concerned, it's just that, of this or any other year."

My cab driving mates handed out the leaflets, doing a sales talk I'd written out for them. And I plastered pubs with posters, black print on a yellow background, which, according to a printer mate of mine, was the most eye catching combination of colours. Meanwhile, when I complained about what seemed to me to be sheer lack of interest, I was told by my publishers that advertising didn't sell books. I couldn't believe this, but I came to believe that in most cases it was true enough. Unless like, say in the case of "Peyton Place" somebody decided to spend a small fortune on setting up a sales machine that could have made Arabs buy sand, the ordinary one line adverts in the literary press made little or no difference to sales.

So it looked like I wasn't going to make any fortunes from book writing. And yet I felt that if somebody injected some time and money, "Butcher Boy" could have taken off like a rocket. I began to feel frustrated and many times I got so mad about all that wasn't being done, that I had to get pissed out of my brains, just to hide from this unwanted truth.

The book did help get me other work, writing scripts for television. Mostly crap work because most of the TV series were pretty awful. But I was glad of the money and the more credits a guy had on the small screen, the more chance he had of graduating to the big one. And it was in movies that the big money lay. The money that could buy a fella time to write another book.

When I sold my first TV script, the story editor asked to see me. He shook my hand furiously, telling me that he hadn't seen such good dialogue in many a long day. This said, he sat down facing me across his great desk and proceeded to change every line.

I didn't know what to do. The man was a prick who couldn't have written home for money. But he was the guy who kept an eye on scripts, ensuring that the running characters weren't asked to do anything that would be out of character, etc., etc. And he did smile at me every time we lost a line that I loved. Which happened to be every single one. No, he didn't think it a good idea for the writer to attend rehearsals. He didn't explain why, and it was years later before I realised that if the writer was in on rehearsals, it made it difficult for actors to say "this is a load of shit" before they changed the lines that the story editor had altered already anyway. But on that first one, the director happened to be a man who believed in writers, admitting without any of the usual hang-ups, that it all began when some fella like me sat down to face a blank sheet of paper. That the finest actors, technicians, producers and directors in the whole fucking world couldn't move until the script, good or bad, appeared, so that they could all make themselves busy by immediately declaring that it was a load of horseshit. So I got into rehearsals, to which the story editor never came after the first day. And little by little, I put my own dialogue back where it belonged. I'll remember till the day I die, the look of gratitude mingled with amazement on the face of the leading actress, when, after she'd complained that a certain line was just too impossible for her to deliver, and I rewrote it on the spot, she said: "Fantastic... how can you possibly do it, just like that?"

"I've just given you back the line as it was when I wrote the script in the first place," I said, very happy that her kiss of gratitude contained a little bit of something else as well.

Working around television, even on a freelance basis, meant a lot of drinking for me. Most people involved in "the tube trade" seemed to do a lot of boozing, and often I told Phil that I had to gargle with these people if I was going to get more work. She didn't really care any more. When she had a go at me about drinking, it was only because of the time I was wasting.

"You used to moan about cabbing, that it didn't give you enough time to write."

And now I was spending my cabbing time drinking all over town.

"You're not really writing any more." Her voice was cold, her attitude free of criticism. She was just stating what she felt were the facts. "You're playing at being a writer... being seen to be a writer has taken precedence over the real thing. And honestly, Maguire, it's not easy to stand by and just watch it happening."

I didn't pay any attention to this. She was bitching because I was seeing a lot of beautiful birds in one TV studio or another. And because I was acting a bit as well, she didn't like any part of the whole set up. But I felt entitled to go after work that I wanted to do, and I had no guilt now about sleeping with the bird I fancied. Phil didn't want me, couldn't bear for me to touch her, so what was I to keep it for?

One director/producer tried to give me a pull, while he was congratulating me on a script I'd just written. Reading the signals loud and clear, I knew that if I played games with him, I'd get all the work I wanted. And I gave it some serious thought. Why not? Look at the number of actors, male and female, who performed in private for the chance to perform in public. Let him get his laughing tackle around it... all he wants to do is blow. They don't call him Mouth Full of Feathers for nothing.

I tried, I really did, to be adult about the whole thing. It was strictly business... bit like being a brass.... Didn't have to mean anything. But, I couldn't get it together, not if I had to wash dishes. A producer who was a bird, all right, even if she was some kind of barracuda, but not a fella. No way. I could remember still, how dirty I'd felt for so long after the one and only time I'd sung for my supper. Walking the streets with newspapers stuffed inside my shirt. Getting a warm bath and a soft bed on a cold night, knowing I'd have to throw a couple into the little poof who was as desperate for a little loving as I was for a good night's sleep.

It just wasn't my scene and there wasn't a thing I could do to change the way I was made. God, some of the sad women I'd woken up with, real alligators some of them, but always female. And though I could have been bottled by a troop of Guardsmen during some of my memory blanks, I somehow knew that I'd never been in the scratcher with a bloke. Not just because my chocolate button felt intact, it was more than that. Deep down in my subconscious there was an easy acceptance that the homo scene wasn't in my repertoire. If it had been, I'd have tried to live with it. To my mind faggots just have a different set of problems to the rest of us, the heteros, or whatever we're called. I had some mates who were bent that way, and I thought of it in the same way as I did about fellas who wanted to screw schoolgirls in uniform. But knowing somehow, that neither one was my bag.

My drinking cost me a lot of work in television, and there's no way I can blame the guys who decided that I was a nutcase. Some of them thought I had talent, others thought I should stick to writing novels, but whatever the reason, I didn't get the amount of work I seemed to be entitled to, taking into account the scripts I'd written, and the fact that I never let even one story editor down. In fact, once or twice, I got a guy out of a real hole, by writing a very fast script, when another writer had failed to deliver. Not getting enough further work, I guess my behaviour, my desperate need to be seen to be Jack the Lad, had something to do with it.

Not that I accepted this. It was the clique thing that was keeping me out. The old pals act, of which I wasn't a part, because I wouldn't lick anybody's arse to be admitted. Then again I knew they were jealous of my novel, that most of them, while they were technicians who could produce workmanlike television scripts, couldn't have put a book together if all they had to do was bind it. My thinking went like this because I just couldn't see things any other way. It had to be the other fellas who were wrong. I was the good guy fighting the system. The rest were a bunch of shits, holding on, terrified, to the security of the work they shared amongst themselves. And all the time it was me, or rather, I, I, I ,I, the guvnor of the personal pronoun, God's gift to story editors, directors, producers, and on a personal level, to anything that moved in skirts. If nobody laughed at me, it could only have been because I was anything but funny.

If Phil hadn't been working, well, truly, I don't know what would have happened to us. She kept our home in one place and in one piece, working night after night, driving into town in the little banger of a car, which mercifully seemed to run on nothing. Phil didn't talk about work, she didn't say much about anything, and I left her to herself unless she spoke to me.

I was into a bank for about a grand, and it was all down to booze. I'd done some great talking about the money I was going to earn from books, but I don't think this would have worked if it hadn't been for my connection with Phil's family. The business account was at the same bank. Not that I mentioned the family as I pleaded for support: but then, I knew I didn't have to....

The phone hadn't rung from my agent in months... "Roads" was finished, but I had to prune it and polish a few bits I wasn't too happy about. I hated the thought of having to touch it again. I found that when I wrote it, it was a dead thing. Like a woman, I suppose, who has given birth to find that the child is stillborn. You've delivered but there's no life.

The only good memory of those days is the time I spent with the children. I guess they saw more of me than most kids did of their father, and I can't count the times I was grateful for my hang-up about rowing or fighting in front of them. If I gave them nothing else, the time that I lived under the same roof with them was terror free. They'd never known violence in their own home. Never seen Daddy belt their mother all over the place. What I did give them was love and fun, all the ingredients for happy days. I urged them to speak and to sing and to dance – to never be afraid to speak the truth and to try and talk straight out of the mouth, never up and never down. And to never say to a little guy what you wouldn't say to a big fella. That way you were trying to give everybody a fair crack of the whip.

I felt marvellous at times like this, forgetting that day after day, I was walking all over the heartbeats of Phil, ignoring as often as possible, what my behaviour was doing to my wife. Too full of shit, ego-shit, to even think of practicing what I preached.

Chapter Twenty-Three

Desperate to earn money, I agreed to write an Irish radio show. I needed bread badly to keep the bank from taking my furniture away, and I needed somebody to employ me before I began to believe that they all couldn't be wrong, that I just didn't have it.

I signed a contract to write one hundred and fifty shows. The money per episode was a joke, but together the scripts would earn enough to keep the home fires burning, put a smile on the impoverished face of a bank with only three hundred and thirty million in assets, and allow me the right to raise my head again around the house.

The day after I took this job, and make no mistake, I was glad to have landed it, the phone began to ring again. Suddenly I was in demand. Producers wanted me to write for television, and a short story of mine had attracted enough attention for a film producer with money to approach me about turning it into a small movie for him.

I know that what happened was meant to be. So there's no point at all in saying "If I hadn't done this, or that, or the other thing!" I did what I did, and though what WAS isn't, it WAS then. So wise or not, I grabbed what was going, and having reached this point in my life, I couldn't have got here any other way.

I got into the radio work quickly. Writing three scripts a day. This represented about forty minutes of radio time, so that at the end of three weeks I had delivered sixty-three episodes. This might seem a lot. It was in terms of labour, with little or no creative writing involved. It was more like tailoring. You had so many acting slots to be filled, say five in each episode. You had a team of fifteen actors or thereabouts, so to keep the thing moving, you had to work people in and out of the story line, keeping them (through a narrator, who linked each script with what was happening OFF), alive in the mind of your listener, until you could bring them back ON THE AIR, to stop the actors from starving, or to be exact, dying of the thirst.

I bashed out five television scripts after this, before moving back to the radio serial in order to keep my script delivery two months ahead of the transmission date. I now wrote my first screenplay and when this was finished, I went back to the serial.

And now I had a phone call from Hollywood, and I felt like a fella tumbling downstairs. An endless staircase with me rolling head over knickers, knowing that this wasn't right. That there was an imbalance or something, that could hurt me very badly. But I'd been out of work for too long, so close to having to admit defeat, say to Phil's father, that I couldn't turn down the chance to make money. I knew I was taking on too much, but I hadn't learned how dangerous it could be to try and make up for time lost or wasted. I didn't know how to allow the past to bury its dead.

The man from Hollywood wanted to make a movie of my book. I told him, thinking it was a good stroke, that I couldn't sell my novel to a man I didn't know. He seemed to appreciate that and told me he'd be in London the next day. He arrived all right, and over dinner I told him something about myself. When he realised I'd written for television, not forgetting my own screenplay, he asked me if I felt I could adapt the novel for the cinema screen. I knew I could do it.... Who better? Despite what some writers have said about adapting their own books for the screen, I consider it easier than adapting the work of another writer. And I told this to Dave Keller, who seemed to like me. I felt good about him. He seemed to care. He was a gentle guy, with a wry sense of fun, and he drank like prohibition was starting a re-run next day.

Daft though it now seems, my estimation of a man depended to a great extend on how he took his liquor.

Within days the deal was signed up and I was reeling at the thought of being solvent. Could it really be true? Or was I going to piss the bed any second, to wake up in a cold sweat? That's a bad moment. When fear, conditioned, by too many hours of doubt, chokes off the ability to accept that something good can ever happen. So I had a large whiskey to push away the chilled finger that insecurity was poking into my ribs. Things were real enough, and maybe now I could do something about refloating my marriage.

I had high hopes. Phil had stopped work, and with a few quid in the little brown jug, it was possible I could drive the worry out of her – make her feel important to me. Not that she hadn't always been, but it was obvious, even to a piss artist like me, that my gallivanting, my indifference to her needs, my lack of regard for the sensitive areas of her gentle nature, had been the concrete slab that helped bury, deep within Phil, the willingness to risk being hurt ever again.

Phil admitted being glad that she had stopped working, but nothing had changed. After an evening out together, when she seemed to sparkle at odd times during dinner, I kissed her passionately, wanting very much to make love to her. She broke away from my mouth, a cry of... "Oh, God!"... horror, ripping out of her.... Her tears then, and her apologies, deep and profound pleas for forgiveness, for not being able to respond, and worse, to her mind, for not managing to find whatever was needed to even pretend.

I thanked God for that.... That she couldn't tolerate me when my touch turned her into a quivering, frightened fawn that didn't know which way to run. I cuddled her then, like a friend, and she knew it was for real.... She sensed the change in me, the response to her need for kindness, for the understanding of a pal, *that* someone who can care, and show it, without asking anything in return. When she finally went to sleep, I got up and went downstairs for a drink. I wasn't angry and just then I wasn't hurting any. But I was a bit annoyed with myself for not knowing, not seeing in advance, that you can't buy back what was freely given. How in hell could I expect to purchase something that had been dormant long enough to be dead? Love was like life, surely. Not to be turned on by the flick of a switch, not when the warmth, heat, passion, all of those things, collectively, the electricity of the relationship, had been allowed to die quietly in the quilt of its own death-wish.

Poor Phil. She had pulled so far back into herself that it seemed she might never emerge to lead a full life again. And I wondered how much of her suffering, when I touched her or tried to make love to her, didn't have something to do with my action being a reminder of just how far she had run from reality. Each of us have felt at sometime or another that reality is unkind, if not often cruel, and I know that if I hadn't been born with a kind of long term resilience, I'd have had to withdraw the way Phil had done, or crack up completely.

If I needed any further proof that Phil no longer loved me, it was written in her expression when I told her I was going to Ireland to write the screenplay of my book. And it was almost funny the way she packed for me. Not that she hadn't always done this for me, but now you'd have thought I was catching the last plane out of England, she was so concerned I might miss it. And I must confess I breathed a sigh of relief when I climbed into O'Casey's cab for the ride to the airport. The responsibility for my behaviour was still there. Every time I looked at Phil, I could see just how deeply she had been affected by it all, but away working in Ireland, at least I wouldn't have to face it each and every day.

I hadn't been home since my visit to the hospital. I hadn't gone home for Pop's funeral. I'd been to one funeral in my life, when we'd buried Larry, and it had burned a deep wound indelibly into my mind. Anyway, if I'd been unable to do anything for Pop while he'd been alive, what could I have done for his body after death? All the mumbo jumbo and the holy water trick meant nothing to me. It hadn't in an awful long time, and though I wasn't against it for people who believed in it, I didn't think it was ever going to be important.

O'Casey was full of envy, with more than half a mind to park the cab at the airport and come with me for the ride.

"Come and stay if you like," I said, meaning it. I was going to have a pad of some kind. Somewhere to live and work. So why not? If that was what he wanted.

"The plates..." he moaned... meaning his wife.... "She'd never stand for it...."

"That's good..." I said, meaning it. "Long time ago, a fella said to me... when they stop fighting with you for staying out all night... when they give up slagging you for getting pissed... when that happens, your marriage is over.... They've stopped caring, and no relationship can survive that...."

"All the same..." Herb said. "I wish she didn't want to get in my bleedin' ear...."

"You can't tell somebody how to love you, prick... that's the way the bird is... that's her way.... Be grateful," I told him, thinking of the state of my own marriage.

He wouldn't take any bread. O'Casey only ever wanted to do things for the people he cared about. But he knew there was a pad for him any time he wanted to come over to Dublin.

I was sad as I left O'Casey. We were very close, without having to be seeing each other all the time. It was as if we'd been brothers who loved one another in a previous existence. Somehow he had moved into my affections, ahead of Theo and Darcy and the others. He had more soul, though he would have laughed out loud had I told him that.

As usual I was terrified on the flight, and as always, I drank my loaf off to try and relax. It was stupid. All the times the drink had failed to help me in that way, yet I persevered with the kind of a blind faith that would have alcohol and not religion.

Sitting there on the plane, trying not to think about the

flight, I allowed my mind to play around with the word, alcohol, and the way it had crept in and taken over so much of my life. Remembering a conversation with Theo's girl, Jilly, the pair of us agreeing that the thought of not being able to have a drink, ever again, for whatever the reason, was enough to make you go out and commit suicide. I know this sounds dramatic and all the rest of it, but Jilly was very serious and I wasn't kidding either. It wasn't that either of us wanted to die, it was to do with just not being able to imagine coping with life, without at least occasionally getting away from it all by wrapping yourself up in the cloak of oblivion produced by enough alcohol.

Phil had produced a form, a questionnaire, a few months before for a drinking mate of mine called Trevor. His missus had come across it, but she'd given it to Phil, hoping that she could give him the message contained in it. If he felt his missus had anything to do with it he'd just go off at a tangent and not come down to earth again for weeks.

At the time it didn't occur to me that I was being conned by my wife. That she was applying in reverse what I believed she was going to pull on Trevor. There were twenty questions to be answered on a straight YES or NO basis. And I went along with it, just for a laugh. At the bottom of the paper was the information that If ONE question had been answered positively, it was POSSIBLE that you had a drinking problem. TWO answers in the affirmative, made it PROBABLE that you had a drinking problem. Three times and you DEFINITELY (underlined) had a problem with your drinking.

I had answered yes eighteen times, cheating on at least one of two negative replies, but I'd laughed in Phil's face, telling her that some religious nut had composed the questions. Questions like, Have you ever had a drink the morning after a heavy bout of drinking?

"Well of course, I did... but only to get rid of the shakes so that I could get working on the typewriter.... Never because

I wanted a drink, or even liked the idea of having one." I'd gone out of the house almost immediately after this "little game" meeting, Trevor in the local, and getting smashed with him as we laughed and joked about such a load of bloody rubbish. I mean, we both knew that alcoholics were people who drank methylated spirits and slept on bomb sites around London and places like that. We were just socialisers, blokes who liked booze and pubs and all the crack that went on in any good boozer. As well as which, you had more chance of pulling a bird in a pub. A good few jars often helped a chick lose her inhibitions, so all in all, drinking just made for more fun all around.

I believed this once I had a few belts inside me. Then, as the guilt and the shyness and the insecurity were pushed into the back room of my mind, I began to enjoy myself. But as my tolerance had developed, it took more and more drink to get me to that stage of intoxication. Which was why in recent years, boozing had interfered with my life, with my work, my beliefs and my standards.

The plane touched down at Dublin, and I didn't kid myself that I was going on the wagon. Not in this town, I thought.... But as soon as I have the movie written, I'm going home and I'll give it up then.... Just stop as I'd done before. Only this time I wouldn't be impatient with Phil. If I had to wait twelve months for her to start coming around... even longer than that, I'd do it. I'd put things right, I would, yes.

Chapter Twenty-Four

Within weeks I was sure I had the answer to the whole question of booze – and not only did it work, it was the perfect way to live. The answer to all the dull colours, the black and grey and the crappy brown moments that could bug me. And it was simple. All I had to do to ensure that it was always a lovely, pale pink world, was to drink all the time.

By this I don't mean that I had to crash booze down like I did when I was doing a bit of serious drinking. That was no good because I eventually got to a point where my system just couldn't take any more. Which meant having another bout of withdrawal, shaking and suffering for days as I came down from Cloud Seven, without being able to drink anything at all to help me back to earth.

The idea was to make a ritual of drinking, give time and thought to making it a real performance, sort of like shaving with hot towels, steaming water and shaving soap, as opposed to just running an electric razor over your skin.

It was fun, apart from being the answer to any problem Phil thought I might have. Morning began with iced champagne, a touch of the Moet & Chandon or a slipper of Veuve Cliquot; either one being a great improvement on tea or coffee as the liquid beginning of another day. And you didn't need milk and sugar either.

Every other day you mixed the bubbly with fresh orange juice, making a vitamin packed quencher called "Buck's Fizz" which troubled the jaded palate not at all. Vodka mixed with orange up to lunch. Going against etiquette and the general good advice given to drinkers, by mixing the grape with the mash, and it not yet lunchtime. But it worked and it was nothing new for me to be going against the book.

Some kind of lunch had to be eaten, if only as an excuse to sip a drop of hock, some brandy over coffee, and more of the same when lunch was over. On into the evening putting the cognac away at a civilised pace, with just a few pints of Guinness in the evening. All the brandy could leave you feeling a bit dehydrated, so apart from being enjoyable, the stout put something back for you to burn up with the late night return to the brandy bottle.

Obviously this kind of drinking took a lot of effort. Not the actual drinking, which came to most of us with such ease that we had to be the latest in a long line of first rate gargle merchants. But regardless, it was worth it, because a fella never got really smashed, and you felt so good about most things that you were good company and always capable of getting it up. Which, to a fella with a keen interest in sex, was important. Brewers' droop might be good for a laugh, but not when the droops on you.

The other great benefit from the new imbibing routine was that I could work with very little effort. Not that I was working, apart from trying to keep the radio serial up to date. But I knew I could, the moment I was ready to sit down and begin writing the screenplay. And I felt the urge moving closer. It wouldn't be long now and I'd just knock it off the machine without any bother at all.

My mind rocks now when I think back on the whole scene. My ability to bullshit myself, make myself believe anything that I felt was a good idea at the time. And I shudder when I think of the bread I squandered. Money that was to buy time to sit down and write a book that would make the knockers say "Christ! I wouldn't have believed it."

But at that time I was too busy living to think about anything accept having a good time. I'd earned the money and why not? So for many weeks I lived on a long party, trying desperately to be the star of every gathering. And nobody seemed to mind me topping the bill as long as I was paying it.

I'm not blaming anybody for taking a free ride on a wagon. I was trying to buy warmth, friendship, love, when all the time, down in the back of the head somewhere, I knew that all three either came your way for nothing, or not at all.

When I'd boxed myself into a deadline corner, I sat like a zombie at the typewriter. My nerves were shot to bits while a man in Hollywood, named Keller, was waiting for his screenplay to arrive. And the time had come when I was afraid to put it off any longer.

I stayed in my flat for three days without getting more than two lines down on paper. I was drinking of course – I had to drink to stop myself from yelling out in terror as the furniture began to move about the room. And by the time I shook most of my paranoia, I was too high to write anything but horseshit.

My new drinking pattern had gone by the board. It was too much trouble when I was so pressed for time, and anyway I needed the charge that whiskey gave me. I seemed to be living on whiskey and canned beer, and I rarely felt hungry when I had enough of both. This apart, I was in a real bind. I had to work but I couldn't get into the screenplay.

Nights were all right because I usually had a bird back to the pad. And though most of the time, I couldn't remember whether we had or whether we hadn't, and consequently, had no idea if it had been any good or not, it was good to find I wasn't on my own when I woke up. But once the girl had left, the pad seemed to close in on me and I couldn't bear it. I couldn't take the pressure of the fear that being alone seemed to inject into my brain. I was sick with this fear, and sweating in the grip of the guilt that had to be the main reason for the fear itself.

I paced the floor, trying but failing to appreciate the heavy handed irony of the situation. Dublin, my home town, and me feeling so alone that I might as well have been a castaway on a rock in some uncharted ocean. I'd lost touch with the people I'd known. Ma couldn't help me. It was doubtful that she would have even understood the bind I found myself in. Yet all I had to do was jump into the car and drive into the Bailey, or Neary's, or Sheehan's, and I could have all the company anybody could want. And was I ever tempted, to do just that...? But I couldn't – I'd run out of time and even if I was to get even more worried about getting into the screenplay, I would be in serious danger of ending up in a padded cell.

There wasn't anybody I could turn to when I needed help. I had no real friends. My own fault, I know. People were only allowed to get so close. All the jokes and the booze and the late night laughter, like a prayer to keep the party going, didn't add up to one person to whom I could admit that I was in splinters. But then I'd forgotten Danny O'Brien, who mercifully, hadn't forgotten me.

Danny was an actor, a real Dublin head. Like, you can't get any more "Dublin" than Meath Street. He'd worked the FIT UP scene, touring the country with a roadshow, just like I'd done myself, so we had a springboard for some good late night chat, often sitting in "The Manhattan" for hours after we'd been kicked out of the last of the late night drinking spots, reminiscing over bowls of good soup, eventually wondering how long it would be before television and the Showband scene would drive the last of the little roadshows out of business.

Danny had the same kind of background as me, but he'd walked away from it, and like O'Casey's "Covey" in "The Plough and the Stars," he didn't go behind the door when it came to yelling about all that was wrong with the city and the country as a whole. More important than this was his dedication to the theatre. Unlike most of the actors I'd come to know, he was less concerned with fame and the money it could bring, than he was with giving the ordinary guy good plays, well produced, at realistic prices. And often in our first days of getting to know each other, his Dublinese had started floods of memories that probably for the first time, made me feel grateful for my origins. I knew that if I ever did get the screenplay of "Butcher Boy" written, he was going to play in it.

When he came into the pad, I could have hugged him. And without having to consider, one way or the other, if I should tell him what I was going through, I poured out the story, warts and all.

"Good bleedin' job I came in, wasn't it?" he grinned, and I felt that somebody had switched on the electric light.

"I've a week off..." Danny said. "If it'll help I'll stick around... do a bitta readin'... haven't read anything decent in bleedin' months...."

It was that simple. No bullshit or dramatics. Just the word of a fella I knew I could trust. Somebody willing to spend what time he could. Helping me to get on with the work without making me feel that he thought I was insane simply because during those weeks in my life, the booze had pushed me to a point where I was terrified to be on my own, even in broad daylight.

Danny read the pages as they came off the typewriter, having promised to pull me up if there was anything that didn't make sense to him. If he couldn't understand it, I didn't want it in the script. Danny was so like me, so very like the people I wanted to reach. I'd no interest in writing for the chosen few, even if I'd been able to do it. There were more ordinary people than brilliant ones, and anyway I felt sure that the book, which was direct and simple, with a fine thread of innocence echoing through the voice of the narrator, would be all the better on screen if I was honest in my treatment of it. I wanted it to be as visual a picture as possible, keeping dialogue down to a minimum. Wasn't that what movies were about? I mean, you didn't get any pictures on the radio.

Ma used to say that God looked after the innocent. Well, when I think of how that screenplay was written, with Danny walking me down to the post office to send off the pages each evening, I can only feel sure that somebody was praying for me. To send to Hollywood, eight or ten pages a day, flimsy foolscap paper, folded and slipped into a buff envelope, like the bills came in, well, I shudder now when I think about it. I'm not forgetting that the words matter most believe me, yet bad presentation could so easily have offended the professionalism of the man who was paying me. He could have been maddened just by the first sight of my early pages so that he might never have read them at all. And he couldn't have been blamed for saying he didn't want to do business with someone who behaved like such a bloody amateur. But he didn't, he loved the screenplay, and we made the movie on location in Ireland. Danny got the part for which he was so right, his performance being one of the best in the movie as far as I was concerned. And this didn't have anything to do with him having saved my brain from snapping on me. Keller auditioned him just like everybody else I recommended, so friend in need, or not, Danny was there on merit.

I still wonder how I survived the spring and the summer of sixty-eight... God! It was the most hectic period of my life and I mean future as well as past, because you can believe I wouldn't want to work at that pace again. It wasn't just the work, I was drinking dangerously to keep going, having a couple of belts the second I began to run out of steam. And a few more to be that much livelier than most people needed to be. The booze made me reckless and promiscuous, but even on nights when I felt sated from the night before, I took a girl home because I couldn't face waking on my own. Often I invited others back to the house I'd rented. The more people there were about, the easier I felt inside.

At the end of the day's shooting I'd sink into a chair in the Intercon, needing about eight large whiskies before I could find the energy to get up and go to the lavatory. After that I'd have a few jars for enjoyment. With the aches moving out of me, I'd begin to relax, and once the discussion for the next day's shooting was over, I'd be on the rampage. And if I ever got into the scratcher before about two o'clock, it was an early night. With me getting up at four thirty or five, to knock out the radio episode in a couple of hours, before the pick up car came to the door to take me to the location. For eight weeks this was more or less my schedule, and if I looked forty years old at the end of it, I felt about seventy-two.

"Roads" was published in September and in general it took a beating from the critics. Not that I cared, it was an honest book, and I knew that whichever way I'd gone with my second novel, I was going to get a panning. If I wrote another "Butcher Boy" I'd be accused of not being able to do anything else; and if I moved away completely from the Dublin scene, I would be advised to stick to the thing I knew best. In the opinion of some critics, writing, regardless of plot, setting, locale, wasn't it.

Whoever it was that said "Critics are rather like eunuchs in a harem… they know everything about how to do it, but they just can't make it" (or words to that effect) was my man. Not that you can be angry for long with a fella who finds himself relegated to such a lousy job. I mean, he has feelings like the rest of us, and he's entitled to take his ire out on whoever he can hit, without being hit back. And if the same fella thinks you're making a fortune from books he could write off the top of his head "If only he could find the time", while he earns a weekly wage that only allows four or six nights a week blind drunk, well, he has to be forgiven. "If only I had the time…." My non-stop cry when I had to drive the cab eight or ten hours six times a week. I thought, and so did Phil, that I wanted the time I spent cabbing to write. But when I got it, I used it to make like a writer in one pub or another, learning that there never IS any time. You have to MAKE time for the things you want to do, and depending on how much you WANT to do whatever it is, well, you'll make the time, believe me. It has to mean cutting into the time given to other pursuits; but it's been done by ordinary people forever, and obviously it's no hardship to go without certain pleasures if what you want to do is important enough. So just to prove that magnanimity is not dead, I forgive critics on the grounds that they can't help being frustrated writers. To be angry for any length of time with a critic, well, it'd be the same as laughing at a fella, who, three parts pissed, was a sensation playing the bones at your cousin's twenty first birthday party. If your man was talked into going for an audition for television, and he found it all a bit different from that cosy front room in your cousin's house, with not so much as a bottle of beer handed to him before he went on to die, well, who could laugh at him?

One last word about critics. Ireland, and Dublin in particular, breeds critics like shamrock. Everybody knows it all about everything, and you can't stand for five minutes sheltering from the rain, without being told just where it was you "made a ballocks of it". And if you happen to be, as I was and hope to remain, an ordinary working guy, well, you are really going to get it. "If an eejet like him can do it, Jaysus?" is the general attitude, whereas if you went upstage and behaved like an arch ballocks, I honestly believe you'd be left alone. Some of the time anyway. It's one of our big failings as a race, this inherent inability to judge the line between cordiality and familiarity, and too many of us have to be seen to be blunt and straightforward with little or no regard for the unfortunate sounding board, off of whom we bounce our hollow voice.

You have to forgive a lot of things in Dublin, but most Dubliners don't seem to notice that there's a thing wrong with it. There's too much drinking, and in relation to the cost of living, wages are bloody low. Social services are in bad shape, education could stand vast improvements, and most kinds of consumer services are almost non-existent. Like, if you buy a vacuum cleaner or a television set, well, it's to be hoped that you've been praying regularly, and lighting the odd candle. If you are unlucky and the thing breaks down, it's the smart guy who goes out and trades it in, right away. Believe me, you could write a volume about having the simplest service carried out in your home without being driven out of your mind. The Americans call it "charming and easy going" but this is nonsense. Feckless, apathetic, and often irresponsible, any serious student of "The Irish and Work" would have to come to the conclusion that "they just don't like it". Which has to be part of the reason why we appear to be turning into a nation of beggars. Year by year, the amount of bums on the streets has been increasing at a fierce rate. And on the fringe of town, you get an endless procession of tinkers to your door, day after day. Women carrying babies that are filthy, either through neglect, which is criminal, or through being made to look filthy for the sympathy stroke, which made my mind boggle when I first came across it. So few people care that very little is being done. And night after night, on the streets of Dublin's Fair City, you'll see people sitting on the pavements of the lesser used streets off Grafton, drinking stout, cheap wine and even methylated spirits. This is bad enough, but you'll often see tiny children of two and three years of age, sitting on the pavement alongside their elders. I called a policeman, having staggered across just such a scene in Clarendon Street at about half ten one night in October. A little girl, without knickers, sat on the winter footpath, while her parents reached out for oblivion. The young copper hated what was happening, but there was little he could do. Move them on and they'd just sit down again as soon as he went back to his beat. It wasn't his fault, but I was determined to do something about it. I'd call one of those influential people I'd come to know. But it was getting on to closing time, so I'd nip in for a quick one while I found the right telephone number. A quintessential Dubliner, a critic of all that was wrong, but just not able to "find the time" to do anything about any of it.

Chapter Twenty-Five
London. '69

By the middle of the year, Phil was back at work, and not because she was bored with housework. And I was kicking myself for not having renewed my contract with the radio show people. It was hard to believe and murderous to accept but I was back on the floor. My money had run out and I hadn't even paid Jackie Williams what he'd loaned me to go and see my father just before he died.

My stupidity, which is my apparent generosity really was.... My thirst for booze, and affection, plus a couple of investments that left me feeling I was some kind of charitable institution, and a final tax demand of the kind that makes a fella pull the sheet back over his head. Together, the contributing factors to my insolvency, assisted by a frightening lack of work in television and movies, and on top of it all, the book I was working on was such crap that even I could see it.

Phil had troubles of her own, the main one seeming to be my presence around the house. She didn't say much at all but I was sure I wasn't over reacting. It was in the air. When she had to face me about the most ordinary things; if she had to ask me to pick up a bag of laundry, she was like a woman terrified in a dentist's chair. It became so bad that I moved into the back bedroom, worried that my being in the bed was interfering with her sleep to a point where she would be ill if I didn't do something about it. Phil had made the first move herself, slipping into the spare bed when she came in from work. After that I told her I'd move out to the other room. She was the worker and the least I could do was allow her to have the decent scratcher. I was worried about the kids... Mammy and Daddy slept in the same bed.... How would it affect them when they came for the early morning cuddle they loved so much? Concerned, yes I was, yet when I had a skinful of drink I could stay out all night, for a week sometimes, without ever giving a thought to what my absence might be doing to the lovely innocents I loved so very much.

We went through a string of *au pair* girls at this time. Phil had to have somebody when she couldn't rely on me, so we had all kinds of Europeans, plus a phlegmatic Scot, and a big sad Irish kid who thought she was Shirley Bassey. Shirley Bassey? Well, I just couldn't work that one out at all. Anyway, there wasn't a tasty bird amongst the lot of them. It might have been deliberate on Phil's part. If it was I didn't mind. Even I wouldn't have pulled the hired help. Christ, you'd never get them to do any work afterwards. I said this to Theo and he fell about laughing, telling me I'd get up on a back rasher. It seemed funny but when Theo had gone, I knew that his joke had been a put down. He had no respect left for me, which probably accounted for the fact that he rarely came around any more. I didn't care, not about Theo, not about my brother Billy who had gone off me since I'd put the bite on him for ten shillings a few weeks before. That was an all time low, asking him for ten bob for a drink, not able to care what he thought of me, but busily cursing myself for not having asked him for a pound.

I was tumbling downhill, very much aware of how helpless I was around booze, but at the same time I just wasn't able to stop. I wanted to give it up if only because I hated being a slave to anything. For Phil and my kids, I wanted to give it up, get some kind of control going in my life again. But I couldn't say it to Phil. She didn't listen any more and who could blame her. She'd seen it and heard it hundreds of times before. Me on my knees in the morning, begging her to stay by me, that I'd beat it, stop it for good. And that evening she'd see me pissed and arrogant, and so totally selfish that she said I was almost unrecognisable. So I didn't make her any more promises. But I made them to myself.... She was worth giving up booze for. But then I'd remember some stupid thing Phil had done, something so small and innocuous that it was a joke to even remember it. That would be the excuse I need to have just one.... And after that it was the same old sad story.

There were a couple of bad scenes between Phil and me. Two nights when I got in just before she arrived home. Drunk as I was, I remember the first time I challenged her about where she'd been. And Phil was so amazed that she actually answered me.

"I've been working, for Christ's sake...."

"Working? Till this hour?"

"What is it, Maguire? What do you want me to say?"

"The truth, that's all... working till nearly four in the morning... working on somebody's cock."

Phil stood looking at me for a few seconds. "I'm tired, too tired to even listen to such shit."

I stood up, grabbing her by her upper arms... wanting her to drive the nail into my palms.... "Who is he? Tell me...."

There was no fear in Phil, but my hands on her arms were giving her a very bad taste in the mouth.

"I'm tired... dream up your fantasies... I want to go to bed."

I let her go and she walked out of the room. I collapsed on the carpet, knowing by the state of my eyes the next morning that I'd been weeping heavily.

The other time I attacked her while she was sorting out her wages, so much for this, so much for that. She did it before she went to bed because mornings hadn't ever become any easier for her.

"You only work to show them I'm not making it..." I said, needing to hurt her as brutally as I could.

Phil looked at me, her hand flying to her face as though I'd slapped her. She cried then, ugly, distorted sobbing that suggested she had to hold it down, that if she really was to let it rip out of her, her brain would be blasted to splinters by the sound of her own misery. I sat in a chair watching her, wondering what it had all been about. Then I would be absolutely clear, knowing I had made her cry, only to find moments later that I was perplexed again.

She didn't speak to me all that night.... There was no need in her to fight back, and I should have realised that I was so pathetic that Phil couldn't bring herself to have a go at me. Her silence was a kindness really, but I didn't appreciate that at the time.... She was treating me with bloody derision, the cow.... After all I'd put up with from her father over the years....

I had no money for drink and my credit ceiling had been reached in most of the places where I was known. So I had to go in search of company with money, people who would buy me drink if I entertained them. Oh Jesus! When I think of the walking from one pub to another.... Pain filled stumbling on legs that didn't seem to fit the feet below.... The strain of going into a routine when I did find a team who would wear me. Just getting my shoulders back, finding that infectious smile, getting the patter into gear.... Kidding myself they didn't know I was on the bum, that I was too clever for them to notice.... And all the time, a voice inside me screaming, what am I doing here? What am I doing with these people? The soreness in my mind because I knew I was a sick animal.... A white hot scar on the mirror I had to face until the booze covered it with a film of temporary relief.

The months that followed revealed nothing new, apart from the odd desperate chance I took to get money for booze.... But it didn't matter.... If I couldn't have drink, they could do what they liked with me. I woke up in Paris on one occasion, having flown over for a jar with money I'd either borrowed or nicked, I can't be sure. And another time I woke up with a beautiful girl who said "Good morning darling" in broken English. It was a nice change to wake up with someone so tasty, and I just assumed I'd pulled an *au pair* girl in London. I waited till she hit the bathroom before I peeped through the blind.... Was I in Hampstead? Or Kensington? Or

Chelsea? I looked for a name plate on the street... Jesus! I was in Amsterdam.... In the Grand Hotel Krasnapolski to be exact, and when I checked I found my passport stamped and my plane ticket in my inside pocket. I sat down, terrified.... It was bad enough not being able to remember meeting the bird, but I couldn't remember getting on the plane at London.... Two days earlier, according to the information on my plane ticket.

A couple of years before, the Amsterdam story would have been a gas.... Good for a laugh for a week at least. But I didn't seem to laugh any more.... All the fun had gone out of my drinking.... Out of my life.... And I had begun to believe that I was meant to die from drink. My grandfather on my mother's side had gone under to alcoholic poisoning at the age of forty-one, so it looked like someone had forgotten to throw out the mould they used for him.

You have to understand that I no longer cared what was to happen to me. Whatever sliver of grit had kept me fighting to give up drinking had been washed away in the perpetual flow of booze that sapped at my spirit. I felt lost, and it didn't matter. I was too helpless to do anything but accept what was meant to be. I was no longer important, even to myself. How could I be when I had changed to such a degree that someone else seemed to be staring at me whenever I found the guts to look at a mirror.

If I'd been able to believe in God, I'd have tried to work out what I'd done that warranted such diabolical treatment. What was happening to me made slow hanging seem like a nice way to spend an afternoon. But then I didn't, couldn't, believe in God. The way I looked at it, if you believed in miracles, the rest was easy. That was my laugh line about religion – one I'd used for years. Never for one second thinking that some day a miracle was going to happen to me.

The day began like any one of hundreds that had gone before, the only difference being that I felt worse than I could ever remember. I seemed to have gone beyond life yet

I wasn't quite dead. Not cold in the clay dead yet I was buried alive.

There was a girl beside me on a bed that wasn't mine. Naked like myself, and attractive, or so I thought when my eyes began to focus. They were sore, feeling like they'd been boiled slowly for a couple of days, and I didn't think they'd improve until I got about half a bottle of something inside me. I had to get up, get out of there, but the idea of standing on the floor without getting drink into me first just increased the intensity of the jigs. I was shaking so much that my teeth were rattling together, making enough noise to sound like a pneumatic drill that stuttered inside my head. The pains all over my body were very real, and I needed to scream out to release the steam valve of my suffering. But I just ground my teeth tight, afraid I'd frighten the girl, whoever she might be.

I moved as tentatively as I could, scared to trigger off the alarm system which only booze could keep quiet. But I fell off the bed, crying out in terror with the most blinding pain. Somebody was rubbing my nerves ends with some kind of electric sandpaper, and if I ever got my hands on the bastard, I'd use his scrotum for a tobacco pouch.

I jerked about that floor as shock after shock seemed to shoot right through me. Somehow then, I got hunched, using my arse to hold my heels down, pushing my hands under my knees, trying to grind the whole jellified mess into a tight ball. If I could only remember where I was, maybe I could break the fucking hold that booze had over me. Just that thought encouraged me to remain hunched.... It was the first time in months, many months.... I'd stopped thinking for so long. Nothing came.... The inside of my head was hurting too much.... Even the padded cover that drink slipped over me was burning me this morning.

I won't describe how I got my clothes on. The jigs were so desperate that I wept with frustration and agony, but an insane need to get out of there drove me to attempt walking across that floor. I moved and it was like walking on the hot glass.... Painful, sure, but really no worse than standing still, or even lying down.... And I needed some air in my lungs before I choked to death.

Outside that little house I leaned my head against the wooden upright supporting trellis-work for flowers. Then, and this is where my miracle began, I seemed to be sucked up and away from myself, stopping about ten or fifteen yards from where I was actually standing. I got time to get a good long look at where I was at.... To see, and I mean really see, what drinking had done to me. Down there below me, stood me, and I didn't have to look any further for that picture like the one of Dorian Gray.

"Maguire, this is fucking ridiculous...." My voice came from behind me, and I felt that somebody, something, outside of myself, had tipped me upright for long enough. As though some wise old men had said: "Listen, the head is in bits... if we give him a tilt, just a little push upright for a few seconds, he might get the message."

That same evening, after a day without one drink, a man, a fella who wishes to be a man anyway, stands outside a house in Redcliffe Gardens. He stands for many minutes, finally moving, a staggering, whiskey sick, suicidal mess. The day without booze had blazed furrows into the desire to get dry.... Up the granite steps to what they call the upper ground floor, which enables landlords to apply the euphemism GARDEN FLAT to the basement.

In the hallway a woman came to meet him, extending her hand, smiling with genuine warmth. "Welcome," Ruth said... "I'm Ruth and I'm an alcoholic."

I gave her my hand, making a deliberate effort to try and remember her slim face with the bright happy blue eyes under the cap of straw coloured hair. She guided me into a room where about thirty people waited. A fella was sitting down at the same time as me.... He was at the other end of the room, behind the table.... And though he wasn't wearing any kind of dog collar, I waited for the sermon. Jesus! I must have been nuts. Coming to this kip.... Still couldn't figure out why I'd phoned.... Maybe it was something to do with that old Susan Hayward movie, "I'll Cry Tomorrow". I mean, up to that second when I'd made the call, AA meant Automobile Association to me....

I badly wanted to leave, but again I moved out of myself, and try as I did, I couldn't come up with any reason as to why I shouldn't sit and listen. And the others sitting around me didn't look like religious maniacs, much as I wanted to believe that this is what they were. They were just people for Christ's sake, just ordinary men and women.

The man at the table began to speak. Maguire sat up when he heard the voice. He seemed to recognise it, and he gave all his attention to the speaker. A few minutes went by... Jack was telling his story, relating the facts about his drinking. Jack? Jack, for God's sake! Maguire had it... Jack from the Fullham Road. One of the biggest lunatics of all time.

I'd been shivering and feeling desperately sorry for myself. The woman named Ruth put a hot drink into my hand... I nodded my thanks, aware that nobody in the room was staring at me. Neither did they seem to be bothered by the way I had to keep moving as my nerves bugged me. I sipped the drink very carefully and I tried to listen to Jack, and never mind remembering what a nutter he used to be.... A fella who'd do anything for drink.... And he was no stranger to the gutter by the time he had disappeared from the scene. I couldn't remember what I'd thought at the time.... Probably assumed he was dead from the gargle.... Smiling at the memory of how he used to smell because he often didn't change his clothes for three weeks at a time. You sing, Maguire and I'll hum a little.... The old jokes we played with forever. What do you mean, a little? Then.... No wonder I have to drink large ones... the whiffa you, I have to do something. Jack baring his chest, flapping the shirt front to spread the smell, share it around. Love it they do, the smell of a man, and none of your poofy deodorants.

I listened to Jack.... This guy was bona fide.... He hadn't been any kind of Mickey Mouse drinker.... And he was no bloody do-gooder, either. He sounded just the same, the Cockney accent was still there, and he obviously didn't give a damn whether the likes of me believed him or not. It was this, and the thought he was probably using one of those poofy deodorants he used to sneer at that made me concentrate on every word coming from behind the table. I finished the hot drink, which stayed down, wrapping my hands around the cup to stop them shaking.

Words began to sink in. Jack talked about hitting his own personal rock bottom, and about his first trip to the house we were sitting in. It was amazing, but he was describing, exactly, the way I'd felt as I'd climbed those granite steps. He began then to mention some of the symptoms of alcoholism as he had come to know them. Here again he seemed to be mentioning them just for me, dropping them right into my lap, until finally all my defences dropped out of the way and I could relate to everything Jack was saying. He spoke of the early morning cure, the times when the drink wasn't coming up fast enough, the way he'd often slipped out to make an imaginary phone call, only to nip into the boozer next door for a couple of quick belts.The self pity. The persecution complex.... Everybody else was at fault, never me.... The TV boys, Keller for not making the movie as I saw it, my publishers.... Even Phil, working nights, being accused of trying to show me up.... Jack went on, enumerating a list of over thirty symptoms, the big one of all being the BLACKOUT.

I learned that the Blackout is not a passout. Not the unconscious bit. But a period of amnesia which the drinker goes through without being aware of it. And most of the times his companions aren't aware of it either. They might notice that his eyes are a bit dead looking, but to all intents and purposes, he is just drunk. I had no trouble admitting that I'd had Blackouts. Christ! I'd had them as far back as Jersey, before meeting Phil. And from New Zealand onwards, there were so many blanks in my memory bag that, in terms of black and white, it must have looked like a pedestrian crossing.

I sat there in that room in Redcliffe Gardens, stunned at first, then Jack made it clear to me that alcoholism was a disease, a killer disease, labelled as third behind heart disease and cancer, by the World Health Organisation. And he told that room full of people... "It's not my fault I was born with a disease... I can't be blamed any more than you can sentence a man for having diabetes.... So I don't have to accept responsibility for a lot of things I did while I was drinking.... If drink made me lose control, how can I be held responsible for being a pig of a wife beater or a thief, which I was...."

He continued, but I'd heard enough for one evening.... And as I sat there, I felt that somebody had lifted the heavy haversack of guilt off my back. I had a disease called alcoholism and whether it was inherent or not, didn't matter. It was in me... not in booze.... If alcohol was responsible for alcoholism, everybody who touched one drop would be an alky.... No, the disease was in the man, and I'd been granted the good luck to realise what was wrong with me. I felt weak with relief, needing to weep my gratitude, knowing that I'd been given a personal miracle. And I heard myself say half aloud:

"Jesus Christ! I'm an alcoholic, that's all that's wrong."

Jack promised me that if I got with the AA programme, I was guaranteed sobriety. That if I stuck with going to the meetings, listening to more experienced members, asking questions when I was uncertain about something, that in time, the urge to drink would pass, and eventually, with luck and application to the programme, the twelve suggested steps for recovery from alcoholism, I'd come to know what was referred to as contented sobriety. I had to learn to live for one day. Cut my life down to twenty-four hours, staying away from one drink for that one day. Why one drink? I asked Jack.

The meeting was over and we were drinking tea. I felt

lousy still, physically battered and beaten, but my mind wasn't cold any more.

"If you don't take that first one, you can't get to the one that screws you up..." Jack said, and the logic of it had me wanting to knock myself on the side of the head because I hadn't thought of it. I was bright enough to have worked out the whole thing, but I didn't. Others who had gone before me had designed the programme I had to learn to live by. Men and women, alcoholics like myself, had found a way to start living again, and it was being handed to me on a plate.

When I got out on the street again that night, I could feel the change. Some kind of spiritual awakening had taken place inside my agnostic spirit. It was nothing to do with religion, not even God, really. It was more to do with coming face to face with myself for the very first time in my life. Somehow getting the break that helped me face me, without any kind of insulation, and even more important, without the need for any.

I turned right into Fulham Road. My legs ached and I needed a warm bed. I wouldn't drink tonight and if the morning came, I'd ask for help to stay away from the first drink for one day. I had a copy of the AA serenity prayer in my pocket. I'd say it word for word, a hundred times a day if I had to. I'd eat a bag of grass every morning if it would help rescue my life. I went into a shop for cigarettes and I smiled a little bit to myself in the backing mirror on the wall.

"The shit Maguire died tonight, head," I told myself. "Forget all the bullshit, bury the past under your fingernails, for all I care." I paid for the fags and walked along the street. I could still see my face in the mirror. "For a while, the only thing that matters is to get with this programme. It works for fucking Jack, Jesus, it can be made to work for me. He's made a new life, so can I.... It means change, head, not all in one day, but he says, you've got to change if you've any chance of staying off the sauce. So we start changing here.... No way can it go on the way it's been... that scumbag, booze has to go The Lad's got to be evicted… that lunatic we've had to live with… Maguire… he's got to get the bullet… he's dead, wire, as we've known him, Maguire is dead."

Chapter Twenty-Six

Phil wasn't impressed and I couldn't blame her. Not after the years of promising, swearing on my bended knees, to give it up. She wasn't interested any more. Whether I drank or not was my own affair. All she wanted was for me to leave her alone. How badly she needed that I didn't know, I told her it hadn't been my fault. She whirled on me; the words had come out the wrong way because I was in bits for want of a drink, desperately afraid it had all come too late to save my marriage, and again I'd started to talk to her before she was really awake.

"No, of course... nothing's ever your fault.... Don't blame poor, hard done by Maguire...." She wept but there was a streak of defiance in her I hadn't seen before.

"I didn't mean it was your fault, Phil...."

"What you mean, what you do, I don't care.... Can't you understand? All I want is that you stop fucking up my life... just get out... do all the drinking and whoring you want, only get out of my sight...."

"You really mean it, don't you?"

"Oh Christ! Do I ever mean it. I packed your bags three days ago.... Is that message enough or should I give it to you in writing?"

She stood in her dressing gown, drawing deeply on a cigarette in her shaking hand. "I don't want to fight with you... saying all this... I don't want to hurt you, but you've driven me to it...."

I had to leave, owing her that much. If things have been even slightly different, I might have been able to reach her. She knew nothing about alcoholism, and in that she was just like most people. Up to the night before I had been ignorant to the same degree.

We didn't speak again until O'Casey had my stuff packed into his cab. The children were out with the latest dozey French bird. Phil would tell them I was away writing a film for a few days.

I tried to be calm, manly if you like, but I was falling apart, desolate that things had come this far. I wanted to hold her in my arms, tell her how much I loved her, somehow willing into her empty heart a thread of warmth that she might direct my way. But it was the wrong time for anything like that. It was time to go.

"I'll keep in touch, kid... for the sake of the kids...."

She nodded, her lips pressed tightly in a straight line of self control. I knew she wasn't going to speak. She had said it all. I walked down the little path and out through the front gate. I climbed into the front luggage compartment beside O'Casey – my stuff was in the back of the cab. He drove off and I held my tears, but Jesus Christ! I should have let them roll. The way I was feeling, well, it was all too much to be held inside.

O'Casey stopped outside the pub and I got out of the cab. I needed a couple of drinks after that scene. How could she have been so heartless after me giving it up to keep things together. I stopped right there. Wait a minute now, wire.... Don't use Phil as an excuse.... You gave it up for yourself.... You went to that meeting last night for you.... To try and stay alive.... There was no qualification about saving the marriage scene.... So if you're going to be a fucking fool, get on with it, but don't go back to being a scumbag on your very first day.... Don't use Phil to excuse your sick, fucking mind....

Herb was standing looking at me. "Okay, Blue?"

I looked up at him. I was okay. "I don't want a drink."

He nodded and we got back into the cab. "Bit early for me anyway, Blue."

I sat there beside him, truly believing that I was going be all right. Getting honest back there at the pub.... That was

something the old Maguire wouldn't have been able to do....
But then he hadn't known anything much about anything....
Well, things had changed already, and with me being lucky enough to fall into that meeting on the very night Jack was in the chair.... With that kind of good fortune, there was every chance for some kind of a decent life. It was all a question of wanting it badly enough.... And I wanted to live.

Chapter Twenty-Seven
London. April '70

The hire car stopped outside the house and I paid the driver before I got out.

Betty opened the door, hugging me in relief. I kissed her face and shut the door.

"How is she?"

Betty nodded: "She's over all the surgery... for the time being...."

"The kids?"

"Oh, they're fine...." She smiled, at a loss. "I haven't told them...."

"Good.... We'll leave it for a few days."

I made coffee and she sat at the table smoking. "You're not to blame yourself, Paddy...."

"It's all right, Bett. That kind of bull, the wallowing bit, is a luxury I can't afford...." I gave her a cup of coffee.

"I'll just take a look at the children.... Bet they've grown...." I went into a room and I stood looking down at my children. They were sleeping easily and I just thanked God they were so healthy and normal. That was something I'd started to do lately.... Thank God.... I didn't give it much thought, even though I knew that something outside myself, a power greater than me had decided I should get sober. I didn't worry about it and I hadn't become a churchgoer or any think like that. And I didn't think I ever would. All I knew for sure was that I was getting help from somewhere. And you better believe I was grabbing it, with both hands.

Also published by Killynon House Books

THE REPUBLICAN

AN IRISH CIVIL WAR STORY

By TS O'Rourke

With the prospect of Civil War looming, Jack Larkin, a veteran of the War of Independence, is torn by his idealistic search for the 'True Republic', the love of his sweetheart and the memory of his dead father.

Set in Dublin during the 1922-23 Civil War, The Republican examines the emotionally charged divisions that the Treaty with England created within the Republican movement and one man's desperate struggle to understand his decision to fight.

The Republican is one man's journey though Ireland's darkest hour - a period that many would like to forget, but which is etched deep in the collective unconscious of the Irish Nation. It is a story of the Irish Civil War in Dublin that has not yet been told, either in novel or film format.

ISBN: 1-905706-00-6